Praise for the Kris Longknife novels

"Shepherd's grasp of timing and intrigue remains solid, and Kris's latest challenge makes for an engaging space opera, seasoned with political machination and the thrills of mysterious ancient technology, that promises to reveal some interesting things about the future Kris inhabits."
—*Booklist*

"Enthralling . . . fast paced . . . A well-crafted space opera with an engaging hero."
—*SFRevu*

"Mike Shepherd has written an action-packed, exciting space opera that starts at light speed and just keeps getting better. This is outer space military science fiction at its adventurous best."
—*Midwest Book Review*

"I'm looking forward to her next adventure."
—*The Weekly Press (Philadelphia)*

"Fans of the Honor Harrington escapades will welcome the adventures of another strong female in outer space starring in a thrill-a-page military space opera." —*Alternative Worlds*

"If you're looking for an entertaining space opera with some colorful characters, this is your book. Shepherd grew up Navy, and he does an excellent job of showing the complex demands and duties of an officer." —*Books 'n' Bytes*

"You don't have to be a military sci-fi enthusiast to appreciate the thrill-a-minute plot and engaging characterization."
—*Romantic Times*

Kris Longknife
AUDACIOUS

Mike Shepherd

ACE BOOKS, NEW YORK

THE BERKLEY PUBLISHING GROUP
Published by the Penguin Group
Penguin Group (USA) Inc.
375 Hudson Street, New York, New York 10014, USA
Penguin Group (Canada), 90 Eglinton Avenue East, Suite 700, Toronto, Ontario M4P 2Y3, Canada
(a division of Pearson Penguin Canada Inc.)
Penguin Books Ltd., 80 Strand, London WC2R 0RL, England
Penguin Group Ireland, 25 St. Stephen's Green, Dublin 2, Ireland (a division of Penguin Books Ltd.)
Penguin Group (Australia), 250 Camberwell Road, Camberwell, Victoria 3124, Australia
(a division of Pearson Australia Group Pty. Ltd.)
Penguin Books India Pvt. Ltd., 11 Community Centre, Panchsheel Park, New Delhi—110 017, India
Penguin Group (NZ), 67 Apollo Drive, Rosedale, North Shore 0632, New Zealand
(a division of Pearson New Zealand Ltd.)
Penguin Books (South Africa) (Pty.) Ltd., 24 Sturdee Avenue, Rosebank, Johannesburg 2196,
South Africa

Penguin Books Ltd., Registered Offices: 80 Strand, London WC2R 0RL, England

This is a work of fiction. Names, characters, places, and incidents either are the product of the author's imagination or are used fictitiously, and any resemblance to actual persons, living or dead, business establishments, events, or locales is entirely coincidental. The publisher does not have any control over and does not assume any responsibility for author or third-party websites or their content.

KRIS LONGKNIFE: AUDACIOUS

An Ace Book / published by arrangement with the author

PRINTING HISTORY
Ace mass-market edition / November 2007

Copyright © 2007 by Mike Moscoe.
Cover art by Scott Grimando.
Cover design by Annette Fiore DeFex.
Interior text design by Kristin del Rosario.

ISBN: 978-0-441-01541-2

ACE
Ace Books are published by The Berkley Publishing Group,
a division of Penguin Group (USA) Inc.,
375 Hudson Street, New York, New York 10014.
ACE and the "A" design are trademarks belonging to Penguin Group (USA) Inc.

PRINTED IN THE UNITED STATES OF AMERICA

10 9 8 7 6 5 4 3 2 1

Lieutenant Kris Longknife, sometimes styled
Princess of Wardhaven, hated running in high heels. To make
matters worse, the street here was paved with uneven cobblestones . . . and they were wet!

The street was also empty. The brick buildings were five-
and six-story-high relics of New Eden's early days four hundred years ago. Rehabilitated and converted to government
offices, they'd emptied at the close of business with amazing
speed. The restaurants and small "shoppes" that serviced
them had also closed down for the day.

Kris had the place to herself—except for tonight's assassins.

The ratcheting back of an arming hammer on an automatic
weapon reminded her that she was once again the hunted.

Kris dodged to the right, heading across the street. Forcing
assassins into a deflection shot had often kept her alive. One
"shoppe" had an open alcove for an entrance. She sharpened her
angle and redoubled her speed despite complaining ankles . . .

And ducked inside the cover not a second too soon.

A spray of rock shards told her the stone front of the store
was real. Only scratches showed on the large display windows

where they'd repulsed shots as well. A glance at the name on the glass told Kris she'd been lucky . . . again. Brevel's Fine Jewelry had paid for bulletproofing.

Kris took all this in as she dropped to the ground and reached for her service automatic.

Abby, Kris's erstwhile maid, had insisted that she show off her figure tonight. "Let the newsies see it once, then we can do what we want." The clingy burgundy sheath had been padded, so Kris almost looked like she had a bust, and it fit nicely over Kris's armored underthings. The short slit up the side reminded her to take graceful little princess steps tonight. Now it was a much less modest long rip; Kris easily got at her weapon.

Kris rested her automatic on the brick pavement and edged it around the corner, then waited for Nelly, Kris's pet computer . . . worth more than several blocks of the surrounding real estate . . . to paint a sight picture on the retina of Kris's eyeball.

Nothing happened.

NELLY, WHERE'S MY TARGET?

KRIS, WE ARE STILL BEING JAMMED. I CANNOT READ THE GUN'S TRANSMISSIONS.

STILL! Kris spat in dismay. SHORT-RANGED PERSONAL NETWORKS *CAN'T* BE JAMMED.

YES, MA'AM. I KNOW, KRIS, BUT WE ARE. The computer voice in Kris's head conveyed disappointment at her failure, but Nelly was absolutely sure of her conclusion. Between woman and computer there was a direct hookup. Kris hadn't known when she signed for the hardwire that she'd face this, but she was grateful she had.

Scowling at what couldn't be—but was—Kris waited. When the next blast of rapid fire ended, Kris risked using her own eyeball to draw a bead on the gunner. In formal black tie and tux, he seemed a bit chunky for the tights he wore in place of the more conservative pantaloons that were in this year for men in Garden City.

Kris put two rounds in the center of his chest.

That only drove his aim high. His next burst smashed windows above Kris . . . government offices didn't rate armor.

Acknowledgments

No manuscript becomes a book without a lot of dedicated work from wonderful people. Ginjer Buchanan deserves a special thanks for all the support she gave a writer she discovered in the slush pile. The gang at Ace has been wonderful to work with. Jennifer Jackson is all the agent that a writer could hope for. And there is no better first reader than my wife, Ellen.

And I will never pass up the opportunity to thank those of you who tell me your stories. Those of you who go "down range" to help folks who hardly know they need helping and may have no idea how to say thank you. You know only too well that Kris Longknife is not the only one whose good deeds never go unpunished. Thanks for sharing.

Shards rained down on Kris, including one that speared her gun hand.

She bit back the pain and raised her aim. The next three rounds did things to his face that Kris didn't need to see. She'd been there, done that . . . and had a long lineup of gory memories for her nightmares. She scanned left for a second shooter.

He'd skidded to a halt poorly, dropping down on one knee. A hand on the cobbles steadied him. He whirled around and headed back the way he'd come.

Kris put two rounds in his head but all it did was knock him down.

SMART MAN, ARMORED TOUPÉ, Nelly observed dryly.

Kris's long ringlets were also borrowed for the night—and similarly fortified. She took off running for the corner while the assassin picked himself up and decided if the game was worth the cost.

"Where is Jack?" Kris growled.

Normally her chief of security was attached to her at the hip and full of nanny advice. As a Navy lieutenant she outranked his Marine first lieutenant. She should have been able to ignore him. Only after she made the mistake of drafting him did she learn that he had absolute say over her security matters. Which he insisted extended much further than she found plausible.

They argued a lot.

Sometimes it was actually fun.

At the moment, Kris would love to have him to argue with.

2

Tonight's assassination attempt had been layered. First the attendant in the ladies' room . . . one of the few places Jack didn't insist on escorting her. After putting that overly helpful and far-too-deadly woman to sleep, Kris found the door locked and even Nelly unable to do anything about it. That blasted jamming.

So Kris threw a chair through the low back window.

Only to find some very fancy dressed men waiting for her.

She'd kicked the closest one in the groin before he realized this Navy lieutenant was not the usual damsel, given to easy swoons when in distress. Both guys went down in a ball and Kris took off running for her life . . . or at least freedom.

Which frequently meant the same. It had for poor little Eddy.

The front of the Hotel Landfall had been a zoo of newsies, cameras, and security. The back was quiet as a Buddhist temple, but Kris lacked the time to contemplate. To her right, at the end of the alley, a car waited with two more thugs. She headed left at full speed.

Running footsteps and the crash of several garbage cans told her it was going to be a long night.

At the end of the alley, Kris found a guy in a full-length, leather coat taking a leak. Bad timing. While he scrambled to finish with one hand, he clutched inside his coat with the other, grabbing for what Kris suspected was an illegal weapon on this wonderland of planets, New Eden.

Or just plain Eden as the locals insisted.

Kris didn't wait to see what he came up with. She chopped him on the side of his neck to put him down.

She'd kept running and had been running ever since.

As Kris ran for the corner, behind her came more sounds of the chase. Either her second pursuer was finding the nerve to keep this up, or whoever was paying for this hit had not stinted on numbers. The quality his money bought had yet to be determined.

Maybe it was the first time for them.

It wasn't for Kris Longknife.

As she neared the corner, a gruff "You're blocking my fire lane" greeted her in Jack's wonderful voice.

Wonderful for at least the moment.

Kris went wide around the corner, then skidded into a turn and a stop. Jack knelt there, in dress red-and-blues, service automatic covering the street. Kris took the situation in as she caught her breath.

Ineye's Qck-Stp. "Lunch in five minutes or it's on me" probably didn't have armored glass, but solid bricks covered the lower half of his store front.

Kris ducked behind Jack. "You got a handkerchief or a bandage?" Kris asked as she eyed the half-inch glass sliver in her gun hand.

"Bandage in my hip pocket," Jack said, and snapped off two rounds. There was a shout out there and the clatter of a weapon bouncing along the cobblestones.

Kris located the bandage, drew the sliver out with her teeth, then spat it out as she wrapped the bleeding hand if not expertly, at least with experience. "What took you so long?"

"How am I supposed to know how long you need to take a leak, put that outfit back together, and powder your too-large nose. Your opinion, not mine," he said, and snapped off two more shots. No noise rewarded him this time. A stream of bullets stitched the glass of the far window but failed to make it through to the window above Kris's head. Other rounds ricocheted off the pavement.

"I am not slow in the head," Kris snapped. Well, there was the time she'd planted bombs to blow up a space station's sewage treatment plant, but that was a special occasion.

"Besides," Jack continued, "the Hotel Landfall did not take well to me shooting the door off their ladies' room. Insisted I wait for someone with a key. And asked dark questions about whether or not I had a permit for this thing." Jack fired two more rounds to punctuate the reference to his Corps-issued weapon, authorized on Wardhaven . . . but illegal on a mature, civilized place like Eden.

Kris had been naive enough to believe that line in the official "Welcome to Eden" handbook given her by the inattentive secretary in the ambassador's office. But not naive enough for her and Jack to leave their backups at home on this night of Kris's coming out as the visiting princess from the Rim.

"You'd have thought they'd give us a couple of free passes," she grumbled. "Two or three quiet nights out."

Kris's complaint was cut short by the roar of a car engine. A gray sedan shot around the corner up from them, an automatic pistol already out the window. But the gunner was busy holding on tight as the car took the corner, giving Kris the first shot.

A major mistake.

Kris aimed one for the gunner, then quickly spaced ten across the front window.

The car wobbled in its turn. Then slammed into a fire hydrant. Water geysered up, showering everything, including the car. No motion there.

"Somebody's got to notice that," Kris said.

"Glad we've heard from the motor brigade," Jack said, then followed it by three shoots down the street he was covering. The storm sewer was backing up fast, turning the street corner beside them into a lake. Water now lapped at Kris's very expensive, if nearly nonexistent shoes.

Jack snapped off two more shots, the last of which brought a scream from someone. "Unless you're planning on walking on water tonight, Your Princesshood, what say we make tracks?"

Kris did not argue. Not tonight. She was already up and running.

3

The Wardhaven Embassy was just a few blocks farther down, its gray stones looking wonderfully bulletproof. Still, Kris figured they'd spent about as much time on this street as they dared and zigged right at the next block. Halfway down that block, in midstreet, Kris's luck ran out—again.

The guy in the leather coat came racing around the corner, so intent on beating feet to get a shot at where Kris's back had been that it took him a second to notice her front. Kris and Jack put a pair of rounds into his jacket.

It must have been armored, the shots just sent him sprawling backward, his feet flying into the air like he'd stepped on a banana peel. His gun clattered halfway across the street.

Kris took a hard left. This government building had a well-sheltered entrance. Surprise, it wasn't locked. Kris held it open for Jack, then followed him through.

"Nelly, can you lock that door?" Kris bit out.

"No. That jamming, Kris."

"I'll belt it shut." Jack whipped off his issue belt and began tying the door handles together. "Check the back door."

Kris galloped the length of the foyer, past a bank of elevators and a tiny coffee stand. Through the glass she could see the front entrance to the Embassy. She tried the door.

"It won't budge," Kris shouted over her shoulder.

"Or unlock," Nelly added.

"Shoot it," Jack said, racing for Kris.

She did. It flew open. Kris took the right side of the granite-sheltered entrance.

The street looked empty. Across it lay the embassy; a stately colonnade lorded it over the center of its many wings. An inviting driveway led to the formal greeting area within the columns. Kris just wanted to slip into the basement entry of the nearest wing. Only an empty, white guardhouse with a red roof offered anything like protection. The black, wrought-iron fence looked strong enough to hold back a mob of very angry cub scouts. On second evaluation, make that preschoolers.

Jack joined her on the left. "I don't see anything."

"But tonight we don't usually see them coming," Kris said. "Lucky amateurs. Make for the guard booth."

They did. Kris covering right, Jack left, they dashed across the street and piled into the stall. "Will this stop anything?" Kris asked Jack, his face on top of hers and tantalizingly close.

"I'm told it will. If it doesn't, I'm writing the captain of the Marine detachment a very angry letter."

"We should live so long," Kris muttered, and tried to sit up enough to look out. The arm around Jack managed to stay there.

The wrought-iron gate began to slide closed. Across the street, three men rounded the corner. Ugly-looking machine pistols came up from under long black coats.

They proceeded to hose down the guard post.

Kris raised her automatic, but Jack pulled her hand down.

"Watch this," he said with a wide grin.

The stall sheltering them didn't puncture or even rock from the hits. Jack disentangled himself from Kris just enough for both of them to get a good look out the guard post's open door.

There was a faint sheen between the flat black of the fence's iron bars. There, suspended in wicked lines, were the incoming 4-mm rounds. As Kris watched, more lines crossed and crisscrossed the space between the bars. The darts that hit the "wrought-iron" bars bounced off.

"That's a spider-silk mesh between the ceramic bars!" Kris chortled. "Our gentle looks are deceiving."

"Like a certain princess," Jack said, climbing off of Kris.

She turned a sigh into a grunt as she helped herself up. Foul words came from across the street. A soft whirling sound came from the top of the guard post's red roof as a camera unfolded itself and turned to take pictures of the shouting, impotent assassins.

"I want copies of those," Kris said.

"Let's talk to the duty sergeant about that."

With a backward wave, that only brought more foul language and frustrated fire, Kris headed up the driveway. Jack cut the walk short as they came to the steps down to the basement entrance of the nearest wing. The door opened for them. LET ME GUESS, WE'RE OUTSIDE THE JAMMING AREA? Kris said.

OR THEY TURNED IT OFF, Nelly answered.

Just to the right, off the wide hallway, a marine sergeant sat at his post, monitoring several screens. "Glad you made it," he said without looking up.

"Glad we made it, too," Kris snapped, a regal frown coming tight to her mouth. "Don't we call out the guard or come to the aid of distressed citizens anymore?"

"We are not permitted to carry weapons on the streets of the capital, Lieutenant," came from behind her. She turned to see Gunny Brown, shipshape and starched as if it was oh-nine early, not twenty-two something late. The buck sergeant on duty kept his eyes on the screens and let the senior NCO take over the education of a certain junior officer.

Kris sighed. Yes, this was New Eden, or Eden if you prefer. Yes this was old humanity, four hundred years settled. Not the raw rim of space, two hundred years since planet fall, like Wardhaven. Or even rawer rim of human settlement where Kris had spent much of her three-year Navy career.

Kris marshaled her thoughts to logic, not an easy thing when the adrenaline was pumping. "One would think automatic-weapon fire deserved attention no matter where it came from."

"I fully concur with you, Your Highness." Smart Gunny. "However, this Marine's orders and my orders are logged and signed. Our detachment is here to protect Wardhaven's sovereign property and do it smartly, Lieutenant."

Before Kris could snap back a rejoiner she'd regret, Jack cut in. "Come morning, I'll have a talk with your detachment's captain. See what we can work out. I definitely want the services of a larger escort. And a female Marine to go where I shouldn't. It's either that or your maid is going to be spending her nights out with us."

"I should hope not," said maid said, plucking a dart from the back of Jack's dress-red blouse. "Better warn your dry cleaner to check for the rest of these."

"Didn't duck fast enough," Kris said with a grin.

Abby pulled a dart from Kris's rear. "You didn't, either."

Kris swallowed her grin.

"And look at what you did to that brand-new and very expensive dress. My, my, girl. What am I going to do with you?"

"Draw me a warm bath," Kris said hopefully.

"The tub is filling. Good thing I didn't go out tonight like I planned," Abby said, putting a guiding hand on Kris's elbow and steering her down the hall. "I put my feet up for a minute to relax and you sneak out and make a mess of yourself."

Kris had made a mistake. She didn't have *a* nanny, she had two. Jack to nag and nanny her outside the perimeter fence, and Abby to do the same inside.

Not for the first, nor the last time did Kris wonder just what was so special about being a princess. So far, all it did was paint a big target on her back. Though, come to think about it, she'd been dodging assassins long before joining the Navy.

She'd been ten when the first attempt was made . . . and Eddy six. She survived. Little Eddy hadn't.

Kris made it back to her room in one piece. Quickly, she was out of her dress, the ceramic-strengthened underalls, and the spider-silk bodysuit. She was in the water and under the bubbles before the shakes caught up with her.

"You got the trembles, girl?" Abby demanded, a foul look on her face as she surveyed the damage done to tonight's gown.

"No," Kris lied.

"The whirlpool may be riling up that water, girl, but your shoulders are doing their own little shake-and-roll. You wanna talk to your Mama Abby?"

"I'm fine," Kris insisted, sinking into the tub up to her neck. "I'm fine."

Kris's mother hired Abby to make Kris presentable. She'd also put forth more than half an effort to provide some of the mothering that Kris never got from her mom. Still, it was now old news that Abby was on more than one payroll.

She also sold news about Kris.

It wasn't unusual for servants to pass along tidbits about their employers to gossipmongers. Abby, however, sold her gossip for top dollar to various intelligence services around human space. Even Kris's own Wardhaven Intelligence subscribed! Kris had chosen to look for the silver lining. Now she got a copy of Abby's reports and used them for her own. Still, Kris was having a hard time trusting Abby with certain things.

Like who did Kris think was behind tonight's fun?

It had been an amateur effort; Jack was right about that. The shooters had not been that prepared. Had whoever bought this gone for a bargain-basement special? Or was what passed locally for hit men that out of practice? Kris frowned in thought. Certainly, that line was the one both the ambassador and the local police would want to believe.

There was just one hole in that story. The jammer.

Jamming a major network was not supposed to be possible. Jamming a computer with Nelly's power was supposed to be in the realm of fantasy. Still, Nelly was being jammed—and had been jammed before. Aunty Tru, Wardhaven's retired Chief of Info Warfare . . . and the woman who'd helped Kris with her math and computer homework and the upgrading of Nelly since first grade . . . was working on the problem.

Tru had no solution to it yet.

One thing was clear: Only someone with a whole planet of software hacking under their thumb could have pulled this off.

The Peterwalds had eighty planets last time Kris checked.

And the last time she'd been jammed, there'd been a Peterwald in the mix.

Kris sighed. The trembling had stopped; she reached for a towel Abby had left within reach. She'd better get a good night's sleep . . . as good a night's sleep as she could. Tomorrow she'd have to start hunting for a Peterwald. Last one that crossed her had ended up dead. She hadn't exactly killed him. She just shot his ship up and he ended up dead. A fine point she couldn't expect his father or other relatives to think much about.

Better to find this Peterwald before he . . . or she . . . found Kris.

4

"The ambassador wants to see you after the nine o'clock staff meeting," Chief Beni hollered Kris's way as she entered the military dining room for breakfast. The embassy, though huge on the outside, was really pressed for space. Now that de-evolution had turned each of the Society of Humanity's six hundred planets into independent and sovereign nations, the Wardhaven Mission to Eden was splitting at the seams.

Wardhaven, under the benign leadership of the recently elected King Raymond I . . . Grampa to Kris . . . had about a hundred planets forming the United Sentients, or maybe it would be a Commonwealth, or Association. No one was quite sure. The politicians from those one hundred planets were still debating the constitution on Pitts Hope.

But what it meant in the real world was that the Wardhaven Embassy on Eden did work for all hundred planets. Kris had been told she'd be buying paper clips, pens, and the likes. "The likes" included business computers and their software. Usually not the actual items, but the right to reproduce them locally.

So someone in the embassy's administrative branch had settled on one dining room for all the military on staff. Not a wardroom for the officers and a mess for the enlisted personnel. Nope, one for all, and all in one.

So the chief usually had the hot dope for Kris even before she had her hotcakes, or bran muffin, or whatever.

Kris nodded and went down the chow line quickly, putting her breakfast on white, bone china rather than the metal trays reserved for the other ranks. Done, she joined the officers at their tables in the back of the room. You could tell the wardroom area. It had napkins and linen tablecloths, rather than the bare tabletops of the enlisted swine.

Kris had gotten a formal invitation to join the diplomatic dining room. Maybe she would . . . later. For now, she preferred the company of the line beasts and their officers.

"I understand you had a rather more exciting evening than you signed on for," Captain DeVar, commander of the Marine detachment, said as she settled into the vacant chair next to Jack.

"Jack tell you all about it?"

"In quite detail," the Marine lieutenant said.

"It sounded like a well-executed withdrawal," the Marine captain said dryly.

"A running gunfight," Kris said. "Them gunning. Me running."

"Yes, there was that unexpected aspect," Captain DeVar said, raising an eyebrow. "You were actually running."

"Can we talk about them gunning," Kris didn't quite screech.

"I've already asked," Jack said, "for four of his hulking Marines to accompany us next time out. And two female Marines to keep an eye on you in the head."

The Marine captain frowned. "There is that matter of the local legality of anything more dangerous than a paper clip." He punctuated that with a smile . . . not a bad look on him.

"Isn't that why we brought Penny along? To liaison between us and the local constabulary?" Jack said.

At that moment, the subject of their conversation entered the dining room. Lieutenant Penny Pasley had started her career in Intelligence, but her father had been a cop and hanging around Longknifes quickly found her drawing on the easy

way she had with local police officials. Today she had a sheaf
of printouts under her arm, but she approached the steam tables first.

Kris concentrated on attacking her bran muffin.

As Penny settled at the table next to the Marine captain,
her face lost a thousand-yard stare and took on a scowl. "That
must have been quite a night, Your Sharpshooting Highness,"
she said as she dumped the printouts on the table before them.
"I woke up to reports from the Garden City P.D., Eden Bureau
of Investigation, Secret Service, and Park Service."

"They glad she's still alive?" Jack asked, fishing the Secret
Service report from the pile and eyeing it with professional interest.

"How about hopping mad about the mess she made."

"You must send them Her Highness's regal regrets for not
letting them kill her quietly," the Marine captain said, not
quite covering his grin with a napkin.

Penny pulled a short printout from the bottom. "A police
lieutenant—uh, Martinez—offers to help you complete the
necessary forms for carrying heat hereabouts."

"There might be one level head among our nervous
grannies."

"Looks that way. Did you really blow up a fire hydrant?"

"No, I got the driver of a car that was shooting at me. The
fire hydrant put a stop to his car's further involvement."

"None of the reports mention a car around the hydrant,"
Penny said, flipping through several of them.

"Any decent field lab should be able to tell whether metal
has been knocked over or blown up," Jack said.

"Don't count on Eden cops to be that observant," Abby
said, entering the conversation. She'd come in the back door.
Sometimes the maid ate in the officer area, sometimes in the
enlisted section. Usually she was invisible in either. Kris made
the mistake of ignoring Abby once . . . for about a day.

"You're from here," Jack said.

"Yep."

"How long you been gone?"

"Not nearly long enough," Abby said, slipping into the

chair next to Jack. She filched an orange from his breakfast and began to peel it with the dinner knife from Jack's napkin.

"Think the cops might have changed in your absence?" Jack said, reaching for his banana before it also was requisitioned.

"They ain't changed in human memory," Abby snapped. "Don't bet on the tiger to change its spots. You'll lose every time."

"Don't tigers have stripes?" Penny said.

"Maybe where you come from. But on Eden, they do things their way."

"*They*," Kris said. "Not *we*?"

"Baby ducks, *they* are the main reason I left this place and, you may remember, said I didn't want to come back. Ever."

Kris had read up on Eden. The Chamber of Commerce had been rosy. The embassy handout was as optimistic as they come. The financial reports, even those available to a major stockholder in Nuu Enterprises said things couldn't be better.

So why last night's little escapade?

One report on Eden was missing. Abby's personal views. She hinted plenty, but when pushed, went silent. Just like now.

Kris pushed back from the table, her eyes narrowing. Around her, the group fell silent. Down the way from them, the table where Commander Malhoney was telling one of his long, rambling jokes broke into chuckles as he finally reached his punch line. He fit his undress whites like a small whale might, bulges here and there. In any Navy still applying up-or-out, he would long ago have been out. But the expansion left room for men who had reached a certain level even if they never would exceed it. Now his table fell into the silence, furtively looking Kris's way.

Her Highness weighed the benefits of keeping secrets verses what she'd gain by inviting the whole crew into what lay ahead of her. She tossed a coin mentally and made her choice.

"I was told," Kris said slowly, voice low. The hush now spread from the officers to the enlisted. Even at the steam tables, the clatter seemed to continue on kitten toes. "That I'd made the Rim too dangerous for me. I was *told* that Eden was about the *only* place I could walk the streets in peace.

"Then last night it turns out I can't even take a piss without someone trying to perforate me." There were soft chuckles at that. Marine Gunnery Sergeant Brown turned to the staff sergeant who'd had the duty last night; they exchanged winks.

"The last time Grampa Ray gave me one set of orders but dumped me into a totally different stew, it turned out that I was supposed to cook that stew and ignore the orders." Around her, there were grins at her family reference to King Raymond I, but the grins were quickly swallowed as Kris finished her thought.

"Since Eden clearly isn't the advertised paradise, I find myself wondering what I'm really supposed to get done here?"

5

By the time Kris presented herself in undress whites for the ambassador's pleasure, she had spent an hour on the phone with Administrative Lieutenant Martinez. He was as helpful as his cheerful smile promised, but it was clear his job was to see that all the T's were crossed, I's dotted, and no firearms permit issued without a tree sacrificed to the paperwork god.

"We need full documentation of no less than three attempts on your life," he said, apparently reading from policy displayed right beside Kris's face on his old computer screen. Kris had long ago noticed that most bureaucrats found old technology far more to their liking than the new stuff.

"Three assassination attempts." Kris tried to sound thoughtful rather than outraged. "I imagine that cuts down on the requests. Those that don't survive the first couple don't trouble your day much do they."

"No, ah, they don't." Lieutenant Martinez had the good sense to at least look apologetic.

"Does last night's shoot-out count as one? Can I just send you two more?"

"Last night?" he said, glancing offscreen. "I don't have any report of an attempt on your life. My morning report says everything was quiet last night."

Which left Kris wondering what it took for the powers that be in this burg to admit there had been a major can of worms crawling around their streets, shooting off automatic weapons. If last night was quiet, did it take the use of a long-forgotten fusion bomb to get noticed. *Is this part of why I'm here?*

Kris turned to Abby. "I'm sure your reports contain several attempts on my life. Would you be kind enough to forward them to Lieutenant Martinez."

"I usually charge for such releases," Abby primly said.

"Put it on my bill," Kris growled. "Send six of them."

"Six," squeaked from the wall screen Kris was addressing.

"Just six. Abby, have you filled out the basic form?"

"Yes, Your Highness," the maid said as if on cue.

"It would be a shame if you had to explain to King Raymond, formerly President Ray Longknife of the Society of Humanity, how it came that I got killed on Eden because me and my escort couldn't shoot back."

"President Longknife. You're related to him!"

"He's my great-grandfather."

His "Oh" took a minute for Martinez to swallow. "And you want an escort."

"My Chief of Security, First Lieutenant Montoya, and at least four other people on my immediate staff. I will also have six Marines rotating in and out of my protection detail. Maybe more in some instances."

"When you are granted a permit, it covers your bodyguards," Martinez muttered.

"You don't have cause to grant many of these, do you?"

"Most requests are legacies. Your father had a permit, so you are authorized one when you move outside his secured area. Your father or mother was a registered bodyguard and you are accepted into one of the guilds. That sort of thing."

More information that didn't make it into Kris's official briefings. NELLY, REMIND ME TO LOOK INTO THE SERVICES OF SUCH AGENCIES.

I AM ALREADY SEARCHING. THEY ARE NOT LISTED IN THE PUBLIC DATABASE.

Curiouser and curiouser.

The call went long, but it left Kris with only five minutes to cool her heels . . . and think . . . in the ambassador's outer office before the staff meeting collapsed and she was invited into the inner holy of holies.

"The ambassador will see you now," his secretary said, a fellow in a three-piece business suit that made him look more like an ambassador than a secretary. But then the entire outer office was overblown in wood desks, expensive wallpaper, and carved filigree.

The ambassador's office was even more palatial. But Kris had seen where the king of a hundred planets lived . . . and he needed none of this folderol. But he was Ray Longknife—*that* Ray Longknife—and he needed little display to highlight his power.

Ambassador VanDerFund apparently felt the need for display. Kris wondered how many other people knew it was all borrowed.

The embassy was known locally as Brown House, not because any streak of brown showed on its facade but because a certain Mr. Brown had built it to display the wealth he'd made on Eden in the first century of its colonization. Several of the first landers had built similar mansions near the center of town before land got so expensive. The great-great-grandkids now preferred to make their show of wealth farther out . . . some complete with hunting forests. Most in-town places, like Mr. Brown's, were taken over for other uses.

This was not the only one that had become an embassy. Somewhere across town, Greenfeld had an even bigger white elephant to feed Henry Peterwald the XII's ego.

"Mr. Ambassador," Kris said, with a nod.

"Your Highness," Samuel VanDerFund said with a slight bow that didn't make it past his chin. Dressed in a suit his secretary might have ordered, his aquiline face, graying hair, and other auroras of strength and power were cut short, literally, by his five and a half feet of stature. Kris placed his age at eighty. Back then, there had been an unforseen genetic blunder attached to offspring bioengineered for just such qualities Sammy exuded. Short stature. Oh, and a sensitivity that went with it. No one called him Sammy to his face.

Maybe a princess could, but Kris wasn't interested in finding out.

Today, Sammy was also short-tempered. He went directly from "Your Highness," with no further preamble, to "What were you trying to do, get us all declared persona non grata on this planet. I was warned that you don't seem to care that there are half a dozen planets that you cannot return to, but some of us have the honor of representing Wardhaven and its growing alliance on planets like Eden. And we don't want to leave."

He finished by pulling several purple folders from a drawer and tossing them across his immaculate marble desk. The reports that slid from them duplicated those Penny had shared with Kris and friends over breakfast. One was new. It showed the seal of the prime minister's office. Kris glanced at it. *It* had the story straight.

"Interesting," Kris said with a frown. "I just finished talking to a police lieutenant about getting a permit for my bodyguards to carry weapons. He said that the police reports from last night show nothing happened."

"Clearly, he is misinformed," the ambassador snorted, dismissing Martinez with a wave of his hand. He then launched into a diatribe on Kris's need to do her job, keep a low profile, and not disturb the tranquility of the embassy to the second most ancient planet in human space . . . and the most important when it came to Wardhaven's growing trade.

Kris nodded in all the right places, made the occasional proper noise of agreement . . . and put her time to better uses.

NELLY, WHAT IS THE MEDIA SAYING ABOUT LAST NIGHT?

I WAS WONDERING WHEN YOU WOULD ASK. NOTHING, FOR THE MOST PART.

NOTHING, ZERO, NADA!

PRETTY MUCH. NO SHOOT-OUT. NO DEAD BODIES. I EVEN

CHECKED THE MORGUE. NO ONE ADMITTED WITH GUNSHOT WOUNDS.

So, NOTHING HAPPENED, Kris said, and barely kept a puzzled frown from her face that wouldn't have been a proper response to where Sammy was in his flow of words, wisdom, and correction.

THERE IS A REPORT IN A SMALL MEDIA OUTLET THAT CONCERNS ITSELF WITH CIVIC MATTERS AND BUSINESS CONTRACTS FOR CITY WORK. IT SAYS A FIRE HYDRANT FAILED, AND POINTS OUT THAT THE SAME HYDRANT FAILED NOT THREE YEARS AGO. IT DEMANDS AN INVESTIGATION INTO SHODDY WORKMANSHIP BY CITY WORKERS AND STRONGLY SUGGESTS SUCH MATTERS SHOULD BE CONTRACTED OUT TO MORE EFFICIENT PRIVATE CONTRACTORS.

THREE YEARS AGO. DID YOU CHECK THAT STORY, NELLY.

YES, KRIS. THAT FLOODING WAS PUT DOWN TO A BAD WELD AT THE FACTORY.

NO WAY TO TELL IF ANYTHING HELPED IT ALONG?

SORRY, KRIS. I CAN ONLY REPORT THE NEWS THAT SOMEONE WRITES.

AND SOMEONE SEEMS TO HAVE A SOLID LOCK ON WHAT THAT IS, Kris said, then nodded for the ambassador's benefit and said, "Yes sir, I will endeavor to not be attacked by assassins in the future."

If Sammy detected the sarcasm, it did not show in his dismissal. "Now, today you have some important negotiations. Thank heavens they are in the embassy. I shall assume you can do that without destroying the building."

"Yes, Mr. Ambassador. I'm sure I can."

He made a point of turning his attention to his desk computer. Kris made a point of nodding and leaving. It looked like it was going to be a busy day.

With luck, it would not be fatal for anyone, especially Kris.

6

Three planets, Lorna Do, Pitts Hope, and Hurtford wanted to build the latest line of business computers coming from IBM loaded with the software that went with them.

The sales rep from IBM was most willing to deal . . . but at a price that was quite out of line for a similar sale just closed between Yamato, Europa, and Columbia.

Kris knew about that deal. A Nuu Enterprises company on Yamato had been involved. The three reps on Kris's side also knew of the deal from their sources. The sales rep had to know they knew. Still, she smiled cheerfully and set the higher price, and the other planet reps smiled just as cheerfully and began their own long-winded campaign to lower the price.

All Kris could think of was that this was another day she'd never have again.

So, had Grampa Ray sent her here to learn to waste time?

Somehow, Kris doubted that.

She set Nelly to doing a more informed search on this planet, and nodded along with the conversation while Nelly searched. And made reports.

Reports that were as useless as the negotiations.

KRIS, I HAVE TRIED RESEARCHING THE LAST HUNDRED YEARS OF THIS PLANET'S HISTORY BUT I KEEP COMING UP AGAINST BABBLE.

BABBLE?

YES, MA'AM. I TRIED SEARCHING THE ARCHIVES OF THE THREE MAIN MEDIA SOURCES ON EDEN. HOWEVER, ALL THREE HAVE THEIR DATA STORED IN A DIFFERENT, NONSTANDARD FORMAT AND I CAN ONLY ACCESS THEM IF I APPLY FOR A SUB-SCRIPTION AND AM APPROVED. THE COST FOR ANY OF THEM IS UNBELIEVABLY HIGH.

HOW HIGH?

Nelly quoted a price, and Kris barely suppressed a whistle that didn't fit into the bargaining. News archive subs would set Kris back the price of several of those overpriced dresses Abby occasionally added to her royal wardrobe.

YOU HAVEN'T APPLIED FOR A SUBSCRIPTION?

NO, KRIS, I DO NOT SPEND THAT KIND OF MONEY WITHOUT PERMISSION. I AM NOT ABBY. ALSO, I WAS NOT SURE YOU WANTED IT KNOWN THAT YOU WERE APPLYING FOR SUCH A SUBSCRIPTION.

Which was Kris's second thought. While getting the straight skinny on this planet might not be easy, she somehow doubted keeping anything a secret was all that easy, either.

"Kris, you have a call coming in," Nelly whispered softly.

"I'll take it," Kris said. While the actual conversation would take place in the privacy of Kris's brain, it was com-mon courtesy to let people in business meetings know that one of their members was going to be somewhat distracted for a while.

Around Kris, the conversation did not pause. That only confirmed her suspicion that while she might be in a Navy lieutenant's uniform, she was here to keep up royal appear-ances.

HELLO, Kris said, using Nelly's net connection.

THIS IS LIEUTENANT MARTINEZ, CALLING ABOUT YOUR WEAPONS PERMIT.

YES, LIEUTENANT, THANK YOU FOR GETTING BACK TO ME SO QUICKLY.

WHAT MY SPEED MAY BE REMAINS TO BE SEEN. I WOULD
LIKE AN OPPORTUNITY TO TALK TO YOU FOR A FEW MINUTES.
PREFERABLY ALONE AND SOMEWHERE WE WON'T BE INTER-
RUPTED. "Or overheard" seemed to be hanging there unsaid.

Of course, anywhere that filled that bill could also be setting her up to be gunned down by any shooter walking by.

COULD YOU MEET ME HERE AT THE EMBASSY?

I'D PREFER NOT TO, came back very quickly.

WHY DON'T YOU MEET ME IN FRONT OF THE EMBASSY AND
WE'LL SETTLE ON A WALK FROM THERE. SAY IN FIFTEEN MIN-
UTES.

I WAS THINKING ABOUT LUNCH.

I WAS THINKING ABOUT NOW. This at least would let her
keep control of part of this potential bit of target practice.

As soon as Martinez rung off, Kris informed Jack.

NO SURPRISE OUR WALLS HAVE EARS. Jack agreed. I *AM* A
BIT SURPRISED THAT A LOCAL COP WOULD NOT WANT TO TALK
TO THEM.

I'M DISCOVERING LESS AND LESS ABOUT THIS PLANET,
JACK. MAYBE I CAN FIND OUT SOMETHING IF THIS FELLOW
FEELS FREE TO TALK?

AND DOESN'T GET YOU KILLED.

AND ON THAT TOPIC, DO YOU THINK YOU COULD SCARE US
UP A HALF DOZEN MARINES. IN CIVVIES. I DON'T WANT TO
LOOK LIKE A PARADE.

I'LL GET THEM IN CIVVIES. NO GUARANTEE THEY WON'T
LOOK LIKE A SQUAD OF MARINES, THOUGH.

MAYBE THEY'LL SCARE OFF MY NEXT ASSASSIN.

THAT WOULD BE A CHANGE.

7

"**Lieutenant** Martinez, so nice of you to come so quickly," Kris said as she offered her hand. He shook it. In a rumpled raincoat and thick-soled shoes, he looked the part of a cop. Kris had ditched her cover and wore a light blue civilian raincoat over her whites. The violation of uniform regs just might make her a harder target. It made Jack happier.

Jack, along with a half dozen other Marines in civilian clothes formed a wedge behind Kris. Martinez took in their tight haircuts with a nod and a smile. "I'll see if I can postdate your application's approval to cover this walk."

"We would greatly appreciate that." Kris left it to Martinez to decide if the "we" was royal or collective. The nod from Jack made either fit.

"So, where shall we walk?" Kris asked.

"There is a mall that many people enjoy on days as sunny as these," the policeman said, eyeing a patch of blue sky where the sun shown through the white, fluffy clouds. The raincoats actually might come in handy.

"You pick the mall, I pick the direction," Kris said.

Martinez smiled tightly and led the way. Jack's team

formed a circle around them. Two blocks over, they found the mall, four- or six-blocks wide with trees and gravel walks. At one end was a stone monument in the classic shape of a rocket. At the other end an imposing building with colonnades.

"Is that where the tricameral legislature meets?" Kris had noted in passing that Eden was unusual in that it had three legislative bodies, not the usual one or two.

Martinez shook his head. "Only the American legislature."

Kris was about to let that pass, but a faint alarm bell went off somewhere. Martinez was leading the way across the mall. They had some time, so Kris asked the dumb question.

"American. Isn't that one of the main powers on Earth? It can't have a legislative body out here on Eden."

"Earth doesn't," Martinez said, then gave a quick jerk of his head toward the domed building. "That thing is all ours."

Kris goaded him on with a quizzical look.

"About a third of the politicians that make the laws of my fair planet work out of that building. The European legislature sits in New Geneva and the Chinese Mandate of Heaven speaks from Guang Zhou Du."

Kris almost missed a step as they crossed from grass to gravel. She'd assumed that the tricameral reference had been to three houses elected by the same people, maybe one by head count, one by regions, and one by wealth or nobility or some such. Why hadn't this been plainer in her briefing. NELLY?

I AM SEARCHING THE RECORDS, KRIS. SUDDENLY WHAT SEEMED PLAIN AS THE NOSE ON YOUR FACE IS TURNING INTO A WHOLE LOT OF NOTHING.

Kris suspected any third-grader on Eden could have told her what she wanted to know. Why should it be written down?

"Those are all from old Earth," Kris said.

"AmeraEx, ReichBank, and some similar association from China funded the loans that got Eden started. Most of the early settlers came from those three. When they paid off the mortgage and demanded the right to set up their own government, they wanted a world government, but one that wouldn't step on any of their toes. Here in the American territories we measure in feet, apply common law, and things like that. They actually use the Napoleonic code I'm told in the Eurolands. And if you can figure out the Mandate of Heaven . . ." He shrugged.

Kris had that feeling she got when she was being attacked by all the information she needed to solve a problem. Only it was nibbling her to death by the bites of a thousand rabbits. And in a moment they'd all be gone and she'd be left bleeding with nothing to show for the effort.

She fell back on the blandest of questions a politician's daughter knew. "So, do you like what your legislator is doing? You plan to vote for him next election?"

"I don't have a representative. I'm not a voter."

And alarm bells went off all through Kris's skull. "Jack, have we got a secure area here?"

"Any beams aimed at us will only get white noise. Unknown nanos within ten meters are toast, Your Highness," he snapped. Was he just as eager to get the next question answered?

"Lieutenant," Kris said, not looking at the police officer, "I assume you wanted to be someplace we could talk without anyone listening in on what you said. I, too, occasionally want my privacy. My security chief assures me we have it, but before we go into your concerns, could you *please* tell me what you meant by your last statement. You're not a voter? The Charter of the Society of Humanity gave all citizens the franchise. Planets could make limits for age, mental condition, and penal status, but . . ." Kris let her words trail off.

The cop looked at Kris like she'd just asked if murder was a felony around here.

Kris called on her perfect source for information. "Nelly, isn't universal suffrage in the Society of Humanity's charter?"

"No, Kris, the basic charter allows each planet to establish its own criteria for the vote."

"I know that," Kris snapped, not happy at being corrected. "But Grampa Ray pushed through the Twenty-fourth Amendment when he was President after the Unity War. He insisted all planets give everyone the vote."

"He did, Kris," Jack said from behind her. "New planets had to. However, existing members were only encouraged to."

"President Ray Longknife made a major effort to get all planets to adopt universal suffrage." Nelly sounded like she was quoting from one of several dozen books on the topic. "But the Iteeche War interrupted him."

"And Eden was quite set in its ways," the policeman added. "And your great-grandfather needed the support of Eden . . . and its industry . . . in the war."

They were in the middle of the mall, on one of the gravel walks. "Which way do you want to go?" Officer Martinez asked.

Kris pointed toward the huge building. It was official and likely to have more security around it. She and the cop ambled toward it. Kris made an effort to swallow being caught short on something she should have known, and asked one more question.

"How did your family come here, and when?"

"We arrived as indentured workers, our future employers paying our way for seven years of cheap labor. My family was from Mexico, but workers came from all over South America. There are also Indians, Pakistanis, and Filipinos. The Eurolands has Turks, Palestinians, and Russians. The Chinese have, well, Chinese or Taiwanese, or Koreans. Cheap or forced labor."

"And none of the late arrivals got the vote?" Kris needed to hear this. She knew it all added up to that, but *knowing* it and *hearing* it were not the same.

"Not unless you married someone who did, and then only your children got franchise if they came out above 50 percent. Some folks invest a lot in keeping their genealogy straight."

Could this be why Grampa Ray sent me here? It didn't make sense. She might have missed the footnote on this part of Eden's history, but King Ray had lived it. *And what could she do about this violation of civil rights, anyway?*

It was time to get down to business. "You said you had

something you wanted to tell us and didn't want to say it where the walls might have ears."

The local cop smiled. "That was a fast turn. Yes, I've reviewed the file you sent. I must say I'm amazed that you're still here to make the request."

"You're not the only one," Jack put in.

"I've had a lot of help," Kris said, smiling at the guards around her. "For which I am truly grateful."

Most of the guards ignored her, concentrating on their section of her perimeter. Some did acknowledge with a smile.

"Anyway, I have recommended authorization of protective services, including automatic weapons and armored transportation. No crew-served weapons such as mortars and heavy machine guns."

Kris tried to keep the surprise off her face. When folks here went for security, they went heavy. What were they afraid of?

"That should do for us," Jack said. "Is there any limit on the number of security personnel she can have at any one event."

"Social graces govern there," Martinez said. "Hostesses don't want their soirees overrun with tight-mouthed men who can't participate in the chitchat, if you know what I mean."

Kris suspected she did. They'd come to a place where a multilane road crossed the mall. A long motorcade, official-looking, was speeding toward them. The light still said her group could walk, so Kris did.

"We better get out of their way," Martinez suggested, and the group of Navy and Marines began to jog.

They were just reaching the other curb when a Marine sang out, "We've got explosives nearby."

"How close?" Jack snapped.

"Don't know. I think we're about on top of it."

Kris glanced down at a spilled box of popcorn. Strange, none of the plentiful pigeons had attacked it.

"Bomb," Kris shouted, and took off running just as Jack made a grab for her as if to push her.

"Run, Marines," Gunnery Sergeant Brown ordered, but he was backpeddling up the road, his automatic out. He gave the entire detachment one quick look, determined them gone enough, and started to empty his weapon.

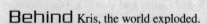

Behind Kris, the world exploded.

She went down hard. Jack hit on top of her even harder.

She hoped it was nice for him.

She rolled out from underneath him and was struggling to her feet even as she took command of the situation. "Anybody injured? Let's hear a report. Sound off."

One by one five of her six Marines reported their presence. Two shouted as if they might be having a hard time hearing. Beside her, Jack got to his feet, licked his finger, and made a mark in the air. "Missed you again," he muttered.

"Gunny," Kris shouted, not interested in Jack's humor.

The sergeant was slower getting to his feet. "It missed me, ma'am. I think it was aimed for the center of the road." He pointed at the trees across the street, now denuded of leaves and branches. Two were nothing but shattered stumps. "Those won't need trimming for a while."

Her primary duty done, Kris turned to look for the local police officer. He was still down. She offered him a hand.

Martinez took it and stood, but his attention was focused behind her. Kris turned to see the motorcade bumping off the mall

to her right, gunning its engines as it used the next road up to
head back where it came from. Tracks on the mall's grass and
gravel showed where heavy vehicles had made fast passage.

"I was going to say, another one to add to my file," Kris
said. "But whoever's in those rigs might dispute that."

"I suspect they would."

"On your knees!" a new voice demanded. "Hands behind
your heads! Twitch a muscle and I'll shoot you, you damn ter-
rorists."

Martinez immediately dropped to his knees, but he shouted
out. "I'm a police officer. I have credentials in my pocket."

Kris made no effort to comply, but slowly turned to face a
young man in full armor, assault rifle aimed at her head. "I am
Princess Kristine of Wardhaven and a serving officer in my
planet's Navy. These men with me are Marines and part of my
security detail. We exploded that damn booby trap. I demand
to see one of your officers."

Kris noted that Jack and Gunny had slowly led their subordinates in complying with the wish of the man with the rifle.
Good of them. But Kris had been accused of too many crimes
she didn't commit. She'd waste as little time with this one as
possible.

She locked eyes with the armed man and didn't blink.

"Stand down, Corporal. I'll take it from here."

The man who stepped forward to place a gentle hand on
the corporal looked a bit older than Jack. The deep tan of his
face matched the soft brown of his suit. "I'm Inspector Johnson. You say you are a princess. Can you prove it?"

The corporal may have been told to stand down, but the rifle
didn't waver from Kris . . . and his finger stayed on the trigger.

"Inspector, I have credentials in my pocket. May I drop
this raincoat?"

"Please do so. Slowly."

Kris did. She got upraised eyebrows from both the inspector and corporal as her uniform emerged.

"The Navy part seems to have some substance," the inspector said, then glanced around at the rest of her party.
"Marines?"

"First Lieutenant Montoya is the chief of my security detail. The others were 'volunteered,' when Lieutenant Martinez of your police asked to talk to me."

Now the inspector glanced at his own officer. "You have credentials handy?"

"In my coat pocket."

"Produce them slowly."

Lieutenant Martinez did. The inspector examined them, whispered something to his personal computer, and seemed happy with the answer he got. "You may get up, Lieutenant. Is she what she says she is?"

"I have every reason to believe so."

"Gentlemen, I'm going to ask you Marines to stay down a moment longer. Your Highness, will you slowly present your ID."

Kris did.

"Lieutenant Montoya?" the inspector said. Jack answered with a grunt. "May I see your ID card?"

Jack slowly produced his. The inspector looked at all three of them together.

"Can any of you explain why our explosives experts swept this area and found nothing. Our advanced guard had no inkling of anything, but a mine exploded for you?"

"Corporal Singe, report," Gunny snapped.

"I was using an MK 38, Mod 9 sensor both to search for illegals and to control our own nano-guards, sir. As I approached the curb, I got the first alarm that there were explosives and electronic devices present. They appeared to be well shielded. I announced the problem and followed the princess. That caused the sensors to spike and I concluded it was either in the popcorn box or being covered by it. Gunny then took action, sir!"

"And that action was?"

"I shot it until it exploded, Inspector," Gunny Brown said.

"You have a permit for that weapon, mister?"

"That was what I was talking to your lieutenant about," Kris put in. "My submitted request for a weapons permit for me and my security detail. I think this proves I need one."

"Hmm," said the inspector.

Lieutenant Martinez shook his head eying the direction of the vanished motorcade. "I'm not so sure you get credited with this one."

"You mean she's now walking into other people's assassinations." Jack shook his head. "That's really not fair."

In the road, four people in civilian clothes organized a thorough search of the bomb scene. One of them came over to talk in dark whispers with the inspector. He waved Kris and company toward a tree ten meters away. They went.

A few minutes later Inspector Johnson rejoined them. "Did that bomb sniffer of yours make a record of findings?"

Kris glanced at Corporal Singe.

"Full and complete, Your Highness."

"I'll need that record," the inspector said.

"We'll make a copy," Kris said.

"I want the original."

"You may have the original. We want a copy."

The inspector nodded. A large, apparently armored, vehicle pulled up. "I will need all of you to accompany me downtown."

"For what reason?" Kris demanded.

The inspector seemed to recognize the error of his ways and moved to explain. "We need as much residue from this new form of bomb as we can get. Your clothes are potentially peppered now with fragments of the explosive, electronics, what have you. Would you please accompany me downtown where our experts can examine you and your clothing."

Put that way, Kris could only answer, "We will be glad to. Let me call my embassy and explain why I will be late returning from lunch. Don't want to be declared a deserter . . . again."

Several hours later, Lieutenant Martinez offered Kris a hand in her dismount from the same armored transport, or its sibling. Her hair was stripped clean down to the second layer of cells; Abby would have a fit. The Marines formed a perimeter around her. Even on the embassy doorstep, they were not taking chances.

"I will do my best to speed the process of awarding you a permit," he said without looking her in the eye.

"Is there a problem?" Kris asked.

"My supervisor did not seem in any rush."

"You could wave this. It's bound to make the media."

The local cop shook his head. "Not in any outlet he's likely to read."

"Well, please tell me which media it will make. After last night vanished into some kind of invisible hole, I'm wondering how to fill up my scrapbook." *Or Abby's.*

"You haven't heard about our alternate press."

"Is it to be trusted?"

"Some more than others. I read the *El Camino Real*. You might want to subscribe."

"I'll look into it." NELLY, SEE ABOUT HAVING PENNY SUBSCRIBE. THAT SHOULD KEEP MY NAME OUT OF IT.

DOING, KRIS.

Kris hardly got in the basement door before she was ambushed by the ambassador's secretary. "Where *have* you been?"

Kris frowned at Jack. "We reported to the Marine Comm Center where we were," he said.

"Well, they didn't tell anyone else. You *can't* just vanish, Your Highness. People *expect* better things of you," he sniffed.

Kris wondered how big a bribe it would take to have one of the Marines behind her pop this guy one. From the looks on their faces, the fellow was rapidly reaching bargain-basement pricing. A few of them looked willing to pay for the privilege.

"Did you check in with the Marines?" Kris asked softly. Dead softly.

The secretary ignored Kris's question and went on to the matter of some importance to him. "We have a request for your presence this evening. Ms. Broadmore is throwing a small party at her city residence and would so like you to serve as the centerpiece of her evening."

"I've had a rough afternoon," Kris bit out.

"Not *doing* your duties, if I may say so. The negotiations *floundered* without you. They'll continue tomorrow. Please *try* to be there."

"Last night, I went to one of Eden's little balls and got shot at." Kris was rapidly losing what temper she had left.

"So *you* say. The ambassador wonders about that. I must say, I do, too. Ms. Broadmore is a *very* important person here on Eden. You *really* must be there. It will be small, so even *you* will likely not foul it up. Here's your invitation. Do be at least fifteen minutes late. Any more is gauche. Any less and, well, you *are* a princess, aren't you."

And apparently, some people figured that made her just the person they could order around.

Before Kris could decide between decking the guy herself or just hanging, drawing, and quartering him, she was interrupted.

"Kris, what have you done to your hair!" And Kris got ready to be ordered around some more.

Unfortunately, the secretary was long gone by the time Kris explained that the condition of her hair was the result of another bomber's near miss.

"I had planned to go out this evening," Abby grumbled, "but it looks like I'll be up to my elbows in princessing you for most of the afternoon. Let's get started."

Kris was freed from Abby's "tender" care just in time to board one of the embassy's armored battlewagons at 1930. Jack was her escort, in dress red-and-blues. The driver and one other Marine were also in dress uniform. Two men and two women in formal dress were too clean-cut to be anything but Marines.

"I'm glad you could arrange things so quickly," Kris said.

"Captain DeVar was already on it when we got back. He seems to be better wired into the embassy rumor mill than the ambassador's secretary."

"Good man," Kris offered.

"He also asked if you might want to go jogging with some Marines. They run their three miles at 0515 every morning. Five miles on Saturday."

"I'd love to join his Marines," Kris said. It would be good to spend an hour with real line beasts every day. The rest of her day was la-la land; a bit of time sweating with people who got their hands dirty might keep her grounded. Heaven knew, with all the food thrown at a princess, if she didn't get some exercise, this desk job might be the death of her.

"I told him you would." Jack grinned. "I am supposed to take care of your security, and if you keep eating like a hog and don't exercise, I'll lose you to a heart attack."

Kris started to swat him, but the limo was already slowing to a stop. A glance at the bright lights showed that now might not be a good time to assault her security chief.

9

If this was Ms. Broadmore's townhome, Kris wondered what she used for her rural retreat. Something the size of Texas? Of course, Kris had never figured out how large Texas was, but the old saying suited this place.

Ms. Broadmore's town house might be smaller than the Wardhaven Embassy. Then again, the huge, column-lined facade before Kris could be hiding a dozen wings . . . or two. Around the grounds, several scores of limos, many larger than Kris's, were parked on concrete or grass, depending on how heavy the liveried men directing traffic took the rig to be.

"Small get-together my well-armored derriere," Kris said.

Jack took it in. "You carrying?"

"And you ain't getting it." She locked eyes with Jack. He looked away. "Now that that's all settled," Kris said, "let's go see what this is all about."

Jack handed her out of the limo. A man in white livery and knee britches took the invitation from Jack and escorted them to the main entrance.

He frowned as the four formal-dressed Marines formed two couples and followed.

"Madam has provided refreshments and entertainment for your servants, Your Highness."

"Good. Then they can rotate, one couple at my elbow, one on break," Kris said, giving one half her detail. But only half.

His "As you wish" dripped with disapproval.

Kris had learned to live with disapproval at an early age. Dead was not something she wanted to live with anytime soon.

Through the glass doors was a marble hall that, apparently, served only as a foyer. This was laying it on thick.

Kris, this design mimics a French palace of the eighteenth century. Earth.

Thank you, Nelly. Let me think, please.

They came to a ballroom that was larger than the drill field at OCS. More marble pillars held up a domed ceiling streaked with gold and lit by chandeliers that actually burned candles. The aroma was very striking. A marbled and carpeted staircase led down into the second level of the ballroom.

Beside Kris, her liveried escort handed off her invitation to a man in a coat of gold cloth holding a huge staff.

"Princess Kristine Anne of Wardhaven and Nuu Enterprises" boomed out in a rich baritone.

"Not bad," Jack whispered.

"And associates" was added a long second later.

"I guess that puts us in our place," Jack added.

"Just stay close," Kris said. "This is not what I signed on for tonight. I do not want any more surprises," she added as she took the steps slowly down into what she could only think of as a gladiator's arena.

But a bloodless one. Most likely.

Kris had been processing all the surprises of the day as Abby prepared her for the evening. She hadn't paid much attention until Abby poured her into the red, floor-length ball gown with the tight bust. At the time, Kris had considered it a bit too much for what she thought she was headed into, but didn't need a fight with her maid to add to all the day's other battles. Now, a glance around the floor showed that Abby was far more plugged in to the social circuits here.

Dress was formal. Very formal. Some of it was into that outlandish area that can only be attempted by stamping it "formal." One woman, either very young, or very well preserved was wearing . . . something. A haze of multicolored lights orbited her, keeping her somewhat modest. And teasing every male eye in range with hopes that the program would fail and leave her, just for a moment, wide open on one side or another.

"That's an interesting use of nanos," Jack murmured.

"Whoever is in charge of our nano-scouts, please keep them away from her," Kris said. "I don't want to be accused of causing the most exciting social blunder of the evening. Some of the men here don't look more than one heart attack away from a coffin."

"I'll see that it doesn't happen," one of the female Marines said, elbowing her escort and deftly removing a small console from his inner coat pocket.

"You don't trust me, Doris."

"Never saw any cause to" cut the Marine off at the knees.

"Let's pay attention folks," Kris said as she approached the bottom of the stairs.

THE WOMAN AT THE FOOT OF THE STEPS IN SHIMMERING BLUE AND BLACK IS MS. BROADMORE, Nelly said in Kris's brain. SHE OWNS AND OPERATES ABOUT FIVE PERCENT OF EDEN'S CAPITAL. THERE IS NO MR. BROADMORE AT THE MOMENT. WHAT SHE OWNS SHE OPERATES.

WHO ARE THE REST AROUND HER?

Nelly started to identify several men and women, then paused. THE WOMAN IN THE WHITE GOWN IS NOT TRANSMITTING.

Kris glanced at the woman, but at just that moment, she disappeared behind a tall man in formal black. Social graces usually required people in public meetings to broadcast their minimum bio. It was similar to the IFF that warcraft had used for centuries. And often the topic of battle jokes. It was not unforgivable for someone to "throttle their squawker." Some people were shy, others just preferred their privacy. Still, in an evening intended for meet and greet, going quiet was . . . interesting.

Ms. Broadmore offered Kris her hand. "So glad you could come. I understand they have this and that to keep you busy at the embassy during the day. I'm so happy you could make it."

"This isn't my first social event," Kris pointed out.

"Yes, I heard you had to leave Marta's little get-together early yesterday. Don't you just hate events thrown at a rented hall. It's so easy for them to go to pieces at the slightest happenstance."

Kris allowed a slight nod. Apparently Ms. Broadmore didn't know what had happened last night or didn't care. Several muscular young men in easy orbit of her looked like they would apply all the caring their patron did not.

Ms. Broadmore introduced Kris to others that stood eagerly about. Since their names and offered bios matched what Nelly knew, Kris left it to her computer to remind her if and when she needed them.

It was the redhead in the white gown that kept snagging Kris's attention. Never center stage, she was always there in the corner of Kris's eye. She would turn or move a hand at just the right moment to draw Kris attention away from whomever she was talking to. It was . . . bothersome.

Finally, Ms. Broadmore took two quick steps and reached for the hand of the unidentified woman. "And have you met my other special guest of the evening. You must know her. Your family and hers are a pair, are you not? But I understand that you have been a bit of a cosmopolitan, and she's been given a sheltered upbringing. This is her first trip into civilized space."

Ms. Broadmore inserted a theatrical pause, and Kris could feel every collar or lapel camera in range clicking away. Kris gritted her teeth and hoped this would not go on much longer.

Apparently their hostess had had fun enough, with a predatory smile she finished. "Kristine Longknife, have you met Victoria Smythe-Peterwald?"

10

Kris had known intense moments in battles to cause it, that heightening of awareness that let you take everything in but no time seemed to pass. How often had Kris joked about her social life being like a battle?

Now she had battle awareness right in the middle of the ballroom floor.

Victoria Smythe-Peterwald looked so much like her brother. The same flashing blue eyes, perfect skin, rigid set of jaw. The white dress was skimpy up top, barely covering a set of boobs Kris would kill for. Original equipment or after-sale add-ons? No way to tell. Vicky was supposed to be totally natural, no genetic engineering, due to a slip up in her birth.

Hank was a totally engineered product, implanted in the womb. Vicky was a natural blowby that should have never made it to birth . . . but here she was.

Those cold blue eyes were full of raw determination. No, this woman would not be easily dismissed.

The gown looked painted on. It flowed over more curves than the law should allow. Men were going to be easily distracted around this woman. Pity them, Kris decided. At the floor, a flair of faux fur covered her feet. Maybe they were too big?

Even as Kris took in the outer display of the woman, she also checked the backup. Three alert men and a woman looked to be clearly in Victoria's orbit.

At least we're even there. While Vicky's weren't Marines, Kris suspected they'd make up in pure viciousness what they lacked in honor and field craft.

Outside the bubble of Kris and Vicky, beyond their guards, the room fell quiet, grew expectant. *So we're Ms. Broadmore's floor show. Let's not keep the paying customers waiting.*

Kris extended her hand. "I am glad to make your acquaintance" seemed like a good, neutral start.

Vicky took Kris's hand in a surprisingly strong grip. Like some men, she then tried to twist it, put her hand on top, Kris's on bottom. Kris was not about to send submissive signals. Her hand stayed where she had it, thumb up, little finger down. Kris could feel her knuckles going white. Vicky's dainty pale hand went pink.

It was Victoria who broke the shake.

Vicky spat, "You killed my brother." So much for chitchat.

"I really don't think I did," Kris said, as matter-of-factly as she could. "His brand-new cruiser was blasting away at my ship. I admit I returned the favor as well as my eighty-year-old command could. It was his choice to start shooting."

"What, and leave you with all that alien technology you'd stumbled upon? Let you Longknifes make a fortune and cut the rest of us out?" *Vicky could teach a cobra how to spit.*

"I told Hank before he started shooting that he was rattling off a pipe dream. No way my family could hog all that. Or would want to. Look at what is going on as we speak. Half the universities in human space have staff in those two systems. Most every major and a whole lot of minor corporations are trying to figure out what they have. 'Trying,' being the operative word. Last I heard, they don't know squat. You heard differently?"

"That doesn't change the fact. You shot up a Greenfeld ship and my brother died."

How much of the woman's anger was that Kris had "shot up a Greenfeld ship," and how much was because her "brother died"? *And I thought my family had interesting dynamics.*

Kris shook her head. "He should have lived through that battle." Then she added, "I did."

"Count your days, Longknife. Count your days."

Even as Kris snapped back the first thing that came to her mouth, she knew it was a mistake. "They'll be long and happy if you don't send anyone better than the ones you hired last night."

Oops, that lovely pale skin, milk white to begin with, was now showing red from—was that a nipple peeking out—to her cheeks. *So, Vicky, you have a temper to go with that red hair. Better learn to control it, girl.*

"That was none of my doing. Some junior employee's idea of a welcoming present for his boss's daughter. He's no longer in our employ. He's paid for his mistake."

Kris tried to gauge whether that last comment referred to losing his job or something worse. Kris wouldn't bet the poor fellow was still breathing. *Now don't get all sympathetic for the guy who tried to kill you last night,* a small voice in the back of Kris's head warned her.

But in my line of work, you got to love the ones that miss, the imp in Kris shot back to her more cautious self.

"I suspect I'll be seeing you around," Kris said, as offhandedly as she could manage and turned her back on the second deadliest woman in the room.

In the end, Vicky could spit her venom all she wanted. It was Kris who had been there, done that, and buried way too many of both the good and the bad.

"That was educational," Jack whispered at her side.

"I hope Ms. Broadmore enjoyed the show," Kris whispered back. "Nelly, we will not be accepting any more of Ms. Broadmore's invitations. The ambassador can hang himself before I'll make another trip to this snake pit."

But Kris could not—would not—cut and run. And the senior

representative of Nuu Enterprises on Eden was right there, with his wife, ready to glom on to Kris's elbow. They exchanged chat about the weather . . . it was going to get hotter as spring turned into summer. That was comforting news. He also deftly guided her around several business associates whom he said she might find interesting.

One had a daughter at his elbow. In her senior year at Eden U., she looked to Kris for support for her decision to join the Navy. Both father and mother were shaking their heads as the words tumbled over their daughter's lips.

"These are interesting times," Kris said. "And if we don't all share the burden evenly . . ." She left that thought for the parents to finish. "Besides, a couple of years with the colors will be educational. I know they have been for me."

"Assuming you and Karen survive the experience," the father put in, tight-lipped.

"What doesn't kill us, makes us stronger," Karen offered.

"You're too young to realize what you're saying," the mother shot back.

Kris beat a retreat from an argument she was not likely to resolve. Her own mother and father were still not happy about her career choice.

Nearly an hour later, Kris withdrew to a tiny table. She edged her feet out of her shoes. *How could something so small be so painful to wear?*

As she mulled that reality of her life, she eyed the room. She'd managed to keep most of it between her and Vicky even as they circulated. The orchestra, a full-size one no less, had launched itself into dance tunes shortly after the shoot-out between Vicky and Kris.

The woman in the flyaway apparel—Kris could not think of it as a ball gown—and the long line of men waiting to see what the view was up close, held down the center of the dance floor. As long as Kris kept Vicky's white dress behind that zoo, they were in no danger of a second battle.

Maybe the almost-not-dressed woman was not an accident of personal choice. Would Ms. Broadmore go so far as to hire

a professional stripper to be a control rod to keep her party below nuclear meltdown? Interesting question.

Kris edged her toes back into Abby's torture device and
prepared to prove she would not flinch first. Not her.

A voice came from behind her. "So, did you kill that poor
girl's brother?"

11

So much for Kris's hope that the Longknife faction would keep a solid hold on its side of the room. Kris swiveled in her chair to face a woman. Her gray hair likely put her over a hundred years old. But it didn't look like she'd put them to use gathering wisdom. Not if she was willing to beard Kris among her own supporters.

NELLY?

SHE IS NOT SQUAWKING. I AM SEARCHING MY MEMORY FOR A FACIAL RECOGNITION.

So Kris would have to go on what she had in her own gray matter. The dress was conservative. Even old-fashioned. And the lapel pin claimed service in the Iteeche War. Somewhere in the back of Kris's head, a soft voice was whispering something. Alarm bells weren't going off. It was more like a kitten's purr. Part of Kris wanted to roll over on her back and let the woman pet her belly.

You're definitely going weird, her paranoid self snapped.

No, she's not what she sounds like, another part of Kris shouted, that young part of her that got lost when little Eddy died under the kidnappers' pile of manure.

"Gramma?" Kris half whispered. "Gramma Ruth?"

The woman opened her arms, and painful shoes or not, Kris ran to hug her.

"I figured for sure your mom had seen that you forgot me, after she ushered Trouble and me out of the house and told us never to come back."

"Did she?" Kris asked, looking down into sparkling gray eyes. "She didn't tell me that. And I had my pictures of you and the general. I didn't exactly leave them out on the dresser for Mother's maids to steal, but how could I ever forget you. You haven't aged a bit."

"Now you're lying like a Longknife," Gramma Ruth said, and swatted Kris gently.

"Is Grampa Trouble here?" A frown crossed Kris's face as the question sneaked out without a lot of thought.

"Let me guess. From that reaction, I'd say the old boy has been up to his usual no good and maybe you're starting to understand why so few of us love that rascal's lopsided smile."

"Let's just say I'm learning to double-check, no, triple-check any advice he gives me."

"Good girl. Now you just be sure to do ten or twenty checks on anything that scamp Ray comes up with and you just might live to have as many gray hairs as I've got."

Good advice, Kris would have to think about how a serving Naval officer did that to a king who had authority over her.

"So, what are you doing here?" Kris asked as she guided her great-grandmother to her table and settled down for a long talk.

"I'm teaching ancient history, you know, the stuff five, ten minutes ago. I have a visiting professorship at Garden City University. I guess they figure a relic of the Unity and Iteeche wars is just the old fart to ramble on about the dusty past."

SHE HAS A PH.D. IN MODERN HISTORY, Nelly put in.

"If you ramble anything like I remember, you're keeping them awake in class." Kris remembered that Gramma Ruth hadn't just talked about the past but dropped reading hints like pedals off a three-day-old rosebud. "And probably burning the midnight oil finishing assignments."

Gramma shrugged. "Don't get too many complaints."

And are you here just for that, or is there more to your travels, like there always seems to be to mine? Kris decided to prod that gently.

"Will Grampa Trouble be joining you here?"

Gramma snorted. "Eden is one of quite a few planets that has a standing invitation for him to be on the next ship out if he should pause here a moment. Probably for good cause, too."

"I'm still working on one of those here," Kris said. She cast a look at the woman Marine that had taken over the nanoscouts. She shook her head curtly. A social event like this took place in a flood of bugs.

Kris nodded, and quickly gave her favorite great-grandmother the official version of the assignment that brought her to Eden.

"Well, honey," Gramma Ruth said, "they also serve who only hang around. Or so I told myself when I was officially just growing vegetables on the old *Patton*. I understand you had a chance to horse that old wreck around space."

"You would have been proud of the vets, turning the *Patton* into a museum, and then into a semidecent fighting ship."

"If they got her up to semidecent, they had her in better shape than we ever did." The old woman laughed. "She always was a mess. Is she a wreck now?"

"I don't know. Last I saw her, she was as attached to High Chance as they could get her, what with all the damage. She's their ship. They'll have to decide."

Gramma paused for a second, then asked, "And what are you deciding?"

Kris looked around, as if she could see the nanos buzzing them. "I really don't know. Any chance we could do lunch?"

"Not like your lunch today, I hope."

"You heard?" Which raised the question: "How?"

Now Gramma Ruth laughed, a hearty belly laugh that got most of her shaking. "One of my students is from the Turkish community on the Euro side. He suggested *The Turkish Truth. Triple T.* A usually reliable source."

"I've had the *El Camino Real* suggested to me."

"Good rag," Ruth said. "I often see them exchanging by-lines with the *Triple T*. Them and the *Banzai*, a source my Japanese students swear by."

Kris fidgeted, wanting to talk more, but unwilling to share it with the rest of human space. There were so many things she wanted to ask someone who'd married into this zoo that was the Longknife legend. Gramma Ruth and Trouble weren't Longknifes . . . exactly. But Grampa Trouble had been Ray's right hand through so much of the Iteeche War. And they'd married into the family; their daughter, Sarah, had been Grampa Al's first wife until a truck driver took off her side of the car. Accident or bungled assassination attempt? It was now too late to determine.

Yes, Gramma Ruth knew the sorrow of being too close to one of those damn Longknifes. Yet here she was, saying hi to a great-granddaughter that she could have walked past.

Hold it? How did Gramma Ruth get into this soiree?

Kris realized she was not holding up her end of the conversation. "Who gave you an invite?" she asked softly.

Again the old campaigner laughed. "Us college professors have our ways. We may be poor, but we're genteel poverty. Don't think my name was ever mentioned." She glanced around. "Some old fart here is without his wife, I suspect. Ah yes, he's in line to dance with the confetti girl. I'll have to tell his wife. Or not."

Kris figured there was one item she wouldn't mind having the whole universe know. "You know anyplace where a girl can get decent shoes to wear that aren't combat boots?"

The two of them studied Kris's feet.

"In your size, I'd suggest the company that made my old milking shoes, back in the days when I was just a poor farm girl looking for a nice boy to settle down with me on Hurtford."

"Boy did you miss. Gramma, I'm thinking you're not the one I should talk to about finding a man."

"Oh, I'm the one, gal. Boy's are easy to find. Men, now, that's a whole lot harder to do. Hey, you, Marine. Yeah, you, Lieutenant."

Jack turned from where he'd been facing out, giving Kris as much privacy as anyone in a social goldfish bowl could have. "Yes, ma'am."

"When you going to make an honest girl of this woman?"

Kris yelped, but Jack held his ground manfully. "Commander Tordon, there is no way I could make an honest woman of a Longknife. They are born into iniquity and it only gets worse as they pass the age of reason. Assuming they ever do. Sorry, ma'am. I'll take a bullet for her, but there is no way to make her honest."

Which, Kris had to admit, was a very neat sidestep of the question Kris would have loved to have a straight answer to. And a warning of what lay ahead if she ever did figure out a way to pop that question to the main man in her life. Oh, pooh!

The night dragged on in mindless chatter. By the grace of some bored god, Victoria Peterwald folded her tent and slipped away before the first yawn attacked Kris. So she got home at a decent hour and actually enjoyed a good night's sleep.

Officially, Kris counted that as a good day.

Interlude 1

Grant von Schrader drummed his fingers on the door of his limo. He drummed them while Miss Victoria Smythe-Peterwald posed for one last photo shot . . . five times.

The young woman was vain. Very vain.

The door finally closed and the driver immediately put the multiton behemoth in motion. Grant continued drumming his fingers until his personal computer, directly plugged into his brain, announced, THE CAR IS SECURE.

"Remind me again why your father sent you to Eden?" Grant said as softly . . . and as deceptively as his temper would allow.

"I believe he said something vague, like you are to show me the ropes," the young heiress said, arranging her dress so that it fell tightly across her breasts, allowing nipples to raise their distracting heads.

Grant swore softly to himself and praised the common sense that came with age and lower hormone levels.

"I believe he also mentioned something about helping you develop enough common sense so that you'd survive a bit longer than your brother."

That got a raised eyebrow from the young woman. Was she wondering if *Pater* had passed along coverage of that meeting . . . or if Dad's security wasn't as tight as he boasted.

But she said nothing . . . and Grant left her unenlightened.

Grant let his student fully measure that thought through a long pause. "It was foolish to confront the Longknife brat."

"And why should it be?" came back without a second for reflection. "She murdered my brother. I can't let her live. She knows that as well as I do."

Grant sighed . . . soundlessly. Thirteen generations and the Peterwalds had come to this. He'd met the thirteenth of that name twice and been unimpressed. His sister was not coming across any better. He warily drew in a deep breath and began— again—the education of this gorgeous pig seated beside him.

"Your brother is dead. There is no doubt about that. However, just how he ended up dead is subject to some conjecture. What there is no doubt about is that he crossed swords with Miss Longknife—frequently. A neutral observer might consider that a bad habit you might want to break."

"She killed my brother. She will pay," Victoria hissed.

So much for lesson one. With little expectation of greater success, Grant went on to lesson two. "No more men will be spending an hour alone with you in your bedroom."

"Oh, and Vennie was so pleasant a companion," the young woman said, licking her lips. "I haven't seen him around recently. Where is the boy?"

On a slow starship back to Greenfeld where he would explain himself personally to Henry Smythe-Peterwald, XII. Grant hoped Harry would be very interested in what he did with his daughter for an hour . . . and why he put at risk a project that had been fifteen years in development. Grant would not want to be in Vitali Gruschka's fashionable shoes for that meeting.

"He has been called to a meeting with your father," was all Grant said.

The young woman smiled as if she knew something Grant did not. Or maybe did not care about a man who'd worked hard and well for Grant for ten years.

"You do not kill a Peterwald and live," was all she said.

"Then kill her someplace else. We have business here on Eden. Profitable business. And I do not care for you washing your dirty linens in my backyard. Your father sent you here to learn about making a profit. You can kill this Longknife troublemaker anywhere else you want. Just not here."

The young woman seemed to mull that over for a while, then smiled. "Yes, Uncle Grant. I most certainly can."

Von Schrader wasn't totally sure what that meant, but he'd done about as much as he could for one evening. He'd learned long ago that Peterwald heads were very dense.

One of the reasons he was here on Eden, about as far as he could comfortably get from Harry.

But if the first package Henry Peterwald dropped on Grant was a pain, the second package was a delight.

Later that evening, when Miss Vicky was hopefully well and solidly put to bed, a door opened in Grant's study that most visitors thought was just his "I-love-me wall," full of pictures of Grant with movers and shakers.

To Grant, it was his target wall.

And an experienced target was the ramrod-straight warrior who came from the secret passage that led to the wall.

"Eginhard Petrovich Müller," Grant said, hugging the man. "I thought you'd be dead by now."

"Who in the old team would have believed that Lucky Grant would live to grow a paunch," the younger man said, patting Grant's flat belly.

"When they told me you would be leading the team, I had it run through the decoding gear twice. But no. It was you. And the rest of the team, is it as hard as you?"

"As hard as you taught me to be." Eginhard grinned back.

And yes, Grant's young lieutenant was showing gray around the temples. So the kid had learned wisdom and now led his own company of storm troopers. *Of course*, Grant told himself, *I am no older*. He laughed.

"And the company, are they arriving soon?"

"Many of them are already here, sir. Everyone has their own cover. No two alike. If one goes south, we will not weep, but, at least so far, all have reported in. Are the police here on Eden blind?"

"Not blind, just old and comfortable in their ways. The place is a ripe fruit, ready to be plucked."

The team leader clicked his heels at attention and saluted. "We dreamed of plucking fruit in the old days. Now we shall."

12

Kris actually jumped out of bed when her alarm woke her at Oh Dark Early. Marines were the best of company to keep early in the morning. For her jog, Kris figured she could go light. She just pulled on a spider-silk body stocking, sweatshirt, gym shorts with ceramic slat inserts, and combat boots with similar armor.

Proof against most personal weapons, she slipped her own automatic into the small of her back . . . and ran into Jack and Penny in the hall.

"Got to stand up to the Marines," Penny said. Her sweatshirt said GO NAVY.

Jack's sweats were still Wardhaven Secret Service, which was to say, blank.

Kris laughed with her friends and strode outside.

And came to a roaring halt.

Captain DeVar stood waiting for her. He saluted as Kris took in what he had arrayed before her. "The Marine Detachment is ready for PT, Your Highness."

"In full battle rattle!" Kris yelped.

That they were. Each Marine stood with his or her M-6 at port arms. Without a full inspection, it was beyond Kris's kin, but it sure looked like each of them were in full-battle gear . . . with a full-battle load.

"Is all this necessary?" Kris whispered.

"Your Highness, I will not take my Marines in harms way without proper armor and equipment."

Kris waved at her eyebrow and the Marine captain smartly dropped his salute. "Gunny Sergeant, open the detachment," he ordered.

Orders were given and half the Marines smartly took three steps forward, leaving room for Kris and company to slip into the space between First and Second Platoon.

"Do we have a permit for this much firepower?" Kris asked.

"I fully expect that anyone concerned about that fine point of the law is still sound asleep. Shall we get started, Your Highness, so we can complete our run before that changes?"

Properly chastised, Kris settled in between Jack and Penny.

"Oh, one more thing, Your Highness. Local marksmanship is reported to be pretty bad, so we'd appreciate if you'd wear this." Captain DeVar handed Kris a bright red sweatshirt. On the front a mean-looking bulldog growled SEMPER FI, from behind a golden globe, anchor, and rocket ship.

On the back was a target in circles of Navy blue and gold.

"Thank you *so* much," Kris said, then pulled the shirt on over her armored one.

"Don't want any Marines ending up as collateral damage," the captain explained with a grin. "If one of my Marines takes a hit, I want it in the front, charging the bastards."

"Ooo-rah,"answered that. Softly, so as not to wake anyone.

"Gunny Sergeant, move the detachment out."

And they headed for the mall. There had been a light rain during the night. The air was cool with the smell of trees and fresh earth. And honest sweat. They had the place to themselves, except for a trash truck carrying off yesterday's refuse. Three miles never went so quickly for Kris.

Though it did leave her a bit breathless. She was spending

way too much time being a social target. She'd better start paying attention to that target on her back or someone just might score a bull's-eye.

As they jogged up to the embassy, a large black sedan pulled to a stop ahead of them. Gunny brought them to a halt as Inspector Johnson got out from the driver's side. No chauffeur today . . . or maybe just at this hour.

Kris broke ranks to trot up and join the inspector. Jack and Captain DeVar hung back in easy hearing and close support.

"Didn't expect to see you this early," Kris said to break the ice of the hard glare the cop was giving the Marines.

"I got a wake-up call from the Sanitation Division. Someone asking if the mall was being invaded. I suspected I knew where the invasion came from." He opened his arms as if in surprise. "Here I am and here you are. And you and you," he said, nodding toward Jack and the captain.

"May I dismiss the troops, Your Highness?" DeVar asked.

"*Please* do," the inspector said.

"Kindly do," Kris said, and quickly, quietly, it was so.

Jack and Penny took guard around Kris, checking out the building roofs, streets, and any other potential site where death might reach for her. The Marines in battle dress raced off, but didn't leave her unprotected for long. A minute hadn't gone by before two marines in khaki double-timed from the embassy. The apparent duty team on sensors were followed only moments later by one Marine hobbling on crutches as quickly as he could, his left foot in a cast, him in a hurriedly donned sweatsuit.

That was when it hit Kris. She'd been adopted into the Marine Corps family. They had made her one of their own. It sent a shiver down her spine. And stiffened it, too. These men and women would lay down their lives for her.

Of course, the unspoken contract flowed both ways. Loyalty went up and down or it didn't go at all. As unlikely as it might seem to some, she now owed her life to them. A stranger to the uniform might not see much prospect for Kris to pay the full price for one of these privates or NCOs.

Kris knew differently. A solemn vow now bound each of them equally.

And that was the only way it could be. One for all. All of them for each other when the mouth of hell was yawning and the piper demanded his pay.

Kris found herself standing a little taller, her back a bit more ramrod, as Gunny would expect of her, even as she passed the time of day with Inspector Johnson.

If he was aware of the change that came over the woman in front of him, he certainly showed no evidence of it.

"Did you bring over my weapons permit?" had been Kris's first gambit.

"Not my job description," the inspector said. Then paused, as if debating whether or not to say more. Kris held him hostage with her eyes. She'd learned at her father's knee that a good politician could often get confessions, concessions, or even extra campaign donations if they just didn't break eye contact.

And unlike other forms of hostage taking, holding someone's eyes against their will was not an indictable offense.

No surprise, it worked in the soft morning light.

"Some of my associates in the police force, maybe other places, are wondering if maybe we shouldn't withhold the permit. Some think it might encourage you to go on your way."

Staying in this shooting gallery with no weapon! She couldn't go on carrying without a permit; sooner or later folks would get tired of her and hers flaunting their gun control laws. If they started frisking her every time she left the embassy . . .

"I would have thought that whoever didn't drive by that roadside bomb we stumbled over yesterday would be oh so happy that I'd get a permit for my reward." She tried batting her eyelashes along with the words. In the movies, it always worked. No doubt, it would work for Victoria Peterwald.

Kris also tried her ace in the hole. NELLY, DO WE KNOW THE NAME OF WHOEVER IT WAS WE SAVED?

NO, KRIS. I AM STILL WORKING ON THAT. IT IS FAR MORE COMPLICATED THAN YOU WOULD BELIEVE. CAN I BRIEF YOU NOW? IT WILL BE A LONG ONE.

LATER, Kris said. Nelly wasn't helping her, and clearly her experiment in feminine wiles hadn't worked, either.

The inspector shook his head. "I'm sorry. I might officially be grateful, if that had officially happened. However, officially, it didn't. And, unofficially, we're not sure what to make of it. Did someone trying to get you almost get one of us? That's not something we'd like to have happen."

And, what with so much of this planet's current events disappearing with no trace, she could hardly defend her honor. Kris scowled. "So you're willing to ship my very expensive casket to King Ray, and Grampa Al and my father with a sincere diplomatic apology that my death happened on your watch?"

"Certainly as sincere as the diplomatic apology Wardhaven sent Greenfeld on the death of Henry Peterwald the Thirteenth," the inspector said with a very straight face.

"There is no sincerity in diplomatic apologies," Kris muttered. *Okay, that didn't work, now what do we try?* Kris noticed that it was now Inspector Johnson who was holding her eyes and not blinking.

What could he want?

"Why are you here?" he said softly.

Behind Kris, Jack snorted.

"Not that question again," Penny whispered through a sigh.

Kris found her eyes raising to the heavens. No surprise, the early morning gray had no answer written on the low clouds. Now it was her turn to take in a deep breath and heave it out with enough dramatics to rival one of Tommy's best Irish sighs.

"Inspector," she finally said, looking him straight in the eye. "Would you believe that your planet, with its established ways, solid gun control laws, and law-abiding population was presented to me as a safe harbor where Wardhaven might send their wayward daughter and she'd stay alive while the Rim cooled down and forgot about her last, deadly escapade?"

"Believe it? Not likely."

"Well, I'm having a harder and harder time believing it, too," Kris muttered softly.

The inspector chuckled.

"It seemed believable before I got here and discovered that the same old, same old happens here. It just never makes it into the official record . . . or the late-night news." Kris bit out those last two words. What a joke they were here.

The inspector swallowed his mirth. "You're serious."

"As serious as that bomb yesterday. I'm here to buy paper clips and spare parts. Arrange for computer sales and software licenses. Stay away from stray bullets until Henry Peterwald the Twelfth forgets I was involved in his son's demise."

"That won't happen anytime soon."

"Tell me about it. And certainly not with Vicky getting in my face." Kris paused, frowning in thought. "Any chance you could find out when the request went in for her visa? Was it before or after mine? If after, how soon after?"

The inspector raised an eyebrow. "An interesting question. I may look into it. Maybe."

"And you might share the results with me? Maybe?" Kris might be weak in femme fatale, but she'd learned to wheedle the cook at Nuu House shortly after learning to walk. Very shortly.

"I might," the inspector said, eyeing her. "I might if you could figure out why you're really here and share it with me."

"It's hard to conclude a bargain with all those mights and maybes in it," Kris said.

"And I'm certainly not interested in shaking on it. Haven't you heard? It's dangerous to shake a Longknife's hand."

"Only since I was in my crib," Kris grumbled.

"Well, I'll be seeing you. No doubt," the inspector said, and departed.

"What was that about?" Jack asked.

"I. Have. No. Idea." Kris slammed all the exasperation she felt into her words. "Any of you have something better, I'd be glad to hear it."

All she got were shaking heads. They headed in to shower, dress, and breakfast. After that, none of them were any the wiser. But there was no summons to the ambassador's office, so, apparently, neither was anyone above them.

Kris was about to leave for exciting negotiations when Nelly broke in. "Kris, I have a message from Great-grandmother Ruth. She wonders if you are interested in lunch today."

"I could be," Kris said, glancing Jack and Captain DeVar's way. They nodded, so she assumed a full escort was available.

"She is teaching today, and asks you to meet her in front of Garden City University Faculty Center shortly after noon."

"Tell her I'll be there."

No doubt, it would be fun talking to Gramma. And maybe she'd slip Kris a sealed envelope under the table. Orders sent by way of an innocent gray head.

Innocent? Ha! Kris's paranoid self wasn't buying.

But why *was* Kris here?

13

Settled into her chair at the bargaining table, Kris put a smile on her lips, a bright look on her face . . . and told Nelly she was ready for a long, informative briefing.

It did turn out to be long. But informative? Maybe . . . if Kris could fit all the pieces together. And guess her way around a whole lot of blanks.

KRIS, EDEN NOT ONLY HAS SOME OF THE BEST ENCRYPTION INVENTED BY HUMANS AND COMPUTERS, BUT THERE ARE FIREWALLS BEHIND FIREWALLS EVERYWHERE I TURN. AND THEN THERE IS DATA THAT IS ONLY AVAILABLE OFF-LINE AND I HAVE TO PAY TO HAVE SOME HUMAN AUTHORIZE ITS RESTORATION. AND THERE IS NOT A SINGLE DATA STANDARD. THE PLACE IS ONE HUGE BABEL AS FAR AS INFORMATION STORAGE AND RETRIEVAL IS CONCERNED.

MOST PLANETS ORGANIZE THEIR DATA SO IT IS READILY AVAILABLE TO PEOPLE. NOT HERE. I DO NOT THINK THEY WANT ANYONE KNOWING WHAT ANYONE ELSE HAS.

Kris kept puzzlement off her face as around her the two sides talked about the cost of each unit and upgrades. Grampa Al had a standing offer of a job for Kris if she'd just resign from the Navy. He promised to keep her safe within the security cocoon he'd built for himself in Nuu Enterprise's headquarters.

Kris made note to send Grampa Al a nice letter declining his gracious offer. And asking him if, in the future she ever did accept, to please shoot her when she showed up for work.

Surely, some space alien had eaten her brain.

But back to Nelly's problem. It looked like the last thing anyone on Eden wanted was to share information. Kris had been raised to think of information as power. Well, Eden was doing its best to see that very few got their hands on it.

What must research be like? Kris would have to ask Gramma.

Nelly was going on at great length about the lack of any data standards. Most individual's files on Wardhaven opened with a person's name, date of birth, and identification number. On Eden, those might be hidden anywhere in the file. And each system assigned them different locations.

AND YOU HAVE TO CRACK EACH SYSTEM. EACH AND EVERY ONE OF THEM!

THERE HAS TO BE A DATA DICTIONARY OF SOME SORT, Kris thought.

OH, THERE IS, Nelly agreed. OFF-LINE OR OFF SOMEWHERE UNDER GOD ONLY KNOWS WHAT TITLE. KRIS, THESE PEOPLE ARE PARANOID. AND SCHIZOPHRENIC. THEY ARE ALL CRAZY. LIKE IN THE BOOKS.

Nelly, of course, had access to all the medical books on Wardhaven, but those weren't the ones she meant. Lately, Kris's computer was analyzing all the action, suspense, and murder fiction she could get. Nelly was curious about the human experience of fear. She blamed it on the penchant Kris had for so often getting them almost killed.

IF YOU ARE GOING TO KILL US ALL, I NEED SOME EARLY WARNING. SOME SENSE THAT WE ARE IN FOR TROUBLE. JACK AND PENNY KNOW IT IS COMING. THEY HAVE FEAR. ALL I HAVE IS MY OWN DATA FORECAST. I NEED SOMETHING BETTER.

So Kris put up with dreams of being chased and mass murders and some really ugly stuff until she demanded that Nelly buffer her nighttime studies better, and those nightmares had stopped.

To be replaced by the usual ones of being chased and people trying to kill her. Or visits from those people who had followed her orders into an early grave.

Kris shivered, something definitely not called for at the bargaining table. "Anyone else cold?" she asked. No one was.

Kris paid attention to the conversation for a while, then went back to Nelly. BUT WHAT ABOUT THE MEDIA? SOMEONE HAS TO KNOW WHAT IS REALLY GOING ON. YOU CAN'T FOOL ALL OF THE PEOPLE ALL OF THE TIME, Kris said, quoting the prime minister quoting someone.

THERE IS A MEDIA, BUT WHAT PASSES FOR MAINSTREAM REPORTING DOES NOT SEEM ALL THAT RELIABLE. NOT IF WE USE OUR OWN OBSERVATIONS. I AM NOW RIDING THE EMBASSY'S SUBSCRIPTION. IT IS AN INTERESTING EXERCISE IN WHAT I SUSPECT YOU WOULD CALL FRUSTRATION. NOT ONLY DID THEY HAVE NOTHING TO SAY ABOUT OUR TWO KNOWN INCIDENTS, BUT THERE IS NOTHING ABOUT ANY POLITICAL ACTS OF PROTEST. YES, THERE WERE THE ODD FAMILY DISTURBANCES, PEOPLE GOT CUT UP IN BARS, THEIR KITCHEN, EVEN AT SCHOOL, BUT NO GUNS. NO BOMBS.

AND SOMETHING I FOUND VERY INTERESTING WAS THE WAY THE NEWS DISAPPEARED.

INTO ARCHIVES? Kris asked.

SOME ARTICLES DID GO INTO ARCHIVES YOU COULD REACH . . . FOR AN EXTRA SUBSCRIPTION . . . WHICH OUR EMBASSY HAS. BUT THERE WOULD BE NEW POLICIES ANNOUNCED AND WHEN I WENT LOOKING FOR THE OLD POLICIES, THERE WAS NOTHING IN THE ARCHIVE. I FOUND REFERENCES TO EARLIER SPEECHES IN STORIES, BUT NO SPEECHES OR EVENTS. NO NOTHING. THE DATA STORAGE IS LARGE ENOUGH FOR A WHOLE LOT MORE DATA. AND IT'S THERE. THEY JUST WILL NOT LET ME GET AT IT. KRIS, I DO NOT LIKE TO FAIL ON MATTERS LIKE THIS. Nelly almost spat in Kris's head.

Kris squelched a chuckle that didn't fit into the present bargaining. Nelly did not have a lot of experience with failure. It would be interesting to see how the present state of her

computer's upgrade dealt with this. WHAT ABOUT THOSE
OTHER NEWS SOURCES? THE ONES LIEUTENANT MARTINEZ
AND GRAMMA RUTH MENTIONED.

THE EMBASSY DOES NOT SUBSCRIBE TO THEM, Nelly
started. I USED PENNY'S ACCOUNT TO SUBSCRIBE TO BOTH,
THEN JACK'S TO SUBSCRIBE TO TWO MORE OF THOSE MEN-
TIONED. THE SUBS WERE NOT CHEAP. I REPAID THEM FROM
YOUR ACCOUNT.

THEY REPORTED BOTH EVENTS WE SAW, BUT NOT ALL
THAT MUCH. THEY KNEW A BOMB EXPLODED ON THE MALL,
BUT NOTHING ABOUT A MOTORCADE. THEY REPORTED SHOTS
FIRED IN THE GOVERNMENT DISTRICT, PROBABLY AUTOMATIC
WEAPONS. THEY HAD NO BODY COUNT. I WAS TEMPTED TO
FILE A REPORT, KRIS. THEY PAY MONEY FOR NEWS.

HAVING ONE REPORTER IN OUR GROUP, NELLY, IS ENOUGH,
Kris said. If Nelly took to selling information along with
Abby, Kris would have no hope of privacy.

The negotiations were getting close; Kris asked Nelly to
keep any more for later. Still, as Kris paid more attention to
the table, her mind gnawed at what her computer had learned.

It wasn't much. Just enough to give Kris a strong hunch
that something was rotten in Eden. Still, using the old religious story as a hook to hang things on, she had no idea who
the snake might be. No idea even where the tree might hang
out. She didn't even know who was filling the shoes—or bare
feet—of the guy and gal.

Before too long, Kris called a halt for lunch and took her
mulling elsewhere.

Maybe Gramma Ruth did know what her orders were. Ab-
sent that, Kris knew she could count on the old woman for
some fun talk . . . and maybe a few more pieces to add to the
puzzle laid out on Eden for Kris. Maybe.

14

Kris did not find a limo waiting to take her to lunch. Instead, three black, hulking, all-terrain city vehicles were parked under the portico of the embassy. Jack joined her, in dress khaki and blues, and flipped a coin.

"Heads," he said. "You ride in the middle one."

"And if it had been tails?"

"I'd have flipped it again to see if you rode in the lead or trailing rig," Jack said, opening the door for her. Penny was already in the far seat, next to the window.

It looked like Jack intended to take the other window seat, leaving her no place but the center one. "You sure I need all this protection?"

"Don't know, Your Highness. But I'm sure that when we get in trouble again, neither one of us will figure you have enough."

Kris sat where Jack pointed. In front were three Marines, all in dress khaki and blues. "How big is my detail?"

"Fifteen, plus us," Penny said. "There also will be an escort from Eden, but they intend to stay back."

"Out of the line of fire," Kris muttered, maybe a split second behind Jack.

"I've got sniper teams in both of the other rigs. They'll go high if things get mortal. Oh, and two women to escort you to the head. Want anything else?"

"Yes, a weapons permit to make this all legal."

"Wish in one hand, spit in the other," Penny said with a quirk of a smile, "and see which one you get the most out of."

"Your grandmother?" Kris asked.

"No, one of Tommy's," Penny said with hardly a flinch.

The convoy was only a few minutes away from the campus when Nelly said, "Kris, I have a call from Great-grandmother Ruth."

"Put her on."

"Kris, I got out of class a bit late, could you pick me up at the back of the Faculty Center?"

"I'd be glad to, Gramma. Where do you want us?"

A map appeared in the air in front of Kris, a green blip on it. A moment later it was repeated on the heads-up display in front of the driver.

"I got it, Your Highness. We'll have to drive around the campus, but no problem."

"We'll see you there," Kris said.

And the green blip was suddenly no longer on the map.

"She throttled her squawker!" Nelly said as she pulled the map from the air in front of Kris. "Civilians aren't supposed to be able to do that," she sniffed.

"Possibly, Commander Tordon has kept her reserve commission on the books," Jack said. "But living close to Longknifes, I suspect she's just paid for more security than the average head-in-the-sand civilian feels a need for. And has her head on straight enough to use it whenever she gets too close to a Longknife. Might explain why she's still got that head."

Kris found nothing to argue with.

The rigs zigged and zagged around a campus that looked very familiar to Kris. In the center of things were a few brick buildings, maybe one or two with pretentious stone pillars.

The next layer out showed a more prosperous planet as granite and stone replaced brick in someone's idea of a neoclassical style. But the population kept growing and money started getting short. The outer layers of classrooms and labs were shoehorned into big, blocky buildings rising not so high that they required more expensive construction materials, nor so low that they took up too much land that was getting expensive. The history of education was writ the same on hundreds of planets.

If Kris smiled at the sameness of the buildings, she almost laughed at the students, products of some cookie-cutter mold kept handy on every planet. The rigs' advance slowed, surrounded by a mob of hungry college students who, though afoot, showed no fear of cars and a near proprietary attitude toward the streets.

"For God's sake, don't hit one," Kris said after a close near encounter with a jaywalking pair of redheads.

"I'm doing my best," Kris's driver said, tapping the brake as two coeds ducked between her and the lead car.

It was a good thing they were going slow, because they found Gramma Ruth waving at them a full two blocks early.

Jack said a bad word, usually reserved for only the worst of situations. Only this time, it oozed admiration. "She is one smart cookie."

Jack opened the door and pulled down a jump seat for himself. Ruth settled in next to Kris. Jack called over his shoulder, "Take the next right and get us out of this mob."

"They don't have the common sense God promised a gnat," Ruth said. "I know. I love them and I'm proud of the ones that actually do learn. But even the ones that can learn smarts may have no concept of what they should do for personal safety.

"The peace has been wonderful, but I can't help but wonder if it's been too long," Gramma added, putting on her safety belt.

"Now that we're headed away from the campus," Kris asked, "where do we eat?"

"Oh, I know just the place. It's about six blocks down the

way, then four to the right." Ruth held up her wrist and squirted something to the driver's computer.

"Got it," she immediately said.

"Do we have reservations?" Jack asked.

"That's what I like about this place. They serve the best Greek food in light-years, and never require a reservation. Oh, and they have separate rooms for those willing to pay extra. You'll like it," she said, giving Jack a wide, knowing grin.

"Kris, I'm starting to think at least some of your relatives can acquire common sense. If they live long enough," Jack said.

"Ah, but remember, I married into this mess. I'm a farmer's daughter," Gramma Ruth said, patting down her gray hairs. "I learned common sense at my mother's knee and my father's worried brow. You spend a few years wondering when it's going to rain and if you'll be able to pay the mortgage on the place, and you'll know what matters and what doesn't."

"You can't have all that much common sense," Kris snorted, not at all liking the way Jack was fawning over this smart old lady. "She's met twice in the last twenty-four hours with a Longknife. Very risky business, I'd say, for an unarmed, unescorted little old lady."

"Who said I'm unarmed," Ruth snapped, and produced a very ladylike, and very dangerous-looking, automatic. It disappeared so fast that Jack didn't have a chance to raise an objection. Or for Kris to see where Gramma had it hiding.

"And didn't you see those two fine, young kids back there, keeping an eye out for me. Fine bodyguards they are."

"Hold it," Jack said, now getting a hand up.

"How'd you get your hands on a gun?" Kris said. "And where did you get a bodyguard?"

"I hired them," Gramma Ruth said very matter-of-factly.

"How?" Kris, Jack, Penny . . . and Nelly asked at once.

"From the guild hall, of course," Gramma answered.

"What guild hall?" Nelly demanded. "I searched the yellow database for armed escorts, bodyguards, security teams. Every title any sensible planet would use. There is no such thing."

"I even asked the ambassador," Kris added.

"You don't know," Gramma Ruth said, eyeing Kris, then Jack.

He shook his head.

She frowned. "When I learned you were coming, I mentioned to several of my friends on campus that I was excited to see you again. Next day, Dean Rosemon, head of graduate studies, an old fart from one of the oldest families on Eden, took me aside. He suggested I might want to see to my security, what with the bad blood between certain families and you Longknifes.

"I, of course, remarked of my surprise, seeing how Eden was so peaceful. Peaceful my eyeteeth. I know this place is seething under the surface. Every time I'm invited back, I'm surprised it's still here. Anyway, despite my most unladylike goading, all Herman Rosemon provided me with was a number for a consulting service."

Gramma Ruth shrugged. "I called the number. A very nice young man came by, looked at my daily schedule and my apartment. Two days later, just before you arrived, these two, hunky young men joined me for my walk to school, and they, or others like them have been with me every day since. I'm told the apartment is covered at night, but I've never met them."

"And your weapon?" Jack asked.

"Comes with the service, or so I'm told."

"Why weren't *we* told?" Kris demanded. "Better yet, why couldn't we even turn up a hint that this guild hall exists?"

Gramma Ruth chuckled. "Honey, haven't you figured it out? Eden presents one face to the universe, and saves its very ugly back side for locals and visitors who notice."

"So I'm finding out," Kris muttered.

"Any chance you could give us the number of that guild hall?" Jack asked, practical as always.

Ruth looked at the front seat, then glanced over her shoulder at the following rig. "You thinking of trading in your Marines for local hires?"

No way would Kris trust some local to take his pay and take her bullet. She wanted *her* Marines in reach.

Jack wasn't so sure. "They might have a better sense of this territory. God only knows we're way too much in the dark."

"But could you trust someone who's only here for the paycheck to *not* take a bigger paycheck to look the other way?" Kris said. Abby was one question mark. How many question marks could she afford to have around her.

"Hey, Marine, up there," Gramma Ruth called. "What's your price to sell out this barbarian princess from the Rim?"

"This fu—ah, planet," the sergeant said, struggling to clean up his language out of respect for the gray hairs in the backseat, "don't have enough money to buy a Marine, ma'am."

Gramma's answer was obscene and pure Corps. "How well I know that Marines don't sell out. I fought pirates and Iteeche with you hardcases, and never found one I wouldn't share a beer or a fighting hole with."

"Ruth?" the sergeant said. "Gramma Ruth? You aren't that Ruth, are you?"

"The Ruth that married General Trouble. Only then he was just a lieutenant. Though I can't say he was that much less trouble. Yes, Marine, I am that selfsame fool. Glad to make your acquaintance."

"Honored to make yours, ma'am." If possible, the Marines in front suddenly were sitting at an even stiffer attention.

"We got General Trouble's wife on board, here," the driver whispered into her mike. "Look sharp."

Kris laughed. "I'm just a princess. You, Gramma, are a legend."

"Not a legend, Kris, just a survivor. And a carcass no Marine wants to have to explain letting get suddenly dead to my esteemed and utterly worthless husband. Am I right, Sergeant?"

"I'd have to express some reservations about that worthless part, ma'am."

"Don't you line beasts still consider anyone above field grade as useless as tits on a boar hog?"

"Not in the presence of his wife, ma'am." But he was grinning. A stiff thing, he was still very much at attention.

"If I may interrupt," Jack said. "Do you think we might hire from the guild hall to give our weapons some veneer of legality? We could at least listen to them before we ignore their advice."

"I'm not sure I want some stranger fully briefed on my scheduled whereabouts," Kris said. "Gramma, did your escort hear you make your lunch appointment."

"Both times," she said, a growing smile on her face.

"And you didn't keep either," Kris said.

Gramma Ruth turned her smile loose on Jack. "You can say a lot about my bloodline, but you got to agree, boy, they do learn fast."

"Never expressed any doubt about that, ma'am. Only reason she's still alive."

"So, I'm guessing that Gramma Ruth would be happy if a Marine or two joined her bodyguard," Kris said.

"No, no, gal. I'm not a target. You are. Not me."

"We'll take that under consideration," Jack said.

From the way the sergeant in the front seat was smiling, Kris suspected the decision had already been referred to Captain De-Var and Gramma Ruth's opinion was no longer relevant.

And if her hired security had any thoughts of selling out, the sudden discovery that they now had Marine shadows could not help but encourage them to think again.

They arrived at the Acropolis; Gramma Ruth went in with three Marines to arrange lunch. Jack and the sergeant set up a perimeter for the three rigs to keep them unbooby-trapped, and set a rotation so everyone got a chance to eat and the rigs were never alone. They finished about the time Gramma Ruth returned.

"We've got their largest room. Jack, you want to see to its debugging? Kris, you're going to love this place."

It turned out one of the Marines on Ruth's initial escort was a defensive tech specialist and had already gotten the room cleared by the time they got there. The walk through the great room was . . . an experience.

The usual clientele totally ignored, or at least did a very good imitation of ignoring, the parade of uniformed marines. Even the snipers with long guns slung down the front of their full-battle rattle got no second looks.

"Interesting place you have here," Kris said to the owner, as he took them down an aisle lined with artificial grapevines. On the wall of the main room was a view of the rebuilt Acropolis above Athens. It looked hand painted.

"I provide what my clients want," the owner said, smiling jovially, then added with a shrug, "If I don't, there are plenty of places in town who will."

Kris tossed Gramma Ruth a glance. Which Ruth let go right by. Clearly any explanation would save for later.

The room was large. Its walls were painted with window views of old Earth's Greece. The sniper teams took seats at the tables beside the two real windows. The one door was quickly surrounded by Marines at the tables closest to it.

Ruth led the way to the table in the room's center. "This should do us fine."

The owner offered to take their orders. "It's lunch. Most people are rushed."

Ruth glanced at the menu, then ordered something in Greek that made the owner smile. "You have excellent taste, Madame."

Kris ordered the same. As did Jack and Penny. The owner left promising them a magnificent experience. Around Kris, most of the Marines were ordering hamburgers, though a few did go for the lamb version of the familiar lunch.

As the waiters left, Gramma Ruth unfolded her linen napkin, sipped from her water, and asked, "So, why are you here?"

Kris gave the usual explanation.

Gramma Ruth barely managed to swallow her water before she spat a mirthless laugh. "No wonder Trouble was so mad at Ray the last time he messaged me. The love of my life was his usual coy self, refusing to tell me what Ray was up to. Said I'd find out soon enough. I guess I have."

Now Kris demurely unfolded her napkin. "So I take it you don't have sealed orders to hand me. I was so looking forward to Grampa Ray telling me just once what he'd sent me into."

Gramma Ruth snorted several times as Kris finished. "The problem is, Kris, that the old boy has no idea what he's doing. Don't you know that by now?"

"Are we talking about the same Ray Longknife, legend from one end of human space to the other. King of some sort over a hundred planets?" Kris asked.

Jack and Penny looked a bit uncomfortable at what some might consider treason . . . if not to the putative royalty, at least to the historical legend. Around the room, Marines got very interested in the wall paintings.

"Kris, girl, haven't you figured out the truth here? Cause if you're still all starry eyed about your lineage, it won't do us any good for me to tell you the answer."

Kris didn't shoot back an immediate response, but chose her words carefully. "Gramma, I knew that what most people take for the Longknife facts are more a product of poor reporting and just plain luck. Unbelievable luck to still be alive, all things considered. We are flesh and blood like everyone else."

"That is nice to hear," Gramma sniffed. "So talk to me about Grampa Ray, named by some king of a hundred planets."

Kris thought for a moment, then, without raising her voice, said. "Marines, I really don't want to read about this in the media tomorrow." A few heads nodded, then she went on, "Grampa Ray comes from a long line of barkers and biters. And if anyone in his lineage ever stopped by a church, it was only to nip and snap at the preacher's heels."

Jack and several other marines looked likely to choke. Penny actually beamed. Probably the first smile Kris had seen on her face since the battle that made her a widow.

Gramma Ruth grinned from gray hair to gray hair. "I don't believe I could have said it better."

"So," Kris immediately went on, "we're agreed Grampa Ray isn't some superman. Doesn't have a crystal ball, and sometimes shoots his way out of the messes he's gotten himself, and half of humanity, into. Stipulating that, why would he send me here?"

There was a harsh rap at the door. A moment later several waiters charged in carrying delightfully aromatic platters.

And Marines made automatics disappear as quickly as they'd appeared. For a long minute, Kris watched as an interesting array of food was set before her. As she had so often when on the campaign trail for Father, Kris prepared to see what and *how* a more knowledgeable elder ate, and would follow her lead.

When the help left, Gramma seemed to have other things on her mind. As she slowly ate from a strange-looking salad with a stranger-smelling cheese, she eyed Kris.

Kris let the silence stretch, then slowly twist itself into a pretzel. Finally, she grabbed the bull by the horns. "Gramma, why doesn't everyone on Eden get to vote?"

Ruth laughed at that. "Ask the old girl a question. Huh. That'll get her talking." She looked at the lunch, mostly untouched. "Well, you folks fill your mouths. The lamb is especially good with the couscous. That's this stuff."

Kris took a small bite to keep Gramma happy. It actually tasted good. Still, she put her fork down and gave the older woman her full attention.

"I can't answer one question without firing up more, so let me start at the beginning. The various space programs on old Earth had just about completed their first fusion-powered spaceships when a lunkhead on a quantum-gravity research grant spotted this weird something out Jupiter's way.

"The Chinese shot off an unmanned high-speed probe that somehow stumbled into the jump point and vanished. Suddenly, the mission to Mars didn't seem so interesting and all three, the *Santa Maria* from Europe, the *Columbia* from America, and the *Smiling Goddess* from China are not quite racing for this little bit of nothing orbiting Jupiter.

"And despite the calmer heads back on Earth telling them to be careful, the three ships, after ducking just one remote through the jump, went charging through themselves.

"You know about the *Santa Maria* getting lost?" Penny and Kris nodded at that. "That kind of set the others back a bit. But only a bit. Alpha Centauri is a bust of a system. But there, not a day's hop from Earth's jump, was this other one, and behind it was lovely, blue-green Eden.

"It took the Chinese all of five seconds to announce they'd be colonizing the place. Which meant the Americans had to.

And the Europeans couldn't be left out. Now, who do you think was ready to come out here?"

"The best and the brightest," Kris said. That *was* the usual answer the teacher expected.

"Thank you for the textbook answer," Ruth drawled. "Now, who do you *really* think got on the ship to leave Earth forever?"

"Didn't the Chinese basically just press-gang their transportees?" Penny said.

"I expect that was in your schoolbook, if you grew up anywhere but the Chinese section of Eden, honey, but I don't think the old lords of Beijing were all that different.

"Eden got some folks that couldn't wait to see what's out here, but they aren't that many. Then came folks the old regime wanted to see gone. Some were in prison; others were just troublemakers. The Europeans and Americans emptied their jails of all but the worst offenders. And there were the religious zealots out to create a perfect world for *their* true believers."

"That's not exactly the mix you hear about in the Lander's Day speeches," Kris said, having sat through many a long-winded one praising the gallant, foresighted founders of Wardhaven.

Gramma chuckled. "Back on old Earth, the Americans were a lot like us, a population made up of folks who fled Europe. Some came on their own. Most were flat broke and came as indentured servants, in hock for their passage. Some were headed for jails when they signed their indenture. Two hundred years later, people might want ancestors from the early boats. But one American businessman of that time, a Benjamin Franklin, I think it was, had a different view. 'We ought to thank King George for his new colonists by shipping him rattlesnakes in return.'"

"Rattlesnakes?" Jack said.

"Yeah," Gramma Ruth answered. "Big, poisonous things. Not what you want to come across in a dark alley."

"And it was like that here on Eden?" Kris said.

"For a while. Then the Americans found their own planet, Columbia. The Chinese got New Canton all to themselves. Same for Europa with the Europeans. Yamoto got the Japanese into the act. And the less said about New Jerusalem, the better. So interest in New Eden, and New Haven, another one-for-all colony kind of dried up.

"And Eden was having enough trouble. Who's in charge? So once the banks weren't running things, the folks had a bit of a problem on their hands, figuring out just what kind of government they wanted telling them what to do. Did I mention that most of them didn't cotton to much telling?"

"So each set up their show to run their side," Kris said.

"With them setting the rules for their territory, and vetoing any law they didn't like for the planetary government. It worked fine at first," Ruth said.

"But they needed more labor than could be done by the babies they were producing," Penny said.

"You can praise technology all you want, but there's still the dirty work, the stuff no one wants their kids to grow up and have to do," Ruth said.

"So they imported them from Earth," Kris said.

"And as these guest workers grew in numbers, the problem of them not having any say in how they were governed got to be more and more of a problem," Gramma Ruth concluded.

Kris pursed her lips in thought. "And no one knows what to do about it."

"Oh, don't kid yourself. They've known what they have to do since before the Iteeche War. Ray probably could have gulled them into it . . . if we hadn't suddenly found ourselves up to our eyeballs in critters with too many eyeballs and no love for us. When you're crossing a raging river, it's really hard to talk folks into changing their horse. Tarnation, girl! Some folks would consider it a damn fool thing to even consider. No, Ray folded his tent real fast, and the way things were stayed the same. Right up to today."

"Everyone knows what needs doing?" Jack said.

"Every year, students throw the same debate. Kids with franchise defending the status quo. Kids from the other side of town pointing out why it can't go on this way. Lots of ideas for working the change. Some want just one big happy parliament, like so many other planets have. That kind of frightens a lot of folks. Big changes tend to.

"So others suggest more of the same. The Spanish should have their own house. And the Turks. Or maybe them and the Arabs. Or maybe not. You begin to see the problem. The African's want theirs, of course. And you don't dare do something like this without giving the Japanese their say-so. What with Yamato looking out for all the sons of Nippon in space, you can't short them. Oh, and then we need one for everyone who isn't covered. Oh, and where do the Filipinos fit, Spanish or other. Or . . . ?"

Gramma Ruth shrugged. "Once you set the wheel in motion, figuring out where to stop gets awfully hard."

"So people who have the franchise figure better the devil you know," Kris said.

"But they aren't paying the devil's piper," Penny added.

"And nothing gets done," Jack finished.

"Until the wheels come off," Gramma pointed out. "And you got to admire how well Eden is doing, keeping folks in the dark about how wobbly those wheels are. Lot of my franchised students never had a serious talk with someone who wasn't, until they got to my class. It's an eye-opening experience, let me tell you."

Kris mulled that over while she took another nibble at her lunch. It was really quite good. It was just that her appetite had done a vanishing act. She'd have to give this place another chance when she could concentrate on the food.

"What would have happened," she said slowly, "if we hadn't caught that bomb yesterday? What if it had gotten who it was intended to? That looked like a very prestigious cavalcade."

"The papers would have said nothing," Ruth said, munching something that she'd unwrapped from a grape leaf.

"And the dead," Kris said, reaching for one of the fig-wrapped items.

"Heart attack, poor dear. Didn't get him to the hospital on

time. Or one of those rare, untreatable cancers. Or maybe a skiing accident. Amazing the number of eighty-year-old types who take up skiing late in life."

"Here on Eden!" Kris said.

"That's true," Nelly said. "I've just checked the database. Kris, the most likely cause of death for people in business or government is heart attack, cancer, or skiing. Five times the planet's average for people not in those lines of work."

"How many skiers died the day after our little shoot-out?" Jack asked.

"None," Nelly reported. "However, a large helicopter went down. It was taking twelve people to ski in Aspen."

"Nelly," Gramma Ruth said with an impish grin. "Could you tell me how many of them had ever been skiing before?"

"No." The computer's response actually sounded like a whimper. "On just about any other planet I could. Not on Eden. Here databases are a babble."

Before Nelly could go into depth on that, Gramma Ruth succeeded in cutting her off. "I know. I've had Trudy send me the best hacking and cracking gear she has. No go. This place is locked down tight."

"You know my Aunt Tru?" Kris asked.

"Since long before you were born. We owe each other a life several times over. I've forgotten who's ahead at the moment."

Kris nodded, taking in the quiet statement of life on the line time after time, and death just one misstep away. But Gramma Ruth had lived to sport all those gray hairs. And Tru was enjoying her retirement. Or near retirement. Or maybe not retirement. Last Kris had heard, Tru was heading for Alien 1.

"So," Kris said thoughtfully, "we all agree Eden has a problem and needs to change. Most folks even seem to know how."

"Though there are the usual suspects who like the way things are and won't take kindly to messing with how it is, was, and ever should be their way," Gramma Ruth cut in.

"Isn't it always." Kris sighed. "But what's one young Longknife supposed to do? Grampa Ray can't expect me to snap my fingers and change this planet. I don't change planets."

"I know a few that might disagree," Penny said dryly.

"Want me to name them," Jack added with a grin.

"But all of them were already headed downhill and in a hurry. All I did was nudge them a bit here. Maybe a bit more there. I affected what happened. I didn't make it happen."

Jack and Penny thought for a moment, then nodded agreement.

Gramma Ruth munched away for a minute on her lunch, then patted her lips and laid her napkin down. "You know, there's a reason why folks don't like change. You start to change a bit, you never can tell where you're going to end up. History is full of changes that started out good, then went bad. People who got a ball rolling, then found that some thugs— Robespierre, Lenin—grabbed it and ran off with it where nobody wanted to go, where no reasonable person would want."

Gramma Ruth eyed them for a moment. "The problem when you've got all the news scrubbed down to just the nice is that you don't know who the players are. I don't. Do you, Kris?"

And with that unsettling thought, they parted company.

A fourth rig joined them for the ride back to campus. It worried Kris a bit, but not for long. When they stopped at Gramma Ruth's apartment, three Marines dismounted. Not uniformed Marines, but individuals in civilian clothes that were way too clean-cut and ramrod straight to be students.

Gramma Ruth spotted them at once. She gave them a cheery wave, then waved at her own hired guard. The guards took a long look at the Marines.

Kris was gone before the next act of that play.

For once, Kris hoped the afternoon bargaining went long. She needed time. She and Nelly needed a serious research session. If the ambassador had plans for Kris's evening, he would find one princess who'd learned to say no. After all, she'd said it a lot at the bargaining table.

Abby intercepted Kris on her way to rejoin her team. "Your Highness, boss, and lord, I've been trying to take some time ever since you landed. You mind if I take the evening off?"

"You can have the afternoon, too," Kris said. "I am not going out tonight. And I still remember how to fill my own tub. You go look up your mommy or daddy or ex-boyfriend or whoever it is you want to see here."

"I'll give them all a hug from you," Abby said, as dry as any bone.

15

Abby found that the old neighborhood had changed a lot . . . and not changed at all.

Tram Line 79 no longer went to Five Corners. It was now Line 128. But the tram Abby rode in could have been the same one she rode out fifteen years ago. She was tempted to peel off the layers of graffiti to find what it had sported back then.

The evil-eye of the tram cop suggested he'd be none too happy if she produced a knife and took it to his bit of Eden. On reflection, the layers of graffiti might be all that held the old wreck together.

Abby had been careful to dress down. Still, she wasn't nearly as shabbily dressed as the young woman whose name Abby refused to remember after she left Five Corners and swore it had seen the last of her.

So why was she coming back?

She'd already been greeted. Twice.

She'd pulled one young girl's hand out of her purse. The kid had her hand already around Abby's wallet. The maid of many faces restrained the urge to break a wrist. The kid, maybe ten, was just trying to make it through the day.

Abby had sent her on her way with five bucks. Eden. Not all that much.

The cutpurse had not gotten off so easy. Abby hadn't returned his knife by plunging it between a rib. Not quite. It had been a close thing. But blood on the streets made the neighbors talk. That was not something Abby wanted.

No, she'd confiscated the knife and shoved the fourteen- or fifteen-year-old boy into a brick wall. Maybe he'd learn something from the lesson.

Maybe not.

Not everything that was the same in the old hood was that exciting. Old man Artork's ice cream cart was still on the same corner. Closer approach showed he wasn't still running it. Had he been late once too often with his "insurance check" and actually ended up sleeping with the fishes . . . as he'd often joked with the kids? Or had he actually lived to retire and turn it over to his son?

Abby ordered a chocolate cone, her old favorite. It was still down there in the frosty cool. One lick and Abby scowled. The memory was much tastier than the having.

She started to toss it. Then caught sight of the wide eyes of a little girl. Seven, maybe eight. Or six. Now that Abby recalled, the kid had been lurking nearby. Not so close as to be accused of trying to steal anything. Not so far as to miss any scent of those wonderful concoctions. How often had a young—no, forget that name.

Abby handed the cone to the girl.

The urchin eyed Abby for a long moment, to see what this icy delight would cost. Only when Abby let the silence stretch, did the girl half run, half skip away.

Hopefully, Abby hadn't taught the little thing a bad lesson. That you could get something for nothing. That someone could give her joy. A very bad lesson in Five Corners.

Abby watched the kid go, trying to remember the taste of cold chocolate on a warm day. Trying to remember a happy moment here. There had been a few.

Then she turned and walked purposefully toward a place that held very few good memories. It was always better to walk as if you knew where you were going. Needed to be there ten minutes ago. Slow down and who knew what might overtake you.

At that pace, it didn't take Abby long to turn the final corner, to bring the last place she'd lived on Eden into view.

Then she had to slow. There wasn't all that much to see.

Half the houses on this block were broken down and abandoned. It had been headed that way back then. The brown house was now among the derelicts.

She really shouldn't be surprised. She'd been gone fifteen years. How long had Momma Ganna ever lived anywhere?

That was a big mistake. Suddenly Abby was flooded by feelings. The feelings of going out in the morning, maybe to school, maybe to something that might earn an Eden dollar for her . . . or Momma.

Only to come back to an empty house. Not just empty of Momma, but swept of anything that Momma called her own. Momma totally gone.

Abby tried asking around among the neighbors to see if anyone knew where Momma had vanished to. None knew. She went looking for a grown-up that might admit to knowing Momma.

People who knew Momma were never that easy to find. Not easy for a short person who couldn't read or write all that well.

The first time had been the worst.

That time, Abby hadn't been much older than the kid she gave the ice cream to. She'd spent a night and a day on her own before she stumbled into someone who knew someone who knew where Momma Ganna had set up shop.

That time Abby got a beating. As if going to school one morning expecting to come home to the same place was somehow wrong. She didn't deserve a beating, not for that.

And it taught Abby a lesson she never forgot.

As Abby slowly ambled by the gutted brown house, she spotted the telltale signs of squatter occupation: the smell of smoke, a bit of movement in the deep shadows.

Her first thought was to keep walking, circle around to the

trolley station, and get back where she belonged. She'd worked hard to get there. To be Abby Nightingale, the maid of many skills. If she was smart, she'd get gone from here.

Abby glanced over her shoulder at the crumpling brown house. She could ferret out any secrets it still held about Momma. *Yeah, me and a squad of Marines.*

Or maybe just me and the chief and Penny.

No way would she take them to the hell that was Five Corners. No way would Abby risk seeing the look on that Longknife girl's face when she saw where her maid came from.

Okay, smart kid. You gonna just give up cause Momma ain't here with no cake? You gonna call it quits that easy? What about Myra? You gonna forget about her?

If this was a job for the princess, you'd think of something.

That jab hurt.

Abby paused. If she went right here, she'd almost be at the green house.

"Computer, mark the brown house, two blocks back. Mark the green house, one block farther down this street." The green house still looked in decent shape.

The brick house would be two blocks farther along that street, and one over, she told her computer. Three data points showed on the map reflecting on the glasses Abby wore today.

The maid walked a few more blocks, remembering two more homes of her youth. And spotted the pattern about the time she spotted the wasteland.

Two blocks beyond, Five Corners came to an end.

Not really. Actually the five corners that gave the place its name was out there, surrounded by the baked ground and struggling weeds of half-begun urban renewal. A few houses still stood out there, surrounded by nothing. They huddled alone, waiting for someone to put up a shopping mall and chic housing for the wealthy, or those on their way to wealth.

But it hadn't happened yet.

With Five Corners's luck, it might never happen.

Abby frowned at the conundrum ahead. Her old homes might still be standing, out there in the baking weeds. On any other planet, all Abby would have to do was call up an orbital photo.

Not on Eden. Not without paying a chunk of money and facing a human with a need to know that met their rules. Abby had almost been killed on Earth before she learned how easy it was elsewhere to get pictures.

With a sigh, Abby turned her back on the hardscrabble that was the only mark left of the first two homes she remembered.

To find a guy sauntering toward her, a leer on his face.

He was no stranger. To the extent that he'd been leaning against a wall in the spare shade of a fallen-down roof with three other guys, Abby knew him. She'd logged and stored the memory of quite a few clumps of local dudes like them since she left the station. She knew their kind from years back.

"Hey, bird, whatcha doing all dolled up for?"

Abby tried to ignore him. "Pardon me," she said, and made to step around him.

"Whatcha doing for the next five minutes," he said, side-stepping to block her way, and reaching for her.

She could smell alcohol on his breath. It came through a wicked, knowing grin that was missing a couple of teeth.

His right hand was in his pants pocket. When he pulled it out, it would hold a switchblade. Abby knew that as sure as she knew the sun would rise in the east.

When she left the embassy compound for this little trip down memory lane, Abby knew things could get terminal. Now her heart didn't so much as skip a beat.

She was trained for this. She'd experienced it many times. Both here in Five Corners and so many light-years from here.

Abby took a step closer to the man, putting on the *face*. Abby's game face had been the last thing many a man had seen in life. If the guy was smart, he'd head back for his friends. "I got no plans," she said, voice level. Deadly level.

"Whatdaya say I make them for you." His grin now got lopsided. Jack had a lopsided grin, but not like this one. There was nothing of a leer when Jack smiled.

"I'd have to think about that," Abby said.

Then closed the distance to him with one quick step.

Her right came up to wipe that grin off his face. Her knee took care of that other matter he had so much on his mind.

In half a breath, the idiot was withering on the ground.

His three friends had ambled around the corner to enjoy the show, maybe get involved if she was easy.

Abby raised a questioning eyebrow. *You want some of this?*

If all three of them jumped her, matters might get a bit exciting. For them, not her. Abby figured she could put all three down without breaking a sweat.

Still, fools had been known to get lucky.

They fled back around the corner.

Abby eyed her would-be assailant. His knife was out. She kicked it into the gutter. It rattled on a sewer grating before falling through. As for this optimistic dude, she didn't want to see him again for a long, long time.

She'd chosen her shoes for walking—maybe running—and for fighting. They were steel reinforced. She gave him a hard kick in the kidney.

He screamed.

Abby doubted she'd done permanent damage. But if she had, that was why he had two of them. Maybe he'd be more careful with the other one.

She crossed the street and took a right, not wasting a backward glance. If she heard footsteps, she'd turn.

She didn't hear anything. At least not for now. Maybe later she'd find out how bad an enemy she'd made.

16

The street ahead looked ready to be bulldozed. But there, waiting for Abby under the awning of the one place on the block not crumbling away, was the little girl she'd given the ice cream to. The kid was still licking sweetness from her fingers.

As Abby came alongside the kid, she fell in step with her.

"You put Promie down good."

"He looked in need of it."

"He's gonna remember you."

"Maybe you shouldn't be seen talking to me," Abby said, not looking down. Those eyes were so huge. So dark. So full of untasted need.

Abby wanted nothing to do with them.

The kid kept walking beside her.

"Whatcha doing here?" she asked.

Abby meant to say no more to this stray. Then found herself muttering, "Looking for something. Or someone."

Abby had just spotted a pattern when she'd been so rudely interrupted. At the moment, all she'd wanted to do was get out of Five Corners. At that moment, she'd noticed the pattern.

Every move Momma Ganna made put her farther from Five Corners.

Maybe Abby wasn't the only one wanting out of this place.

Then again, Five Corners was pretty much rotting from the inside. Maybe Momma didn't have a choice. Abby doubted she'd get a straight answer to that question from Momma.

At that moment, the kid beside Abby stooped to pick up a passing cat. The cat allowed that she could be petted and suffered the kid to do so. It even purred.

"You want to pet her?"

Being mauled by a stray cat was very low on Abby's list of things to do. She declined softly. So the girl put the cat down and it proceeded to wrap itself around Abby's legs.

"I think the Goddess likes you," the girl opined. "She don't like many people. You must be nice to lots of people. Not just me and giving me an ice cream you didn't like. Why'd you buy it if you didn't like it?"

Abby was glad the cat approved of her being in her part of town. The kid, however, was turning into a talker. Not something Abby needed.

"Once upon a time, I used to like that kind of ice cream. Guess I don't anymore."

"Your glasses are nice. I see all the colors on them. You have a nice computer. You must be rich."

Abby hadn't planned on anyone getting close enough to see her computer interface. This could go bad in so very many ways. "Not rich," she said. "Now, someone who has her computer jacked right into her head. That's rich for you. Or the ones that don't wear glasses, but contact lenses. Those are rich."

"Yeah, I guess. But Bronc uses a reader. All the time he wishes he had a better one."

"Who's Bronc?"

"A kid I know. He knows everything. If you want to find someone, he'd know them."

"For a whole six blocks."

"No, a whole lot more. All the gangs let him run in their territory. He helps them with their stuff. Not nothing that

would help them against each other. He took their beatings
and showed he didn't want nothing of that. But if they got music that ain't working, he can usually fix it." The kid seemed
quite proud that she knew someone that even the gangs respected.

And who might know Mamma Ganna.

Or be a setup for an ambush.

*You knew you were taking stupid risks when you left the
embassy compound.*

With a shrug, Abby took the next risk.

"Why don't you take me to Bronc and we'll see what we
can do for each other that might make us all happy. Like this
here computer. You think Bronc would like it? Or one like it?"

Not the actual computer. Too much data on it. But maybe
one like it. Well, maybe a bit cheaper. Abby's computer wasn't
anything like Kris's Nelly. Still, it was not something you got
at the local drugstore, either.

To Abby's surprise, the kid just eyed her. If anything, her
reaction got a whole lot harder. "Bronc don't give no one up
to be hurt. You a cop?"

"Nope, I'm not a cop."

"Who are you?"

Stupid, stupid, stupid. That was one question Abby hadn't
brought an answer for.

So she tried the best lie. "I left here fifteen years ago. I'm
wondering if I can find my mother."

"And turn her over to the jawbreakers," the kid added.

"They still calling the antiterrorist squads jawbreakers?"

"I don't know. That's what we always called them as long
as I've known."

"All I can say is that there's no way I'd work for them."

The kid eyed Abby, those deep brown eyes seeming to take
all of her in. Weigh her. Decide her fate.

And Abby did a wipe of all her assumptions about the girl.
Then she studied her again. Stringy hair needed washing. The
dirty face and skinned elbows were part of a stick-figure body
that looked to be years away from womanhood. Or could blos-
som tomorrow. Hard to tell, kids from Five Corners were so

underfed. Maybe Abby had been low on the age. Ten, plus or minus one, might be closer.

But it was the eyes that gave the experienced maid pause. No way to tell what they'd seen. What they'd done. Abby started to credit them with what she'd known at ten or so.

Then shook that thought off.

Five Corners had been going to hell fifteen years ago. And it had gotten worse. No, this kid had seen worse than what drove Abby out of here.

There really was no reason to trust her. Certainly not her and a smart kid with connections to all the gangs.

It was time to walk . . . fast.

"You see that corner down the way," the girl said, pointing. "The one with two stores on it and a couple of good-looking houses. One's even got some grass they cut."

Abby looked and saw it.

"Uncle Joe and Auntie Mong don't allow no drug sales on their corner. No nothing. And they got shotguns to back them up. That's neutral territory. You go there. I'll bring Bronc there, so you can talk, and maybe Bronc will help you."

"How about Uncle Joe. Could he help me?"

"Uncle Joe don't know nothing. You can ask him if you want, but all he ever says is that he don't know nothing."

"Smart man." Abby had known Uncle Joe's in her time. She sauntered that way.

A second later, when she looked back, the cat was cleaning its paws, but the girl had vanished.

Uncle Joe's provided shade, and a lazy fan only slightly disturbing the warm air.

An old man of dusky origins took her measure, said, "You're not from around here," and pointed Abby at a soda cooler when she agreed she wasn't.

Abby paid her rent for taking up space in the store by buying an orange soda.

"I'm adding a deposit on the bottle. You drink it here, you can turn it in for the deposit."

"Sounds fair," Abby said, paid, and turned away to examine the merchandise. It was mostly food and essential items for the home. Or the hovel. Abby noticed a good supply of Sterno stoves and candles. Oh, and one entire wall was taken up with cheap wines and fortified beers.

It wasn't much different from the stores Abby'd spent her quarters and dimes at. Only now, everything was a buck or more.

Uncle Joe's "You start any trouble and I'll finish it" told Abby she was no longer alone in the store. The girl was back, but no one was with her.

"You want an orange soda?" Abby asked.

"I like the grape kind better," the kid said, her face intent as she checked out the store.

"It's just me and Uncle Joe," Abby offered.

"She lying?"

"Not that I can see," Uncle Joe said, but quickly turned his attention to stocking cigarettes on the shelves behind him.

The kid sidled up to Abby. "Bronc says your rig is making all kinds of music. Stuff he don't know how to work."

Abby glanced at her wrist unit. "Is it making music like a cop or jawbreaker?"

"No, or we'd have run. Then again, Bronc says you might be some kind of superbreaker. How's he to know?"

"I work out on the Rim. We got better stuff than the fools who think they're running Eden."

Brown eyes went wide. "The Rim! You been in space?"

"It ain't all the stories crack it up to be."

"What part of the Rim you from?" a young man's voice asked, cracking on "Rim." He was a head taller than his girl-friend. Maybe a shade cleaner, at least his elbows weren't scabbed. His eyes were an intense blue that seemed to overflow with questions.

"Wardhaven," Abby said. "And other places."

"Didn't they just have a big space battle around Ward-haven?" the youth asked.

"I wasn't in that fight. Some of my friends were. Some of them died."

The two youths seemed to put their heads together over that one. Now, seeing two samples together, Abby figured the boy for thirteen, fourteen. The girl for maybe twelve, tops.

"What kind of work you do?" Bronc finally asked.

"Interesting stuff," Abby said. "A little of this. A little of that. The less said about it the more I like it."

"And you're from here?"

"Not in the last fifteen years."

"It would be nice to be fifteen years away from here," the boy muttered.

"And she wants to find her 'mother,' " the girl added.

"Everyone's got a mother. You get away from yours for fifteen years and even you might want to see her again. Maybe even your gram."

"I'd be happy if I never saw Granny Ganna ever again."

Abby let herself blink twice at that name. She also made a point of not skipping a breath. "You two want a drink? What's her name asked for a grape soda. What do you want, Bronc?"

"I'll have a beer," he said, pulling himself up to his full height.

"He likes a strawberry soda," Uncle Joe snapped from two rows over. "And that's all he'll have from my place."

"Auntie Mong would sell me a beer," the boy said in not quite a whine.

"Over her cold, dead body. Don't you kids think us gray heads talk to each other?"

Grateful for the distraction, Abby pulled a grape and a strawberry soda from the cooler, and headed her two, ah, unreliable information sources to the counter. Business done, and more deposits made, Abby quick marched the youngsters to a couple of chairs around a dusty space heater.

The bottles were half empty before Abby asked. "What's your name, dirty face."

"Cara," the girl answered. "And don't you go telling me to wash. You want me to look like I'm ready to sell something I don't see no reason to part with just yet." That was said with a glare Bronc's way.

"What's you mother's name?" Abby tried to slip that in gently, softly.

It didn't work. "None of your business. Who you hunting for, anyway? Bronc's the one that knows everyone. He's the one that wants to earn a 'puter like the one on your wrist. And he told me you'd never give him that one. Were you lying to me? People never give away a 'puter with their own stuff on it."

"Let's say I got ahead of myself," Abby said, and turned her attention to the boy. Interrogating a fourteen-year-old boy ought to be easy. He had hormones. She didn't. Although on closer examination, the boy seemed to have eyes only for the unit on her wrist.

"So, Bronc, does Cara's mom have light hair? Some call it platinum blond. Others call it white or something like that."

He glanced up from the computer. "Yeah, only it's starting to get browner now. If you wash that mess on Cara's head, it would look like that. Real pretty."

The girl stuck her tongue out. "You and what army."

"No, really, Cara, you'd look real hot, like your mom."

"And what did that get her?"

That was not something Abby would ask. With luck, she'd see Myra in a few minutes and make her own assessment. Daughters were never a reliable judge of their elders.

"Is her mom named Myra?"

"She goes by Ruby now," Bronc said, "but my momma says she's just putting on airs. She had a real name before that."

"Yeah, my mom used to be Myra," Cara whispered.

"And you just mentioned Granny Ganna." Abby shot the last words out.

Cara fidgeted. "I guess so."

"She's about as tall as me. Pretty in an old-fashion kind of way." Abby knew it for classical beauty. But what do you say to an angry twelve-year-old?

"She's old and fat and, and she ought to behave like a gramma-ma."

"She's still hot?" Abby asked Bronc.

"If you're an old man and like old women, I guess so."

"I'm, ah . . ." Even now, Abby had problems getting her tongue around that old name. She tried a different tact. "Ganna or Myra ever talk about another daughter?"

Both kids shook their head.

Which shouldn't have come as a surprise to Abby. Still, it was a kick in the gut. Apparently, they'd dusted her dirt from their shoes just as completely as she'd washed them out of her hair.

Abby took in a deep breath. "I think your folks are who I've come looking for. Could you take me home?"

17

"Well look what the cat done brung in," was Momma Ganna's greeting for her long lost daughter. Why was Abby not surprised.

"She followed me home," Cara said, grin stretching from ear to ear as she enjoyed the scene. "Can I keep her?"

Momma Ganna snorted at Abby, the old disapproving snort the teenager in Abby remembered so well. "You keep her, she'll break your heart, like she breaks any heart that lets her in."

Abby had been surprised at the house Cara led them to. The block was solid row houses, stone and brick, three- or four-stories tall. None were abandoned. Yep, Momma was coming up in the world. Two blocks over and she'd be in Hepner neighborhood. It'd been gated once, to keep the riffraff of Five Corners out.

And Momma had aged well. Cara was wrong about her being fat; Momma was pleasantly round with hardly a sag or wrinkle. *Wonder who's paying for the body work?* was Abby's professional question.

"What kind of name you going by?" Ganna asked.

"Nightingale. Abby Nightingale. Who are you, Momma?"

"Topaz. A nice name, isn't it? Expensive name."

"A hard name, but one that can be broken," Abby said.

"Momma, what's all the racket?" came from the shadows at the top of the stairs. But it couldn't hide the slender form of Myra, not from Abby's hungry eyes.

But Sis wasn't right. Whereas Abby remembered a willowy figure, what she saw today seemed more out of focus. The way she leaned against the wall . . .

"Myra, are you using?" Abby snapped before she thought.

"No," she said, but the scowl on Cara's face gave it a lie.

Abby turned on her mother. "Your own daughter!"

"It's either that or she eats all the time. A hippo ain't no use to me."

"And you couldn't bring in some kid from the streets to handle your customers?"

"I got clients now, baby ducks. Clients that want their privacy. Got to keep things in the family now."

"You're even more disgusting than you were when I left."

"To empty bedpans at that fancy home. Bedpans better than what your momma does to put food on the table."

"There was more of a future there." Abby bit off that line. If she let it all out, she'd have to march out the door.

And she did want to see more of Myra.

"Yeah. Now you're working for that princess. What you doing for her and all those pretty boys around her?"

Abby was about to fire back a "Nothing!" when the full impact of what Momma just said hit her.

"How do you know who I'm working for?"

Momma's laugh was more a cackle. "Got you there. Look around some time at one of your fancy balls. You may just see your mamma on some well-turned-out guy's elbow. Topaz has lots of surprises for you."

And alarm bells went off all through that part of Abby that was a trained operative.

"I can see I'm not welcome here. It's been nice seeing you again. Myra, hope we get to spend some time together while I'm here. It was good meeting you Cara, Bronc." Abby turned to beat a well-ordered retreat.

Abby half expected a butler, or small tactical team, to try to stop her. She was relieved when she made it out the door.

Bronc was at her elbow. Cara had been halted with a "Where do you think you're going, young lady."

Abby would miss the little imp, but she kept walking.

Walking her anger out, Abby wanted to quick march for the trolley. Bronc, however, had gotten a bad case of the slows.

And Abby kicked herself as she quickly reacquired the situation she was in. There were guys—in threes and fours—on a lot of street corners.

"This place suddenly popular or is this the normal crowd?" Abby said, under her breath.

"There's too many dudes here, and I think some of them are hot," Bronc said.

Was that why he was slowing down?

The real reason for his delay arrived a moment later. "Hi, Auntie," Cara said.

"What took you so long?" was Bronc's greeting. "You gonna get in trouble?" was Abby's.

A stuck-out tongue was all that Bronc got. "Momma's going out tonight. I'll sneak back in when she's gone. She won't remember nothing by tomorrow."

"Ruby going out, too?"

"Yeah."

"Why am I getting all this attention?" Abby asked. The guys were closing in.

"A couple of nights ago, your princess got jumped," Bronc whispered. "Some of the folks she put down were from here. I think they figure you owe them."

"Now wouldn't that be a terrible end for me, paying for Kris Longknife's doings while I was home in bed."

"You didn't do nothing?" Cara said.

"I swear it's so. On my mother's grave."

Cara giggled at the image, and took off, half running, half skipping for one of the clumps. This one had a tall dude in white wearing a belt with a huge gold buckle.

Cara talked to him. He listened. Then he shook his head.

It looked like Abby was about to get whopped for that damn Longknife's good luck.

No use wasting time getting it on, Abby thought.

With one swift motion, her automatic was in her hand. She sighted it on the big fellow Cara had talked with, cycled a dart into the chamber, but reduced the charge. Then lowered her aim.

A second later, the dart was sticking out of the big dudes belt-buckle.

"I could have aimed for an eye," Abby said in a voice that carried. "How much you willing to pay for your fun?"

The big guy eyed his buckle, then Abby. Around him, gangers had started to go for heat. Now they waited for his signal.

Abby was glad Cara was out of the line of fire. Bronc had taken the time to back away from her. He looked ready to hit the ground at the slightest hint that the call was against Abby.

Then the big fellow laughed.

It wasn't a nice laugh, but it was full. Suddenly the gangers were all laughing.

Abby allowed herself a chuckle.

"Cara says you weren't out that night our boys got wasted."

"Home in bed where I belong."

"I hope with a nice guy?"

Abby gave that a noncommittal shrug.

"You be sure and stay away from that princess girl."

"I'm just her maid. I only wash her hair."

"Why don't you wash Cara's hair. She'd be some looker if she just cleaned up."

Cara was trotting back to Abby. She answered that with a raspberry. That got a second laugh. Little girls could get away with what would get the head slapped off a woman a few months older.

They got to the trolley with no further surprises.

18

The tram was in the station. Abby risked running, but it pulled out before they got to it. That left Abby with an awkward twenty minutes for dudes to reconsider.

And two very quiet kids that wouldn't look her in the eye.

"What's going on? Cara wouldn't shut up when I first met her. Now you two look like someone stole your allocation of nouns for the rest of the month?"

Cara didn't meet Abby's eyes as she mumbled. "You going to go away and never come back. You did for fifteen years," she blurted out. And locked eyes with Abby.

"I did that. But I'm here now, and my employer is like to be here for a while. I'll be coming back. Besides. I owe Bronc a computer."

The relief on his face showed he figured her to stiff him.

Abby tried to show her commitment without letting him know she'd seen the doubt. "Let me see what you're using for a 'puter. That doesn't look like anything more than a reader like you see in the doctor's office."

"I wouldn't know. Never been to one," the boy said, but offered her the unit.

The thing didn't look to be more than a reader, but its screen was blank. Then Bronc said, "'Puter, what's the name of the princess visiting from Wardhaven?"

"Princess Kristine Longknife," a voice that sounded a lot like Cara's said. "She recently commanded several squadrons at the Battle of Wardhaven and . . ."

"End that," Abby said. If the kids wanted to know more about her employer, they could do that on their own time. And without Abby at their elbow to be asked, with those big, truth-demanding eyes, if that was all true.

"What do you have in there?" Abby demanded.

Bronc had the cover off his darling in a second, and Abby was looking at the most convoluted spaghetti that she'd ever seen under a computer hood. Barely visible under all kinds of stuff was the standard innards of a ten-year-old magazine reader. Jacked into that were what looked like a main processor that might have been top of the line fifteen years ago. And several memory units that might have been taken from used washing machines or who knows what.

There were other chips and boards that didn't immediately declare their purpose, but Bronc had identified noise coming from Abby's unit, and that couldn't have been easy.

"I thought I passed a Ryes on the way in here," Abby said.

"All the time he likes to go and look," Cara snorted. "They frisk him every time to make sure he's not walking out with the store. They don't dare frisk me."

"So you walk out with the store?" Abby said to her niece.

"No," Bronc snapped. "I'm gonna get a job there. I can't have a record. Or even be near a record."

"Lot of dumb kids from Five Corners have a hard time remembering things like that," Abby said softly. "Glad to know Cara's with a smart one."

"Cara's pretty smart, too."

Cara seemed to like that. At least she didn't stick her tongue out at it.

"And how did you come to learn so much about computers?" Abby said. The next tram was in sight. Maybe it was early, or maybe the one they missed had been a really late one. Around Five Corners, schedules meant nothing.

"Mick and Trang have been kind of teaching me. Not everything they know. Some of what they know would get me in jail. But I've learned a lot. A whole lot."

Cara nodded proud agreement with him.

Abby paid for them. The kids tried not to stare as she just slipped her palm over the pay scale and it took her at her word. From the way she'd had to use coins to buy the sodas, Abby was pretty sure the hood was still on the cash system.

They settled into seats far from the snoozing eye of the cop, an old man so oversize he hardly fit on the provided stool. Only then did Abby question her computer. "Any bugs here."

Before her own computer had a chance to reply, Bronc was talking. "There's an eye, ownership unidentified. And an ear. Same on the ID. You want them dead or just out for a while?"

"What's legal here?"

"Actually, bugs are illegal, so there's no rules against burning them," Cara said.

"But it's considered bad form to burn them unless they're really obnoxious. Or if you want people to know your gang owns this territory."

"Make them go to sleep," Abby said.

There was a static discharge near them, another a bit farther back. Impressive for "just a reader."

"Computer, how many bugs in Momma Ganna's house?" Abby asked her own computer the question she'd been wanting answered since she stomped out of there.

"None," Bronc said. "She keeps it real clean. You can't get any cleaner than Granny's place, not even the gang hangs."

"And you know that because . . ." Abby said, eyeing Bronc.

"The Bones, the folks you just met, and the Rockets pay Mick and Trong to keep their places clean," Cara cut in. "You know, the places they eat. Where they hang. They don't want any breakers eyeing them or listening in. Or some other gang, either. So they pay Mick, and Bronc does the actual cleaning."

"They trust Mick?" Abby asked.

"I also get something extra to do my own checks. They paid for some of the extra stuff in my reader."

"You good?"

"They think so," Bronc said. "And I think so, too."

"Me, too," Cara said. And, since they'd ended up on the same seat, gave him a bit of a hug. He actually reddened.

Which made it a good time to change the topic. "Tell me about what happened back there. How'd the guys from the hood get mixed up with my princess?"

Bronc shrugged. "Word came down from somewhere that there was going to be a big hit. No one usual, some guy from off planet. None of the usual clans were taking the hit, not at least with their own shooters. You got to understand, ma'am, this was a big chance for some of the best heat in the hood. Make a good showing and you might get tapped by a real security guild for a job. That don't happen a whole lot around here."

"And anyone that turned up facedown on the street would have no tracks back to anyone respectable," Abby added.

"I guess so. None of the gangers were thinking much about that, not when they left."

"What happened to them?" Abby asked. Was there a mass grave somewhere out there in the wastes of Five Corners?

But Bronc just shrugged. "You want me to find out?"

"No! For God's sake. Stay clear of anything like that."

"We hear about more hiring, you want to know?" Cara asked.

"No! I mean yes! I mean I don't want you two getting close to something for me. But if you hear anything, I wouldn't mind getting an info copy. But stay clear of this Longknife woman. Lots of people have tried to collect on her head. They're dead and I'm still washing her hair."

The two kids eyed Abby, still undecided.

"Listen, when you get a chance, you see what your 'puter can tell you about her. Listen carefully. Then, oh, double what it told you cause I can tell you a lot about her ain't on the news. A whole lot." Abby paused for a second. "And I was there for most of it. Okay."

The kids nodded, then raced for the exit as the familiar Ryes stop was called. Buying a computer with Bronc at your elbow had to be about the most fun Abby'd had with her clothes on in fifteen years. Only he didn't want to buy a computer.

He turned up his nose at the completed units . . . and headed for where they sold the components. Why was Abby not surprised.

He started with the box. They had everything, from tiny ear and glasses units to a few obsolete reader-type boxes. He picked the cheapest. It actually had a black-and-white screen.

"You don't have to go for the absolute bottom," Abby said.

"I want a box so it's got plenty of room to add stuff. And I don't want it looking too fancy or, you know . . ."

"But color is nice to have when you need to read plans, stuff that's using color. You can always have black and white for your default," Abby added.

Bronc didn't need more persuading.

He settled for a midlevel processor and storage. Abby bought him the high-end sniffer submodule. He grinned at that. "I better not tell Mick I got that. He'll get jealous."

All the parts in a bag, they were ready to check out and head for a pizza parlor the kids knew. There they'd find a quiet corner and put all the pieces together. But Cara pulled Abby aside. "Could I have something?"

"What do you want?"

Cara led Abby to the jewelry counter . . . not the expensive end, but the counter with the cheap costume stuff. There, a fake, green emerald had an image of the Madonna and Child etched into it. On the other side, it was a full-function phone.

As much as Abby wanted to say "sold," she paused. "You know this isn't just a phone. When you're carrying it . . ."

"They can track where you are without you knowing. They can turn it on and listen even if you don't have it on. Yeah, Bronc's told me. He also says he can fix it so it don't."

Abby glanced at the boy. He nodded his head confidently.

"If Granny Ganna has security in her house, it will sniff this out even if you do squelch it."

"So I don't take it home. I got a place I can hide it."

Twelve years old and already briefed in on spying basics. Said something about the home she was brought up in. Abby would have to think about all that said about Momma Ganna, but for now she'd buy the bobble. She also needed to think about why a twelve-year-old kid was attracted to a picture of a mother cuddling her child close.

Bronc won a five-dollar bet with Abby. He had his machine up and running before the pizza arrived. "The screen is up. I got a lot of stuff still to do, but it's awake and working."

So Abby paid.

It was doing more before they finished the pizza. Abby paid for software downloads. She'd arrange for more later under special instruction. One thing she made sure of. She didn't leave until he'd squelched Cara's new commlink.

It was not yet dark when Abby paid their fare back to Five Corners. "Don't tangle with a Longknife. And if you know anyone that you wouldn't like to get suddenly dead, tell them the same."

"Don't worry about us, Auntie Abby. We know how to take care of ourselves," they both answered.

They were so young. So confident.

If only Abby felt half so sure.

19

Princess Kris Longknife wondered whose good day she was having. It couldn't be anything she deserved.

The morning started with a fine run with the Marines. Some Navy and Army personnel attached to the embassy jogged along with them. Even Chief Beni and Commander Malhoney were up early, leading a small detachment in a spirited walk. Strange what having a princess around did to middle-aged men.

And the business hagglers had finally talked themselves out. They settled within pennies of where Kris figured they would three days earlier. But they'd spent those days arriving at it, and both sides seemed delighted at how hard fought their victory had been. Their bosses would be so proud of them.

And there'd be no questioning that they'd earned their expense accounts.

You'd think they'd won a battle.

Kris did her best to join the victory spirit, including lunch at The Vault, one of the most expensive places Garden City had to offer.

It should have been a fabulous time. Four men paid court to

her, each trying to outdo themselves in their wittiness and praise for their home planets and reasons Kris should visit. Two had sons her age she might enjoy meeting.

But Kris watched this three-martini lunch while drinking soda water. From that perspective, none of them were quite as witty as they thought.

She was saved from having to stay as lunch ran into happy hour, and maybe even supper, by a call from Inspector Johnson. "Can we talk?"

Five minutes later, the inspector picked her up in front of The Vault. "Do you lunch there often?" the inspector asked, giving her an investigative eye that would make even one of those Longknifes feel guilty. Maybe.

"We just finished bargaining for some of Eden's computer technology. Some real sharp types wanted to impress me with their expense accounts."

"Did they?"

"Oh, they impressed me. Just not the way they figured."

"Clearly, they haven't studied the reports on you. Money does not impress you."

"What someone does with it might. Waving the raw stuff around . . ." Kris shrugged. "Did you call me out here to discuss business ethics. I don't mind. I needed out of that lunch sometime between now and breakfast. Thank you."

"Actually, I do have a reason for taking you off on this little drive." Now Kris noticed that they were not heading back to the embassy. NELLY, ANY IDEA WHERE WE'RE GOING?

NOT A CLUE, KRIS. LET ME KNOW WHEN YOU FIND OUT.

It was bad enough when a computer wasn't helpful. *But one that sassed you back to boot!* Kris really needed to schedule some time with Trudy.

Kris edged around to face Johnson . . . and make it easier to reach for her automatic. She also rechecked the backseat of the sedan. It was empty.

The inspector must have felt the tension. "No, I am not kidnapping you, poor fool who tries."

"That's nice to hear. So, where are we going?"

"Nowhere in particular. I've got the car set for random

turns. Anyone starts following us, and I may be calling on your weapons expertise to save my hide."

"What about yours?"

"Ten-for-ten at twenty-five feet. But I have never had to actually shoot a man."

"Lucky you," Kris said, dryly.

"I believe so. Now, the cause for our peripatetic journey is some good news for you. And, as is the custom around you, some bad news."

"And as is my custom, I'll take the good news first."

"Higher-ups have decided that we should grant you a temporary license to carry arms and a special protective contingent. That particular stunt yesterday of mixing your team with those guarding Mrs. Tordon was quite brilliant. With some of your Marines guarding her, she already having a permit, and then switching off guarding you, it might well result in a plea that they had a weapon on her detail and got switched so suddenly to your detail that they didn't have time to return their arms to the armory. A brilliant sleight of hand. But then, General Trouble is also your great-grandfather."

Kris considered relieving the inspector of his illusion, but thought better of it. Once in a while a good deed should get the kind of reward it deserved. The Marines had taken it upon themselves to stand up a guard for their general's woman with not a second's thought. If it now got them the freedom to shoot back when shot at in the cause of protecting his great-grandbrat, well. Good for them.

Kris felt good for all of three seconds, then remembered the lead-in to this little chat. "And the bad news is . . . ?"

"Since this is a temporary permit, any security used that is not already under license by the Personal Security Administration of Garden City, such as your Marines, will have to use only nonlethal protection devices."

Kris considered that for a long moment. Then said, "I am going to produce my weapon, since it is now, I assume, legal."

"It is legal. I will not feel any obligation to confiscate it. Assuming it shoots nonlethal darts."

"There is that issue," Kris said, bringing out her Browning

automatic. "This little puppy was given to me by, well, never mind. It chambers a 4-mm dart, either from the right magazine, which loads Colt-Pfizer's highest-quality sleepy darts. Or, at the flick of a switch, armor-piercing rounds from the left magazine. I assume if I and my Marines promise to always keep the selector on the right side, you won't be all that concerned if the left magazine is not empty?"

"It could complicate an investigation," the inspector said, but he didn't contradict her.

"You are aware that with enough of a propellant charge a sleepy dart will smash flesh, bone, and skulls?"

"Oh, it can? I hadn't heard" didn't reach the usual level of conviction that Kris had come to expect in the most two-faced of diplomatic exchanges.

And Kris suddenly felt very tired of playing guessing games and "Thimble, thimble, who's got the thimble," where the thimble probably wasn't anywhere within a day's drive.

"Inspector, you and I both know that my exit from Hotel Landfall a few days back was not by the normal route. And I left a rather high body count on the pavement between there and the embassy. Yet none of that made it into the papers; none of the bodies showed up at the morgue. You want to tell me where they went? More important, if my Marines need to put a similar number, or more, of such optimists down hard, will their bodies do a similar disappearing act or be used as evidence against me and my Marines in a court of what passes for law on Eden?"

"Why don't you ask your maid?"

That answer from deep in left field knocked Kris off her stride. "What does Abby have to do with this?"

"Yesterday afternoon, she visited the hood where most of those shooters were hired. She met with the gang bosses, at least one of them. She spent quite a bit of time with several members of the gang and even gave one of them a computer and bought supper for him and his girlfriend."

Kris felt like she'd launched herself for a skiff drop from orbit . . . but forgot the skiff.

NELLY, DID YOU TRACK ABBY'S WHEREABOUTS YESTER-
DAY?

NO, KRIS, SHE THROTTLED HER SQUAWKER. SHE SENT A
MESSAGE TO HERSELF WITH A CC COPY TO YOU FOR OPENING
LATER LAST NIGHT, BUT SHE ERASED BOTH WHEN SHE GOT IN.
I DID NOT OPEN IT AND HAVE NOTHING AVAILABLE TO LOOK
AT NOW.

NELLY, I'M VERY UNIMPRESSED WITH YOUR WORK PERFOR-
MANCE.

I KNOW, KRIS. BUT YOU ALWAYS KNEW THAT ABBY WAS
BUYING THE TOP-OF-THE-LINE ENCRYPTION SYSTEMS. AND
SHE CHANGES IT TOO OFTEN FOR ME TO CRACK IT.

WE NEED TO TALK ABOUT THIS LATER. "Inspector, can you
share with me where my most *loyal* maid went yesterday?
Royal courtesy or what have you?"

"I shouldn't," he responded, but he was clearly enjoying
being ahead of Kris on something. A map of Garden City suddenly reflected off the sedan's front window. A line appeared
in red, with various other colored lines intersecting it. Sometimes they merely crossed. Other times, they went quite aways
together.

KRIS, THE MESSAGE WAS SENT FROM THERE. And a green X
appeared along with the red and black line late in the day. It
was on Kris's vision, not something the inspector could see.

"Well, Inspector, it appears that you know something I
don't know—ah, didn't know. I will need to look into this."

He grinned proudly.

"Oh, and could you tell me why you're the one letting me
know about my new permit? Shouldn't Lieutenant Martinez
have delivered it?" That put a dint in his grin.

"Your case has been elevated. I'll be handling all your is-
sues for the time being."

And thus keeps me from talking to someone who can't
vote and might give me an interesting perspective on your
planet.

Kris gave the inspector the empty-headed socialite grin she
occasionally got away with. Clearly, she had a lot on her plate

at the moment. And the inspector had played his distraction game very well.

Kris made a mental note. There had to be something in the fine print that would leave her with a question or two. A question that she really didn't need to bother a full-fledged inspector about.

But first, matters close to home. Why was Abby talking to the people who had done their best to kill Kris?

20

Nelly, TELL JACK, ABBY, AND PENNY I WANT THEM IN MY QUARTERS NOW! Kris thought as she marched into the embassy. TELL THEM FIVE MINUTES AGO WOULD BE EVEN BETTER. OH, AND TELL PENNY SHE CAN BRING HER THUMB SCREWS.

YOU ARE JOKING, KRIS?

JUST TELL EACH OF THEM WHAT I TOLD YOU TO TELL THEM.

YES, YOUR HIGHNESS, MA'AM, BOSS.

Kris found Abby already in her quarters.

"You got a command performance, baby duck," she said, removing Kris's cover and running a testing hand through her hair. "Ambassador says there's this charity art show that you just must make an appearance at. Oh, and he suggests that you spend some of that Longknife money buying some of this art . . . for goodwill sake."

Kris stepped away from her maid. Was this for real, or was Abby just doing another one of her Oh-we're-so-busy-no-time-to-talk song and dances?

The arrival of Jack and Penny interrupted that dance. To

Kris's disappointment, the professional interrogator was not juggling thumb screws or pushing a rack.

And people said Kris had problems following orders!

Abby raised an eyebrow at the intrusions, then did her best disappearing act, backing herself up against a wall and leaving the floor to the others.

"Not this time," Kris said, and used Abby's own movement to corner her. "What were you doing yesterday?" Kris demanded.

"You gave me the afternoon off. I was on personal business. Even a poor maid needs a bit of time to herself," Abby said as self-righteous as any who spoke for the downtrodden masses.

Kris shook her head. "Not good enough. What were you doing yesterday meeting with the very gangs that provided the shooters that I was running from three days ago? Why did you have supper with two of those gang members?"

Now Kris found Jack at her right elbow, Penny at her left. They said nothing, getting their briefing, as it were, from Kris's own questions. But what they heard caused narrowing eyes to go hard as they locked on Abby.

"I thought everyone had a right to some privacy. Isn't there any time a poor working woman can call her own. And why were you spying on me?" Abby shot back. It hadn't taken the maid very long to find grounds for a counterattack.

She was good.

"I was not spying on you, though the next time you throttle the GPS squawker on your computer you better have a good reason. No, Inspector Johnson seems to have all of us under surveillance. Don't spit on the sidewalk, any of you, or you'll end up with a rap sheet. But let's get back to the questions I'm asking. Why were you meeting with gang leaders?"

Abby pulled herself to her full height, and if possible, her back got even more rigid. She sniffed. "I was *not* meeting with them. I failed to avoid them while getting the hell out of Dodge. They demanded to know why they shouldn't take out on me some of Your Highness's bad karma with them. My argument was brilliant, and they bowed to my logic."

"How many did you kill?" Jack demanded.

"None. I said they bowed to my logic."

"Am I the only one having a hard time swallowing this?" Penny said.

Once again, Abby was doing a great job of misdirecting her interrogators. Kris held up three fingers. "Okay, let's say you answered one. Why buy a couple of gangers supper?"

"Because Bronc needed the time to put together the computer I'd bought him. The cops did mention that I bought one of them a set, or rather the parts to build a set."

This was getting weird. Kris still had two fingers up. She would not let Abby confuse her . . . or deflect this line of questioning.

"You bought two ganger's supper?"

"No, I bought pizza for my niece, who I assure you is not part of any gang. And I bought a computer for her boyfriend, also not part of any gang, for helping me do what I went there to do," Abby said very slowly. "He also liked the pizza. I hear most teenage boys do."

"So why were you in that part of town? With your squawker off!" Kris demanded.

"I. Was. Looking. For. My. Mother."

"Your mother" came in three separate gasps.

"Yes, my mother. Everybody has one, don't you know, Kris." Abby gave Kris one of her dry scowls. "Didn't your mother give you the basic talk about the birds and bees? Princesses have mothers. Maids have mothers. Princess's usually have fathers. For a maid it is optional. Makes it easier. If you're born a bastard you don't have to work so hard to earn the title . . . as some around here do."

"She did say she was from Eden," Penny pointed out.

"And I didn't want to come back here, may I remind you."

"So you went looking for you mom . . . on the worst side of this town," Kris said.

"When you're born and raised on that side of town, where else you gonna look?"

"So you found your niece," Jack said.

"With a whole lot of help from her boyfriend. I'd promised

him a computer. You wouldn't believe what he was doing with just an old magazine reader."

"With a whole lot of help . . ." Penny said. Kris gave her a glance. Maybe they had taught her something in interrogator's school.

"With a whole lot of help," Abby said slowly, "we talked Cara into taking me home to meet the family."

"Why's that?" Penny asked.

"Why do you think? Princess here was born and raised in Nuu House. Fancy place. The first couple of houses I lived in got bulldozed for urban renewal. Nothing growing there but a few weeds, but trust me, it's an improvement."

Abby paused, swallowed hard. "When I was twelve, I didn't take a lot of friends home, either." Then again she stiffened. "And I killed my squawker 'cause I wasn't all that interested in any of you knowing where I was . . . what I was looking for."

"I'm sorry, Abby," Kris said, wondering if she just bought another ticket for a ride. "Did you see your mother again?"

"Yeah, and my sister. And Cara. A good kid. She deserves better."

That got three nods.

"Well, if you need time off to visit . . ." Kris started.

Abby cut her off. "If I had my druthers, I wouldn't be going back there anytime soon."

Again three people nodded, knowing that whatever feelings were going through Abby, they had no idea what they were.

"But I will be going back a whole lot sooner than I want."

"Why?" Kris asked.

"Because I bought Bronc a whole lot more computer than I'd planned on. He'll need it if he's going to stay alive with a Longknife on this planet."

"Huh?" This conversation was going round and round. Was there a center to it?

"Kris, my mom knows I'm working for you. My momma's gotten herself uptown. Says you might be surprised to find her being squired around on some fancy man's elbow at a party or two."

"That's, ah, nice," Kris said, but tried to leave half a question mark hanging.

"Not nice . . . at all. There's no reason for her to know I'm working for you. Your name was in all the papers. I wasn't even in the background of any of your pictures."

Kris took a step back, no longer pinning Abby to the wall. The others beside her were backpeddling, too.

"Maybe she saw your name in some landing report?" Penny offered.

"For a planet like Eden, where everything's a secret, the chances of that are poor. And when you consider I am now Abby Nightingale, a name my mother never knew me by, it gets harder and harder to match her knowing I was back—and working for you—to just coincidence."

Kris nodded slowly. Yes, this was a whole new development. An entirely different can of worms.

"There's a whole lot of people knowing a whole lot of stuff about us," Abby said slowly. "A whole lot of people who are working real hard to know what they know. Me, I want to know a bit more about them."

To Kris, that sounded like a great idea, too.

"Oh, and Kris . . ." Abby seemed to add as an afterthought. Though coming from her maid, Kris suspected she'd been leading up to it the entire time. "If I was you, I'd reimburse me for my little investment in Bronc's hacking skills.

"Oh, and if you can arrange it, you might want to have Chief Beni buy the kid pizza a couple of times. The more software on Bronc's new computer, the safer we all might be."

21

Kris had a lot to think about, and as usual, the only time she had was in the tub . . . while Abby did her hair.

Abby had a mother. Not all that surprising. Kris had a mother . . . and did her best to avoid her. Interesting that Abby seemed inclined to do the same.

But it wasn't Abby's family dynamics that might kill Kris.

Somehow, despite all Eden did to hide things, said mother knew Abby was back in town . . . and working for one Princess Longknife. That must have taken a lot of pull.

How did Abby's mom do that? Why?

Or was it just blowby? . . . Some crumb of information that dropped into that motherly ear. From whom? And what was *their* interest in Kris's safety?

Kris reviewed her thoughts and came away with way too many question marks. Given a chance, she'd gladly vote to outlaw that particular punctuation.

Kris snorted and almost got soap up her nose.

All the money she'd spent on Nelly. All that computer to make sure she'd have information at her fingertips, and Eden was stonewalling her.

I AM SORRY, KRIS. I AM TRYING.

Oops, Kris had forgotten her latest gadget. Having a computer plugged directly into your brain was a great way to stay alive. However, at certain moments, like in the bath, Kris really didn't want Nelly around her neck. The surgery had come with a plug to seal the extra hole in Kris's head when Nelly was elsewhere.

But there was this really nifty new gadget. A plug that included a short-range network. And Kris was now doing her ruminating with Nelly listening nearby.

SORRY, NELLY, THAT WASN'T MEANT FOR YOU. I KNOW YOU ARE DOING YOUR BEST. IT'S JUST THAT WE ARE UP AGAINST A STONE WALL. AND IT'S NOT AN ACCIDENT. THEY DON'T WANT US TO KNOW WHAT'S GOING ON AND THEY'RE SURE DOING A GOOD JOB OF IT.

DO YOU THINK THIS BRONC MIGHT HELP US WITH THE NEW COMPUTER ABBY GAVE HIM?

HE MIGHT. Then again, he might just get himself killed. Kris did not want more blood on her hands. Especially a kid's.

"Abby, how good is this boy . . . and your niece?"

"At staying alive. Not too bad. They grew up in Five Corners and they're still breathing."

"But are they ready for the hand they're being dealt?"

Abby took awhile to answer. "Your Royal Highness, I can only guess. All I know is that I made the mistake of going home and suddenly those poor kids are in this up to their cute button noses and all I can hope to do is give them a helping hand at staying one step ahead of dead. You got any better ideas?"

"Your mom won't protect your niece?"

"My mom has my sister on drugs to keep her figure in the high price range."

On that thought, Abby rinsed Kris's hair with more than the usual fury. Kris's scalp took quite a beating.

As Kris rose from the tub and toweled herself off, she offered what she could. "Arrange for the kids to have a session with the chief. See what he can offer this Bronc. I'll pay for any software the chief says they need. And add on anything you know and the chief is weak in."

"It won't be eating," Abby said and went to select a dress for tonight as Kris started pulling on a spider-silk armored bodystocking. Tonight she'd add ceramics and anything else she had armored in her lingerie drawer.

No telling who'd be at this shindig.

Or what they'd be doing—to Kris.

"That big, white rig up there," Gunny Brown said, pointing out a limo that looked more like a space liner than a ground car. "Story is that Miss Victoria Peterwald is renting that showboat."

"How'd you get that bit of intell?" Kris asked.

"I got one of the woman Marines reading the social columns. She likes that stuff and I'm shaking my head at all the information you can get from those gossips. You'd think people would know a bit about operational security."

" 'War by social means,' as Billy Longknife is want to call it, doesn't mean that all its participants are up-to-date on their Clausewitz," Kris said.

"Beggars ought to learn."

"But not too fast, Gunny," Jack said. "Their poor security gives us a moment to adjust. Thank heavens for minor favors."

But other than tightening her gut muscles, there wasn't a lot Kris could do.

And the big, white whale of a limo wasn't necessarily a sign of poor planning on Vicky's part. Showmanship might not belong on the battlefield, but it sure worked on the society pages. Winning by intimidation was a well-practiced tactic in business . . . and bitch fights.

Somehow Kris doubted Vicky was much interested in that kind of a win. "How large is my detail tonight?"

"I've got the inside with six good shooters, all in civilian and all armored," Gunny said. "Corporal Jorhat has three uniformed to keep the rolling stock secure. The captain has a response team ready to roll at the embassy. Mrs. General Trouble is with a group of students at a pub this evening. Captain wants to be able to reinforce in either direction."

Kris hoped Gramma Ruth had a quiet evening; heaven knows she deserved a few. It looked to be a few more years before Kris could make a claim on quiet.

Kris was hardly out of her limo when Marta Whitebread attached herself to Kris's elbow. And stayed there.

"I am so sorry you missed the autumn show. They really are quite fantastic. The horticulturalists and genetic people showed a lot more than just flowers."

"More than flowers?" Kris said, just to see if she could get a word in . . . edgewise.

"Well, it's still flowers mostly, but there were some fantastic animals. Last year, we actually had a Pegasus. You know, a flying horse. Tiny thing. Gossamer wings."

"Did it fly?" Another successful intervention for Kris.

But if it wasn't Marta at Kris's elbow, it would have been one of five or six standing nearby . . . and one of them was Ms. Broadmore. That woman Kris had sworn never to talk to again . . . if she could avoid it.

So Marta kept rattling on about how the genetic engineers created a tiny horse that could fly. "They lightened the poor creature as much as they could. Hollow bones, just like birds. I just never realized how strong bird's legs are."

"Oh?"

"Poor thing must have taken a fright. Ms. Broadmore swore her trainer was only supposed to let it do short flights. Anyway it took off, circled the rafters several times. It seemed to be greatly enjoying itself. But when it came in to land, it shattered all four of its legs. They had to put it to sleep, immediately. It's crying was so painful to hear."

"No doubt, its broken legs were quite painful to bear," Kris added dryly.

"Oh? Can animals feel pain?"

Kris suspected the woman would have had the same reaction if she'd suggested that her household staff and the workers who earned those dividend checks that appeared in her bank account could also feel pain.

Maybe Ms. Broadmore would be better to talk to.

BUT SHE HAD THE POOR CREATURE MADE, Nelly pointed out.

Isn't there anyone worth talking to on this entire planet!
Or maybe it's just the company I keep.

Kris managed to steer Marta into the larger group. In a matter of moments they were disagreeing with each other as to what the best artifacts of the autumn show had been. With a bit of battle tactics and judicious application of hip checks, Kris ended up beside a young woman. A docent's name badge with Samatha printed on it identified the freshly scrubbed and thoroughly curvaceous woman as someone that might know what was actually going on this evening.

"So, what is special this season?"

"Holovids," the young woman answered with a friendly smile.

Kris directed Jack to provide a momentary picket fence, and soon Kris was walking rapidly away with just the docent and a woman Marine.

"I'm Princess Kristine. Most people call me Kris."

"I'm Samatha Tidings, an art student at Eden U."

"And you bring me tidings of great art?" Kris said, smiling.

"Gosh, I haven't heard that joke for, oh, five minutes."

"Yes, but now you can say you suffered it from a princess."

"My granddad was a union organizer. I don't know how he'll take to me hobnobbing with princesses and Longknifes."

"Ah, yes, but Longknifes send their kids off to college to give them an education, widen their horizons, and the brats end up doing all sorts of nasty things. My folks still haven't forgiven me for joining the Navy." Kris chuckled.

"Well, it's not like the Navy does any fighting these days."

The woman Marine beside Kris was very unsuccessful at swallowing a snicker.

"You haven't done any fighting, have you?" the young woman said, eyes growing wide.

"Let's just say that out on the Rim, folks are a bit less law-abiding than around here," Kris answered vaguely. "So, what would you suggest we look at? I'm told I should buy some of this. Any suggestions?" should change the topic.

"There's a lot to see. The central ballroom is one hologram after another. Most of those are pastoral or landscapes. Each conference room has been allocated a specialty. One of my favorites is impressionist."

"Well, there's a strike against you. My mother drools over that stuff."

"Oh."

"Yes. I was eleven when she took me through several of those holograms. Colors flowing in all kinds of weird patterns. It scared the stuffing out of me. Course it was after lunch and I was high as a space station. Not a good combination. Left me with nightmares for a week."

"And you were eleven?" Now Kris had scandalized the coed.

"Just part of my misspent youth." Kris didn't add that those nightmares had been preferable to the ones of poor Eddy, suffocating under a manure pile.

They entered the ballroom just as Jack was catching up. A Marine now joined the woman trigger-puller and the two of them established a pattern of staying one hologram ahead of Kris, checking each out before their princess arrived.

The huge room didn't look all that big as they entered it. A stone wall, covered with creeping vines in flower was quite close at hand. In these close quarters, the aroma of the honeysuckles was almost overpowering.

But Samatha walked them right up to the stone wall . . . and into it.

And the next breath they took was winter crisp as a snow-covered landscape spread out before them.

Kris almost stumbled as the vertigo took her.

Ahead, range upon range of snow-covered mountains marched off into the distance. Here, close at hand, a deer nibbled on a tree. Foolishly, Kris reached out to touch the animal. Her hand went right through it.

"That was not well done," Samatha said.

"Yes, I do feel rather foolish," Kris said with a chuckle.

"No. Not you. The artist's work is quite primitive. That deer should have reacted to you moving your hand by bounding away. There have been routines available for that for years. It's inexcusable to be that sloppy."

It didn't look sloppy to Kris, but then she'd never been a connoisseur of holograms. "Do you have something in the show?" she asked Samatha.

"No, students at my level may work with a master on some project, but we don't actually enter on our own. But my boyfriend does. He's a graduate in Historical Environmental Designs. He has a wonderful scene from early Earth. The arrival of the first men and women on the American continent. When his mammoths stampede, the ground shakes. It's quite a show."

"I hope we get a chance to see it," Kris said, making a note to herself not to shoot any stampeding mammoths. No telling where her rounds might end up.

The next several scenes introduced Kris to desert and arctic views, rocky coasts at glimmering sunset and formal gardens. It was very tempting to try sitting down on one of the stone benches in the garden.

"Not real," Kris said as her hand went through the bench.

"Nothing is real here," Samatha answered. "Well, actually, a few of the rocks or stumps may be real. At least real enough to touch. They contain the projectors. That's why you are supposed to stay to the path. No way to tell when you'd stumble on a rock that's really there."

"And probably loaded with several millions of dollars of projection equipment," Jack added in a droll aside.

"So true. Lots of students are in hock to their eyeballs. If they make a sale here, they'll be set for life. If not, well, it was slightly used equipment when they rented it."

Kris and Jack were sharing Samatha's light chuckle when one of the rocks suddenly unfolded like a flower petal.

Kris recognized the auto-gun immediately.

"Don't move," she whispered through unmoving lips as she froze herself in midstride. NELLY, GET THE MARINES BACK IN HERE!

ALREADY DOING IT, KRIS.

22

In the stories and the vids, the grizzled sergeant shouts freeze and all the troops do just that. Possibly, if you're moving carefully through a battlefield, you can do it.

Kris had tried it, once, moving across a minefield, and done a passably good job of freezing.

But who takes the same care walking through an art show?

Kris was fast learning that she could end up just as dead either place.

Even as Kris ordered those around her not to move, she knew she was in no position to take her own advice. One foot was up and way too far out for her to keep from finishing the step.

Everything depended on what sensors the auto-gun had.

If it had motion sensors, the last one to move just might get away with it . . . assuming the magazine had run empty on those that moved first.

If it had Kris's picture in its brain, nothing much mattered.

If it was under the remote control of some assassin, again, nothing much mattered.

Or it might just aim for sound. In which case, Kris was again in trouble. She did have to issue an order. Jack didn't need any. As for the girl . . .

It turned out she couldn't take them.

First the college docent screamed as she recognized the barrel of a gun. Then she bolted.

And the gun homed on her.

Jack, God bless him, kicked the girl's knees out from under her before she could take a second step. Then, he threw himself on top of her.

Kris could understand the male desire to do something like that. Samatha was certainly strategically well-padded enough that neither of them should be hurt. Kris hoped Jack lived long enough to enjoy it.

It also put the back of his armored dress blues to the gun. When the gun spat a long stream of darts, most of them finished sticking out of his blouse. Still, that had to hurt.

Someone was going to be black-and-blue tomorrow.

And grumpy.

But Kris had her own problems. Gravity was having its inevitable effect. She turned her fall into a tumble to the left, and went for her automatic at the same time.

And brought her weapon up as the pea brain controlling the auto-gun swept it toward her.

Kris aimed her automatic at the rock. It kicked in her hand on full auto, full power, armor-piercing magazine.

Let's see which of us can take it the longest, Kris thought.

It was a close run thing.

Kris felt the impact of darts, starting at her right foot and coming up her leg. It was purely an information dump to the brain. In the heat of battle, pain didn't arrive—yet.

She kept her aim on the rock. Sparks flew along with small parts of things. No way to tell what she was hitting. The hologram's illusion hid whatever damage her slugs were doing.

She felt the darts hitting her hip, and climbing up her belly. Here, the ceramic slats in her girdle earned their pay.

Kris let her fire wander, a bit down, a bit up. Maybe if she hit the auto-gun in the right place . . . ?

Two Marines rushed into the scene, machine pistols held up before their eyes, tracking for the sound of the fire.

They put long bursts into the auto-gun even as it turned toward them.

Now Kris had a broadside view of the gun. She aimed for the arming bolt's slot. Mess that up and it had to do bad things to the gun. Why else were Gunny's all the time saying you had to keep the slot clean.

Jack took a few more hits as the auto-gun swept past him.

Even as Kris fired at the arming bolt, another part of her brain was processing the trajectories of the rounds that didn't connect with her or Jack's armor.

Outside this hologram must be a slaughter.

The chatter of the gun hicupped. Regained its rhythm, then slowed down to nothing.

A hush went over the scene.

Then the lights went out.

Now Kris heard people screaming, crying, moaning, and weeping throughout the huge ballroom.

"Somebody's cut power to the whole show," Jack said.

The two Marines showed that they took the business of being ever ready, or was that the Coasties motto. Anyway, they produced lights and a moment later, two beams were searching around the room.

"Somebody hit the goddamn lights" echoed through the room in a voice only a Gunny Sergeant could manage.

And there was light.

Proving that God truly is spelled G-U-N-N-Y.

The harsh glare of the newly reborn lights showed carnage. Kris, Jack, and the Marines were the only ones who had felt the need to wear armor to an art show. Scores of bleeding people now suffered the full effects of their civilian optimism.

Across this gory scene, a dozen men and women moved with purpose toward Kris, their machine pistols out.

If anyone wished to take up arms against Kris now, there would be hell to pay.

Scattered in with the fallen were other hologram generators, now off.

Were any of them rigged with auto-guns?

Kris wasn't the only one mulling that thought. One or two Marines paused to eye rocks, tree stumps, what have you. As per their training, they eyed the things over weapon sights.

"Don't shoot the gear," Kris said, taking responsibility for several million dollars of equipment that struggling artists would have a hard time explaining to their rental agents why it came back in shot-up pieces.

Hopefully, she would not have to pay for this good deed.

"If any of them start shooting, nail 'em," Gunny added.

Once at Kris's side, the Marines formed a wall around their princess. In the distance sirens began to sound. But the bleeding people in the ballroom needed help now. "Any of you have lifesaving gear?" Kris asked.

Most of the Marines nodded.

"Gunny, please select your best shooters to stay with me. Detach the rest of your team to help these people."

"If you wish it, Your Highness." The statement clearly reflected what Gunny thought of that idea.

"Of course she does, Gunny," Jack drawled as he rolled off the docent. "She's a Longknife. They always want to take more risks than any sane person would." Then Jack groaned.

At the entrance to the ballroom, two Marines rushed in, no weapons out, but instead loaded with medical emergency kits. They immediately fell to, working with the bleeding. "Those Marines from the truck park? The ones Nelly called for?"

"Yes, ma'am," Gunny agreed. And with a nod from him, all but two of the Marines around Kris joined in lifesaving.

Over the next several minutes, civilians straggled in. Apparently, some owners of the limos parked outside also traveled with medical emergency kits. Several EMTs rushed to where someone was down, either relieving a Marine or starting initial care. Others stood around until a Marine yelled at them, and got them helping where they were needed.

"Jack, you okay?" Kris asked.

"Shouldn't I be asking you that question, Your Highness?"

"I'm fine," Kris said.

"You're bleeding."

"If I am, I'll have Abby write a very nasty letter to some lingerie manufacturer."

"Check your leg, ma'am," Gunny said.

Kris did. Trickles of blood showed where several darts stuck out of her spider-silk stocking.

"I think the darts were small enough to work their way through the weave of the thing," Jack said.

"What about you?" Kris demanded again.

"I'm okay," Jack said, but then groaned.

"Check him out, Gunny," Kris said, and took an offered hand from a woman Marine to get herself up. The leg was definitely starting to smart. And the hang of her gown was now all wrong, as darts imbedded in her ceramic understuff held its fall.

"Anybody see a Vicky Peterwald?" Kris asked.

Just as the source of her query exited the ladies' room, surrounded by a mass of hulking security. They made for the exit without looking back.

"Lucky timing," Jack muttered.

"Or informed timing," Kris added.

"Sir," Gunny said, "you have darts sticking out of your skull. I know Marine officers are supposed to be hardheaded, sir, but this goes beyond my usual experience of the Corps."

Jack chuckled, or at least tried to. He also pulled a wig off his scalp.

"I thought you looked terribly shaggy on formal occasions," Gunny muttered, examining the armored toupee. On the inside of the hairpiece, where its outside had stopped a dart, was now a lump. The armor had both stopped the slug and tried to spread or absorb the impact.

"Looks like it done good," Gunny said.

"How is your neck, Jack?" Kris demanded. "All that force had to go somewhere. You took, what, three slugs?"

"I'm fine, Kris," Jack said, squinting at her. "And you are as beautiful as ever. Both of you."

"He's concussed," Gunny said.

"Let's get out of here. Is there a hospital close?"

"My orders are to transport you to the embassy's clinic,

Your Highness," Gunny said. "Captain is about one minute out with the reaction team. I am instructed to await his arrival before moving you. Either of you, sirs."

"Then by all means let's do what the captain ordered," Kris said, and, suddenly feeling the need, plopped back down.

"Bad idea," she muttered through gritted teeth. "Blasted leg isn't happy with me standing, and doesn't much like me sitting, either.

"Captain, we'll need two stretchers, here. Yes, sir, the princess is bleeding a mite bit, and the lieutenant is going to have one whale of a headache in the morning."

"Who said anything about the morning," Jack groaned and put his head gently down.

Samatha was shaking like a twig in a tornado. "You saved my life," she managed to get out through chattering teeth, as she reached out to caress Jack's face.

"I wouldn't do that, ma'am," Gunny said. "We don't know what all is busted there."

And then the reinforcements arrived.

23

Captain DeVar moved them out as quickly and smartly as Kris expected of a Marine. Kris only tossed two monkey wrenches into his well-ordered plan.

Kris might not have been perforated by the darts, but she was quickly coming to feel like she'd been worked over with a baseball bat. Several of them. Despite the pain, there were things Kris had to do while the moment was right.

"Captain, assign your best electronic tech to that pile of wreckage," Kris ordered, though gritted teeth, managing to give the auto-gun a limp wave.

"Already in the works," Captain DeVar snapped.

"Nelly, get Chief Beni down here. I don't want that auto-gun vanishing without us getting a complete workup on it."

"Definitely will do. Now, ma'am, I want you out of here," the good captain insisted.

"Take me over there on the way out," Kris insisted. "By those women at that table."

With an exasperated sigh, the captain waved the stretcher bearers in that direction.

Hotel employees were busily rolling out tables and setting

up chairs around them for the well-heeled customers who were not bleeding out on the carpet. Kris pointed her bearers at what she suspected was the first table up. What else could explain why both Ms. Broadmore and Marta Whitebread allowed themselves to collapse around the same table.

"Was this *another* attempt to kill you," Ms. Broadmore demanded. Clearly, in her mind, Kris bore full responsibility for this disruption of her art show.

"Probably," Kris admitted with a sigh. "And I didn't get a chance to buy a thing."

"None of us did." Marta scowled.

From the glare both women aimed at Kris she suspected her name was rapidly plunging toward the bottom of the list of people who *just must* be invited to every little thing.

Hurray!

Kris put a frown on her face and, leveling herself up on one elbow, said in as dumb a voice as she could manage through the pain. "There's one thing I don't understand."

"What *could* that be," Ms. Broadmore sniffed.

"Every other time I've arrived on a new planet, by now I'd have met the president and half of the congress. Being Billy Longknife's brat or Ray Longknife's great-granddaughter usually has them coming out in droves to at least pay their respects."

Both women just eyed Kris, not at all grasping where this rambling was going. Kris would have to paint a very clear picture for these two.

"Didn't you invite any of the political powers that be to this show? Or to either of your soirees this week?"

"Of *course* I did," both women shot back immediately.

Then paused.

Then looked at each other. The lights going off behind their eyes had to be a least forty watts, maybe more.

But neither said a word to Kris.

"Your Highness, can we *please* get you out of here?" Captain DeVar said, as if on cue.

Kris let herself be hauled away. But the two women were in rapid conversation before Kris was out of earshot.

It would be interesting to see what came of that little land mine she'd planted.

As they headed for the car park, the captain glanced over his shoulder. "Ma'am, I'm pretty well schooled in platoon and company tactics, but I'm not quite sure what I just saw."

Kris relaxed onto her stretcher. That didn't make it hurt less, just hurt different. "Captain, in social circles, there is an A-list, a B-list, and a C-list. Me, I suspect today I've sunk to some F- or G-list."

The captain raised an eyebrow at that.

"But two very proud A-list social harpies have just found out that they have been had by the real As. Used as stalking horses. Everyone likes to be in the know. I just told those two biddies that there are people in the know that knew not to show up. And those people didn't let them know.

"How do you think that makes them feel, Captain?"

"Interesting, ma'am, very interesting."

Kris spotted Inspector Johnson getting out of his car as she was loaded into a transport. The captain now brooked no delay; Kris ended up fighting just to get her and Jack in the same hulking all-terrain rig.

It could have passed for a tank. The only thing missing was a main battery gun. There were plenty of automatic weapons out. All the traffic now headed for the art show; her rig covered the distance to the embassy in no time at all.

The two police cycles driving shotgun, sirens blaring, might have helped. Tomorrow, Kris would have to thank Inspector Johnson for at least one good deed.

Kris's tour of the embassy had not included a stop by the clinic. She had noticed that an Army doctor shared the mess with the troops. Kris, flat on her back on a gurney, did her first assessment of the doc as he did his assessment of her leg.

Well, at least there was no alcohol on his breath.

Captain DeVar had whispered a quiet prayer—that Kris was supposed to not have noticed—that the good doc would not have drank his supper today. The captain had asked for sobriety, what with two of his primaries out in the shooting gallery, and had sent the doc off to supper with Commander Malhoney to help him remember. Since Kris knew the good commander was much taken by the drink, she was grateful that the two of them had held themselves to the captain's high demands.

"Your leg is stitched, but not deeply," the doc said. "We'll need to cut you out of those stockings and dress."

"I doubt you can," Abby said, materializing at Kris's side. "I see you had a good time tonight."

"Nope," Kris said. "No one to shoot back at. Auto-gun."

"Oh, pooh," the maid said.

"Why don't you concentrate on Jack, Doc, who I think is in worse shape, while Abby and I get me out of this getup."

The doc glanced at Kris's vitals, flashed a light in both of her eyes, let her count his fingers, and then went away.

Abby closed the curtains behind him, giving Kris a bit of modesty, put both her hands on her hips, and scowled down at Kris. "You are a mess."

"Could you scold me later?" Kris said. "The pain is nasty, and I doubt that horse doctor will give me anything until he's had a chance to see all my black-and-blue spots.

"I heard that and you got it right, Your Highness" came from across the partition.

"Let's get you out of that dress," Abby said, reaching for scissors. "I'm not going to tell you how much you paid for it."

"Somebody will get a bill for this," Kris said darkly.

"No doubt. Now hold still. I don't want to cut nothing off you that you can't afford to lose." The dress came off in pieces. The darts held it solidly in place, not letting go from where they had dug themselves into the reactive section of the ceramic body girdle. That girdle had done its job; it and all the darts came off together. Only from the inside could Kris see the cracks and spalling. It had held—but just barely.

Peeling off the bodystocking was almost work as usual, except that every time Kris twisted or turned to work the spider silk down her body she wanted to scream.

Her right side was an ugly line of black and blue where the rounds had hit, been stopped, but demanded payment for the energy they gave up from the soft flesh beneath. At least the ceramic armor had done a good job of spreading the energy.

Spider silk stopped a round. As far as its energy went, that was a matter not mentioned in the promotional material.

When the bodystocking was down to just Kris's right leg, Abby wrapped her in a modest blue gown and said. "Doc, when you can pry yourself away from that hardheaded Marine, this Navy type is ready for a look-see."

"Sorry, Princess, but you'll have to wait. You aren't nearly as interesting a collection of bruises and contusions as this fellow I've got in my clutches right now."

"What?" Kris yelped, and tried to roll off the table. That produced another yelp. A very real one.

Abby made sure that Kris laid back down, then called over the curtain. "Jack, you decent? Mind if I let this nosey neighbor of yours at least look at your ugly mug?"

"I'm not sure if I'm decent or not. They kind of got me locked down" came back in a way-too-shaky voice.

"Abby, open that curtain," Kris demanded.

"I could point out that only family are allowed in here," came back from the doc.

"I drafted him. He's head of my security team. Doc, open up," Kris almost pleaded.

"Well, since you put it that way. Open the curtain. She drafted you, boy, and you're still speaking to her?"

"Seems that way, Doc."

So a corpsman slid the curtain aside.

And Kris swallowed the first five things she tried to say.

Jack's dress uniform was in shreds on the floor. No, on closer examination, it was in distinct pieces. Apparently, whoever designed armored dress uniforms made allowances for taking them apart after heavy use.

But that wasn't what held Kris's eyes.

Jack was splayed out in some kind of traction. His back, his neck, and his skull were surrounded by things that held him. It looked like he was being eaten by a huge metal spider.

They had stripped him down to the bare nothing, revealing a back and butt that was a sickly gray in the few places it wasn't livid black and blue. His minimum modesty was preserved by a towel someone had thrown over the vitals.

Kris finally emitted something like a gasp.

"Does he need all that?" she whispered.

"Most likely not," the doc said, stepping away from Jack. "But you ever met a doc who don't like to play with all his toys when he gets a chance. Especially when someone else is picking up the tab." The doc had gray eyes that sparkled and white hair that gave him the look of a father everyone could use. Only the lines around his eyes showed worry. At the moment, those lines were etched deeply as he took in Jack.

"I can't look all that bad," Jack insisted feebly. "You sound like I'm dying or something."

"More like the something," Abby put in. "I don't think the doc here would let you out of his care that easily."

"He ain't nearly tortured enough," the corpsman put in through a smile.

"So much for your performance rating," the doc grumbled, but with too much smile to make the threat real. Then he turned to Kris and took her still-stockinged leg in hand and turned it gingerly. The creases around his eyes failed to soften.

"Corpsman, you keep an eye on what that jarhead claims is his brain," Doc said without looking back at Jack. "If that meatloaf starts to swell any little bit, I want to know about it before it happens. You hear."

"Loud and clear, Your Godhood," said the unconcerned medic.

"Now, Your Highness, let's see what you've done to your perfectly usable collection of flesh and bones."

"It's been in better shape," Kris agreed.

The doc struggled to pull one dart from where it had buried its point in the spider silk. "Nasty little thing. And it does like where it's at. Captain, quit holding up the wall and bring your strong right arm over here. Nobody's going to commit assault and mayhem in my clinic. I won't allow it. Already writ the prescription agin' it."

Captain DeVar came over from where he'd established himself, able to observe both casualties and keep a weather eye on the entrance to both the emergency room and, through the window in the door, the clinic's front door.

"Grab a pair of pliers and see how much work it is for you to pry one of those darts loose. Pull it straight out."

Even the Marine ended up grunting from the effort as the first dart came out.

"That's just the way it is. My second wife always complained that I had those strong surgeon hands for cutting someone open, but hand me a jar of pickles and forget it. Officially, young lady, I'm declaring you a jar of pickles."

"Or olives," Abby added dryly.

"With very nice stuffing," the doc said, not letting a mere maid get in the last word.

"Would you two quit it," Jack said. "I'm in enough pain without you trying to get me laughing."

"Ain't you heard, laughter's great medicine," Doc insisted.

"Not just now it isn't," Jack and Kris said in harmony.

"Patients," the doc spat. "Don't know why we let them in the door." But for someone who didn't seem to have much use for patients, the doc was very reluctant to let them out of his sight. "Commander Malhoney will just have to find someone else to drink with tonight," he said when he was done with Kris.

"You two look fine, but then, I've buried a few patents who were, or claimed they were when they walked out on this old sawbone. So settle in, get comfortable, and get ready to pay attention to my whole collection of horrific patient stories."

Kris had better things to do with her time. She'd had about enough of playing target in somebody's shooting gallery. It was time for a Longknife to take charge of her own life. Start kicking butt and taking names.

Maybe it was the lame stories. Or maybe it was something she got poked with. But Kris was asleep before Doc finished his third one.

Interlude 2

Grant von Schrader smashed the Close button. The latest report on the afternoon's happenings vanished. "Is that little idiot back yet?" he demanded of his supervisory computer.

"If by 'little idiot' you mean Ms. Victoria Smythe-Peterwald," his computer answered dutifully, "she has just returned. Should I ask her to come to your office?"

"For the duration of her stay you may assume that 'little idiot' means only Ms. Victoria, and yes, you may tell her that I want her here right now."

Grant returned to his overview of the situation while he waited. He did not like what he was watching. Unlike most news stories that were reported once and stayed the same, this evening's events were changing. Growing. Couldn't anyone shut up those two old biddies!

No, that was not the problem. Why were those two still getting face time? Why hadn't those two's ramblings been buried?

Ms. Victoria entered, looking very smug. He would have to stomp on that . . . hard.

"I see you missed that Longknife bitch again." That should cut Vicky off at the knees.

Instead of penitent, the little twit shrugged diffidently. "She may still be alive, but it was close. Very close. She has to know that next time it will be closer. And sooner or later, she dies. Kris Longknife will die. Let her think of that in her hospital bed tonight"

"There will not be another time. Not on *my* planet."

Victoria plopped herself into one of the padded guest chairs around his discussion table. "Oh, Uncle Grantie, you sound upset. Is something bothering you?"

Grant detested·being reduced to "Uncle Grantie." He took an extra moment to get a firm handle on his temper, then another second to examine exactly how he should approach this offspring of his boss's loins. He was supposed to be teaching her. So he called up his best educational tone.

"The initial news reports blamed the incident at the Spring Charity Art Extravaganza on a gas-line explosion."

"Good. Some newsie used his imagination," Victoria purred.

"Unfortunately, whoever you hired for this hit didn't use his imagination," Grant shot back. "A nice bomb would have left little enough to challenge that bit of creative reporting."

All that got from Victoria were raised eyebrows.

"Your man used an auto-gun that left plenty of bullets in victims, and pieces of the gun in the wreckage."

"And your police can't handle a little problem like that," Vicky said, shaking her head. Suddenly, the discovery of her poor planning was his fault.

He made a mental grab for his temper, caught it barely by his fingernails, and stuffed it back in his hip pocket.

"Reporters can get the scoops we lay out for them. Police reports can be 'corrected.' Unfortunately, Ms. Broadmore and Mrs. Whitebread say they saw the gun and all the shooting and they're talking a lot and it's all off story."

"Can't you have them popped?"

"They are major players on Eden. They die later," Grant snapped, cutting that line of thought off at the root.

"Heart attacks?" Vicky said, arching an eyebrow.

"Not fast enough today. And all of your solutions involve risk for minor gains when fifteen years of work is our main concern. Hasn't your father mentioned the benefit of staying focused on the prize and not being distracted by mere glitter."

"Longknife's death is not mere glitter."

"It is right now."

"Well, if you hadn't sent poor Vennie packing, he might have done a better job for me."

Grant got out from behind his desk and walked over to personally confront his boss's daughter. He stood there, towering over her, hands on hips.

"Longknife is not an objective of the Peterwald Empire on Eden. We have more important work to concentrate on. You will make no further attacks on Kris Longknife."

Victoria shrugged. "If you say so, Uncle Grant."

Uncle Grant. He was now "Uncle Grant." Maybe he had gotten something through that thick, red head of hers.

He better have. They couldn't afford any more blundering around.

24

"Hey, you alive" was deadly cheerful, coming from Abby *way* too early the next morning.

"Not sure," Kris mumbled. "I feel like I'm being tormented by little devils like Tommy's grandmum warned him about. Come close and let me see if I can move my arm enough to throttle you. Tommy said you can't kill the real demons."

With a thoroughly ugly grin, Abby approached Kris's bed.

After further thought . . . and an effort to move that sent her whole body screaming in pain . . . Kris decided to let Abby live.

"You two hungry?" Abby asked. "Cause the President of the Officer's Mess has declared dirty rules. You can show up in sweats." Abby tossed a Navy blue-and-gold set in Kris's lap.

"Hey, that hurt."

"Can't this clinic arrange for hospital chow?" Jack asked as Marine red and gold dropped on his blanket-draped belly.

"Hate to tell you" came in Doc's happy tones. "But this is just an embassy clinic. We aren't staffed to handle really hard cases."

"So what are we doing here?" Kris asked.

"Well, we didn't want to send you to any old hospital where you could be strangled overnight, or doped and rolled out with the dirty laundry. I hate it when that happens to my patients. Besides, your armor did its job," he said glancing at Jack's readouts. "Both of you are in great shape."

"I've been doped. I'm hungover, and I hurt in every muscle in my body. And you're telling me I'm okay?" Kris said.

The doc smiled, and tapped her left arm. That was one of the few parts of her that didn't hurt.

"You're stiff. You hurt," Abby lectured like somebody's mother, "and if you don't get moving, you'll stay stiff. Now, let's get you dressed and some food in you before we ply you with morning meds. No more drugs on an empty stomach. Don't want an addicted princess showing up to wave at little kids."

Two hulking Marines showed up to dress Jack, with two women Marines right behind them. Kris found herself dressed and marched down to the wardroom.

If the President of the Mess had suspended the uniform rules, no one else had the Word. But Kris ate the oatmeal and the stewed prunes that Abby set before her. After all, Jack ate the same, with Captain DeVar and two large Marines looking over his shoulder and offering encouragement . . . or else.

"I've come to accept that no good deed goes unpunished, but you'd think that saving that poor college girl's life would be worth some slack," Jack didn't quite whine.

"Oh, I'm sure she'll find a way to pay you back," the captain snickered.

Kris caught the doc's ear. "Abby wasn't kidding about overdrugging me. I haven't been this stoned since I was twelve, thirteen. I don't want to go there again."

Doc frowned. "Your file has nothing about addiction risk."

"If you're the prime minister's brat, there's a lot of stuff that doesn't make it into your permanent record."

Doc nodded thoughtfully, then looked at the pile of pills he'd laid next to Kris . . . and took a few of them back.

"Let me know how the pain is. And if you start taking

heads off, you will take the pills I tell you to if I have to have the Marines shoot them down your gullet."

"Yes, Doc, your Godhoodness," Kris said with a grin.

"I got to have the Marines shoot that corpsman. I got to," Doc said as he went off to fill his own plate with pancakes.

But he'd left orders for Kris with Abby. No sooner than she finished a very light breakfast than Abby was herding her back to her room. "Doc wants you to get some heat therapy for those bruises. This time we're going to use that bath of yours for something other than a pleasure dip."

Then she handed Kris a little bit of something. "And since the only other whirlpool in this embassy is in the ambassador's quarters, you're going to have to share your bath with Jack."

"What's this," Kris said, holding up two bits of . . .

"That's a string bikini. It don't cover all that much of you, so if I need to, I can see about all of you."

"And Jack?" Kris said, her eyes measuring the tub. She'd always thought of it as big enough for two . . . or four.

"Jack won't peek, and besides, once you're in the tub, he won't be able to see much more than your pretty smile anyhow."

Kris's doubts must have still showed.

"If you don't complain, you'll stay in the tub and no one will get a look. And you'll get to check Jack out. Unless, of course, you want him to get warmed up after you. We can do it that way. We got all day," Abby said as if she hadn't a care.

"I want a staff meeting as soon as we're done here," Kris snapped. "Where's Nelly?"

"On your desk," Abby said as she helped Kris out of the sweat suit and into what little she offered Kris.

"Nelly, tell my usual suspects I want to see them in here in a half hour. Oh, and add Doc and Captain DeVar to the collection."

"Will do," came from the next room.

Kris was deep in the water when Jack came in, wearing a blue hospital robe. When he dropped it, Kris got quite a view. There wasn't any back to Jack's suit, at least not much. Which gave her a good look at the ugly black-and-blue circles that covered his back and butt, circles that in several places merged into several huge blobs. Around the edges, they were healing already, swapping black and blue for sickening green and yellow.

"You look quite colorful," Kris said, trying to sound chipper.

"You don't look half bad yourself," Jack said. Causing Kris to look down. Abby had the jets going on gentle. Still, there wasn't all that much of her to see.

"Made you look," Jack said, with only a small chip of his lopsided grin.

After that, they lapsed into quiet contemplation, or serious concentration on their bodies and how they were taking to the warm and gentle workings of the water. Nothing broke loose to spur an embolism.

Jack left first, now having added a warm pink to the few square inches of his skin that hadn't been battered.

"We really ought to get you better protection. How about a ceramic girdle?" Kris offered.

"I never have figured out how you run in one of those damn things," Jack said. "No, thank you. But I will tell the manufacturer that they need to thicken up their blues. There's nasty stuff out on the street."

"You tell'em, Jack," Kris said.

She'd had enough of sweats. "Undress whites," she ordered from Abby. She dressed herself . . . mostly. Abby saved her from bending over by tying her shoes. At 1000 sharp, Kris walked into her sitting room.

Around the large table that occupied its center sat Penny and Chief Beni, Doc, and Captain DeVar. Jack was just arriving, having switched into undress khakis. Abby started to settle onto the couch, but Kris silently pointed her to a chair at the table. If Doc or the captain thought it strange to have a maid in their counsel, they kept it to themselves. But then, the Corps had seen Abby's shooting skill more than once and probably had spread the word to beat clear of her.

"Ladies and gentlemen, I am tired of being a target. I will not walk into any more shooting galleries that anyone hereabouts sets up," Kris said, opening the meeting as soon as Abby and Jack declared the room free of bugs.

"Here, here," "I'll say," and "About time" greeted that.

"How do you propose to avoid said galleries?" Jack asked.

"That's why we're having this meeting. I'm open to suggestions," Kris said, throwing it open to the floor.

The floor just lay there, saying nothing.

Kris shook her head after a moment. "Thank you for your sage advice. Okay, lets do this by the numbers. Nelly, Beni, Captain DeVar, what do we know about yesterday's autogun?"

The two flesh-and-blood types eyed each other. Even Nelly stayed quiet, leaving Kris with a mental image of her pet computer joining the very human ritual.

"Nelly, what do we know?" Kris snapped.

"The auto-gun is a standard make readily available on this planet," the computer started slowly.

Doc snorted. "So much for our vaunted gun-control laws."

"Actually," Nelly answered, "estates with security systems often enforce their perimeters with auto-guns like these. Usually monitored by the security agents."

"Was this one under human monitoring?" Kris asked.

"There was no net connection in the wreckage," Beni put in. "I would have caught the gun earlier if it was sending on a net. It was jury-rigged with a sound and movement-control system."

"Any identifiers on the gun. Unique aspects of the chips?" Kris shot back.

"Serial number on the gun was filed off, if it ever was there," Captain DeVar put in. "The fire-control system had a incendiary device that burned the system when we tried to take it apart. Not a lot left," he finished with a scowl.

Kris let that bounce around her brain for a long moment. "First time out, someone managed to jam Nelly's network. This time out, they've put together dual-use parts to make a unique—for this planet—targeting system. Anyone see a pattern?"

"Electronics," Beni said, sitting up from his eternal slouch. "Whoever is after you has one large pot full of electronics capability."

"And here on Eden where most of the computer stuff is about the most complicated in human space," Penny added.

"Nelly, start a search on new computer chips and software companies in town."

"I will try, Kris, but it will not be easy."

"Why?"

"Kris, advertising seems to be mostly by word of mouth or through select industry-type journals. I don't know which ones to subscribe to. The records and reports of the Federal Bureau of Financial Statistics are not a publicly available database. Even using the access you have as a Nuu Enterprises stockholder, what I get back is little more than the addresses of home offices and the dividends they paid out last year."

"And with that they keep the business's around here legal?" Kris muttered.

"I'm not sure they really do," Penny said. "Until a scandal gets huge, it doesn't even make the news."

"Father tries to keep the government from getting too much in business's face. If he gets too heavy into regulations, Grampa Al comes screaming into his office. But you have to keep the playing field level. Who's doing that?" Kris eyed Doc. "How long have you been here?"

"Twelve, thirteen years, I think. My third wife definitely wanted me gone and she had pull with the right staff. Or was it me that wanted to be as far away from her as possible?" He looked up, those gray eyes sparkling. "I don't remember."

"You do remember the difference between the skull and the pelvis bones, don't you?" Captain DeVar asked.

"Usually, young man, but for you I can make an exception."

"Doc, who really runs this embassy?" Kris shot into that round of chuckles.

"I was wondering when you'd ask," Doc said, eyeing DeVar.

"It's pretty obvious the ambassador is a figurehead," Kris said. "So, who does the heavy lifting. Who's reporting to Admiral Crossenshield?"

That brought a sigh from Doc and a raised eyebrow from the Marine captain.

"We've gone though nine or ten political affairs officers in the time I've been here, Your Highness," Doc said slowly. "They keep being declared persona non grata for a whole raft of reasons, usually involving young women or men. More correctly, girls and boys."

"That's disgusting," Kris snapped, then thought. "All of them?"

"Rather routinely," Doc said with a shrug.

"Couldn't Eden come up with a new excuse?" Penny asked. "Isn't it obvious when you rerun the same play year after year?"

The only answer Doc gave was another shrug.

"So you get to know too much about Eden and you get shipped out of here with a smear on your name," Kris said.

"Last one left about a month ago," DeVar added.

"About the time I got orders," Kris said with a sigh that would have made any of Tommy's Irish grandmum's proud.

"Okay, if I want to stay alive, I've got to get to the bottom of this planet. While avoiding compromising involvement with little boys and girls."

"Don't bet on that being possible, Your Highness," Doc said. "They've shipped our people off on some pretty flimsy excuses."

"But this time they're dealing with a princess. And a Longknife. Enough said?" Kris growled.

"That does make this round interesting," Jack said through a painful-looking grin.

"Captain, what do you bring to the table?" Kris asked.

"I command the largest Embassy Marine detachment we've deployed. A reinforced rifle company, say a hundred and twenty-five trigger pullers. Supporting them are another fifty technical- and heavy-weapons specialists. We drill monthly on evacuating the embassy and getting the entire staff up the beanstalk for transport on the first available U.S. merchant or warship." The captain rattled off the words of his mission and capability like he said them every night before bed. And being a Marine officer, he just might.

"Special operations capable?" Penny asked.

"Of course, Lieutenant. But we don't advertise."

"Nelly, have you finished your analysis of the underground media? Any pattern? Any reporters better at hitting the mark?"

"Yes Kris, but I am not finding much gold in this gravel."

"Good metaphor, Nelly," Penny said. "But why no gold?"

"Some reporters are better at getting the hot stories, but they get hired away to main media. And even the best are wrong half the time. This place is an enigma even to its residents."

"And the opposition party hasn't bothered to drop by and say hi to me," Kris said with a frown.

"I think all the folks with the power kind of like things the way they are," Doc said.

"So why is someone trying to bump me off?" Kris asked.

The room was quiet for a long time on that one. Finally Jack said the obvious. "Vicky Peterwald?"

Kris nodded, but wasn't about to swallow it whole. "Is this just the usual Peterwald thing? Does Eden have nothing to do with it? Come on crew. Where there's smoke, there's usually fire, and where there's a cover-up, there's usually something being covered? I don't buy that it's just me. There's something being hidden and they're spending a lot to hide it. And they ship off planet anyone who gets too close to it."

Kris eyed those around the table. She had their interest. "I want to know what it is. Now, before it kills me."

"The best source we have," Abby said softly, "may well be the two kids I made friends with."

Kris shook her head. "I am not involving kids. They get too close to one of those damn Longknifes, they could get dead."

"I believe Sherlock Holmes did quite well with the Baker Street Irregulars," Doc put in.

"Sherlock Holmes is a fictional character," Kris shot back. "These kids are real people and they could get real dead. No, Doc, Abby, and you, too, Jack. We do this with grown-ups. No kids. Doc, you've been here the longest. You know many locals?"

"Not many. The embassy stays pretty closed in. And as you

know, those that concentrate outward seem to get shipped home rather quickly."

Captain DeVar raised an eyebrow at Doc.

"Okay, I do have a lady friend, but no, no way am I getting her involved with a Longknife. You hear me?"

They listened to the silence of that for a long moment.

Abby sat bolt upright. "Kris, I've got to take a call."

The maid listened to her earbud for a second, then tapped it. "Please repeat that?"

Now the sound came loud and clear to the group. The voice was young and high-pitched and clearly frightened.

"Auntie, Bronc's vanished. A gang has kidnapped him."

25

"Are you sure?" Abby asked.

"Auntie, Bronc's not like other men. When he says he'll do something, he does it. He said he was going by the shop today to show off his new gear. He spent yesterday playing with it, getting it tuned in. Figuring out what it would do. He was like a baby with a new rattle, I told him. He was fun.

"But he didn't make it to the shop. Mick didn't see him. And the Bones, they aren't on the street today. At least none of the ones I spotted would talk to me. They're avoiding me. The Bone Man has to have taken him. Abby, I don't dare go to the Crypt to see the head Bone Man. Not by myself."

"No. Don't. Can you make it to the tram station?"

"Yes."

"I'll meet you there as quickly as I can. It may take a bit. I need to get some things."

Kris could only guess what those things were. But she knew for sure what one of them was.

A princess.

Abby offered further hope and advice to take care before

cutting the line. "You'll excuse me, I seem to have pressing business elsewhere," the maid said, getting up from the table.

"I'm going with you," Kris said.

"Did you hear Cara? Don't you know why her Bronc is up to his ears in trouble, Kris? He got too close to you! He doesn't need more proof of that."

"No, the guys giving him grief need reminding that you don't mess with a Longknife. Or someone close to a Longknife. I'm with you, Abby," Kris said . . . and managed to stand without too much of a groan.

"Need I remind you that you're in no shape for a fight," Abby snapped.

"So I guess someone else will have to do her fighting for her," Captain DeVar said with a hungry grin. He tapped his wrist comm. "Gunny, I want three squads, in civvies, armed for a street fight of escalating violence, ready to depart in fifteen minutes. Include general tech support and two teams of snipers."

An "Aye aye" answered him.

"Your Highness, I would recommend that you not be in uniform, either. If we're about to give a hard lesson to street punks, no need to show the flag."

"Can your Marines take these punks?"

"Oh, yes, ma'am," Captain DeVar said with an evil chuckle. "Quite a few of my Marines started on the streets, ma'am. They know how those punks fight. And it took about fifteen minutes at boot camp for some drill instructor to knock the shiny off them. I know what those gangers are good for. And you know what Marines can do. This will be quite a lesson. And who knows. Some of the survivors just might show up tomorrow to sign themselves in. It's been known to happen."

Fifteen minutes later, the Marines began deploying . . . according to their captain's battle plan.

26

Abby hurried off the tram, trying not to look frantic as she searched the station for Cara. Behind her, she could hear the Marines moving more slowly, more carefully. She'd let them take the safe route. For Cara, Abby hurried in where any smart operator would fear to tread.

No surprise, Cara wasn't in the station. To hang here for too long would only invite trouble. So Abby beat feet for the street, getting way ahead of her Marine squad. She liked Sergeant Bruce and his squad of King Ray's Misguided Children.

He'd protect her back . . . if she didn't outrun him too much.

The captain's orders to his troops were quite clear. "I want you all back. I don't want to break more heads than we have to. If it's a street fight, use brass knuckles. If it's a knife fight, pull your automatics. If they shoot, Sergeant, go to fully automatic and snipers, take down the ones with guns. Hard. I repeat, I want all of you back for chow."

"Ooo-Rah" had answered that.

The street in front of the tram station was hot, dusty . . . and deserted. It was the middle of the day and those that had jobs were working them. Those without work were staying in what cool they could find. Cara was nowhere in sight.

Abby tapped her commlink. "Cara, you anywhere around."

"I can see you, Auntie. But there is a batch of hardcases behind you. I'll come out when they go away."

"Those folks are no problem to you and me, Cara. They're just a few of my friends. A few of my *best* friends."

A head ducked out from the shadows of an alley. The look on Cara's face was dubious to the extreme, but there was also trust for her auntie, even if Auntie had taken to keeping the company of hard men.

The girl half ran, half skipped to Abby, flooding the maid with memories of when she'd been at that wonderful butterfly stage of not quite woman, no longer child. For a moment, Abby felt young again.

But Abby was back in the old neighborhood for ancient reasons. Ancient distrust. Ancient hatred. Ancient died blood.

A moment after Cara gave her a hug and quick peck on the cheek, Sergeant Bruce joined them.

"Do you have any idea where your young man is being held?" he asked, the words clipped, demanding. His eyes did not lock on either Abby or Cara, but roved the street, measuring it, looking for any movement. Behind him, other men and women in casual slacks and shirts did the same from the limited safety of the tram station's small shadow.

Cara glanced up at Abby. At her nod, she spoke quickly to the man. "The Bones hang at the Burrito Palace. They're the ones that made a grab for you when you were here, Auntie. The streets emptied of Bones awhile ago. I think they got Bronc and maybe don't know what to do about that." The words trailed off, Cara running low on hope.

"Where's this Palace?" Sergeant Bruce asked, his computer projecting a photo map into the space between them. Cara pointed to a large roof several blocks away.

There were lots of abandoned houses between here and there. Lots of places to set up an ambush.

"Do you want to wait for second squad?" Abby said, offering him an option she hoped he would not take.

"Ma'am, I don't really like the idea of taking my Marines into this . . . with or without a second squad. However, gangers are not the kind of people who spend a whole lot of time thinking about what's the up and down side of the stupid stuff they do. So let's not give them a lot of time to think about us showing up on their turf. Corporal Nugent, take A team down the right side of the street. Corporal Ding, your team has the left. Oh, and you get this young lady. Take good care of her," the sergeant said, pointing Cara to a group of four marines led by a woman."

Cara went where she was pointed once Abby added a quick wave of encouragement.

"I'll take the center of the street," Abby offered.

"I expected you'd want to be out here with me," the sergeant said, with just a hint of a smile. "What do you say we go find ourselves some trouble?"

The sun was hot. The streets were dusty and what little wind was only good to blow around the uncollected trash. Abby hated to be here, showing all the Marines the kind of place she hailed from.

"I'm feeling downright homey," Sergeant Bruce said, as they came to the end of the first block. "Course, this place is upscale from where I came from. I actually saw three shacks back there that might have still had running water." His smile was tight and friendly, his voice actually gentle.

"This place is about the way I remember it," Abby said. "The kind of place nobody wants to admit they're from."

"But can't wait to be from." He tapped his wrist. "Gabby, am I seeing movement on a roof up ahead."

"Two men, no long guns in sight, but no bet they don't have something short, Sarge."

The discovery of the gang's overwatch was no surprise to Abby. She'd caught the smell of wood smoke and human excrement wafting from one abandoned building. And the glint off of something peeking out a window.

Where will the trap be?

They were closing on the building with the rooftop observers when one of them jumped up and fired off two rounds that threw dust but hit nothing.

Abby pumped a sleepy dart into him about the same time the sergeant did. The young man slumped to the roof and would have slid off it if the other one with him hadn't grabbed for him.

Shouting, "Don't shoot. Don't shoot me," a girl got him stabilized beside her. "He wasn't supposed to do that," she added.

Abby and Sergeant Bruce kept walking.

"That's the problem with gangers," Bruce muttered. "No discipline. You Marines, you hear me," he said, raising his voice. "I want somebody dead, you make them so. I don't want any shooting, you keep'em cocked and locked. You hear me?"

"Ooo-Rah" came back at him.

Abby measured the words . . . and the voice. He could have said it on net, but he'd said it loud . . . to the hood. Be interesting to see how the other side took it.

They walked another dusty block.

Abby could make out movement now in the shadows behind shattered windows. Broken and rotted floors creaked as people tried, unsuccessfully, to either stay out of sight and out of mind . . . or keep up with the squad as it advanced on their Crypt.

"These Bones rattle too much," Sergeant Bruce said with a professional smile.

"You know if they're carrying heat?" Abby asked. She was discovering just how glad she was not to be doing this alone.

"Gabby, any report on weapons in sight or sensor range?"

"Sarge, we got a lot of rapid heartbeats around us, a few are following along with us, but I'm not sniffing any explosives. You'll know the second I do."

"You be sure of that," Bruce said, then said aside to Abby, "You keeping track of Second and the motor brigade's doing?"

Abby glanced at her wrist unit. "Second squad is just pulling into the tram station. The motorized contingent should reach the station about the same time as Second."

"So lets try not to start anything before they get here, what do you say, Ms. Custer?"

"You're Marines, Sarge, not Army cavalry," Abby said, proud that she could match the sergeant's historical reference.

"If you could cook, I'd have to consider marrying you. By the way, that was good shooting back there. I hit the right shoulder, you hit the left."

"Hate to tell you, but I can't even boil water safely," Abby said, deflecting something she might want to come back to later.

"Tend to dump it over some obnoxious guy's head, huh? Well, us Marines are many things, but not obnoxious."

"I'll think about that. I think that's the Burrito Palace in the next block. I see folks on the roof and the front porch." That ended conversation.

The gang's hangout was a wood and stucco two story. Once it might have been a nice home, when it was painted and the stucco wasn't falling off. The front porch was shaded by a balcony that had it's own tables under sun-faded umbrellas.

Over a dozen men, with a similar count of women, slouched in the chairs above and below.

"Gabby, talk to me about this Palace."

"I got the pitter-patter of thirty fast-beating hearts inside. These folks are nervous. I'm picking up ammo. Lots of exits from that building. Back, sides, as well as front."

"What about the place across the street?"

"Empty. Totally empty. You think, Sarge, maybe these folks know better than to set up an ambush that puts themselves in their own crossfire?"

"Wouldn't put them past it. Nugent, bring your team across the street. We'll let them have the right side of the street. We'll take the left."

A minute later, the squad was deployed across from the Bones, relaxing in the shade. But not taking their eyes off the Palace. Or their hands far from their service automatics.

In the morning heat, the tram bell rang out. Second would be arriving at the station. Did Abby pick up the deep throated hum of the motor rigs with Kris and the Marine captain?

It was time to act.

Abby stepped forward . . . and found Bruce ambling along at her side.

"You don't have to do this."

"But nobody said I couldn't. I got good corporals. Lets me have some fun now and then."

"Marines!" Abby said in exasperation.

"Ain't this why you love us so much" was no question.

But "What you doing at our Crypt. You ready to be Bones?" was what got Abby's attention.

"I've come to talk," Abby said, voice even and clear.

Across the street from her, a punk with bad acne and a worse leer shook his head. "Shows what you know about the Bones. We don't *talk* to you. We *do* you."

That got a laugh from the porch. Abby could almost hear pistols slipping out of their hidden holsters. These were the best the Bones had. These were the ones that carried the heat.

Do this wrong, Abby girl, and there will be a lot of blood and guts on the street, but not one ounce of brains.

"I heard tell that you might have happened on a friend of mine. Young kid. About as tall as me."

"You like'em young" came from another punk, and brought snickers.

"My niece likes him," was all Abby said.

"Maybe I like her," said another lounger. He got even more snickers, and suggestions of what to do with Cara, and how.

Abby found her hold on her temper slipping.

And a firm hand gripped her right elbow.

"We didn't come here to banter with nadas," Sergeant Bruce's voice rang out loud and clear. "Why don't you take your jokes inside and tell the Bone Man he's got company that wants to discuss some serious shit with him?"

"And who might that be?" said the first slick punk with the sly grin Abby so wanted to wipe off his face.

"Princess Kristine of Wardhaven" blasted loud.

Three black, all-terrain rigs gunned down the street, sending a cloud of dust out that could have passed for a smoke screen. The "sunroof" was open on all three, with gunners manning mean-looking machine guns from well-defended positions. Second squad rode the running boards.

A moment later, the three rigs came to a halt behind Abby and Sergeant Bruce. Marines poured off them and came out of the shade behind them to fill in the intervals with armed and ready shooters.

"Now that's the way the cavalry is supposed to do it," Bruce whispered in Abby's ear.

27

Kris let the Marines do their thing, waiting in the back seat of the middle rig, careful not to step on any of the captain's sparkles. Though she was only seeing it from the rear, so to speak, the show was quite impressive.

With full-battle rattle, it would be as intimidating as all get out.

It was probably the lack of full-battle gear that left someone with the guts to shoot.

Kris was about to let Captain DeVar hand her out of the rig. That would normally have been Jack's job, but what with both of them beat up, it would not have been very impressive for them to fall flat on their asses. So Kris was just that extra second longer in dismounting and someone was just recovered enough to take a shot.

It was a strange battle to listen to. Or maybe this battle was a unique affair.

A pistol snapped off full-power rounds as fast as someone could pull the trigger. Another joined it. Then more.

From around Kris, she heard the pop of one low-powered sleepy dart. Then another single shot. Then more.

Very quickly there was nothing coming in on full power.

Just as quickly, the sleepy darts fell silent.

Captain DeVar stood up on the running board, giving Kris a good view of the sharp creases in even his civilian pants. "You dudes had enough fun? Any more of you want to try that?"

Apparently the survivors declined the offer.

"Any Marines down?"

"No, sir," the sergeants answered quickly.

The captain dropped gracefully down to the ground and faced Kris. "Your Highness, you sure you want to do this? I imagine about now, there's a lot of folks in great need of changing their underwear. I figure I can get the kid back just fine."

"What, and miss a chance to talk to a local," Kris said with all the panache the pain and drugs allowed her. "Who knows, this one might tell me the truth for a change."

"I will never understand Longknifes," Captain DeVar said, offering Kris his hand.

"Nobody does, Captain," Kris said, dismounting. "Not even Longknifes. But you didn't hear that from me. It's top secret."

The captain mumbled something under his breath. Kris made a point of not hearing it.

Marines held their automatics at high port; there was nothing coy now. They escorted Kris, Abby, and a darling girl Kris took for Cara, across the street and into the shade of the front porch.

No one lounged at the tables now. Those still mobile were as far to the left or right as the porch rails allowed.

Several were no longer able to move.

The center of the porch had tables upended and seven, eight men down. Most were sleeping the sleep of Pfizer-Colt's best. Two, no three, were bleeding.

"Did we do that?" Kris asked Captain DeVar.

"No, Your Highness, those rounds came from the back or side. My guess is these boys weren't all that good at shooting. Hopped up on adrenaline and fear, they couldn't hit the broad side of a barn at five paces, much less my Marines at ten. But they sure could hit the guy next to them, or ahead of them. What were the heartbeats on this bunch, Sergeant Bruce?"

"Gabby says they were pounding near out of their chests, sir."

"Amateurs. Sergeant, how's your heart?"

"Been higher on the shooting range with Gunny Brown breathing down my neck, sir." That came with a grin.

"How I like working with pros," the captain finished. "Your Highness, you stay here while I take a gander inside."

So Kris stayed put, but the sight of a few women trying to render what aid they could to bleeding gangers was not something she could ignore. "Sarge, do we have any medics with the team?"

"Of course, ma'am, er, Your Highness," Sergeant Bruce answered, apparently having more problems with a princess than a shoot-out.

"If they aren't busy with Marines, could you have them render what assistance they can here?"

The sergeant spoke into his wrist unit and a moment later two Marines with Red Cross bags slid to a stop beside the bleeders. They finished a quick exam with "They'll live," just as Captain DeVar and his two escorting Marines returned.

"There's a lot of nervous people in there. No telling what some idiot will do, Your Highness. I would not recommend you go in there."

"You're spending too much time around Jack," Kris said and headed for the door.

The captain shook his head, but only muttered into his wrist unit. By the time Kris was at the door, she had all three sergeants at her back, as well as the two sniper teams.

Two Marines opened the doors wide for Kris's entrance. It was showtime.

28

The tables in the restaurant showed evidence of hasty abandonment; not all the chairs were upright. The diners, men and women, now lined the side walls and back. Very nervous men. Scared women.

Then again, the nervous were likely scared, too. And the same with the scared. The captain was right. This was no place for a lady.

But Kris was a Longknife, not a lady.

She left the bystanders to her Marines and concentrated on the two guys trying to look cool at the one occupied table toward the back of the room. One wore a white shirt and slacks. The head Bone Man? The other sported red slacks and a bright yellow shirt with poet sleeves. If that was the Rocket Man, he'd certainly never seen rocket exhaust. Two women sat behind them in skimpy, but colorful garb. Were they adornments . . . or the brains?

That was only one of several questions Kris needed fast answers to.

Why were there two bosses here? Had her Marines interrupted a gang confab? Would one gang come to another gang's hangout?

Clearly, Kris needed to know more about gang diplomacy and etiquette.

But then, maybe there was nothing in the handbook for what a gang did when it kidnapped the buddy of a princess.

Maybe she wasn't the only one making this up as she went along.

Not waiting for answers, Kris repeated her opener from the street. "I am Princess Kristine of Wardhaven and you have a friend of mine."

The guy in white diffidently tossed that away with a flip of his wrist. "If you are this Princess Kristine, then there's a big pot of gold on your head."

Kris spotted the movement out of the corner of her eye. A man, half hidden by the woman in front of him, whipped out a pistol and fired.

The first shot went high, burying itself in the ceiling.

The second shot smashed into Kris's left arm.

The obsolete lead slug stung like the blazes through the spider-silk bodysuit. It held, though more of Kris would be black-and-blue tomorrow.

The three sergeants' automatics barked once . . . and within a split second of each other. The darts made a tiny triangle between the eyes of the shooter.

What they did to the back of his head was indescribable, but quickly revealed. He was slammed back against the wall and pinned there . . . but only for a second. Then his lifeless body began to slide down to the floor. Behind his shattered skull was a smear of blood and gore.

On the way down, his bowels let loose, proving again— unnecessarily for Kris—that sudden death is a messy, undignified affair.

All this must have come as news for some of the gangers. Many turned green. Several emptied their stomachs.

Kris plucked the 6-mm pistol slug from her arm and tossed

it aside. Obsolete, it was just the thing the spider silk was made to stop.

Jack took a step forward, his pistol held low and ready. He let his eyes rove the room. "Anyone else want to try something?"

He got no takers.

Jack and the three sergeants took station beside Kris, quartering the room between them. "I don't suggest any of you move until we finish here," Jack said. "Breathe if you must."

Kris took three steps forward, and settled herself in the empty chair at the two boss guys table. "Yes, I'm the Princess Kristine with a pot of gold on her head. Now you see why I'm still doing my hair every morning . . . and no one has collected on that pot of gold. Shall we ignore that topic for a moment?"

Both guys nodded silent agreement.

"Now, then," Kris went on, "I understand that you are holding a young man by the name of Bronc. I have never met the fellow. He is not in my service. But he seems to have gotten too close to one of these damn Longknifes and this has caused grief to him and others who treasure his company. I do not like that." Kris let that sink in. She allowed plenty of silence because neither gang boss looked like thinking was his forte.

Leastwise, not what most people considered thinking.

"I think you have him. I want him back. Will you return him? Please." Kris learned early that a wise politician always said please . . . even when he was breaking someone's arm.

Polite costs you nothing. Always be polite, Father said.

The two guys eyed each other, apparently not willing to be the first to make the concession. Behind them, the women were having some sort of silent communication between themselves, but Kris's view was blocked by the guys.

Kris let the silence stretch. Then stretched it some more. About the time it started to bend and twist, the guy in white broke eye contact with the other, looked around nervously at the gangers lining the wall, . . . and the Marines looking at them over their automatics and said, "Fran, get that little hot dog."

The young woman in white didn't seem to like the order,

but she didn't argue. Instead, she sashayed out, distracting most of the males in the place.

Not the Marine sergeants. They kept hard eyes on their quarter of the room.

As did Jack.

A long moment later, Fran returned with a beanpole of a young fellow that Kris took for the requested Bronc from the yelp of the young girl beside Abby. Though terror still gripped the dining room, at least two pairs of eyes lit up in joy.

And then everything changed.

From somewhere, Fran produced a dinky little pistol. Though small, held at the nape of Bronc's neck, it looked ready to do lethal business.

"Now we do some real talking," Fran snarled.

"Wrong," Kris snapped. "Longknifes never negotiate with hostage takers."

The look the woman gave Kris actually seemed like surprise.

But the other woman was out of her chair, and moving to take station beside the two, now a pistol in her hand.

"Lars, you get the Longknife broad here, and you piss it all away. I always knew you were stupid, but, I thought here was something even you couldn't foul up. But you did!"

"Trixie, you're not supposed to talk like that in front of the gang," the red and yellow man pleaded, showing which color was really his.

Kris shook her head. She had walked into an intravarsity dustup! It was bad enough to have all these guns out, but to have the lines of command among those she was bargaining with go all poof! Bad day.

Enough of this.

"Snipers, do you have a shot?" she barked.

"I have the white one" and "I have the colored one" shot back. The snipers didn't have their long guns out, but looked over the sights of automatics with extended barrels and laser sights.

Kris blinked, and Nelly showed Kris what she wanted to see. Both lasers were solid on the foreheads of the two women.

"Put your guns down and step away from the boy or both

of you will be dead before Fran can pull the trigger," Kris said. "Do this very calmly and very smoothly, because if the sniper that has Fran in his sights even thinks she might be starting to think of pulling the trigger, he will scramble her brain before she can form the thought."

"Yes, Your Highness" came from one sniper.

Fran took her eyes off Bronc for a second to look at Trixie. For a second longer, the two of them seemed undecided.

Then their gun trained from Bronc to the table where "their" men sat.

The boss men had been eyeing "their" ladies and seemed ready for this. It must have been clear to all that, having started something, there was no way to finish it with all four of them alive.

The boss men went for their guns as the women rounded on them. It looked like it would be a close run thing.

But two pistols fired from among those against the wall.

The women didn't go down easy. Six rounds as fast as a revolver could fire spun them around in a horrid dance.

Fran got off one round. Trixie two. The shots only tore up the floor.

Which left four men with guns out. And Jack and a Marine sergeant staring at them over sights. Maybe two snipers as well.

"Check fire, Marines," Kris ordered in a soft, but no less commanding voice.

"Holding fire" came from several points behind Kris.

"We came here for our man," Kris said. "He should not have been taken. We will leave now."

"He wouldn't have been taken," the Bone Man said. "But he was bugging us."

"Bugging both of us for you," Rocket put in.

"I have ordered no bugging of any establishments on Eden," Kris began slowly. "Young man, have you talked with me before?"

"No, ma'am, ah, Hiner."

Kris let the young man's problems of what to say to a princess go by. "Abby is my personal maid. She has visited this neighborhood. Abby, did you ask anyone to bug anything?"

"No, Your Highness. I specifically told Bronc and Cara to stay clear of you and anything involving you. You have always been adamant that we do not involve children, and I know better than to cross you on that."

"We're not children" came from two directions. Kris ignored that, but made a mental note to explore later just what areas Abby did feel fine crossing her on.

"Jack, Abby, are there any bugs operating in this room?"

"Captain, would you cover my quarter for a moment?" Jack said.

"My pleasure," the captain said, and metal sliding on leather told Kris what was going on behind her.

Abby and Jack both produced debugging gear and began to roam the room. Both of them soon reported negative findings, then Abby frowned and stooped to run her bug finder over the bodies of the two former gang-boss mistresses. "The only thing live here are two bugs, one on each of them, high-end, very expensive, and still transmitting. Do I burn them?"

Kris shook her head. "Capture them. Let's see if they tell us anything. Bronc, do you have your bug cleaner?"

The boy nodded.

"Take it over to Abby and see if your gizmo can find what she found."

He did, with no results.

"I'd say that your girls have been messing with you," Kris said to the two fellows across the table from her. They did not look happy at that.

"I wonder who they were passing that info to? Who gave them bugs so good, so expensive? Interested in finding out?"

The two guys looked like they'd rather be stripped and whipped before their gang members than say yes, but they did.

"Abby, you able to corral those bugs?"

"Contained, Your Bossiness."

The gangs seemed to enjoy the irreverence. Kris shrugged it off. "Bronc, would you mind taking a contract to work with one of my techs, a chief by the name of Beni? He likes strange things that eat electricity."

"But Abby told me to stay clear of you," the kid said. But he was grinning.

"Don't look to me like you can," Kris said. She stood. "Gentlemen, it seems to me that our interests are flowing, if only temporarily, in the same gutter. I want to know who your girls were working with. I suspect you do, too. I remind you that Bronc and Cara are now under my protection. You don't want to have anything happen to them or the next visit from me and mine will leave nobody standing. You understand me."

The two guys eyed each other, like scorpions . . . under the foot of a very big camel.

"Hey, if your enemy is our enemy, don't that make you our friends," Bone Man said.

"That's the usual way of looking at it," Kris agreed.

So all was ending well, Kris thought, as she turned to the captain.

But he was standing stiff, only his hand moved to tap his earbud. Kris caught the last half of a sentence spoken in Gunny's familiar drawl. ". . . alert message. Repeat, Red alert message. Two Marines down and dead. General Trouble's wife is gone."

29

A white-hot rage the likes of which Kris had never felt in her life swept over her.

Kris whirled back to face the gang leaders. Had all this been just a ploy to lure her and half the Marines away from the embassy? If they had . . .

The same thought was passing through a lot of Marines' heads, too. Safeties clicked off weapons. Slaughter was but a word away.

Before Kris's glare, the two gang bosses melted into boneless puddles.

One held up his hand, as if he might ward off her wrath with mere flesh. "I swear to God, Blessed Madonna, and Child, I don't know nothing about this other lift."

"Me, neither," the other said. "Two of my boys, they brought the kid in. They thought it would be fun. I swear. You want them, they're yours. Gordo, get them out here."

There was movement along the wall as two fellows were half pushed, half thrown out to fall to their knees between the gangers and the Marines.

But Kris had lost her interest in the gangs . . . for now.

Captain DeVar had said the words that held her. "Sarge, repeat your comments and expand."

"Four minutes ago, the two Marines escorting Mrs. Ruth Tordon went off net. When I got no reply to my call, I dispatched the backup squad, as per the order book. When the reaction squad arrived, they found the two Marines down. We are awaiting arrival of local EMTs to verify initial reading of no vitals for either Marine. Captain, they were put down awfully hard." It was a personal aside, one Marine to another.

"Continue, Gunny" was ice. Cold. Sharp. Full of death.

"A search of the area turned up no Mrs. Trouble, sir. She often kills her squawker, and had done so most of the day. We'd been tracking her by the Marines. We're getting nothing at all now, and we've done our best to activate her communicator and interrogate it. No joy, sir."

The pause was brittle. Pregnant. Explosive. Kris stepped into it.

"Gramma Ruth hired some local protection people. Have you found their bodies?"

"No evidence of them, their bodies or their presence, Your Highness. Like her, they're just gone."

"When we find them, they'll either be dead or lead us straight to her," Kris snapped. The captain nodded agreement.

Kris turned back to the gang leaders. Their eyes locked.

"Let's assume for the moment that this is as big a surprise to you as it is to me."

Heads nodded vigorously.

"Let's assume that we can keep on being friends. Business partners, maybe."

Heads nodded faster.

"You want some money? Money that you will live long enough to take to the bank. Not like that pot of gold on my head?"

Heads stopped nodding. Kris suspected they saw it as a trick question. Didn't know how to respond.

"Help me find my grandmother. Any little bit. Anything that leads me to my grandmother alive will be paid for very

well. You'll like me as a friend. You don't want me as your enemy. Do we understand each other?"

They eyed each other, the gangers and the princess. Maybe
her need was more understandable to them than her power.
That was fine by Kris. She *wanted* her Gramma Ruth back.
Alive.

Kris turned and marched out of the restaurant. Behind her,
Marines did their retrograde movement with professional efficiency. The punks seemed to shrink as the chance that they
would live to see the sunset increased.

There was talk in a low hum behind Kris as she went down
the steps two at a time. The gangers had gotten too close to
one of those damn Longknifes. They'd dealt themselves into
the situation. They had no one to blame but themselves. As so
often happened around Longknifes, it was time to take sides.

The middle was washing away.

Only the Longknife side and the losing side would soon be
left.

But there was always the chance that this time might be
different. For the first time, the Longknifes and the losing side
might be the same.

Among themselves, the gangs would decide where to place
their bet. Who they thought would win.

Kris had already placed her bet. Damn the odds. Everything on Longknife to win.

30

The Marines lay where they fell.

Verifying their death had not required moving them.

10-mm grenades in the face don't leave much chance that even a Marine can survive the initial attack.

The Marine techs and Chief Beni joined the local cops trying to scrape some evidence from a scene that offered little.

The other Marines joined the cops patrolling the perimeter, keeping out the gawkers. Officially, that was the job of the local police. But the police lieutenant detailed to tell the Marines to stand down took one look at Gunny Brown's face and quickly offered to share the patrol duty with the Marines.

Smart cop.

Kris found Inspector Johnson at her elbow within a minute of her arrival. No surprise there. Nelly was taking the raw feed from the Marines and anything else they could capture from the police and passing it along to Kris. It wasn't much.

Rather than wait for the local cop to say something inane, Kris said, "What do you think?"

Johnson rubbed his chin. "Hard to say. Could be related to those two attempts on your life. Then again, it could be some local campus issue. Heavens knows, General Trouble has made enemies in his long life of terrorizing whoever he was paid to. His evil past could be catching up with his wife."

Terrorizing whoever he was paid to. Did the inspector actually think that was a soldier's job? Did he suppose it was because it was his job? Kris filed that away and asked the easy question, "That what you're going to put in your report?"

"It would certainly make it easier for me."

"You know she is my great-grandmother?"

"I think I read that somewhere."

"I want her back."

"No doubt."

Kris did not like the attitude she was hearing from the local cop in charge of her handling. She turned to face him and chose her words with a club.

"I want my gramma back. I will have my gramma back. I will not face my great-grandfather when next I see him and try explaining why I was not able to get his wife back to him."

"We'll do everything we can" might have sounded good. But the vagueness around Johnson's eyes gave Kris no comfort.

"You *will* do more. You *will* get Ruth back. Alive."

The cop scowled at Kris's demand. "May I remind you that Eden operates under the rule of law?"

Kris snorted. Her father made the laws of Wardhaven . . . and occasionally ignored them. "Make sure this is one time that the rule of law works for the victim."

"We shall see," Johnson said.

Kris didn't have time to waste repeating demands that should be clear to a concrete block . . . and that blockhead's boss. She turned her back on the inspector and strode away.

"Captain," she said, coming up beside DeVar.

"Your Highness."

"Are you busy?"

He looked around as if hunting for some killer to throttle. He scowled at the nothingness. "Not at the moment."

"Captain, if you could afford me the help of a few good Marines, Jack and I are about to pay a visit to the dean of graduate studies at this place."

"Isn't he the one that helped Mrs. Tordon hire some protection?" Jack asked.

"The selfsame."

"I was hoping to have a quiet discussion with him," Captain DeVar said. He signaled half a dozen marines in full dress blues and reds . . . and long rifles at the ready.

The small group moved purposefully across the campus, staying as inconspicuous as possible. That is to say that anyone who saw them took one look and quickly scurried off to find something important to do elsewhere.

A glance over Kris's shoulder showed that several had added themselves to her visitation team. Abby she understood. Chief Beni and the kid, and his girl were there, too. Kris made a note to see about cutting down on the menagerie following her. If she wasn't careful, she'd end up with a full zoo.

No, make that *worst* zoo.

The dean of graduate studies had a top floor corner office in an old brick building. Kris took the stairs two at a time. Only Chief Beni ended up huffing and puffing.

"You better take up jogging, Chief," Abby upbraided him, "or one of these day Kris will take off and you're going to get left behind."

"You really think so?" He sounded more hopeful than repentant.

Kris led the charge into the dean's front office.

"Do you have an appointment," a middle-aged secretary said, trying to interpose herself between Kris and the door marked Dean of Graduate Studies in gold leaf.

Kris got to the doorknob first. "The Dean has an appointment with *me*," Kris said as she let herself in. A very tight-lipped light brigade charged right behind her.

"I'm sorry, Professor Rosemon, I tried to stop her."

Kris quickly crossed the distance to a wide wooden desk. She used the name so kindly provided and offered her hand.

"Good afternoon, Professor Rosemon. I am Princess Kristine of Wardhaven, and a major stockholder in Nuu Enterprises. You know the company. I think we fund several research projects your university is working on." Battle armor might not melt in Kris's mouth, but butter definitely would. It seemed like a good way to start with a man who spent his days in a wood-paneled office, lined with rows of leather-bound books.

She could switch to lasers and tongs later.

"Ah, yes, yes," said a man with graying hair, bow tie and suit coat on even at his desk, alone in his office. He stood and took Kris's offered hand across a pristine desk. No clutter here.

Kris clamped on to his hand and stepped around the desk. The man seemed surprised, but his eyes were on two Marine sergeants. They were cleaning under their fingernails with very large knifes. Professor Rosemon looked shaken. Maybe even afraid.

Then he looked at Kris and knew terror.

Kris used his hand to back him into his chair. Now Kris towered over him, putting every inch of her six feet to good use. The Marine captain and the two sergeants, knives still out, moved to completely surround him.

Mouth hanging open, the professor looked like he had finally grasped that he was mortal and might die some day.

Like today.

"Professor, we need some answers from you," Kris said, trying to warm the cold in her words with a smile. But the smile was mostly teeth.

The professor blanched and tried to make himself smaller in his seat. Eyes locked to Kris's, he muttered, "Yes, yes. What can I do for you?"

"Mrs. Ruth Tordon is on your staff, a visiting professor," Kris said.

"Maybe. I don't know. There are so many visiting professors."

"Yes, I imagine there are," Kris agreed. "But few are the wife of General Tordon, known to most as Trouble. She's also my great-grandmother. Remember her now?"

Faced with that, the professor's memory improved. "Yes, yes, now that you remind me, I do remember her. Fine old woman."

"You suggested that she might want to improve her security situation when she told you I was coming to Eden."

"Did I?"

"She told me that you did." Mentally, Kris dared him to call Gramma a liar.

"Then I guess I did," he agreed. And seemed proud of himself for it.

"Fifteen minutes ago, Gramma Ruth was kidnapped," Kris bit out. "Right here on *your* campus."

"Oh dear. We haven't had a kidnapping on campus in, oh, years," he answered.

Kris ignored him, but filed the data away for later examination. "Two Marine embassy guards are dead. She is gone. And the two security rentals that you suggested to her are nowhere to be seen." Kris paused to let that sink in to the professor's balding dome.

For the second that the man of learning took to absorb that, there was silence. Followed by a quiet "Oh."

"Yes. Oh," Kris snapped. "You suggested she hire those guards and they did nothing to guard her. Or worse, they threw in with the thugs that kidnapped her."

"Oh, they couldn't have" didn't have much assurance in it.

"Why don't you tell me where they came from and let me go find out."

"Oh yes." The idea of getting these invaders of his quiet corner of the world gone to somewhere else lit up his eyes. But only for a moment. "Oh, but I can't."

"And why not?"

"Because I don't know who she did business with. I called a provider of temporary security. They passed her needs along to several bidders who offered services and she chose from them. That's the way it's done here. You are new, aren't you."

"Hardly been here a week," Kris said while her brain whirled. "So, who's the provider?"

"I don't know. I have his number here." He pulled a Rolodex from a drawer. A Rolodex! Kris had only seen such things in ancient movies.

He held up the number. "Here it is. Security. That's all I know about it. That and the number. I'll call them."

Kris let go of his hand so he could happily bumble about

with an ancient phone, one with numbers on its face. Kris glanced at Chief Beni and the techs with him. They had their black boxes out.

"The number you have dialed is no longer in service" came from several speakers in the room.

"Oh dear, I must have misdialed."

"No he didn't," Nelly said from around Kris's neck. The professor eyed Kris as if she was infested with a demon.

"Do you have another number for security?"

"No," the professor said.

"Any way to get in touch with them?" Kris demanded.

"No ma'am, er, Your Highness. Security guilds contact you."

"They don't advertise?" Jack said.

"Oh no, no, no, my boy. If you need security, and security wants your business, they contact you."

"And you came by that number how?" Kris asked.

"Oh, years ago. Someone approached me and offered me his card. You don't buy security the same way you buy soap," he said indignantly.

"We do on Wardhaven," Kris said.

"Well, that's the Rim. This is Eden," he sniffed.

Kris did not like dead ends. But even she could see one when it slapped her in the face with a several-day-old fish.

The return trip down the stairs was at a slower pace. Jack stayed behind just long enough to advise the professor that he should not kill his squawker. The princess might want further words with him tonight. The professor huffed something about that being illegal. He never did anything like that.

Kris was back on the wide walkway in front of the administrative building before she turned to her team. "Anybody got any ideas, pipe up."

Only the background rumble of college life answered her.

No, Abby was huddled together with the two youths. For several seconds they continued at a low hum. Then Abby looked up, a frown on her face. "We may have something here."

Kris, Jack, and DeVar came close. The trigger pullers formed an outer circle looking out. The chief and his techs did things with their black boxes and the air lit up as several nearby bugs met their doom.

"Area's secure," Chief Beni announced.

"What do you know that we don't?" Kris asked.

"I can back-trace phone numbers to addresses," the boy said.

"On most planets, that's quite easy," Kris said. "Here, it seems to range from impossible to illegal."

"Ah, yes, ma'am, I know. But you see, ma'am, I know some folks that do illegal things. For a fee, you know," the boy said with an uncomfortable shrug.

"And how long can we get away with this illegal thing if we pay?" Jack asked.

"I don't know. Mick and Trang, they pay their money and they get what they pay for, and nobody comes looking for them. Princess Kris here pays money, she'll get what she paid for—I think—but some alarm is bound to go off. Someone's likely to start something. Don't know what it will be, but . . ."

Smart kid, Kris nodded in agreement. What might work for the locals was bound to get folks excited if a Longknife started poking around in it.

"Abby, you have a few credit chits that don't have Longknife on them."

"I have a few that might take the best of them a week or more to trace back to you. Shall I give one to Bronc?"

"Not here. Not now. I don't want to make it any easier for them that aren't making it easy for us. Let's get moving."

31

Five minutes later, Kris was moving in a random pattern away from the university but not toward the embassy. Crammed into what had once seemed a huge rig were most of her usual crew, plus the two kids, Chief Beni, and several Marine techs.

Two Marine transports full of armed Marines followed them.

"Abby, give the kid, Bronc, right, a safe chit."

A moment later, the kid had found a site on the net that offered the goods they wanted.

"That's strange," Nelly said. "I just ran those keywords using the best search engines Eden offers and I got no hits."

"You wouldn't," the girl answered. "On Eden if you have to search for it, you won't find it. That's what I hear from Bronc all the time."

The kid just said, "How good a system do you want to buy?"

"How good?" Kris asked.

"Micky, Trang, they just buy the basic, and you get only so much for that. They know that some folks pay to stay out of the basic list. You pay more, you get a bigger list, and you get more privacy about what you bought."

"They sell the list of who's bought the list?" Jack asked.

The kid gave Jack a funny look. "Well, of course."

"When in Rome, wash your dirty linens at a Roman bath," Kris said. "Okay, what's the basic list cost? How many higher levels are there, and what do they cost?"

"There's five," Bronc said. He named a price for the first level that made even Kris cringe. The price doubled for the second level, then redoubled. The last level was high even for a major shareholder of Nuu Enterprises.

"If you buy that level," Abby said, "I suspect the folks who buy the sixth level will know about it in five minutes or less."

"Right, you're from here," Kris said. "Bronc, hit them for the fourth level."

The boy did, though it was clear that he had trouble typing in that many zeros after the five. The girl beside him whistled.

"Even momma don't spend money like that."

"Momma don't have as much trouble staying alive as this woman," Abby said.

The girl's eyes were wide as she watched Kris.

"I have an address to match the phone number," Bronc said, a moment later. "At least it was active yesterday."

"Somebody's running," Captain DeVar muttered. "Let's see if they run into us on the way out." He passed along the address to his drivers.

The rig accelerated fast enough to force Kris back into her seat.

Five minutes later, it was easy spotting the building they were interested in. It had a moving van out front.

Captain DeVar issued crisp orders. "Block in the van. I want to talk to its crew."

That turned out to be easy. A burley fellow was screaming the moment they screeched to a halt in front of his van.

"Hey, what do you think you're doing?"

With hardly a groan for her pain, Kris was first out of the rig. "Just need to ask you some questions," she said.

"You and what army, pretty lady" was answered quickly as the Marines formed a circle around him.

The guy suddenly looked very chastened. "What do you want to know?" His tone was much more cooperative.

"Who are you moving?" Kris asked.

"Not moving anyone. Just taking back the rented furniture somebody just canceled his lease on. Guy in Suite 401."

Which just happened to be where Kris was headed next.

"Van's empty," a Marine reported.

"Let's see what 401 has to offer," Kris said.

Without an order, a Marine took the driver aside. The civilian didn't seem too happy, but a "What do you think of the Dodgers this year?" got him talking and they left him happy.

In the tiled foyer, there was a creaky elevator and stairs. While sergeants led Marines up the stairs, Kris waited with Jack and the rest.

"So you're learning caution," her security nanny said.

"I am not climbing those stairs. Not the way I feel."

"Thank you," was all Jack said.

"We're holding just below deck four," came from Captain DeVar's commlink.

An elderly couple hobbled out of the elevator, eyed Kris and company, and quickly shuffled away. Inside, the elevator had room for just six. Chief Beni did his usual safety check, then happily held his techs for the next trip. Abby stayed with the kids though this was one time Kris would gladly have had the maid at her elbow.

Kris punched the elevator for the fourth floor. Noisily, it obeyed. The ride was interrupted at two. The young office worker took one look at them and backed away. "I'll wait."

On four, they stepped out into a hallway, the Marines from the stairs at their elbows. Captain DeVar silently signaled his team and they advanced before them to Suite 401.

Guns out, they slammed open the door and rushed the room.

To find themselves facing three very startled men in shirts identifying them as workers for George's Careful Movers. Facing guns, their hands just naturally reached for the ceiling.

"What the . . ." came from the one that seemed to lead.

"I am Princess Kristine of Wardhaven," Kris said, to cut him off. "The former occupants of this office may have been involved in murder and kidnapping. Please stand aside while our Marines search for evidence."

"If this fellow wasn't on the up-and-up, where are the cops?" the boss demanded.

"No doubt, they will be along shortly. Now, if you don't mind, Chief Beni, this is your crime scene."

He and the Marine techs began to search the room.

"Hey, Princess Whoever, me and my guys is paid by the hour. How much money is this going to cost us?"

"Who asked you to remove this furniture?" Jack asked.

"The guy that leased it. Quan Tre's Best Office Rentals."

"You have a phone number for this Quan Tre?"

"I don't. Maybe the office."

"Let's you and me go out into the hall and call him," Jack offered. The milk of human kindness flowing over the carpet.

The boss and his two men left.

"Chief, is this place bug infested?" Kris asked.

"I don't know, Lieutenant. You kind of emphasized doing a crime walk-through."

"Tell me about the bug situation first. I want to know what you find here. No need to let anyone listening know."

"Yes, ma'am, Your Highness, boss lady."

The Marines snickered, but the air began to sparkle as bugs died. Abby did her bit.

The boy at her elbow just shook his head. "I thought the place was clean."

"It's high-end stuff, Bronc," Abby said. "We're playing in the big leagues. Before you got hauled off, I suggested the chief add some stuff to your computer. Now it's past time."

"It is *so* time, Auntie Abby," the girl said, holding on tight to the boy's arm.

Fifteen minutes later, the room had given up absolutely nothing. "Not a thing, ma'am," Chief Beni said.

"So go hit the trash cans out back," Kris snapped.

"Had a Marine doing that, ma'am. Found three fresh trash

bags. Media was wiped and fried. Flimsies were degaussed, blacked, and degaussed again. Not so much as a static charge left on them. Ma'am, whoever this fellow was, he bought the best security and he used it."

"Blast it," Kris snapped. "The bad guys are supposed to be dumb. Make mistakes. Haven't these fellows read the rules?"

"Suspect not, Kris," Jack said, now back from his talk with the movers. "Maybe they don't think of themselves as the bad guys, so they don't feel any need to be dumb."

"You find anything?"

"The movers got their orders about an hour ago. They'd just got here. Quan got a quick call canceling the lease on this gear about two hours ago."

"Who was that call from?"

"John Smith, Associates. I already checked. There's about a million John Smith, Associates in the phone directory. This guy's phone number wasn't one of them."

"And Johnny paid for this how?"

"From a limited bank account, now closed. I guess we could chase that end of it, but I doubt we'd get far on Eden."

"Chase what?" came from Inspector Johnson.

Penny followed him into the room. "He called and asked where you were. Then offered me a ride," she said.

"What exactly do you think you're doing, Rim Princess?"

"Looking for things," Kris said vaguely.

"That's my job on Eden, you know," he shot back.

"*I* hadn't noticed," Kris said, putting a solid bite into it.

"I am *doing* my job. Or at least I was before I was inundated with complaints about you. We've got a formal complaint from this moving company, and several complaints from private security firms about your burning their alarm systems."

Somebody was moving fast.

"As I said, I'm looking for things."

"And finding a lot of dead ends. And making me come out here to tell you to get your nose back to the embassy so real cops can do what we do best. Find criminals and free hostages."

There were several million comebacks at the tip of Kris's tongue . . . all explosive. She swallowed them all and chose honey . . . for the moment.

"I'm sorry we've caused these men trouble. Why don't my Marines help them."

The inspector frowned at Kris, but the moving boss was already issuing orders. A nod from Captain DeVar sent Marines to collect up the chairs. And with only slightly puzzled looks they headed for the elevator. Some helped the two workers push the desk toward the freight elevator. Others helped the boss get the credenza up on a dolly.

Inspector Johnson turned toward the door, encouraged on his way by Penny's promise of keeping Kris on a tighter leash.

And Cara stooped to pick up a piece of trash revealed when the credenza was moved. She palmed it, but winked at Kris.

Kris winked back. No dumb bunnies in Abby's family.

And that may be what I was looking for. Kris had so wanted to throw a royal-size hissy fit. But she'd seen the treasures often found when furniture was moved around Nuu House. She'd once found a draft of one of Grampa Ray's first speeches.

No, Kris was not leaving here until this room was down to the bare walls.

Well, maybe Kris was, now that she knew she could trust Cara . . . and her boy, Bronc, was prowling the place as well.

So Kris hurried to catch up with the inspector and made nice noises about being good. And doing anything that she could to help the inspector find Gramma Ruth.

Which he quickly declined.

His big mistake.

32

Kris held her tongue—and acted like a good little princess—all the way back to the embassy.

The Marine transports had picked up all sorts of bugs while parked in front of the office building. Kris refrained from burning them lest the inspector have to peel more of his time away from the hunt for Gramma Ruth to chide her for destroying private property.

"Burn those bugs," was her first order the moment they crossed onto the Embassy driveway.

"Ooo-Rah" answered that order.

"The ambassador wants to see you" greeted Kris the moment the rig's door was opened.

"I'll see him later," Kris snapped. "Captain DeVar, do you have a Tac Center?"

"A small one." He led her to it.

It was tiny. The next room down was the huge conference room Kris had whiled away many a negotiating hour. "Take over that room. I'll clear it with the ambassador."

"Ooh-Rah" was the captain's reply.

Kris quick marched for the ambassador's office. She found

him sitting at a long table in his huge office, holding a budget meeting with his key staff.

"We need this room. Wait outside," Kris ordered.

The ambassador started to say something but flinched when Kris snapped at the others, "You. Out!"

They went.

Door closed, the ambassador tried to seize the initiative. "What do you think you are doing, young lady?"

Kris stood at the opposite end of the table. Leaning forcefully on it, she corrected him. "*I* am not a 'young lady.' *I* am a serving Lieutenant in the Wardhaven Navy. *I* am a princess of the blood and a Longknife. I am *presently* conducting a search for Ruth Tordon. *You* have two choices."

At the other end of the table, the little man began to fidget. If there was a question of which end of the table was the head—and which the foot—it was now resolved.

"When next I meet with General Trouble and his good friend King Raymond, I can tell them that you rendered all assistance to the search for Ruth. And you will still have a career."

Kris paused to let that sink in. "Alternately, you can attempt to interfere, and I will send a priority message to both king and prime minister. You will receive your recall in the next priority mail."

That might or might not be true. While there was no doubt that Grampa Ray would do anything for his old war buddies, both Trouble and Ruth, Father might not like getting a demand from his daughter concerning *his* Foreign Service.

Kris tossed the bluff out and waited.

Sammy folded. "Yes, yes, of course, you may have anything the embassy can provide."

"Thank you very much," Kris said. She did a quick about-face and quick marched from the office. In the outer office, the staff members were waiting. "You may continue your meeting," she said, and did not look back.

So, she could have anything the embassy had, Kris thought. *I could get to like this.*

If only Gramma Ruth's life didn't hang in the balance.

* * *

"What have you got for me?" Kris asked as she stepped into the conference room that was now a Tac Center.

"Cara's scrap of paper has a phone number on it," Jack said.

"A phone number. Isn't that a bit slipshod for this bunch?"

"Not so much a phone number," Chief Beni replied, "as the impression of the number written on the paper above it."

"And the number is . . . ?" Kris asked.

"Not on the list I bought," Bronc said.

"What are the chances it will be in the level five?"

That got Kris shrugs.

She took a moment to familiarize herself with the Tac Center. Across from the door, one wall was already sprouting photos relevant to the case. Front and center was a picture of Grampa Trouble and Gramma Ruth: he in full military splendor, she in a golden gown. They were lovely together.

Beside that photo was a recent portrait of her that might have been from her passport. Next were pictures of the Marines, one showing each facedown and dead. Then their ID pictures. If anyone wondered why they were here, the photos answered that.

"Let's go for level-five access," Kris decided.

"Ah, Kris, there may be a problem with that," Abby said.

"How so?" Kris asked, turning to her maid . . . and the two kids that now seemed permanently attached to her.

The boy had a major case of the fidgets. "Every computer has a permanent ID branded into it. Anything you do on net can get back to you. Even Micky hasn't been able to figure out a way to change that." Micky apparently was quite a whiz at this.

"If I buy level five," Bronc said, "someone will be checking back on me in like, five minutes ago."

"You're safe with us," Kris said.

"But my mom. I had to give my home address when I registered the computer. My mom." It was almost a plea.

"Is a problem," Kris finished. Without knowing it, she was

endangering the most precious thing this poor young fellow had. But then, everyone knew Longknifes used up people. *What say we get Gramma Ruth back without using up anyone this time.*

She turned. "Captain DeVar, can we solve this before it becomes a problem?"

"Certainly, Your Highness. Gunny."

"Yes, sir," Gunny said, and turned to two Marines. "You just volunteered for detached duty."

The two, a man and woman snapped to attention. "Yes, sir."

"Draw a credit chit and see that this man's mother is out of the line of fire. Try to avoid hurting anyone if you can."

"Yes, Gunny." The woman Marine grinned. The guy scowled.

"Should they be using one of my credit chits?" Kris asked.

Captain DeVar shook his head. "This is official Corps business," he said, glancing at the photos.

Kris didn't argue.

"You folks will need a car that doesn't scream Marine in that burg," Captain DeVar said, pulling keys from his pocket. "Try not to dent it in too many places."

"Ooh-Rah." Now it was the Marine's turn to grin as he caught the keys. The woman Marine muttered something about extra, extra hazardous duty pay as they trotted out the door.

"Nelly, call this place and charge the fifth level?"

"I can't, ma'am. If I am not a computer registered to this planet, much of the web is invisible to me."

The captain nodded. "One of my Marines' local girlfriend hooked him on a computer game. He had to buy a local computer to play. Several of my troopers have them. Gunny, get a couple of those local 'puters in here."

"Belay that order" came from Kris's collarbone.

"And why might that be, Nelly," Kris said, rolling her eyes at the ceiling as her décolletage, or lack of it, became the center of attention. *I got to figure a way to wear Nelly on my head, my wrist.*

BE HONEST, YOU REALLY LIKE THE ATTENTION, Nelly told her, before going on out loud. "I just ordered a top-of-the-line computer from Ryes. In the process, I acquired both the ID codes of the new computer and am organizing a tiny portion of myself to be that computer. I'll even download basic software from the net to look like a real local computer."

"Yes," shouted Bronc, who with Cara had been jumping up and down and shouting, "Go, girl," at Nelly's announcement.

"I am tired of this planet giving me the runaround. It is time I start showing it why I am the one and only Nelly."

For a computer, Nelly sounded in full huff. This looked to get interesting.

"Whose name you going to register it in?" Kris asked.

"Oh, I thought I might put it in the chief's name."

"Why me?" Chief Beni demanded.

"You need something interesting in your life," Nelly shot back. Clearly, the relationship between Nelly and the chief was changing. Kris hoped she could survive whatever came next.

"You buffering this new computer?" Kris asked. "If the downloaded software from Eden is half as obnoxious as this planet's people . . ."

"It is triple buffered," Nelly said. "Eew, that was not nice. Bother, Kris! This software is very controlling. I begin to see why this planet is so messed up."

"Something we are just starting to tackle," Kris said. "Let me know when you are ready to start buying stuff."

"I am good to go. That is what you Marines say. Right?"

"Good to go, girl. Let's get this show on the road. Abby, give Nelly a credit."

"No need, Kris. I have set up a line of credit myself. That was what I have been using. They will not be able to trace anything back to here."

That got raised eyebrows between Kris and Abby. Jack tried to cover a grin. The Marines, including the captain, looked ready to roll on the floor, laughing. Except Marines don't do that. Not with a princess present.

"I have loaded the fifth level. I will pass it to Bronc. Kris, there is an option to buy the archives for a somewhat larger fee."

"Archives?"

"Yes, it says some phones that are no longer in use may be in the archives."

"Do it!"

"Oh, that was not nice."

"Yes, Nelly."

"They declined my credit. I thought I'd made it large enough, but I guess not."

"Abby, pass Nelly a new chit number."

"I have it. Now, let me see. There is more available."

"There is?" Kris asked at the same time Jack and Penny did.

"I am clicking on every aspect of the site, and I am opening up what I think you call Easter eggs."

"Micky didn't mention anything about Easter eggs," Bronc said, mouth hanging open.

"Maybe he doesn't know everything there is to know," Kris said. "Talk to us, Nelly."

"I have an offer for every street address, occupant, financial status, and social coding. The price is steep."

"Buy it," Kris snapped. "Now we'll have something more to cross-check our number against than just a raw address."

"Kris, they also have bank records for sale, but they want quite a bit for them. And I do not know if they will have any of the more interesting people in them."

"Will they let you do a sample run?"

"No, ma'am. You pay to play or you go home empty."

"Let's wait a bit for that."

"Your Princess, ah, whatever—" Bronc started.

"Call me Kris."

"I found Cara's number. It wasn't in the fifth-level list. It was in the archives."

"Does it have an address?"

"Ah, yes, but, ah, it's way up town," he said slowly. "And it could be old, you know."

"We won't go busting in doors," Kris said, then added, "unless we have to."

"Kris, I have a phone call coming in for you," Nelly said.

"Who?"

"A Frederico Miguel O'Hallihan."

"That's the Bones's head man," Cara whispered.

"I'll take it."

"Hey there, Princess, you still in town."

"I still have unfinished business, Frederico."

"Nobody calls me that."

"Sorry, Bone Man," Kris corrected as both Bronc and Cara loudly mouthed the proper form for addressing the thug.

"Well, now that we got that straight, I was wondering if you was interested in what was happening in my part of town."

"You know it's important to me."

"Good," he preened. "Cause the boys that kind of ran off with your boy. We been talking to them and maybe they remember now some guy helping them jump to the conclusion that your boy wasn't our boy no more. You see."

"I do."

"Good, cause this very same dude that caused us so much trouble this morning is back in town, looking to hire some heat. Says it won't be for long. Lots of money in it if things go down right. You curious about this?"

"I am very curious," Kris said, deadly spicing her words.

"You want maybe to put one of your boys in with five, six of ours and see where this takes him?"

Kris eyed her team. "Let me think on this for a second." NELLY, MUTE THE LINE.

"Line muted," Nelly announced.

"Captain, could one of your men pass for a ganger?"

DeVar was shaking his head even before Gunny added his own curt nod. "This world is just too flaky," Gunny said.

"Could you tail them?" Kris asked.

"Nothing beats a try but a failure. We'll need a car," Captain DeVar said, an evil grin capturing his face. He tapped his commlink. "Doc, you know that old rattletrap of yours?"

"The one that beats any rig you got?" came back at him.

"You need to loan it to a couple of carefree jarheads."

"And why would I do that?"

"Because a princess asks you," Kris said, raising her voice to carry to the captain's commlink.

"Oh, that damsel in distress thing."

"You heard about Ruth Tordon being kidnapped?" Kris asked.

"Oh, that. How fast can you get a runner up here? No, I'll head down to you. Time I got involved."

"We've taken over the conference room forward of the Tac Center," the captain said, signed off, and turned to Gunny. "Who's good for a tailing and will call for backup before doing something we'll all regret?"

"Don't know about that regretting part," Gunny said, but nodded at two Marines. "Amy, Brute, you saw what they were wearing this morning. Can you look like that?"

Both nodded and headed for the door.

Penny did, too. "I'm going with them."

"Penny?" Kris said.

"This isn't storm-trooper work. This is good, old-fashioned police work like my dad told me about when I was still small enough to sit on his knee. And I did some field work in my intel days, Kris. And besides, I'm sick and tired of watching, observing, and reporting. I want to *do* something for a change."

Kris wanted to say no. But hadn't she said that what Penny needed most was work? And Penny was right. This was standard police work, not something even a Special Ops–capable Marine company trained for. She glanced at Jack. His face showed only the sadness of someone watching a friend head in harms way. There was no judgment there for Kris, sending another one of her people into the line of fire.

"Keep your head down and call in if you find anything."

"Ain't that the mission, boss," Penny said. She flashed Kris a smile for the first time in months and was gone.

But Captain DeVar was frowning. "Is there something I should know about her? Will my Marines be safe with her?"

"As safe as with their own mother," Kris said. "Lieutenant Pasley-Lien is good to go."

Kris turned to the photos and let the last few minutes roll by in her mind. She'd sent two Marines out to keep Bronc's mother safe. She'd sent Penny and two Marines to tail some-one hiring shooters from a local, now probably friendly, gang.

And she had a phone number that might or might not be of any value. "That phone number is from uptown," Kris said.

"Real high priced," Bronc answered.

"Gramma Ganna says we'll move up there soon," Cara added.

"Sounds dangerous," Abby said.

"Guess I'll cover that one myself," Kris said. "Abby, what would you suggest I wear?"

33

The kids were right, this neighborhood was Garden City's high-priced district. The estates were huge and set far apart by well-appointed grounds. Some looked new. Others showed the gradual growth that marked Nuu House. Add-ons . . . not always according to the best of architectural taste . . . as it passed from one generation to the next.

It hadn't been at all easy for Kris to find it.

The archived phone number said a Mr. Ohi Tristram, VII, lived there. The social database agreed that he still lived there . . . but gave no further information. All of the data elements on income, social status, and the likes were blank.

"I guess you can buy your way out of just about anything on this planet," Kris muttered.

"Should I buy the next database up?" Nelly asked.

"Not for that present computer you're operating. Nelly, buy a new one and start all over again, clean." While Nelly was doing that, Doc arrived, tossed his car keys to the Marine captain, and went to meditate at the photo wall.

"We need to send someone to pick up these computers," Gunny said.

"Nelly, buy two more," Kris ordered. "We'll give them to the company rec room later. And have them if we need them now."

And another Marine in civvies headed out the door.

Which meant a lot of Marines were going in a lot of directions using just about every vehicle available. NELLY, RENT A DOZEN RIGS, COMPACTS TO ALL-TERRAIN.

I WAS WONDERING WHEN YOU WOULD ASK ME. I WILL USE SEVERAL DIFFERENT RENTAL SITES AND DIFFERENT CREDIT CHITS.

OH, AND WE MAY NEED TO BE READY TO TRAVEL FARTHER AND FASTER THAN A CAR CAN HANDLE.

I WAS ABOUT TO ASK THAT, TOO, Nelly said, about as proud of herself as a computer can get.

"Kris, Your Highness," Bronc said. "The new database isn't showing anything more than the old one."

"Who is this guy?" Jack grumbled under his breath.

"Who you looking for?" Doc said, turning from the pictures.

"Ohi Tristram the Seventh," Kris rattled off the address.

"Oh, O'Heidi. Why didn't you say so," Doc said with a grin. "I've partied at his place several times."

"Heidi," Kris said.

"You'd have to meet him to understand."

"What can you tell us about him?" Jack demanded.

Doc shrugged. "A bit of a fop. Doing the only thing he learned from his daddy, which is spend down the family trust. The family was very prominent in the early years, but I don't think a penny has been added to the trust in three generations. But he throws nice parties. Madge, my girlfriend, introduced me to his scene. A good place to meet Garden City's B-list."

"Kris, I am running Tristram through the social section of the media," Nelly said. "He does regularly make the end filler section."

"Been there lately?" Jack asked Doc.

"Can't say that I have. The eating was good, but I can pay for my own chow and eat it in better company."

"What about the company?" Kris asked.

"A lot of bellyaching. Mostly younger kids who didn't

inherit the family business. They sit around complaining about how hard it is to start up new businesses these days. Not good for my digestion," Doc said, rubbing his well-padded belly.

"And eight years ago, he paid to make himself disappear from most Eden databases," Kris said, rubbing her chin.

"Why would a playboy spend money to dig a hole and pull the lid over it?" Jack said, drumming his hands on the table that showed, for now, only a map of Garden City.

"Eight years ago, you say," Doc said, taking a chair at their table. "It was about that time the eats went sour. Four years ago I quit going."

Kris thought about that as she let Abby dress her to impress. Flowing red slacks and a loose-fitting golden shirt covered her thick body armor very well.

Pulling up to the mansion in an armored Marine transport, Kris eyed the setup as an auto-security station scanned her ID. High stone wall. Overgrown. Rather obvious security cameras were either very old or meant to be seen. Were they backed up with less visible ones?

KRIS, I'M GETTING NO EMISSIONS FROM ANYTHING BUT THE VISIBLE ONES.

THANK YOU, NELLY.

Kris had to give a palm print before the gate opened. *Wonder if he did this to all his party guests?* She'd left Doc back at the embassy, so she had no answer.

At the big house, Kris once again had to go through the security formalities, as did Jack and Abby. Kris left Captain DeVar in the car. No need letting these folks know who all she was in cahoots with.

An auto-servant greeted Kris. Little more than a pole on six wheels, it led Kris threw a long entrance hall. The chairs showed wear. A glass of white wine, half empty, was on the fireplace's mantelpiece. Some machine's opticals needed mending.

Mr. Ohi Tristram the Seventh, O'Heidi to some, awaited them at his desk in a huge library. The walls were lined with musty smelling books in imitation leather bindings. Overstuffed loungers offered partygoers places to relax in small groups. The quiet room for the party?

Mr. Tristram stood and offered Kris his hand. Did he get his nickname from the way he hid behind the desk or from his short stature . . . say five feet and a smidgen?

"What can I do for you?" he mumbled as Kris shook a very weak, moist hand. She let go of it with relief.

Kris saw no benefit in a long introduction. "My great-grandmother, Ruth Tordon, has disappeared."

"Oh, I'm sorry to hear that." He didn't sound very. "I hadn't heard about it on the news."

"It probably hasn't made it there yet."

Tristram's face went rubbery at that. First he showed confusion, probably at the speed Kris was moving. Speed that brought her to him. He finally put on a smirk and waited for Kris to go on.

She did. "It seems that your telephone number was found at the office of the security advisory firm that sent her the guards that vanished with her."

O'Heidi took a moment to absorb the words. Then he shook his head. "Oh, I am sad to hear that. About the guards disappearing. I hope they weren't hurt." His reply didn't sound like anything more than an attempt to dodge the obvious.

"I was wondering how your phone number came to be there?"

Mr. Tristram shrugged. At least his shoulders moved. His face stayed in a vacant grin. "I have no idea. Lots of people attend my parties. Many tell their friends about them. Some come. Others don't. Birds of each feather seek their own."

"Who provides your security?" Kris asked.

He giggled. "I really don't know. I leave that to the house 'puter. It lets the contract to bidding every few years and takes the lowest bidder. 'Puter's do it so much better than people. With 'puters, there's no risk of someone hanging their hand out for a kickback, don't you know."

"Could your computer tell us who's providing the service these days?" Jack asked.

"Oh no, that's never done. You must be new to Eden. That privacy is never violated. Strictly a business matter."

"It's really important. I want to find my grandmother very much," Kris pointed out. She considered coming around the desk and towering over O'Heidi, but gave it up. If this fellow was going to lead them anywhere, it would not be intentionally.

O'Heidi steepled his fingers and leaned back in his chair. "I am very sorry, but I certainly can't violate Eden's laws, now can I? Besides, I doubt if it would really help. These things usually work themselves out. Have you been asked for ransom?"

"We've had no call from the criminals," Kris bit out.

"Well, you should stay close to your phone," the man said, glancing at his, a rather antique-looking affair. "If you miss that first call, you may not get another," he said helpfully.

"I'm sure we'll get the call when it comes in," Kris said.

"Well, sorry I can't be of more help. Why don't you come to my party next Friday? I'm sure this will all be settled by then. Bring your grandmother. Or was it great-grandmother?"

"The latter," Kris said and turned to go.

"That did us a lot of good," Jack muttered under his breath as they retraced their way out of the house.

"As you were, Marine," Kris snapped, under her breath as much as she could.

Back in the Marine rig, Kris's first words were "Debug us."

Then she sat silent for the next half minute as listening bugs sparkled in death.

"We are clean," Nelly finally announced.

"That was a major infestation," Jack noted.

"That house is a plague," Nelly added. "I was getting all kinds of reports. Every word you said, Kris, was being rebroadcasted as fast as you said it."

"Different bugs?"

"No. In there, and in this transport, almost all of the bugs were of three basic models. I also picked up some hunter bugs as well. All the bugs are playing the same tune, Kris."

"And he has security to see that only he is doing the bugging," Jack concluded.

"Not as good a security as he thinks," Nelly reported. "Our tap bug is on his phone line." If a computer could grin in pride, Nelly would be grinning from ear to ear.

If she had ears.

"And he's making a call," she said.

"He ought to, after Jack let him know how good he did," Kris said, elbowing her security chief.

"If I hadn't done it, you would have. And it sounded better coming from me."

"Everyone believes a man in uniform," Captain DeVar added with a grin.

"I've got the number," Nelly crowed.

A second later, the celebration was over. "Oh, pooh, he's using a scrambler system."

"Crack it," Kris ordered.

"I can't," Nelly said, with an almost audible sigh in her voice. "The scrambler key changes every couple of words."

"What's the number?" Bronc asked.

Nelly passed it to him.

"Is it in the database?" Kris asked.

Bronc looked stricken. "I've never heard of a nine-oh-nine exchange."

"Neither have I," Cara added.

"Another brick wall," Jack sighed.

"Well, I can tell you a few things," Nelly said, jumping in like a ray of sunshine. "Maybe not what they are saying, but I can tell you that O'Heidi said something, then got cut off, and then he said something back, in a rather contrite voice."

"Oh ho," Captain DeVar said. "Someone didn't like being called, I bet. I'd love to hear what's going on here."

"I suspect O'Heidi really wishes he wasn't," Kris said.

And wasn't far from right.

Interlude 3

"YOU never call me," Grant von Schrader snapped at O'Heidi's interruption.

"Don't you want to know what hasn't hit the news yet?"

"And what makes you think I have to wait for the news to know what's happening on Eden?"

"So you already know what Kris Longknife told me just a moment ago."

"I don't like guessing games, Heidi." Few used that *nomme de party* to Ohi's face. It reminded the playboy just who was boss here.

"She's looking for her great-grandmother. Someone seems to have kidnapped Mrs. Ruth, ah . . ."

"Tordon. If you will excuse me, some of us have work to do," Grant snapped and quashed the line. A moment later, his computer briefed him on the latest news to come in from his sources in Garden City's police department.

Grant had flagged Kris Longknife. He hadn't thought to flag Ruth Tordon. A major mistake, it now appeared.

"Where is Victoria?" he demanded.

"She is just leaving," his house computer answered.

"Tell her I wish to see her."

"I don't want to see you" came in Vicky's own voice a moment later. "I have business of my own."

"Which it seems also impacts my business and your father's. You may either come to my study, or my men will carry you."

"I could drop them before they laid a hand on me."

"Then the armored security guards will collect you, and you can sample the hospitality of my lower basements until such time as your father asks about you. I expect that might be a very long time, all things considered."

A few moments later, Victoria Smythe-Peterwald stormed into his study, four security guards trailing her warily.

"You don't have the right to stop me," she shouted after hardly crossing the threshold.

"I imagine your brother told his mentor that about the time he tried breathing vacuum. It didn't work all that well."

"It was that damn Longknife."

"So you were going to get her," Grant said, trying his best to sound reasonable.

"Her and that old bag, both," the lovely girl spat.

Grant sighed. This educational assignment was not going well. "That old bag was surviving Iteeche killer pods long before your father was born."

"And I caught her up like a blind cow at feeding time," the young woman said proudly.

"No doubt. However, your father and I cannot afford another kidnapping bandied about human space at the moment. Her husband, General Trouble, is not a man who takes offense well."

"He'll never know what killed her. Her and that Longknife brat."

"Ah, but I know. And you just bragged about it in front of four security guards. That is not how your father or I arrived at our places in human space. If your right hand slits a throat, your left hand should know nothing about it. That is something you should meditate on."

The girl actually stomped her foot. "I don't have time to waste doing that meditating thing of yours."

"I'm afraid you do." Grant raised his voice slightly. "Ms. Rotterdame."

"Yes, sir," Vicky's personal maid's voice answered immediately.

"I am sending Miss Victoria up to her suites. She is to stay there, meditating on the meaning of security. I do not want her out of your sight for any reason. You understand me. Any. Reason!"

"I understand you perfectly, Mr. Von Schrader. She will be under the personal observation of either me or one of my assistants at all times, no matter how personal or odoriferous her activity. And I will bring out the shock cane if she proves too headstrong."

"We understand each other," he said, then scowled at his boss's offspring. "I will also have guards at your door and on the grounds below your suite. You were quite good at slipping out of the nursery back on Greenfeld. Do not mistake my house for such a play area. You have created a problem that I must now solve. Go to your rooms while I do it."

Miss Vicky kicked an end table, that proved heavier than she thought, so she slapped the lamp on it. Since it was bolted to the table, all she did was knock the shade askew.

"I would have expected better from a Peterwald," Grant said, eliciting a primal scream from the girl. When he showed no reaction to the noise, she stomped out.

Grant eyed the senior of the guards. "Had she told you where she was going?"

"No, sir."

"And you knew nothing of this plan of hers."

Any answer would damn him. "No, sir," the man said simply.

"Inform your supervisor that someone in her guard detail must know what she planned and helped her plan it. I expect your company to investigate it and take appropriate action."

"Yes, sir" came quickly back.

And Grant von Schrader turned back to his desk and fiddled with minor matters until he was once more alone. Only then did he tap his most secure commlink.

"Major, I need a quick report on all the assets we have in place. I fear some of them may have been compromised. We should also assume that Operation Barbarossa may require immediate implementation.

"That will involve more risk than we intended," his old associate replied.

"Report back to me in half an hour on how far we may have been compromised and then we will assess the risk."

At the sound of the link being cut, Grant called up his plan for Barbarossa. No doubt more time would reduce the risks. However, if the dolts who ran Eden finally pulled their heads out of the sand, more time might ruin everything.

Grant smiled. With luck, he could still add another star to the Greenfeld banner . . . and return the boss's daughter to him alive . . . if not educated.

34

Kris told Nelly to put off trying to decipher O'Heidi's phone call when a report came in from the Tac Center.

"Our tails have found something interesting."

A new location appeared on Captain DeVar's tactical board. The target was a large warehouse in a district full of them. It was also under heavy and sophisticated security.

"Approach will be tough without all kinds of unshirted hell getting in the way," the captain muttered.

"Nelly, have those new cars arrived?"

"Yes, ma'am. Twelve cars ranging from family boxy to sporty to junkers are parked a block from the embassy."

"Way to go, girl." Thirty minutes later, a major chunk of a Marine company descended from all points of the compass on a nondescript warehouse.

Kris was in the backseat of a red sports car. Jack drove; Captain DeVar rode shotgun. Jack gunned the engine and did a very noisy circuit of the warehouse. Kris had her knees up around her ears; the back of the sports car was never intended for six-footers. Likely never intended for anyone.

Despite the discomfort, Kris didn't miss two human guards—one at the front and one at the back door of their target.

And they didn't miss the car. Lust for shiny, fast wheels filled their eyes.

"Bet they can't describe who was in the red sports car," Jack chortled.

"But they got the make and model of this little number," Kris said. "Let's go find Penny."

The intelligence officer was in the parking lot of a drive-in, munching a hamburger as she studied a portable battle board.

Kris leaned against her sporty wheels, filing her nails. The red short shorts and rhinestone-speckled tank top made her the perfect accessory for the car. No one noticed the amount of whispering she was doing with the car next to her.

"How tight is the security?" Kris asked softly.

"About as tight as it gets," Penny answered. "Cameras on each corner of the building. More in the middle of the block. Human guards at the door. Nanos floating around the street both for attack and recon. If we storm that place, they are so going to know we're coming."

"Anything inside yet?" Kris asked.

"I cruised my standard probes around the building," Penny said. "But all met defensive nanos and I pulled them back. No chance of anything normal getting in and out of there."

"Nelly, we could use something not normal," Jack said.

Nelly had been a half kilo of self-organizing computer matrix around Kris's shoulders. But of late, Nelly had put on weight. About a hundred grams of extra matrix and Smart Metal.

"I think Auntie Tru gave me just the right trick for this bunch," the computer said softly. "Five or six recording bugs, and a dozen or so relay stations. The bugs conduct their own recon, then tight beam out a fast report by the relays."

"Do it," Kris ordered.

A gray junker pulled up on the other side of Penny's blue sedan. This station wagon had Abby in the backseat with

Bronc and Cara. The three tough-looking dudes in the front seat were Marines, though the one in the middle was a woman Marine.

"Does anyone have a layout for the insides of that warehouse?" Kris asked softly.

Bronc eyed Kris like she'd grown two heads. Once again, Eden was making it hard for Princess Kristine Longknife to pull the required rabbit out of a very locked-down hat.

Jack ordered a hamburger and a malt for himself, and another set for Kris. She snorted, but accepted the atavistic requirement of the locale that she must belong to some male.

"Don't make this a habit," she muttered under her breath.

The hamburger wasn't too bad, and while the malt didn't match the quality of the milkshakes at the Smuggler's Roost, it was quite decent. Kris was nursing the last few drops from the glass when Nelly said, "I am getting answers from my scouts."

"Show us," Kris said. And watched DeVar's battle board fill with the flight in of one of the scouts.

Nelly merged the scout's reports into one informative burst. Kris and her team got an overview of the lower floor of a very box-laden warehouse. Up on the second deck, down a hall, and into a back room showed Gramma Ruth, taped to a chair.

Beside her, one man paced. Another rocked comfortably in a desk chair. At a table set up across the room, but near the entrance, six young punks were taking apart pistols, cleaning them, and putting them back together . . . very lovingly.

There also was a monitor with its screen split into a half-dozen sections. Pictures from both inside and out flashed on it. The pictures didn't always come up; some segments were blank, others showed a very hazy picture. It didn't seem to matter, none of the men in the room paid it much attention.

Maybe Kris had just gotten her first bit of luck. Maybe.

"The two guys nearest the door are ours," Penny reported. "The guy doing the tiger pacing act is the fellow that hired them. Don't know who the others are."

"Nelly, how safe are your scouts?" Kris asked. The pacing guy regularly turned to the seated fellow and said something, but there was no sound.

"I am getting noise from a few defensive units. Unless one of them stumbles into the line out, they should stay dumb. And when any of them get close to one of my active scouts, I put it to sleep for a while."

"I want to hear what's going on between those two guys."

"Sound coming up," Nelly said.

"Where is that bitch?" the pacer snapped.

"Which bitch?" the seated guy said. He didn't look up from playing his handheld computer game.

"The rich bitch."

"They are both quite a bit richer than me or thee, and I must once again ask you not speak of our employer like that."

"It ain't like she's going to sashay in on us unannounced. She's got guns around her, and even your blind gate guards would have to notice that limo of hers."

"Quite likely. So sit down and relax like the rest of us."

In the background, the talk at the table centered lovingly on the guns the new hires had been issued and what they would do when given the chance. Every shooter was sure he could make head shots at fifty, no now it was up to seventy-five paces.

For a few moments only that conversation came through as the pacer went back to pacing.

Suddenly, he turned on Gramma Ruth. A gun appeared in his hand. "What do you say we pop her right now?"

"What do you say you put that gun away," the game player said, still not looking up.

"Why not pop the old bag?"

"Because our young bag wants the other young bag to be here when we pop the old bag. She's the one paying. I don't know about you, but I was taught to follow the golden rule. She's got the gold. She rules."

"But she should be here by now," the pacer almost shrieked.

The calm one nodded at that. "She should be."

"Call her."

"Don't make me add stupid to your long list of failings."

"I'm going to pop the old broad. I am if we don't see that rich bitch real soon."

"She will come."

"Before the cops."

"Don't worry about the cops. They are taken care of."

"Yeah, and you were so sure that rich bitch would be here what, half an hour ago."

"She will come."

"I'm gonna pop this old bag."

The conversation looked ready to go into a repeat loop. One Kris did not like.

"Captain, I do not think we can wait for the other 'rich bitch' to show up."

"Looks that way," Captain DeVar said.

"So, how do we take down the two guards at the doors without them raising a stink?" Kris said, a smile growing on her face. These fellows had shown themselves easily distracted by a flashy car. Kris suspected she knew another way.

In the car, Jack nudged Captain DeVar. "I hope you have some ideas on this, because if you don't get ahead of that woman, we're all going to be racing to catch up, and I'm not at all sure we'll like what we're racing into."

"Yeah, I think you're right," the captain muttered, then called out the window. "Becky, Trish, I think we're going to need that decoy stunt you've been talking about for so long."

"Whoopee" came from the next car, as a white T-shirt came off and a knife came out. A moment later, the shirt was back on, a door opened, and a woman Marine wiggled her way out of the car. Not much of the shirt was left, what with the sleeves hacked off, the neck now much more open, and a whole lot gone from the bottom.

A second later, the redhead pulled her bra out from under the remnant of the shirt. To wolf whistles from the Marines in the cars around her, she wiggled, showing she had the right curves in all the right places. She held every male eye.

Well, maybe she shared those eyes with the short blonde who joined her.

"As you were," the blonde growled under her breath. That brought laughs.

"What we women do in the line of duty." The redhead sighed.

"Abe, Hamma, trail the girls. You know what to do when the guards get distracted."

Two of the shortest members of the company, in white tees and baggy slacks of the latest fashion: one plaid, the other checkered, sauntered after the women as they sashayed off.

"They big enough to take down those guards?" Kris asked.

"They're Marines, ma'am," Captain DeVar said. "The guards will go down. And if their eyes are where I suspect they'll be, they won't even know what hit them. Now then, my fabulous Nelly, I know those guys are not paying a lot of attention to the monitor, and the pictures on the monitor regularly go blank, but is there anything you can do to encourage it to be on the fritz when I want it on the fritz."

"Fritz," Nelly said. "Interesting word. And yes, while most of you were watching those poor girls turn themselves into sex objects, I was launching new nanos."

Kris found herself staring at two wide-eyed Marine officers. It looked like Nelly was entering a feminist stage of her development. Just what Kris needed, more interesting behavior from her pet computer."

"What kind of new nanos?" Kris said, keeping the discussion on what would help Gramma Ruth.

Jack shook his head. *We need to talk,* he mouthed silently.

"My new nano will access the feed line from the cameras. They are protected and alarmed against just such an intervention, but, if Auntie Tru and Sam are as smart as they think they are, I just may be able to get in there."

"Please leave me alone for a moment," Nelly ordered.

Kris turned back to Captain DeVar. On his battle board he was lighting up cars, giving them assignments to the front or back door and the order for their arrival. "First go in troops that your maid gave spider-silk undies to. The very first have ceramic plates. The unarmored go in last." He tapped his board. "Drivers, stay in the rigs. Move them out of the way for the next one coming. I don't want to see a stack-up of unloading or empty rigs at the doors."

No reply came back, but around the drive-in, heads nodded to the orders.

"What about me?" Kris asked. "I'm fully armored."

"Last," DeVar spat. "If I thought I could make you."

Kris shook her head.

The captain glanced at Jack. "Can you make this woman see reason."

"She's a Longknife," Jack said with a shrug. "Reason is not something they're noted for." He did lean over to look up at Kris. "For God's sake, woman, do not try to be first in. So help me, God, I will personally trip you up if you try."

"You'd have to be ahead of me to trip me," Kris said.

"I am so glad that she's not in my chain of command, or I in hers," the Marine captain said with a groan.

"Where will you be in the assault order?" Kris asked the company commander.

"If I wasn't in the same car with you, I'd fit myself somewhere in the middle."

"Sounds like a reasonable place for me," Kris said.

Jack eyed her in open shock. "Who are you, and what have you aliens done with my primary?"

"My two women are about to walk past the doors," Captain DeVar noted. "Drivers, start you engines. Let's make this look good and not do anything that will get the neighbors talking."

Kris edged around the door, DeVar leaned his seat forward a bit, and she slid into the back.

Around Kris, some cars took off in a squealing of tires and similar teenage panache. Others left at the sedate pace you'd expect of a respectable family car. Two old hulks chugged and smoked, but got under way. In a moment, the lot was empty.

"Jack, are you going to stay with the car?" Kris asked, just as Jack backed the sports car out . . . squealing tires burning rubber. Gears ground as he changed into drive and took off like a rocket.

Once Kris had recovered from being thrown hard against her seat belt, and then deep into a seat way too small for her . . . or anyone for that matter . . . he grinned at her in the rearview mirror. "Wait until you see what I have planned, honey cakes."

What was it about bright red sport cars that cut the male

IQ in half? Kris thought, but didn't say. Jack was getting her to Gramma Ruth.

Assuming he didn't kill her in traffic.

"Front door guard is down" came over the net.

"Back door is down."

"Rig one is unloading" came almost immediately, followed by rig two through five about as fast as notice could be given.

That made it time for Jack and Kris.

The ragtop on the sporty thing folded back.

Jack mashed the gas pedal and his little red rocket took off for the space by the front door just vacated by a station wagon.

Then Jack did a hard left turn. There were two large pickup trucks parked parallel to the curb across the street from their target. Jack brought the sports car to a hard stop, nose to the curb, its side doors with at least an inch between them and the front of one truck, the tailgate of the other.

Kris was on her feet, sliding herself over the tiny trunk and running for the door before the car even stopped swaying.

Jack and Captain DeVar were only a step behind her.

"A fine bit of driving," Kris called over her shoulder.

"Don't get a chance to do something like that nearly often enough." Jack chortled.

"Let's hope you don't need to do something like that for a very long time," Kris shouted back as she charged through the door and into the hot shadowed cavern of the warehouse.

"She dishes it out," Jack growled, "but she can't take it."

Inside, Kris started to ask where to go, but green chem lights lit a path. She followed.

NELLY, WHAT ABOUT THE BUGS? ARE WE UNDER OBSERVATION?

I AM TAKING DOWN THEIR BUGS AND SENDING MY OWN REPORT. THEIR BUGS SEND A RECOGNITION SIGNAL EVERY SIXTY SECONDS. THAT IS ALL THE TIME WE HAVE.

"We got sixty seconds before they notice their bugs are dead," Kris reported.

"I'd planned for only thirty seconds," DeVar replied as they took the stairs two or three at a time.

The hall before Kris was lined with Marines in civvies,

armed with automatics mostly, but a few had M-6s. They awaited their captain's orders.

Captain DeVar signaled to four M-6 gunners. They and a pistol-armed sergeant moved to the head of the line.

SOMETHING IS SPOOFING THE NERVOUS GUY, Nelly told Kris.

Kris slowed down to glance at Captain DeVar's battle board. The scene in the hostage room was getting rambunctious. The calm fellow signaled to the shooters to put their guns back together and for two of them, the ones closest to him, to check the door.

"It's going down," Captain DeVar said, alerting his team in a soft voice.

The four Marines closest to the door moved farther down the hall, leaving room for the new, heavily armed arrivals.

"Protect the hostage," the Marine Captain whispered.

"I'd love to talk to those two suits," Kris added. "Take'em alive if you can."

"But they're not worth a dead Marine," the captain snapped.

And the door opened a crack.

35

The kidnappers tried to peek into the hall without exposing themselves. Not a bad approach.

They didn't expect Marines to kick the door in.

The sergeant not only kicked the door in, but rolled into the room himself. Behind him, his fire team took the gunners on at full automatic.

The two men trying so carefully to open the door were blasted across the room. Their blood splattered the walls behind them. Around them.

The two shooters from Kris's favorite gang dropped to the floor and tossed their pistols as far from themselves as they could.

That left two gunners and two suits. The gunners tried to take the Marines on, about a second after the Marines transferred their fire to them. That second's delay was deadly. Like the first two gunners, they became gory renditions of modern art decorating the dirty gray walls of the room.

Both of the suits now had guns in their hands.

Both swung around to blow a hole in Gramma Ruth's head.

Gramma Ruth showed why she was still around after going

toe-to-toe with Iteeche warriors. They had figured that taping her to a chair would inhibit her movements.

They hadn't planned on her taking the entire chair and laying it over on its back. Suddenly, a metal chair was blocking their aim at Ruth's skull.

They started to take the two steps they needed to get a good aim at her head. At least they tried.

Neither quite made that second step. The sergeant took one. Kris got the other.

The sergeant put one round in the flaky one's pistol arm, then moved aim and put three in his body.

Kris didn't trust her skills. She put one round into her target's shoulder, then two more into his side.

Neither man got off a shot before they were spinning around. Going down.

"Check fire. Check fire!" Captain DeVar shouted.

The Marines did. The silence was deafening.

"Medic. Medic, we got two bad guys down that we want to talk to," Captain DeVar shouted into the quiet.

Two Marines with Red Cross–marked bags raced into the room. They raised an eyebrow at the bodies and parts sliding off the walls and went to where Captain DeVar stood over two suits.

"You want to check Mrs. General Trouble," DeVar said to Kris, but she was already sliding to a stop beside Gramma Ruth.

"You okay?" Kris said as she tugged at the tape over Ruth's mouth. Tugged gently . . . then ripped it free when it didn't want to come.

The bad guys had really taped Gramma's mouth. Kris could guess why.

"What took you so long?" Gramma Ruth growled.

Kris tackled the tape that held Ruth's arms to the chair. "We took the scenic route," she muttered. Just like a Longknife to have nothing but complaints for her rescuers, Kris thought.

Her hands free, Ruth helped Kris rip off the tape on her body and legs. Then started to stand up.

Ruth quickly gave that up as a bad idea.

A medic dropped down beside Kris even before she called

for one. She shined a light into the old woman's eyes, asked and was told she had two fingers up. "And now I'm getting up," Ruth grumbled, and they helped her stand.

She did stand, swaying a bit, but up. "From the looks of this bunch of hardcases and heartbreakers, I'd say I've fallen into the company of Marines."

That got an "Ooo-Rah" from around the room.

"Well, in the name of General Trouble and my grandkids, may I give you my thanks on a job well done. Very well done" got another "Ooo-Rah."

Then Gramma Ruth turned to the two suits. "What a pair of sacks of shit," she said.

"Dumber and dumberist," she growled. "I knew they wanted to pop me one between the eyes. Pacer here kept saying it, and game player never showed anything but concern for the timing. So I figured out what I'd do ahead of time.

"Then you wonderful folks come busting in, and all they can think of is to notch my eyebrows. So I do what I knew I'd do."

Ruth walked over and looked down at the nervous one. He was on a stretcher. The other was being loaded. "I did what I'd planned on doing, and what did you do? You idiot, you followed right after me. That chair was no real protection. You could have ripped me a new one. You could have perforated my thighs so much they'd never find an artery to patch."

She shook her head. "One of you couldn't quit complaining about that 'rich bitch,' and the other never put down his game long enough to do any thinking. If that 'bitch' hadn't been doing your thinking for you, you'd never have gotten me here."

Then Gramma Ruth spun on her heels to face Captain DeVar. "I am very sorry about your Marines. They never had a chance. No one could have seen what was coming."

"Your two local security guards?" DeVar asked.

"Yes. That's them on the wall. What you left of them."

Outside, the distant wail of a siren started up.

"Company's coming, troops. Let's police up the area and clear this scene," DeVar said firmly.

Kris held Gramma Ruth's elbow as they headed out. "Thanks," the older woman said. "I don't think I quite have my balance back. Oh, and I do need to go to the bathroom."

"As soon as we get to the embassy," Kris said.

"Please hurry."

But they paused among the boxes when a sergeant said, "You might want to see what we found."

A Marine was busy attacking more boxes with a crowbar, but it was easy to see from the ones open what the closed ones would show: rifles, automatic pistols, rocket grenade launchers, and boxes and boxes of ammunition for the same. A tarp had been pulled aside to show several mortars.

"This place is an armory," a corporal observed.

"Should we blow it up, ma'am?" the sergeant asked.

"As much as I'd love to," Kris said, "I don't think the neighborhood would much enjoy the experience. Let's leave it for the local cops to figure out. It will be interesting to see what they make of it," Kris said, exchanging a glance with Ruth.

There was no senior to junior in that glance. No vet to neophyte. In Ruth's eyes, Kris saw an equal approving of an equal's call.

Garage-size doors had been opened, turning the warehouse into a drive-through. Three large Marine rigs had been driven in. Two were outfitted as ambulances, the first in line was not, and looked raring to go. Kris aimed Ruth for that one.

And ran into Abby with the kids. "Kris, I have to get these youngsters home. At least Cara. Not sure where Bronc's mom is."

"See if you can find one of the Marines that took care of her," Kris said. "I'll see you when I see you. There's lots of loose ends to tie up here."

Abby looked around at the munitions. "Sure looks that way. You know, a guy could start a revolution with all these toys. I wonder what they had in mind?"

"So do I," Kris said. "And I think I have at least one guy alive who knows what's going on. Take all the time you need to take care of the kids . . . but don't take too long."

"Oh, I just love working for you," Abby said, but Ruth was in the rig and the driver was gunning the engine. Kris piled in and in a second, they were headed for the embassy.

And safety.

36

Kris made it to the embassy with no further delays. They pulled up to a side entrance and Kris hustled Ruth inside . . . and pointed her at a restroom.

While Kris waited, the announcement came over the net that all hands had successfully withdrawn. Two scouts had been left to observe the arrival of the cops. One patrol car had been followed by two, which were reinforced by five that led to the arrival . . . very quickly . . . of, well, just about all of them.

Kris was glad to hear that. Her one fear was that the first car would relock the place and make it disappear again. If that happened, she might have to rethink her revulsion to blowing it up. But now whoever ran Eden would have to take a good, hard look at those shake-and-bake revolutionary fixings.

This time, they might even do something about it.

Revolution. Was that the word for this trip? Was a budding regime change the real reason Grampa Ray had sent her here?

So, Grampa, am I supposed to help it . . . or stop it?

No way for him to tell her this far from Wardhaven. But since the movers for the shake-up had been impolite—in the extreme—to Gramma Ruth, Kris was pretty much coming down on the other side. Assuming there was another side and what Kris did mattered a fig to them.

Further reflection ended when Gramma Ruth rejoined her.

And several Marines entered, weapons drawn, and proceeded to encourage the few civilian and Foreign Service types who happened to be in Marine country to make a hasty exit.

One diplomatic type was talking with Commander Malhoney, the often-passed-over officer whose gut was actually shrinking, now that he was jogging along with the rest of the Navy contingent as a third platoon behind the Marines each morning.

The civilian was still there as a blood-covered gurney was wheeled in from the transport outside and pushed into sick bay.

"Did I just see what I thought I just saw?" the Foreign Service officer asked.

"Most certainly you did not," the commander said, a tight smile edging across his face. "And if you still think you saw what you saw, may I suggest you immediately forget seeing it."

The civilian frowned, then glanced again down the hall as a second gore-covered gurney was wheeled toward sick bay.

Then he spotted Kris standing at the end of the hallway from which all the bodies appeared. His eyes widened, then narrowed quickly. "Right, Commander. I didn't see a thing."

"Smart man. You'll go far."

"Just like you."

That brought a laugh from both, and they headed in the other direction.

Kris and Ruth followed the smell of blood to sick bay.

"I figured you'd bring me extra work," Doc said, greeting Kris as she walked into sick bay, "when that maid of yours waltzed in here with two steamer trunks full of some of the finest medical gadgets I ever hoped to see in my life. But I was

hoping to be working on your fine body, not just any near ca-
daver the jarheads dragged in."

"You can never tell, Doc, when there's a Longknife involved," Gramma Ruth said.

"And who might you be, young woman," Doc said.

"Ruth Tordon, Doc. My eldest girl had the misfortune to
marry into the Longknifes."

"How's she doing?"

"Dead some sixty years."

"I'm sorry," Doc said, and seemed to mean it. "Now, if the
two of you will excuse me, I think my nurses have stabilized
the patients, and I need to see if there is anything that I can do
to keep them out of the morgue."

"Try, Doc," Kris said. "I—no—both of us, really want to
talk with them while they're still drugged and pliable."

"That old wives' tale is overrated. This your handiwork?"

"I nailed one. Sergeant Bruce got the other."

"They were both trying to nail me," Ruth said dryly.

"Horrible behavior. I ought to let them die for such poor
taste."

"We think they were paid to develop that poor taste," Kris
said. "We want to know who was passing around the money."

"Then I shall let them live. If that is within my poor powers," Doc said and entered his surgery.

Kris found herself with nothing to do but pace the room.

Ruth settled into a chair. "Could you please not do that?"
she said a minute later.

"Do what?"

"Pace. The last fellow to do that tried to kill me. By the
way, do you have a weapon I can borrow?"

They dropped down to the Marine armory. An old staff sergeant there was delighted when Ruth asked if he had an ancient relic of a gun to fit her old paw. With a sigh of pure
pride, he produced from the back of his horde an old 6-mm
Special.

"You don't see many like this old baby around these days,"
he told Ruth. "You want me to show you how it works."

Gramma popped the magazine out, pulled the action back,

and checked to make sure it was unloaded. "Works about the same as my old one, my lad."

"Foolish me," the sergeant said, "trying to teach my granny to suck eggs."

"Or to plug those guilty of outrageously inappropriate behavior."

Kris was about to suggest that Abby would have a holster for the weapon, but the sergeant pulled one from the lower shelf that fit Gramma's new weapon nicely and let it ride comfortably in the middle of her back.

"You know," Kris started, "Jack would insist that primaries are not supposed to go armed."

"Jack was that nice Secret Service agent trying to keep up with you. What's he doing in Marine green?"

"Didn't Grampa Trouble tell you about that?"

"Oh no! Did my darling Terry do you in? I thought by now you'd have learned why they all call him Trouble."

Kris made a face. "Let's say that I don't need any more lessons on that."

"I have yet to figure out whether you Longknifes are just natural-born optimists or horribly slow learners."

"I think we're both," Kris said.

"Well, I am not going anywhere without my new pet," Ruth said, sliding the arrangement into the rear of her slacks. "Whatever started this morning is not finished. Not with all those hot boy-toys and go-boom boxes left at the warehouse. How did that finish out?" she said, turning back to sick bay.

"Our scouts say half the local police department is presently parked outside the place. I doubt anyone can vanish that revolution in a box now."

"Good," Ruth said, nodding. "However, with that stuff now in the public domain, or at least brought to the attention of management, whoever stocked that arsenal will have two choices."

Kris nodded and started to enumerate them. "Run away, go to ground, and hope it blows over before starting again."

Gramma nodded.

"Or throw the revolution into high gear, move H-hour to right now, and roll the dice."

"Sadly, I don't see a third option," the older woman said.

"Kris, the ambassador wants to see you in his office," Nelly announced.

"You want to go back to sick bay?" Kris asked.

Gramma shook her head. "Hasn't been nearly long enough for Doc's workup."

"Want to tag along for my little visit to the ambassador?"

"Wouldn't miss it for the world," Gramma said with a grin of evil pleasure.

The secretary didn't look up from his computer as Kris came in. "The ambassador is expecting you." Then he did look up and frowned as Ruth followed Kris in.

She flashed him a smile and went right along with Kris. Kris had noticed, following Father around, that if someone acted like they knew what they were doing, people usually let them go right ahead and do what they wanted.

Gramma Ruth had that I-know-what-I'm-doing-don't-juggle-my-elbow act down perfectly.

"What do you think you are doing, young lady" greeted Kris inside as Ambassador VanDerFund came out of his chair.

Since Kris had quite a few fish in the frying pan at the moment, she didn't dare risk an answer to a question that vague. She chose to punt. "No more than the usual." Then she spotted the person seated with his back to her at the ambassador's desk.

He stood and she found herself offering a hand. "Inspector Johnson. Haven't seen you for, oh, a couple of hours."

"Yes, it's been a pleasant interlude for me, too. So, how are you doing? And who is this fine woman with you?"

"Ruth Tordon," Ruth said, and offered her hand.

"I heard you were kidnapped," the inspector said, raising an eyebrow.

"I believe I was. Sloppy bunch. I managed to escape and took public transportation straight away to *my* embassy. Met Kris in the hallway just as I was going to pay Mr. VanDerFund my respects about the same time she was called into a meeting with him. Wonderful how things somehow work out."

"Yes. Isn't it," the inspector said.

The ambassador looked like he might be having an attack of some horrible debilitating disease, but it was a silent attack, allowing everyone to ignore it . . . and him.

"This tenement you escaped from—" the inspector started, but Ruth cut him off.

"I believe it was a warehouse."

"Did you have a chance to look into the boxes?"

"I was more concerned with hiding behind the boxes rather than looking in them," Gramma Ruth said with a very straight face. "Come to think about it, I don't remember even looking at the markings on the boxes. I was in rather a hurry to catch a bus, you know."

The inspector scratched his ear. "I imagine you were."

There was a break in the conversation at that point. Actually, it more like died. Kris filled in the space with a wide-eyed question. "Ambassador, you wanted to see me?"

VanDerFund blinked as if just waking up to a harsh light. He looked at Inspector Johnson, then at Kris. Then back at Johnson. "I thought the inspector had some questions for you."

"I did, but I believe that Ms. Tordon has answered them for me," the inspector said with a smile that didn't touch his face. "Ma'am, I can't believe you are the great-grandmother to this, ah . . ." Troublesome brat was clearly intended but "young woman" came out. "You are far too lovely. You must have had your children very young."

Ruth gave him a smile. The kind that babies give just before they throw up all over adults. Inspector Johnson must have had children of his own. He took a step back.

"Well, if no one has further business, I am still rather rushed with work," Kris said.

That got another raised eyebrow from the inspector. "Anything I should know about?"

"A little of this, a little of that," Kris said with a shrug. "Nothing to bother you about. You know me. I'm often outside the box."

Inspector Johnson glanced at Kris sideways. "An interesting choice of words. Since I found a lot of opened boxes earlier today."

"Oh, what was in them?" Ruth asked, her face amazingly straight. Kris suspected she was seeing where she inherited a lot of her skills for unsociable behavior.

"Nothing," Inspector Johnson said with a ruler-straight face. "Nothing of interest to a college professor and a Rim princess, I'd imagine."

"You'd be amazed what interests me," Kris said.

"Amazed, very likely," Johnson said, heading for the door. "Interested in it. Not at all likely." Hand on the door, he turned to Kris and Ruth. "Take my word for it. It is none of your interest. Keep out of it," he said, and slipped out.

"Good advice. Good advice," VanDerFund added. "What's this I hear about the Marines being gone most of the day?"

"An exercise," Kris said. "Just a bit of practice."

"Well, if you say so."

"Don't take her word for it," Ruth said, heading for the exit also. "Check with that handsome captain. Captain what's-his-name. I bumped in to him as I was coming in. Reminded me of my husband. Say ninety years ago."

And with that, the two women beat a hasty victory parade.

As they made their way back to sick bay, Kris glanced at Gramma Ruth. "Now I suspect I know where my love for creative fiction comes from."

The older woman chuckled dryly. "Not me, Kris. I'm just a simple farm girl that married a Marine. God, but that Marine can come up with the most outrageous tall tales and keep the straightest of faces. Heaven help Saint Peter when the two of them cross paths."

"Then how do you know to trust him?" Kris asked.

"Oh, my child. He never lies to me. And he never lies to the chain of command or to any of his Marines. He's one hundred percent loyal there. But take that fellow. He was offering us nothing. In return what right had he to the truth from us? And he knew it. He gave nothing. He got nothing."

"And we don't know anything more about that weapons stash."

"It's pretty clear he knows even less."

Captain DeVar joined them, with Jack at his side, a few paces from sick bay. "Doc says he's got something," he said.

They entered sick bay, but the door to the surgery was still closed. Kris just finished bringing the others up-to-date on Inspector Johnson's latest fishing expedition when the door opened and Doc entered, removing his gloves.

They waited while he finished that and retrieved a pad of paper from his hip pocket. "Your guy is a talker," he told Kris.

"Will he live?" she asked.

"More than likely. Can't say the same for the guy the sarge plugged. Captain, it's been a long peace. That the first man your sergeant has likely killed?"

Captain DeVar nodded.

"You might want to send him around for some counseling. Even sergeants can get the shakes the first time they come face-to-face with how fragile life is."

"I'll see to that," the captain said.

"Now, as to your guy," Doc said, turning to Kris, but eyeing his pad. "Since you were hoping he'd talk, I used that new gear your maid dropped by, using an IV rather than running tubes down his mouth . . . and tried some of the anesthesia your maid had in her kit. Where'd she get that stuff?" Doc said, then waved his hand. "No, don't tell me. Cause then you'd have to kill me, and if you didn't I'd be stuck knowing something I really didn't need to know . . . and likely didn't like knowing."

"What did he say?" Kris finally let herself say. Clearly, Doc was enjoying being the center of attention. Enjoying it way too much not to be sinful.

"Hold your horses, gal. I'm coming to that. You know a Miss Victory or something like that?"

"Victoria Peterwald?" Kris offered.

"Oh, so that was the second word. He kept mangling it. Or my corpsman's handwriting is even worse than mine. You know, all the time they complain about us docs' poor penmanship, but I say corpsmen are the worse of the lot."

"What did he say?" Now it was Captain DeVar's turn.

"Well, Kris here said she wanted to know where the money came from. So once he started muttering, I had my anesthesia tech keep whispering 'money' in his ear while I'm doing my cutting thing. 'Money' and 'Where's the money?' It must have worked cause he started talking about Miss Victory—no Vicky—and how he needed to get the money from her with no one around or the others would know how much he was making on this gig."

"No trust among bandits," Jack noted.

"Not that I ever noticed," Doc said. "There was also something else. Something about a Mr. Grant, or Shredder. Not sure about that last name. Anyway your guy is scared to death of him. And scared to death of ruining something. Kept saying he wish he'd found a better place. Another place. That make any sense to you?"

Kris nodded. "We found them in an arsenal. The cops are now crawling all over it wondering what it's doing on a nice gun-controlled planet like Eden."

Doc whistled. "That's perforating someone's stomach lining. I can see why he's scared." There was a high, steady tone from inside the surgery. "I better get back to the meat business. Hope this helps." And Doc was gone.

"I think he helped us," Kris said. "Captain, can we make use of your Tac Center for a new project?"

"I suspect we better," Captain DeVar said.

37

Kris found herself standing next to Gramma Ruth as the old campaigner studied the pictures on the wall. Ruth reached out and yanked hers down, then turned to Captain DeVar.

"I will respect your opinion, but in my book, the scales aren't balanced. Me free, two Marines dead. Somebody still owes us."

"My mission is to protect the embassy," the captain said slowly. "And I will not throw good lives after good lives." He said the words, but his face said something else. "Your Highness, what would you like to do next?"

"Captain, as happens so many times, I don't have a clue . . . at this specific moment. Let's look at what we have and see if it tells us anything."

"Be glad to, Your Highness. Where do we start?"

"First, I want to add one more person to our group, a police lieutenant by the name of Martinez. I have a right to ask him about my gun permit and there are a few things I'd like to get a straight answer to about things local."

The captain didn't look sold on bringing in a stranger, but, as Kris had come to notice, people found it hard to tell a Longknife, and a princess, no.

"If you think he has something important for us," he said.

"Won't know until I ask him, but this place is pretty strange, and you can never tell. Nelly, make the call. And if you can, make a search on Grant, or that other name . . . Shredder?"

"I can make a simple phone call and search my databases at the same time," Nelly snapped. "But I don't have to. I figured you would want to know about Grant and Shredder. I have already done that search, though I doubt you will like my results."

"Nelly, do you have tact in your database?" Kris asked.

"Yes. In my dictionary under T. But if you insist on insulting my capabilities, don't expect me to be Miss Sunshine."

"Note taken," Kris said, rolling her eyes as her team muffled laughs or raised eyebrows. "Now, about Mr. Grant."

"There are several hundreds in the database. All were available at the most basic level. None higher. Most have middle-class jobs and lives. If you want, I can download my findings and you can review them."

"No need to be snippy, Miss Nelly. And the other name."

"I assume Shredder got shredded by the drug-induced haze," Nelly said, and then paused.

"Good joke, gal," Kris said.

"Thank you, I am trying. I searched on various spellings of Schroder, with similar luck to Grant. Oh, Kris, Martinez can be here in five minutes. I told him to come right in."

"Good, Nelly, was there any Grant Schroder types."

"No, Kris."

"So whoever we're dealing with, he's bought himself out of every database on the planet," Kris said.

"Did you search the news archives?" Jack said.

"Searched all the mainstream media for a negative. Still working on the independent stuff. There's a lot of it."

"No surprise, there," Kris said. "If he can buy himself out of the databases, he's either very camera shy or able to make sure no reporter writes about him."

"Interesting guy," the captain observed.

"But he's with Vicky Peterwald," Penny pointed out. She'd come in late and been quiet. "Nelly, do a search of the social pages for both Vicky and this fellow."

"I searched the business, current events, and government areas," Nelly said. "Kris has never expressed much interest in the social whirl."

"I think I am now. And Vicky's only been here for a week or two. Maybe three. That should narrow the search frame."

"Mainstream is negative. Plenty about Vicky. Nothing about any escort."

"Anybody surprised?" Kris asked.

"I have a hit. The *Ankara Picayune*—what kind of a name is that—mentions that Miss Victoria was escorted by the noted 'philanthropic' Grant van Schrader. The philanthropic is in quotes. I suspect sarcasm. I am searching on Grant van-Schrader," Nelly said before Kris could tell her to.

In the silence of the room, Kris could almost hear every heartbeat quickening.

"Mainstream media has zip on our philanthropist. No business, no current events. He, or a Grant *von* Schrader does pop up in the small media. There was a strike at a software company. Every employee was fired. He was one of the people subpoenaed. That was squashed. There are other reports of him being involved in labor unrest. Buying property up cheap for development. Stealing patents. Courts always friendly. I don't like this guy, Kris."

"I suspect we don't, either. Is there anything that shows him as a Peterwald man?"

"Not until Vicky arrived."

"Does the Nuu Enterprises reports from Eden mention this joker?" Kris asked.

"Bingo, we hit the jackpot here," Nelly quickly reported. "They do not much like this fellow, either. He seems to be on the shabby side of a lot of stuff. Drugs are even mentioned. After getting uncertified parts from shops in his holding company, they are ignoring his bids. Which is not easy. His companies do quite a name shuffle. Buying each other, selling, renaming. A Nuu manager keeps track of this guy full-time."

"Get me his reports. Also, see if you can find who owns that warehouse where we found Ruth," Kris said.

"I was about to suggest that," Ruth said.

That did not turn out to be easy. The government's available property database was almost a year out of date and Mr. von Schrader seemed to sell his property on a much faster rotation. A database was available—for a very expensive fee—that was more up-to-date. Nelly bought it.

"Mr. Schrader owns several warehouses," Nelly reported. "Including that one. I have identified six that are as big."

Penny stood. "Captain, may I borrow those two Marines I had this morning. They're good at this skulking business."

"They're yours. Better take a different rig."

"And a few of my nanos," Nelly put in.

And Penny was off at a trot. She opened the door just in time to run into a rather surprised Police Lieutenant Martinez.

"I was told Princess Kris was here," he said, then noticed Kris and entered the room. Kris waved him to a chair. He took it, but had his eyes on the wall . . . and the pictures of dead Marines. "What have I walked in on?" he asked softly.

"Nothing your government need concern itself with," Kris said.

"I hope," Martinez added under his breath.

"Us, too," Jack appended.

"Are you aware," Kris asked, "that my great-grandmother Ruth Tordon was kidnapped this morning and two Marines killed?"

"I had heard it from some news sources," the policeman said. "I am happy to see you returned to your family," he added, nodding toward Ruth.

"I . . . am disturbed," Ruth said. "I have visited your planet many times. It is an enigma to me, but still I come back, hoping to teach something to your children. I doubt I will return again."

"My brother's youngest boy was one of your students. That will be a great loss for us."

"Will it?" Ruth said. "Am I really making any difference?"

"Steve thought you were, my nephew. You opened his eyes to what other planets have done. What we can do."

"As I recall, Steven Martinez told me he wanted to immigrate."

The policeman flinched, and eyed the table. "He has not told his family that."

"So, why don't you immigrate?" Kris said.

"This is my home."

"But you can't vote. Can't participate in your government."

"I am a police officer. I serve my government. I like to think that I make a difference."

"Have you heard about the contents of the warehouse where I was held captive?" Ruth asked.

"No. I had not heard you had escaped."

Kris turned to Captain DeVar. "Do we have pictures?"

A "Gunny," resulted in pictures appearing of the various boxed weapons. The cop rose from his chair and approached the screen on the wall. His hands traced the barrels and firing mechanisms of the machine pistols and assault rifles.

"Holy Mother of God," he whispered. "Does anyone else know about this weapons hoard?"

"There are quite a few police cruisers stopped outside the warehouse. I assume they're doing something about them."

"I should have been informed. Investigating illegal weapons is my job."

"I don't think Inspector Johnson thinks so," Kris said.

"Johnson." The cop almost spat. "I would have expected him to be at the bottom of something like this."

"Importing the guns?" Kris asked.

"No, making them disappear. Our third vice president is very much a believer that if a tree falls in the woods and no one hears it, then it did not happen. Johnson is his man."

"Well, this tree is down," Kris said. "I don't care about it, but I can't help but wonder if there are more trees getting ready to fall and who they'll fall on. You have any idea?"

Martinez just shook his head for a long time. "My poppa told me it would be like this. But who's going to listen to just a street cop. He told me the state was going rotten. And someday someone would come along and shove it over."

"That sounds like a good idea," Ruth said.

"Yes, but will the guy who pushes it over be any less rotten than the state? I know the state, as much as I'm allowed to know it. But what do I know about this other bunch?"

"So, is the devil you know," Jack said, "better than the devil that just walked in off the street?"

"That's our question," Kris said.

"And while I live here, I don't know much more about it than you do. Is this the only arms hoard?"

"We don't know," Kris said.

Martinez laughed bitterly. "I should know, but who's going to tell me."

The conversation might have ended on that point, but Kris did a quick survey of Jack and Captain DeVar, and chose to toss some more information on the fire.

"A friend of mine's dad was a cop. She's heading out in a few minutes to look over a few places we think just might have more guns. You want to go with her?"

"And do some real police work for a change?" the cop said.

Kris shrugged.

"Count me in. I'll call the office and sign for annual leave."

"And if they need you to look at any arms dump they find?" Jack asked.

"They know my mobile number. But I'm betting they won't call. Not me."

Jack left to connect Martinez with Penny. That left Kris staring at the pictures on the wall.

"You decided what you're going to do?" DeVar asked.

"Would it surprise you to know that I often make these things up as I go along?"

"What?" he said, shock in full fake. "You're human like the rest of us?"

"Oh so true. Well, at least one weapons dump is out of play," Kris said with a sigh.

"Are you sure?" Ruth said.

"The cops have it."

"And I bet every one of those cops is carrying something as deadly as what I'm lugging. How would they stand against a full assault team that wants those guns for their screaming hordes?"

"You think I made a mistake, Gramma? Not blowing it up."

"No, I think it looked like a good idea at the time. But keep an eye on it. It may not stay so good. Just keep an eye on that call."

"And everything else that isn't hidden," Kris sighed. "Did you have days like this, Gramma?"

"Days, months, years, Kris. Some of the best things I thought I'd ever done went sour on me. And some of the worst things turned out a whole lot better than I had any right to."

Kris leaned back in her chair, mulling that over for a while. "Are you telling me that even movers and shakers don't always get the moves and shakes they expected?"

Ruth grinned. "And a smart one learns to be grateful for the help."

Further reflection on that ended as Abby came in.

"The kids safe?" Kris asked.

"Cara's with her grandmum, so safe is not the word I'd use. Bronc had work he needed to do. Some gang hangs to sanitize."

"Does he know where his mom is?" Ruth asked.

"No, and doesn't want to. Not yet. He has a place he can crash for a few nights. He's no dumb kid. If he's survived this long in Five Corners, he couldn't be."

For a minute, they sat around the table, Kris and Abby, Ruth and Captain DeVar. Then Kris said, "Vacation over. Back to work. What do we know now that we didn't know yesterday?"

"I am noticing a pattern, Kris" came from around her neck.

"Talk to me, Nelly."

"The bugs at O'Heidi's place were the same as the bugs on those two gang gals. Same types. Apparently the same make, though I can't seem to match the manufacture's mark to any in known space."

"Eden strikes again," Jack said as he rejoined them.

"And the ones at the warehouse?" Kris said.

"I was getting to that. Similar design but more sophisticated. And no maker's marks."

"Isn't that illegal even on Eden?" Kris said.

"I do believe so," Ruth agreed.

"Any similarity between those and the chip in that autogun yesterday?" Jack asked as he rejoined them.

"No maker's mark on those units, but they use the same manufacturing methods. I found the same 'fingerprints' on them. They are likely from the same chip foundry."

"I'd really like to meet Grant von Schrader," Kris said.

"Kris, I cannot find any home address for him, in either our databases or the Nuu reports."

"So let's try a different approach," Kris muttered. "That monster limo Vicky is being showboated around in. Captain, did your social intel researchers notice anything about it?"

"I don't know. Gunny?"

A moment later a tech sergeant presented herself. "Betty, the princess here wonders if you found out anything about that limo Vicky Peterwald is using?" DeVar said.

"Let me check my computer, sir." It took only a minute. The screen on the wall began to flash with pictures of Vicky. Most were close-ups of her smiling self, boobs threatening to fall out of this dress or that, Kris noted.

One showed her walking away from her limo. "There's the plates for it, sir. Can that help you?"

"I will need to buy another expensive database." Nelly almost managed a sigh.

"Abby, this assignment is putting a major dent in even my monthly allowance," Kris said. "Could you put together a reimbursement voucher for Admiral Crossenshield?"

"I could, but don't bet on getting this much money out of that fussbudget."

"Maybe you can negotiate something halfway. The way things are going, I won't be able to afford to replace that dress you cut off me. Or give Nelly her quarterly upgrade."

"You better get something out of Crossie," Nelly said.

Betty and the captain managed to swallow any reaction to this insight into the finances of one of human space's wealthiest women. Or her computer's familiar view of the head of Ward-haven's intelligence community. Gunny just scowled.

A moment later Nelly had the number of Prestige Travel.

"Kris, what are you going to do?" Jack asked with alarm.

"Why don't you watch and see? Nelly, get ready to tap a phone line."

"If I can," Nelly replied quickly.

"Now make the call."

A moment later, "Prestige Travel. We get you there in comfort and awe."

"Oh, good. I hear tell you have this huge white limo," Kris said, dripping hayseeds with every word. "The hugest on this here planet."

"Ah, yes we do." The agent's reply was carefully balanced, neither to inspire a penniless hick to go on, nor to frighten off a hick that had a lot of money she needed separating from.

"Well, this is Print-cess Kristine Longknife from Ward-haven way. I'd like to rent that showboat of yours. I got some-place to be tonight and I'm tired of showing up second best."

"Let me see what we can do about that, Your Highness. Can I call you back in just a second?"

"A second, maybe. A minute and I'll be talking to someone about having my own limo built."

"Yes, ma'am. Er, Your Highness. I'll be right back," and the call ended.

"I didn't know you had a hillbilly voice," Jack said. "Do you really think this guy is dumb enough to fall for it?"

"So far he's over the side and headed down," Kris said through a grin. "I don't think that fellow has any idea who I am and everyone here seemed to expect some kind of redneck from the Rim. So, let's see what happens when I give 'em one."

"Kris, he's calling a number. It's another one of those nine-oh-nine numbers that don't exist."

Kris didn't like that.

"Oh happy days," Nelly almost shouted. "He didn't pay for all that much encryption. I have him."

"Al, Al" came from Nelly in the Prestige Travel man's

voice. "Your tub hasn't moved all afternoon. I thought that brat wanted to go places."

"She was right here, then suddenly, her bodyguard grabbed her and hustled her back in the house and I ain't heard a squeak from them all afternoon. So I'm just sitting here watching the flowers grow at this place. And boy do they got flowers."

NELLY, CAN YOU GET A LOCATION ON THE PHONE RECEIVING THIS?

I CAN AND DO HAVE IT.

On the wall screen, a map replaced Vicky's smiling face. The flashing green dot was far out on the outskirts of town in a gated area of large twenty-acre plots.

"Well, at least we know that much," Captain DeVar said.

That call ended and a second call opened, but not to the same area. This one managed to avoid giving out its location. It turned out the limo was no longer needed and would be available for the evening.

And Kris got rung back.

"Abby, I'm going to turn this over for you to negotiate. Are we going anywhere tonight?"

"Not so far. No one seems interested in your gorgeous presence after that art show."

"Gee, I wonder why?" Jack said.

"Try to rent the limo for tomorrow," Kris said, and took the incoming call. "Howdy, I'm so glad you called back. Let my personal assistant take it from here." Kris waved at Abby.

"Abby Nightingale, how may I help you?" came as smooth as honey. "Ah, yes, the princess does occasionally make calls herself. It causes us no end of trouble."

Kris scrunched up a face at Abby and might have thrown something, but nothing was handy.

"Oh dear, I'm afraid my employer is a mite bit addled where dates are concerned. That party is tomorrow night. She's going to spend a quiet night drinking at home tonight."

Now Kris would have thrown something.

"Very well. Send me the contract and I will return it with a payment voucher. Always glad to do business with a professional." And the call ended.

"Here's hoping we have somewhere to go tomorrow," Abby said.

38

While the problem of what to do with a limo tomorrow night hung ignored in the air, matters for today continued.

Penny reported that the first three warehouses they looked at had only normal security, and apparently just normal contents. They had three more to check.

Abby, with Sergeant Bruce tagging along to supervise a Marine tech, was dispatched to see how close they could get to Mr. von Schrader's apparent residence and examine it as best they could. Nelly sent them off with several of her best experimental probes.

Which left Kris with nothing better to do than immerse herself in the Nuu report on this fellow. She didn't find anything she liked.

"Where did this guy come from?" she said, surfacing a half hour later. "Ten years ago he shows up, loaded with money and starts buying up distressed companies, doing some kind of a hack job on them, then selling off the profitable parts and dumping the rest. Or not."

"What do you mean?" Captain DeVar said, looking over her shoulder.

"My Grandfather Al would be laughing his head off at me," Kris said. "He's the moneybags in the family. He keeps wanting me to ditch the Navy and go into his business."

"Might be safer," the Marine noted.

"But where's the fun in that," Jack said before Kris could. She scowled at him, but he kept grinning.

"Anyway, I took enough business courses and interned a few summers with Grampa Al when there wasn't a pressing election to worry about, so I do have some kind of head for business."

"And what does it tell you that this blind Marine isn't noticing?" Captain DeVar asked again.

"Take this small electronics company," Kris said, calling up a page she'd marked. "It was undercapitalized and losing money when he bought it. It needed to be folded into a larger company with access to more tools, more contracts. He closed down this software unit, sold the game design part of it to a competitor, but he kept the tiny chip foundry going."

"Chip foundry?" Captain DeVar's eyes lit up.

"Yep, a small boutique chip-printing shop. Hold it, Nelly, isn't that the firm where he closed down the union and fired the entire workforce?"

"The name is the same, but my report said it was a software company," Nelly said.

"There was a software portion, but Nuu says there was also this specialized chip section. But if he fired the entire workforce, who kept the thing going?"

"I guess a new staff," Jack said thoughtfully. "Maybe one that wouldn't ask the boss why he needed a unique chip?"

"Looks like that," Kris said. "But that doesn't answer any of my questions. Where did the Grant fellow come from? Who gave him start-up funds?"

"He came from Earth," Nelly said. "Or at least that is what it says in the records of his acquiring his residence."

"You can get your hands on that?" Jack said.

"The plot ownership files are not up-do-date," Nelly said, almost with an audible sniff, "but he did buy his place eight years ago. You can only stall a file clerk so long."

"So he came from Earth," Kris said, not at all convinced.

"*I* said that was what *he* said," Nelly answered, "but I have the citizen rolls from Earth in my permanent data storage and he does not show up on any of them."

"So he's not from Earth," Jack said.

"That may or may not be true," Kris said. "Some regions of Earth aren't all that careful about entering all their citizens on the rolls. If you're a taxpayer, you're on the list, but if you're not paying taxes and haven't registered to vote they get slipshod. At least a college friend I had from Earth said so."

"But where would a mere citizen get start-up money like this fellow was throwing around?" Gramma Ruth asked.

"Any other planet and I'd have Nelly go into the bank records and follow it back."

"Not on Eden," Ruth pointed out.

"Should I buy the bank records datafile that I was offered," Nelly asked.

"The ones where you don't get to see what's in them until you've paid for them?" Kris said.

"And having bought them, shown someone that you are a dumb enough optimist to think they might help you?" Gramma added.

"There is that. It could just be a trap," Jack said.

"Let's put that off for a while," Kris concluded.

And then Abby called in.

"Kris, Cedar Estates is not a gated community," began the maid's recon report.

"That's nice to hear," Jack said.

"It's more like a walled-and-moated fortress. I make the stone wall to be five, six meters high, with wire at the top, probably electrified. Cameras at regular intervals, and guys in pairs walking the outside."

"Real friendly, huh?" Kris said.

"Don't know, I ain't about to stop and chat up one. I tried sending a couple of scouts over the wall. None got more than fifty feet inside. I haven't tried any of Nelly's specials. Not sure I want to give them away."

"I think she might be right," Jack said. Kris nodded, along with Gramma Ruth.

"Let's keep some powder dry," Kris said.

"I'm going to drive around the place, as much as I can, see if it gets any easier. Kind of looking forward to a nice drive in the country with Bruce here." It actually sounded like a smile might be attached to that statement.

"Be careful. Don't stay gone too long," Kris said, and cut the link. "No surprise. Grant von Schrader likes his privacy."

Jack nodded, then rotated his shoulders, his mouth tight against the pain. "While we wait for Penny to report in, you mind if I do another soak in your tub?" he asked Kris.

"Only if you don't mind sharing it," Kris said, realizing that she was due for more pain meds and another soak might let her get by on less."

"I think I still have my lifeguard certificate," Gramma Ruth said. "I'll keep an eye on you two. Call for Doc if things get out of hand."

"You going to be a duenna? Slap him down if he tries to kiss me?" Kris said.

Jack gave her an ugly face, but it was too much fun teasing him at the moment for her to feel too penitent. Then she stood and stretched . . . as gently as she could. It still hurt.

"Slap him? Lordy no, Miss Longknife. Remember me. I want"—and here Gramma Ruth held up her fingers and counted them off—"great, great, great, however many great-grandkids. You two start misbehaving and I'll hitch up my skirt and run, cackling, for the door."

Now it was Jack's turn to stand slowly and very carefully stretch. He winced at the pain. "I think your honor is safe with me. At least for the moment, Your Highness."

Captain DeVar shook his head. Whether at this verbal tripping of the line of fraternizing or some failure of Jack to uphold the masculine tradition of the Corps, he said not.

Kris was just getting comfortable in the tub when Nelly spoke up from the dressing table where Kris had left her. "Call coming in from Penny."

Gramma Ruth had taken one look at the string bikini that

Abby had left for Kris and whistled. "I'm not sure that's better than nothing." But she helped Kris into it and into the tub before Jack arrived.

He had gotten a soft whistle from Kris's gramma. Whether for the fine-looking man that he was or for all the pretty black and blue, yellow and brown that he sported, she said not.

And Kris was just starting to feel the knots of pain unwind when duty called.

"Yes, Penny?"

"Is that you?" Penny seemed to shout back. "I can't hear you over all the background noise. What's going on?"

Ruth killed the jets.

"Oh, that's better. We're at the last of the warehouses. It's wide open. Also empty. Someone got here before us and cleaned it out."

"Any leads about what was in there and where it went?"

"I've got scouts covering the place, and my woman Marine volunteered to do a physical look around. She figured she could talk her way out of trouble better than her hardcase friend could shoot his way out."

That produced some reply in the background, but Kris ignored it.

"I think we better assume that this is a dead end," Penny said. "And someone got away with a lot of revolution in a box."

"I'm afraid you're right," Kris concluded. "We are running into a lot of dead ends at the moment. See if you can find anything, then come back."

"Will do, Kris." And Penny rung off.

"So no luck there," Ruth said.

"You know, with the jets off, there's a lot of you to see," Jack said.

Kris glanced down. The water was amazingly clear.

"Gramma, would you please turn the jets back on."

"I don't know. If I want those grandkids, maybe I should hightail it for the door."

Kris reached out. It was a stretch, and it hurt, but she could reach the jets. She hammered hard on the plunger, and the jets once again filled the water with bubbles that cut visibility to nothing.

"Oh, darn," Jack said. "Haven't seen that much of you since, what, Turantic?"

"Oh, you must tell me about Turantic," Gramma Ruth cooed.

"You must not," Kris said dryly.

So they lounged in the hot tub for several long minutes. Kris tried working her muscles. At least in the warmth of the water, they didn't hurt the way they did normally. Jack moved in the same slow way, stretching, pushing, trying to make muscles that didn't want to move obey his bidding.

It went on that way for what seemed like forever.

Then Nelly spoke up again.

"Kris, Abby is calling. She's very agitated."

"Gramma, kill the jets," Kris said. "Abby talk to us."

"I just got a call from Cara," Abby said, and her voice was replaced by the young woman's. "Bronc's gone. A guy we both know on the street said he left with Mick and Trang and a couple of gang heaters. I tried to call him, but found he'd left a message on my phone."

Now the girl's voice was replaced by static. Then Bronc's voice came through in a whisper. "They're going to kill them all. Tell . . ."

39

Jack was out of the tub without a backward glance.

Gramma Ruth helped Kris out, dried her off, and got her dressed again in whites. Nelly passed along the call to Captain DeVar; he immediately began assembling the Tac team.

"I'll have the two Marines who took Bronc's mom to hiding bring Cara in. We need to know what she knows," he said.

Fifteen minutes later the Tac Center was full when Kris marched in, Jack to one side, Gramma Ruth on the other. She was about to take her seat at the head of a full table when Nelly said, "Kris, you have a call from the ambassador's secretary."

Kris rolled her eyes at the overhead. "I'll take it." She paused, and then added, "Can we make this quick?"

"Why? You don't ever seem to be doing much of anything," the young man answered. Now the whole room rolled their eyes.

"It has come to my attention that you have not acknowledged your invitation to the presidential reception tomorrow evening. I assume you are going."

"Tomorrow evening," Kris answered slowly.

"It was sent out over a week ago. You did not reply."

"I don't think I got it."

"Or that computer of yours lost it."

I DID NOT LOSE IT!

DOWN, NELLY.

"I'm sure the invitation will turn up somewhere. Tell me about this reception," Kris said.

"Just *everybody* who is *anybody* will be there. You'll meet the president, the vice presidents, and most of the senate. Don't expect to say much to them. It's a cattle call. You go down the reception line, smile, say a word or two, and get passed on to the next. Lots of fast pressing of the flesh. You know how it goes."

"And it's tomorrow night," Kris said, eyeing Captain DeVar. He nodded. Faces around the table got grim.

"I said it was."

"Where?"

"The National Gallery of the Arts. Lovely place. Modeled after some Earth place, the Versailles Palace I think."

Captain DeVar messed with his battle board. A map appeared on the wall. A huge building surrounded by gardens and lush trees appeared. He zoomed out, and Kris saw it was several miles from the embassy, along a riverfront.

"Yes," Kris said, "you may tell the ambassador that I will be glad to represent Wardhaven at the reception."

"Good. He expects to be your escort. I'll tell him you'll be ready early. Say seven o'clock."

"I'll talk to my maid about that," Kris said.

Kris waited until the commlink clicked off. "Is the line broken, Nelly?"

"As broken as I can make it."

"Everyone will be there," Kris said slowly.

Abby nodded. "Bronc says they're going to kill them all."

"And I wondered what I was going to be doing with that huge limo tomorrow night," Kris said, letting a tight smile free to play on her lips. "Captain DeVar, shall we look at the security problems that huge, drafty place must have."

Instead, the wall screens' map was replaced by . . . a sailing schedule from High Eden.

Captain DeVar stood, and cleared his throat. "Before we do our best to do something well, may we first consider if we should do it at all."

"Thank you," Jack said.

"What do you mean, Captain?" Kris said, not sure whether to scowl or just sigh at this turn of events.

"Your Highness," DeVar started off respectfully. "My responsibilities are to assure the safety of the embassy and its personnel. The lieutenant, here, is supposed to specifically see that you keep on breathing, right?"

"I'm supposed to try," Jack said, grinning from ear to ear.

"Therefore, I must ask," the Marine captain went on, "if it wouldn't be best if we got you out of Dodge? Fast! *The Great Panda Maru* seals locks in four hours, twenty, ah, two minutes. I may just be a dumb Marine, but it seems to me that the best way for us to assure you stay not dead would be to have you on that ship. Quarters ain't luxurious, but it is headed for Yamato and you could catch a liner for Wardhaven."

He paused. "I am merely offering this for discussion." And he sat down.

Sometime during that spiel, Penny had come in. She took her spot at the table. Police Lieutenant Martinez took a chair along the wall.

Kris found herself standing alone in a terrible silence. A quick glance around the table showed a clear majority. No, a vast majority for the captain's proposal.

Kris would have to avoid putting it to a vote.

She chose to break the tension with a laugh. All she managed was a tiny one, but it was a laugh, and it drew quizzical looks from her audience.

"Sorry, but you see every time I get into one of these deadly messes, everybody wants me to go away. Get out of the line of fire. Captain, you planning on coming along with me?"

"No ma'am."

"You going to load the whole Marine company on the *Panda* with me?"

"Definitely not."

"So, dangerous as it may be, you're going to do your job?"

"Yes, ma'am."

No surprise to Kris, none of the Marine techs or support staff in the Tac Center seemed at all bothered by that. A couple of them sported wolfish grins at the prospects.

"So, what is my job?" Kris asked.

"Buy paper clips and other odds and ends," Abby drawled.

"Yeah, right," Kris drawled right back.

Kris paused for a moment to let that work its way through thick skulls, like Jack's and DeVar's. "King Ray sent me here for a reason. That reason had nothing to do with paper clips. But as is Ray Longknife's bad habit, he didn't tell me what the real reason was, did he, Penny?"

"He never does," the intel officer said.

"He never does," Kris reinforced for the slow thinkers at the table. "He has a Longknife-size problem so he sends a Longknife out to solve it, but old Ray never does bother to let me know anything."

"One revolution, one Longknife," Gramma Ruth said dryly. "Even odds."

"That, my friends, is one of the bad things I'm discovering about being a Longknife. Doesn't make it into the history books, but it's a fact, big as any in the books. Any of you doubt it?"

No one said a word.

"Okay, so let's see. Anyone here really think King Ray sent me here to grab the first ship out at the first peep of trouble?"

The people around the table glanced at one another. Kris locked eyes with Captain DeVar. The Marine blinked first.

"I felt obliged to offer that out, Your Highness."

"Understandable," Kris said. "Gramma Ruth, you want to be on that boat?"

"Oh, my, no. I'm not quite as spry as I used to be, but I think the old girl has a few more good days in her."

"Have you kept your reserve commission on the shelf?"

"No way, honey. It's active," the old gal said with a proud grin. "At my age, they don't seem to think it matters whether it's active or inactive. You'd think that my dear Terrence would have shown them the error of their ways."

"Commander?" Kris asked.

"At your service," the Iteeche vet said with a slight bow.

"So that's settled," Kris said, eyeing DeVar.

He replied with a grin and a nod.

"Okay, it's agreed who will be doing something to someone. Before we go on to how we will be doing it, let's follow the captain's well-ordered process and examine if we should be doing anything at all," Kris said.

That got puzzled looks around the table.

"Clearly that wasn't the most logical thing I've ever said, so let's take a second try. I can develop a cold. We could slash the tires on the ambassador's limo. Simply put, there is no reason to involve Wardhaven in what is about to go down on Eden.

"Yes, I believe a Peterwald is at the bottom of this, but my proof hangs on Vicky showing up at the right time. This Grant von Schrader has managed to do whatever it is he's doing without any visible ties back to Henry Peterwald.

"So, Police Lieutenant Martinez," Kris said, turning to the local man. "Are you briefed on what we think is going down?"

"Penny told me. And call me Juan."

"Thank you, Juan. Do you have any objections to someone massacring these politicians you aren't permitted to vote for?"

The man stayed in his seat, quiet for a long minute, then he stood. "They tell us we are second-class citizens. We cannot vote. We cannot run for elected office," he said, raising his right hand and looking searchingly at the palm.

"Yet"—now his left hand came up—"I am a police officer, sworn to protect this government I cannot elect. I, and my father before me, found this kind of funny.

"But we didn't laugh. The ones we did laugh at were those who had the vote and sat out elections. Now there be fools."

He let his hands fall to his sides. "My grandfather used to say that you are only powerless if you say you are. If you accept that you are."

Juan pursed his lips, then went on. "They say that people like me cannot run for office or vote for anyone. Yet we often decide who will be on the ballot."

Kris raised an eyebrow at that. Juan grinned.

"I know a big man. Big, empty man. He sees himself in the senate someday. But there are five of us cops who have busted him for driving drunk. Five times the fool got behind the wheel and endangered those on the road. If he tries to run, I will talk quietly to one of the small media outlets that cater to me and my people. They will publish a story. A story that will be too hot not to be picked up by the mainstreams. And that man's expectations of high political office will vanish like the wind.

"They are right. I cannot run or elect my government. But I can keep someone out of the government. There is power in that.

"Are the men someone has condemned to death mine? Maybe not, but at least they are not theirs. So, Princess Kristine, in the name of all of us who have no voice, may I ask you to shout for us, even at the risk of your life."

Juan paused, then an evil smile swept his face. "And who knows? Maybe this time there will be enough reports. Enough reporters with balls, to tell what actually happens. Maybe some reporter standing around will get the story straight." He paused. "But nothing must risk the security of what you do."

"Security must be kept," Kris growled. "Surprise is all we have going for us."

"So, Princess, what will you have me do? Stay here where I can only listen to you, or let me go to find enough honest cops to back you up when you need it?"

"Juan, what do you have in mind?"

The man laughed at the joy of the question. "First, there is that warehouse full of arms. The cops guarding it could hardly hold it against a determined assault."

"That is something Gramma Ruth worries about," Kris said.

"Then let me get a few of my friends there. Maybe arm themselves from what they are protecting. That should turn an easily plucked pomegranate into a prickly cactus.

"And if I can get enough men rotated through that warehouse, I may have something like a SWAT team. I've read about them in the literature. It would be nice to have one. We cops do not like that the security hacks have all the automatic weapons and we walk beats with just a revolver or nightstick. I can show this government many eager young men ready to fight for it. And who deserve something better from it."

"Captain," Kris said, "you mind releasing the lieutenant?"

"Unity of command is something we're supposed to strive for, but it looks to me like if we keep Juan here, he might not be able to round up a command. Good luck, Lieutenant. Hopefully, we'll see you when we need you."

"Penny told me that we may not be able to count on our communications when time comes."

"Somebody does seem to have a very good jammer," Kris said.

"Then my caballeros may have to ride for the sound of the guns." The lieutenant tossed the captain a salute and left.

"Gramma, were things this bad fighting the Iteeche. I know the history books make it—"

"You know where you can stuff the history books," Ruth interrupted. "Kris, I'm afraid it never gets better. Only worse."

Kris walked over to the map of the National Gallery of the Arts. "So, how do we defend this thing?"

"More likely, how do we attack this thing while someone else is attacking it?" Captain DeVar offered as a slight correction.

"This could get awfully confusing," Penny said.

"Confusing even for a place like Eden," Abby added.

40

Most of Kris's team had missed lunch, so they broke for supper early. Kris found herself collecting a tray when Lieutenant Commander Malhoney appeared at her elbow.

"I understand there's a command performance at the Art Gallery tomorrow night," he said.

"So I'm told," Kris admitted.

"You'll need an escort. Your Marine here may be, ah, busy elsewhere," he said with a slight cough. "I'd like to offer my arm for your official use."

Kris frowned at the commander; no one would ever mistake him for a line beast. Still, he had been out every morning of late jogging along behind the Marines. His claim to have the biggest belly in the Wardhaven Navy was no longer true. Still.

"Tomorrow night might not be the best time," Kris said.

"Yes, I've heard that scuttlebutt. I've been practicing with my service automatic at the Marine indoor range. The sergeant rates my shooting as 'not half bad.' "

Kris raised an eyebrow. "Not half bad" might not be nearly good enough for tomorrow night. "The ambassador says he wants to squire me around." Kris offered him an out, but waved him into line with her. The double doors to the mess hall were wide open; anyone could pass by and overhear this.

He took the place she offered, and reached past her for a tray. "But if we make it an all Navy affair," the commander said, "he can't really complain. I may not be all that much better than Sammy, but I'll know when to duck and how to stay out of your line of fire. If you have to take care of him, it might just cost you the second you don't have."

Kris went down the steam table, serving herself or taking what was handed to her. What was it about a Longknife? Let one of them charge into harms way and everyone seemed to stand in line to be a target with them. Or step in front of them.

No, that wasn't quite right. Her brother or father didn't get folks into a battle line. Kris did.

And she did it by being there, first in line.

"Jack, you have an opinion?"

"It would be better if I could freelance myself tomorrow rather than being tied to your arm." Captain DeVar would lead the external contingent, the Marines in full-battle armor standing ready to charge to the rescue.

"You really want to do this?" Kris asked.

The commander paused, then sucked up his gut and launched himself into his future . . . or lack of one. "Your Highness, I haven't exactly had a brilliant career in this man's Navy." He snorted. "If things hadn't gotten as tough as they are just now, I would have been shown the door four, five years ago. I've done my job. Good, never great. But then, none of the jobs really needed much doing. Who would send me to do something really important?" he spat out.

"I know who I am. And I can't say that I like it much. Tomorrow, maybe I'll get myself killed doing the job I'm asking for. And I'll just be doing what little bit I can so that better men than me can do what they do best. But you'll be better off with a shooter at your elbow than with a nothing.

"And who knows, maybe someone will take an extra second deciding whether to shoot me rather than you . . . and give you the second you need to survive."

"Abby, do we have spider-silk underwear we can spare the commander?"

Abby shook her head from where she stood behind Jack. "I'm sorry, sir. Your Highness. I don't have anything in the commander's size."

The man half chuckled. "Why don't I find that surprising? And no, my fancy dress mess uniform isn't armored, like the Marine here," he said, nodding at Jack.

"It's not safe being around a Longknife without body armor," Jack said.

"I didn't ask for safe. I asked for a chance to get a few shots off."

Kris looked at her tray, full and ready to be taken to a table. She picked it up, turned, and found a table just emptying, as if waiting for her and hers.

What should she do with the commander? She pondered that as she made her way to her seat.

She'd sworn she would lead no more children's crusades. Yet everything she was doing today, tomorrow, turned on the curt message Bronc had sent. At what risk?

But the commander was no child. He might sound like some cockeyed optimist, but it wasn't because he didn't know the odds. He'd served in the uniform that barely fit him for almost twenty years. No, he'd looked the risk in the eye and despite the obviously terrible odds, was asking Kris for a chance to earn his pay. His pay for tomorrow . . . and for quite a few years when no one had given him credit for earning a dime.

"Commander, why don't you sit with us? I'd be honored to have you escort me to the reception."

And the worried lines on the commander's face were replaced by a happy smile.

Would he still be smiling when they buried him?

The table talk that night at the unsecured wardroom tables was subdued, but seemed to center on how to armor up formal dress uniforms.

* * *

Bronc did his best to stand at attention in front of the one they all called the colonel. Still, his knees were shaking, barely holding him up.

"I'm told you have a very fancy and new computer," the colonel told Bronc, then glanced at the sergeant who'd been working with Bronc and Mick and Trang.

"Ya, yes, sir, sir. An old lady gave it to me, sir." Bronc tried not to stammer, and failed miserably.

"And why did she give this nice toy to you?"

"Ah, sir, she asked me, ah, what I wanted and I told her, sir. Then, ah, she, she told me what she wanted, sir." This time he did stammer and hoped he was turning beet red.

The colonel actually smiled. "I hope you had fun, boy."

"I think I did, sir," Bronc answered. That got him a laugh from both soldiers.

Of course, what Abby really did was tell him to stay clear of Longknifes. At the moment, Bronc really wished he had.

"How good is that antique he's got?" the colonel asked.

"Surprisingly good, Colonel, compared with the crap those other two dunderheads brought. He still had the receipt from a local computer store in his pocket. His story checks out. No doubt he earned his pay."

Both men chuckled at that. Bronc could feel himself going hot in the face again.

"How old are you, boy?" the commander asked.

"Fourteen, sir. Almost fifteen."

"Do you know how to use that computer?"

"Yes, sir. Ah, no, sir. I mean, I'm learning to use it."

The colonel frowned, but the sergeant stepped in. "The two young fools that have been teaching him don't know how to use half of what they've got. I think the kid's got what it takes. Let me work with him for a day and I'll let you know for sure."

"We may not have a day," the colonel growled. "Young man, these are momentous times for Eden. A new day is coming. Bright people like you will find that the sky is the limit if you play your cards right. Are you a card player?"

"Na, no, sir," Bronc said, then quickly added softly. "I never had the money, sir."

"Stick with us and you'll have that money. Sergeant, do what you need to do, but get me what I have to have."

Bronc followed the sergeant out of the colonel's tiny command center. It was little more than a tent with loads of computers. Real ones, ones like Bronc had only heard about.

Only after he was halfway back to the shelter he shared with Mick and Trang, did Bronc breathe easy. The last couple of guys who had been taken up to see the colonel had not returned. Rumor was their bodies had been dumped behind the rifle range.

Bronc hadn't been trained to use a rifle, so he didn't even know where the range was. And he didn't want to know.

He had managed to get a message off to Cara when he picked up the talk that they were going to kill everyone.

He still didn't know who the everyone was, nor did he know a where for the killing.

From what the colonel said, the when must be getting close. The who that would be do the killing was pretty clear. Scores of men walked around the camp with long rifles or short machine pistols slung in front of them.

Bronc so wanted to get another note off to Cara, but knew better than to even think of it. He was getting music on his new computer in areas he had no idea how to interpret. This place had electronic security like he'd never dreamed of.

No question, Abby and the chief had given him a whole lot more computer than he knew how to use.

Maybe, if he listened to it, he'd manage to stay alive.

41

Kris slept amazingly well that night, and was halfway through her morning jog with the Marines when Nelly ruined her day.

"Inspector Johnson just took an encrypted call from someone. He is parked in front of the embassy."

Kris considered dropping out of the morning run, then decided that the good inspector could just wait. In the fullness of time, a Marine company in full-battle rattle, trailed by a platoon of very sweaty sailors, double-timed up to the embassy's front door.

Kris fell out when Gunny gave the order. While the Marines trotted off to quarters, Kris and her team, with Captain DeVar at their elbow, turned to face the inspector.

"It still looks like you're ready to invade my planet," the inspector started off. So much for small talk.

"My orders are strictly defensive," Captain DeVar said, when Kris tossed him the question with a nod of her head.

"Though you could hardly do worse with his Marines than you're doing by yourself," Penny added.

That drew a frown from the local cop. He fixed Kris with a stare. "What do you know?"

"Good Morning, Inspector, and a fine one your planet is offering us, isn't it," Kris said, insisting on some friendly chit-chat before the heavy stuff.

"I wouldn't know about the morning. I didn't sleep much last night."

"Get to the bottom of all your boxes?" Kris asked, cheerily.

"No. And now I have all kinds of people arguing over jurisdiction." He snorted. "Some of them I didn't think were even supposed to know about the boxes. Do I owe you for that?"

Kris shrugged. "Eden is very good about keeping its secrets, Inspector. Very good except when it is very bad. Doesn't seem to be anywhere in the middle."

The inspector turned and walked across the broad driveway of the embassy. Kris followed, her crew on sniper lookout.

In the middle of the parking lot, he turned on her and whispered. "I need to know what you know."

Kris nodded . . . and gave him an accurate answer that probably had nothing to do with his question. "Eden is going to have to change. The corruption, the secrecy, the marginalizing of some of your best can't go on."

"Says you, and anyone who isn't a complete fool," snapped the inspector. "You have a penny solution or have you invested a whole dime in the problem of making it happen?"

Kris shrugged, not at all surprised by his reaction. "I'm just a tourist giving you my observation. The status quo on Eden has very little time left. Eden will either change itself or be changed by those who don't care a fig for her."

"Thanks for your helpful advice," the inspector growled and looked ready to storm away.

And Kris chose to gamble that he was as sincere as his voice had been. "They plan to kill everyone," she said.

The inspector stopped before his second stomp and whirled back to face Kris. "Who is going to kill all of who?"

"I don't know."

"Can't you get back to your source?"

"What was sent to us was sent at great personal risk. No, I am not going to demand more."

"You trust this source?"

"I have no reason not to."

"That's an interesting conclusion from someone who's been on the planet less than a month."

"Take it as you will."

"*They* are going to kill *everyone*," the inspector repeated.

"Whoever the 'they' are and whoever the 'everyone' are. Assuming the 'they' can pull it off."

"When?"

"Your guess is as good as mine, Inspector."

He shook his head and began pacing. "There is no way that any 'they' can kill 'everyone.'"

Kris eyed the inspector. The answer to that question had slapped her in the face only moments after the intel. How could the inspector not see what she saw?

"I've been invited to a reception this evening. I'm told everyone who is anyone will be there," she said slowly.

Inspector Johnson glanced up from his pacing. "Yes, the reception at the National Gallery of the Arts. I know about that."

"Everyone who is anyone?" Kris repeated.

He shook his head forcefully. "Not a chance. Vice President McLyndon had me review security on the place. It will be airtight. That's why we use the Gallery for those things. The actual building is solid stone. The gardens and arboretum around it give us open kill fields. You're as safe there as in your mother's arms."

Did the inspector know just how much Kris did not care for that imagery?

"I can't tell you how glad that makes me feel," Kris said, pouring as much sarcasm as she could manage into "glad."

"Trust me, you don't have anything to worry about tonight."

Kris glanced at Jack and DeVar. Between them they'd come up with dozens of lines of assault on that big stone hulk. Did

Johnson know something they didn't? Or was he totally unable to weigh the power of a modern assault team against it?

At her father's knee, Kris had learned that there are none so blind as those with eyes but unwilling to see. By high school, Kris had her own way of putting it: There was no way to solve a problem for people who didn't know they had one.

Clearly, Inspector Johnson was a man with a problem that he wanted Kris to help him solve. But the National Gallery was *not* that problem.

Maybe he was right.

Kris shrugged and said, "Thank you. I feel so much better about tonight already," and almost made it sound sincere.

"You have any other ideas?"

Kris glanced at her team. They slowly shook their heads.

"Well, you let me know if you have any other information. Maybe your source is wrong about that 'killing everyone.'"

"Maybe," Kris said. "You find any more weapons dumps?"

"No. Maybe that was the only one. I think we've put a solid stop on that. Maybe we're already on the downward slope of this crisis. Who knows?"

"Optimists have fewer ulcers," Penny said.

"Pessimists live longer," Jack said softly as the inspector drove away.

"Captain, better have your tech team go over the approaches to the Gallery as soon as possible. Use Nelly's best scouts. We can't afford to have you run into good guys in your approach march."

"Blue on blue is truly a waste of good effort," Captain De-Var agreed.

"So, now you feeling better about tonight," Penny said with a grin.

"I sure do," Kris answered. "My stomach's down to less than a hundred flip-flops per minute.

42

Kris waited until almost seven to call the ambassador. And did it from her tub as Abby poured water over her head.

"Mr. Ambassador, I think you're going to have to leave without me. I'm running late." Her statement was not quite drowned out by a sprayer working soap suds out of her hair.

"How will you get to the reception if I leave you?" He didn't sound all that worried. Kris had never been told why Sammy wanted to leave a full two hours early, but she suspected this might be the height of his social season.

Apparently, even Wardhaven's ambassador didn't get to see the real power on Eden all that often. That was something she ought to mention to Father when next they met.

"Oh, don't worry. I rented that love boat that Vicky Peterwald has been riding around in for the last week or more. This time I'm showing up in the biggest limo."

"So long as you're paying for it" came through the line just before it went dead.

"Was that too easy?" Kris asked Abby.

"Baby ducks, I hope this don't come as too painful a reve-
lation, but I don't think that man likes you."

Kris modeled wide-eyed shock. "You think so!"

And got soap in her eyes for the dramatics.

"Hey, you're supposed to be looking after my safety," Kris
sputtered as she wiped her eyes.

"Honey, how can you talk safety with you going where
you're going."

Which kind of let all the funny out of the situation.

"There is that," Kris said soberly and stood to dry herself
off. Pulling on her new spider-silk bodysuit, Kris found herself remembering how the last one had earned its retirement.
The black-and-blue places were still on her leg and belly, covered now by a layer of tanning cream.

The bra Abby handed Kris had extra room in it. "Be careful how you use these, they're high explosives," Abby said, as
she slipped the inserts in.

Suddenly Kris had boobs. Boobs she knew all too well how
to make go boom.

The girdle was reinforced with ceramics. This gave Kris a
bit of a rear, though not one man gave a second glance.

Abby must have read Kris's mind. "Don't worry. Tonight,
you'll have buns."

"You're padding my rear?"

"What do you think of this dress?" Abby asked as she
slipped it over Kris's head.

"It's different," Kris agreed. Most of Kris's dresses had a
narrow waist, then flounced out to leave the illusion of hips.
That also left Kris with plenty of room to hide the odd
grenade among her crinolines.

Tonight's dress was a sparkly gray affair that fit her like a
second skin.

Except where it grew suddenly thick. Which it did around
her butt. "What have you got there? More armor?"

"Nope, baby cakes, offense, ma'am, offense. Feel around.
See what opens up."

Kris brushed her hand over her bottom and found extra

thickness. She worked her hand over it a bit slower and found a pocket opening up.

From said pocket she pulled a . . . something. It was square and thin and invited her to toss it like a Frisbee.

"The gray ones are all whizbangs. Flash, smoke, and noise," Abby said. "Depress the bump in the center of it and it's armed. Five-second delay. Turn it right for a four second. Left for a three second."

Kris eyed the device. Clearly this was not something she'd find in any Marine armory. Then again, few Marines were trained to close and engage the enemy on the dance floor.

"The next row on your butt are green and carry disabling gas. I've included a filter in your purse," Abby said.

Kris felt and found there was a second row. And a third row.

"Last row is more of the whizbangs."

Abby worked Kris's head into a wig with long, cascading blond curls to hide her automatic, then placed a lovely tiara to top it all. Not the usual Navy one, but a filigree confection that served better as an antenna for Nelly's search routines.

Being made of Smart Metal, the crown also afforded Nelly more raw material if she found herself needing to reinforce her nano-scouts.

As Kris rose from her dressing table, she found the shoes, unfortunately, were just as uncomfortable. "Can't you do anything about these?" Kris said, lifting one foot as high as the tight dress would allow.

And discovered the dress opened a slit when she needed it. She almost did a high kick.

"Sorry, my tinder-footed Highness," Abby said, "but three-inch heels are three-inch heels. You should try wearing them more often and getting your feet comfortable in them."

"Three-inch heels are not uniform compliant," Kris said.

"Or you could buy from the right place. Nelly, why don't you show Kris what she's really wearing this evening."

"Oh, boy, can I," the computer said. Kris could almost hear hands rubbing together in glee.

And suddenly Kris found herself staring into her mirror at

a Kris wearing a Kelly-green dress, with perfect cream-white skin and red hair. She had to squint hard to notice the tiara.

Kris's eyes widened as she thought of possibilities. "How much can you change this?"

Abby laughed. "If someone's looking for a blonde princess in a gray dress, they're gonna have to look long and hard to find you."

And the dress was a royal blue, and Kris was a brunette.

"Just how far can this go?"

And Kris stared at a black hole in the mirror. Her face, her hair, her dress, her skin were as dark as a black cat in a coal bin at midnight.

And her shoes were pumps, great for running.

"Now that's what I call an outfit, but my nose is still too big," she muttered.

"I am only licensed to take care of so many of your problems," Abby sniffed. "By the way, you've got a carbon copy of yourself running around tonight. One of your woman Marines has a dress just like yours. In black. For now."

"That should provide some interesting options," Kris muttered thoughtfully, then centered herself on the moment.

"Okay, so how do I look tonight? Nelly, make the dress red. Easy for someone to spot if they're looking for little old me. Blond hair like usual." Kris paused, considered just what she could get away with and sighed. "And three-inch heels."

Abby handed Kris a tiny purse on a golden chain. "It changes colors, too."

"What if Nelly gets jammed?"

"Put the purse next to the dress. It will get the message," Nelly said.

And so Kris took one more look in the mirror, scowled at her usual self, and turned to face her future.

Outside, she ran into her team. Jack was magnificent in his red and blues. "New set?" Kris asked.

"My backup pair. Armored as well as the old set."

"Good luck," Kris said.

Commander Malhoney offered Kris an elbow. He was resplendent in his white and blue formal dress uniform.

"You manage to armor up that?" Kris asked.

He opened his white jacket. Someone had sewn sections of a spider-silk bodystocking into its lining. It might do some good there. Then again, it might not. And the wide expanse of white dress shirt covering his gut was likely backed up by nothing more impervious than his skivvy shirt.

The man is taking the risks he asked for, Kris reminded herself. Penny was next in a floor-length, soft orange taffeta gown. At her elbow was an unfashionably oversize purse.

"You monitoring the bugs tonight?" Jack asked.

"Someone's got to cover for the chief. He's outside with Captain DeVar and his hardcases."

Jack frowned at Kris's tight dress, then turned to Penny. "I hope you've got some extra artillery mixed in with your petticoats."

"What kind of question is that to ask a young lady," Penny quipped, then flipped up her wide skirts, showing two rows of bandoleers for grenades and spare magazines. "Especially when the poor girl is feeling like a pack mule."

"Or a gunrunner," the commander said with a raised eyebrow.

"Oh, I forgot, this is your first trip out with our princess," Jack said. "Early on it always looks hopeless. We're all doomed. There's no escaping."

"And then it gets better," the commander said, hopefully.

"No, it gets worse," Penny said. "And worse, and worse."

"And then we see daylight," the commander drawled.

"Nope, that's usually an oncoming train," Kris deadpanned.

"But you must get out. You're here, ruining what's left of my digestion."

"Hey, this guy has the right attitude," Penny said.

"Kris, maybe you should keep him around," Jack said.

"Abby, where are you going to be?" Kris said, turning back to her maid.

"In the Tac Center. Cara spent the afternoon there, with

Gramma Ruth, hoping something might come in about Bronc.
I can't think of a better place for me."

"Keep an eye on Gramma Ruth," Kris said.

"Gosh, and I was feeling safer just having her nearby."

And with that, they headed out to do their duty, assuming
they could figure out what it was.

43

The limo was everything Kris expected, and quite a bit more. It had a bed! When the driver saw that Kris's entourage included two couples and six hulking Marines in dress red and blues as well as two women marines in ball gowns, he made the bed disappear and jump seats appear.

There were sounds of sadness at the change, but Kris was careful not to note where that noise came from. There are some things an officer does not need to know.

Especially when the noise comes from her fellow officers.

Marine escorts pulled up ahead and behind the limo, adding to Kris's security. The driver did not seem surprised when one of Kris's Marines settled in on the seat next to him.

The drive to the National Gallery of the Arts took longer than Kris had expected. It was north of town, along the river in a park. The limo driver seemed to think his job included a running commentary on the local scene . . . or he figured to wreak some revenge on his passengers by boring them with trivia.

"Local soccer leagues use the sports fields as well as track and cross-country racings. We have an annual marathon that people come from light-years away to run in."

Kris had a hard time buying that.

"On your right are the National Rose Gardens. We have every variation of rose in abundance." And at that, the air in the limo took on a whiff of rose scent.

"And the Japanese Gardens to your left"—which directed Kris to a hilly affair—"are renown even on Yamato. Eden hired away Yamato's most expensive gardener for several years to lay out the design and implement it."

Leaving Kris to wonder if the most expensive was also the most respected. Rarely were they.

"Notice the fields of fire," Jack whispered in Kris's ear.

She nodded, the wide expanse of playing fields gave easy search of the approaches to the huge gray building ahead.

"The rose gardens?" Kris said.

"Fully under observation and easy to trim with automatic weapons fire," Jack offered.

"Roses do have a propensity to grow back," Penny offered.

And a poor rose harvest for a year or two was a small price to pay for the lives of your political elite.

Maybe Inspector Johnson was right. This was no place for "them" to "kill them all."

So why didn't that make Kris's stomach feel better.

The limo entered a large expanse of crushed rock in front of the Gallery. A huge fountain filled the center of it. A group of horses and figures spewed water in all directions.

"This is an exact replica of a fountain on the grounds of the Palace of Versailles outside Paris on Earth," the driver said. Which might explain the secretary's mistake about their final goal. "The actual building is an expanded replica of the National Gallery of Art in Washington on Earth. The Gallery of the Arts here covers most of the ground and main floor.

"The floors above it are the official residence of the President of Eden."

"All Eden?" Kris asked.

"Well, if you insist, the American nation on Eden. But it amounts to the same," he said with unquestioning chauvinism.

Kris eyed the marble building. A ground floor. Stone steps leading up to the large portico in front of the main floor. There were at least two floors above that. Maybe a couple more, depending on how the roof was used.

Plenty of rooms to hide in if the upper floors were as divided up as the lower ones. But if they had guns and you had none, any running might only delay the inevitable.

But Kris did have guns and was ready for a fight.

Tonight looked to be interesting.

Jack handed her out of the limo onto the commander's arm, then helped Penny. She took a moment to arrange the fall of her dress. The Marines and their ladies followed quickly.

Kris looked around. She saw men and women in formal evening dress. But nothing to get alarmed about.

There was no sign of the ambassador, but by now, he should be far to the head of the line. She joined the official procession and began to climb—in three-inch heels.

"Isn't that the Longknife woman," Grant von Schrader said from the west portico where he watched the arrival of future corpses.

Topaz had also been watching the arrivals, making catty comments on this or that dress. Now she focused on the column of what could only be soldiers being led by the woman in the tight red dress.

"So that is her? I've never seen her."

"Yes, you can always tell by the uniforms around her. Only, usually it's a Marine beside her. One of those in blue and red. Now she's got someone in white and blue."

"Guess my daughter's rich employer can't keep a man."

"Speaking of your daughter, now might be a good time to get Cara out of wherever she's run off to. Why don't you call her now, and ask her to come home while you're out? She could be asleep when you get in tonight."

"Cara has a phone?" her grandmother said.

Grant gave her the number of the new unit.

Topaz made a show of considering Grant's suggestion, but

as she always did, she obeyed. She moved a distance away on the balcony and made the call. For a minute, Grant was treated to the discord of grandmother-granddaughter argument, but when Topaz rang off, she seemed pleased with herself.

"She is headed home. We'll talk in the morning."

"Young girls need firm guidance," Grant assured her. And notched off another requirement for tonight.

Another limo came to a stop. Another pair of sacrificial cattle dismounted. Grant added them to the list of obits that would not be on tomorrow's news.

The list was filling in nicely.

44

Security at the top of the steps was stiff ... if you didn't have a weapons permit. Kris presented hers and she and her Marines were ushered around the metal detectors and explosive sniffers. In the few minutes Kris watched, several other groups were similarly treated.

A lot of personal heat here.

Were some of these in on the plan?

Now that was an ugly thought.

Kris circulated quickly among the milling crowd. Here she shook a hand, there she accepted a quick kiss on the cheek. Few people waved her down, so she was able to move almost as rapidly as she wanted to.

Quickly, she made a recon of what she could only think of as tonight's battlefield.

She didn't much care for what she saw.

The security setup on the west portico guided her through wide doors into a huge rotunda. The place of honor in the center of that was an immense bronze sculpture that portrayed the first settlers setting foot on Eden.

Maybe it was accurate for the American Express team.

Two expansive halls went north and south off the rotunda. Both were expensively done in marble and lined with sculptures. Off of each hall, doors led into specific rooms with exhibits. Rooms two or three deep on both sides.

So people could be ambushed in small rooms or machine gunned in the two halls. Not a pretty picture either way.

"What's the nano situation?" Kris asked Penny.

"Top of the line," was the answer from Penny and Nelly.

"About half of them are scouts," Nelly added. "The other half are hunter-killers."

"Doesn't sound like a good idea to launch our own," Kris said. Both woman and computer agreed.

Kris finished her review of the south wing just as police in formal uniforms began to close it off to prepare for the arrival of government officials.

"I need to find a little girls room," Kris said to one of them. The one she was pointed to had a long line in front.

"There's two more on the ground floor. Hook a left at the bottom of the stairs."

Kris shed most of her escort and it was just Jack and a Marine couple that took the stairs down.

And Kris hooked a right.

"You should have gone left," Jack said.

"No, it's right," Kris said.

And they ran into a guard.

"May I help you?" It didn't sound like he wanted to.

"I'm looking for the ladies' room," Kris said.

"It's that away. You should have turned left off the stairs."

"That's what I told her," Jack said.

"I hear that a lot," the guard said.

Kris retreated with ill grace.

"What did you see?" Jack asked when they were out of the guard's earshot.

"That the offices are not locked off or all that well guarded," Kris said. "Also, did you see that guard?"

"No body armor and I doubt if he's carrying more than a revolver or automatic."

"Exactly. If he's what Inspector Johnson is counting on to

handle a serious assault with the weapons we found in the warehouse, there's going to be lots of blood and guts on the floor but not an ounce of brain."

Kris actually did make use of the ladies' room.

She was just coming out when Nelly said, "Kris, you have a call coming in from Abby."

"What's happening?" Kris said.

"Cara's gone."

"Where'd she go?"

"That's the problem, we don't know. She got a call, which she took outside the Tac Center. When she came back in she said it was not from Bronc, but that she needed to go to the bathroom. That was fifteen minutes ago. She's not in the bathroom and she's nowhere in the embassy."

"Have you tried to trace her phone?" Kris asked.

"Yep. She's got it throttled. Twelve and already breaking the law. I suspect it's the company she keeps."

"She's got good teachers," Kris said. "Where do you think she headed?"

"I bet either her mom or grandmom told her to go home," Abby said.

"Where she'll be safe?" Kris asked.

That brought a long pause. "I wouldn't bet an Earth penny on that," Abby said.

"You think Cara's included in the 'kill them all,' coverage," Kris said, not really believing her own words.

"I'm thinking that tonight is supposed to be bigger than any of us can get our minds around."

Kris let that hang in the air for a long moment. Apparently long enough for Abby to make up her mind.

"Kris, I'm headed down to Five Corners to pick up Cara."

"Abby, I figured you to keep an eye on the place there, maybe lead some last desperate reaction team."

"Gramma Ruth is doing a fine job of eyeballing this place. She's enjoying using her commander's commission."

"What's your reserve commission?" Kris asked. The last thing she expected was an answer. But now that things were getting interesting and deadly, any sort of answer from Abby would be enlightening.

"I hold a reserve first lieutenant's commission in Wardhaven Army Intelligence."

"Admiral Crossenshield made you a first lieutenant!"

"I started as a second louie," Abby said. "Having survived chasing you around space, I got a promotion awhile back."

Kris didn't know which shocked her more. That Abby held a reserve commission . . . or that she'd admitted it. She was very worried about her niece. "You really want to get Cara back."

"I haven't been much use to her, my own flesh and blood. I will not let her down now."

"Then you better go get her," Kris said. Only after the order was given did she glance at Jack. He was smiling proudly, like maybe a papa does when his little hellion is showing signs of becoming a civilized human being.

"Gramma Ruth, here" came over the line. "I'm looking at a Marine sergeant that sure looks in need of going with Abby. Sergeant Bruce, isn't it?" A "yes, ma'am" came in the background.

"Can you cover the center without him?" Kris asked, not at all happy asking the old woman to take on that responsibility.

"I don't see a problem, Kris. And if things go south, I can always call them back. You do understand, Abby, I call and you come running no matter where you are."

"Understood, Commander."

Kris rang off and found a bench to sit down on.

"Abby holds a reserve commission," she marveled. Jack was busy looking up and down the lower halls, the north a duplicate of the one above. The south offices. He nodded agreement.

"And our forces are getting scattered all to hell in a hand basket," Kris growled.

"Somehow I don't think that is by accident," Jack said.

"These folks haven't been dumb since that first shoot-out. Why should they start dumbing down now?" Kris sighed.

Chimes sounded upstairs.

"I suspect that either means dinner is served or the cattle are being lined up. Want to bet which?"

Jack offered Kris his arm and, with the Marine couple trailing them, they headed back the way they'd come.

Through the east-facing rear doors of the ground floor, Kris got a gorgeous view of a river reflecting back bloodred clouds on fire with the sunset.

Kris hoped that wasn't a harbinger of things to come as she turned to ascend the stairs and do her part in what would happen next.

45

For once, the order of presentation put Kris nowhere near the head of the line.

Three visiting dignitaries from Geneva had the honor of first place, followed by several representatives of the Mandate from Heaven. After that, the pecking order seemed to fall by corporate wealth. Even there, several corporations ranked ahead of Nuu Enterprises on Eden.

It didn't bother Kris a bit.

She spent the time getting to know the killing zone better.

Two floors above the main one had wide balconies looking down on the halls. And men in dark glasses who regularly talked into their sleeves standing watch beside marble columns.

They didn't look any more heavily armed than the fellow on the ground floor.

Clearly, Eden was making a try, but was totally out of their league.

Penny leaned close to Kris's ear. "You think on Wardhaven your old man would have this many guards?"

Which was a good point. Kris mulled it over for a full

second, then answered. "He'd have more if he knew a coup was in the works. And if I had any say-so in the matter."

Jack chuckled dryly.

Commander Malhoney listened stoically through the entire exchange. He didn't so much as twitch.

However, unless very pale was his normal skin coloring, he was more scared than he let on.

Kris reached the beginning of the reception line and began shaking hands with this senator or that senator's spouse.

Kris smiled and shook hands or exchanged gentle hugs. Formal introductions went quickly. Nelly offered to back up the brief name and main political office with something more, but Kris declined.

The line was clearly paced to move fast. If there was to be any serious talking, it would be after the formal meet and greet.

Assuming the hostile assault team gave them a few spare moments.

Nelly, are you getting any jamming?

No, Kris. I will tell you as soon as I do.

And Kris moved on to shake another hand.

"We don't want to get a speeding ticket," Abby pointed out. "Or wrap this car around a light post."

Beside her, Sergeant Bruce didn't noticeably slow down. He'd picked one of the rentals. Not the hottest, but a middling type that had a surprising amount under the hood.

And he was using all of it.

"You sure you know where the kid is headed?" he asked Abby.

"I'm pretty sure she's headed home," Abby said. Still, she activated a subroutine on her computer that she'd paid very good money for.

Everyone knew a phone could be located at any time by the authorities using the correct remote command. Many people paid good money for the illegal option that allowed them to eliminate that function. Abby had paid very good money for a bit of software that was supposed to get around that option.

It would be interesting to see if Bronc was better than all the money Abby had paid.

Surprise, surprise, the kid had a bit to learn. A map was projected onto the car's front screen. A green dot moved along the trolley line toward Five Corners.

"She's on her way home. Please tell me why."

The sergeant offered no explanation. After a bit of silence he did change the subject.

"So you're a first lieutenant?" he said, not taking his eyes off the road.

"I guess so." Abby sniffed. "It's not like I own a uniform or would know how to put one on. Someone . . . who shall remain unnamed . . . suggested that my job of looking after a certain princess might be easier if I had the protection of the Geneva Convention to fall back on.

"Possibly I made a mistake," Abby shrugged, then did a longer review of the last few minutes, trying to get to the bottom of the strange reaction she was getting from this, until now, friendly man who was driving like a maniac.

"I thought you and yours would be less embarrassed about being out-shot by a Longknife maid if she had a commission."

"Being out-shot by an Army puck, and an intel weenie to boot. Nope, sorry, sister. Color me embarrassed. Just who did teach you to shoot?"

"One of my former employers on Earth. Nicest little old lady. Who would have thought she had so many enemies gunning for her? Anyway, she sent me to a range to learn. Two old sergeants, one Army, one Gunny, did their best to show me how."

"And you didn't learn?"

"Not at first. Kept closing my eyes against the noise. Then my lady's security guards went down and my gun and the pistol she had hid in her long johns were all that stood between us and a future as a widening pool of blood.

"I kept my eyes open. Plugged two of them. The sergeants said my shooting was much improved after that."

"I would imagine," Sergeant Bruce said as the car took a corner on two wheels.

* * *

Captain DeVar was in the forefront of his two platoons as he waved them to a pause on their way downriver. On both sides of him, the troops halted and braced against the current.

Captain DeVar had realized very quickly that every approach to the Gallery was a dead giveaway, with dead being the operative word.

The river looked to be the only way in that might not be fully covered.

Actually, the river was very well covered. He had to wonder if the couples paddling canoes and sailing small boats up river on lazy weekends knew the amount of heavy weapons sighted in on them. Some might if their personal electronics were designed to isolate the radars that tracked them.

But that likely wasn't very many.

A Marine couple outfitted with a picnic basket and full electronic countermeasures suite had verified expectations this morning.

So, DeVar was walking his Marines downriver.

The difference between full combat gear for a submerged entry and the same for space or worse wasn't all that different. His Marines were breathing canned air and lugging enough weights to settle them onto the bottom of the Patowmack River.

Of course, just because the boaters this morning hadn't found any evidence of underwater defenses didn't mean there weren't any.

And if this looked like the best approach for the Marines, the other side just might be using it for their own approach. Now wouldn't that be an interesting coincidence.

Captain DeVar looked at the heads-up display on the face of his helmet, found it acceptable, and blinked his right eye once.

The display changed to what Gabby was getting on her sensor display. He eyed it for a long minute and found it also good.

He rose to his feet and motioned the platoons to advance.

* * *

Bronc huddled among the other young men. They had assault rifles. He had his computer.

He kept it going up and down the electromagnetic spectrum, doing searches. It kept coming back with nothing.

Actually, it was coming back with a lot of stuff, but none of it was in the area the sensor sergeant had told him was not supposed to be there.

So long as there was nothing there, he was supposed to keep quiet.

Around him, some of the riflemen would start to whisper among themselves. A moment later, one of the gun-toting sergeants would scowl at the talkers, and they'd shut up.

Bronc kept his silence.

If he could manage it, he'd keep his silence as long as he could even after his fabulous computer started to report something these people were interested in.

Cara's life might depend on it.

46

Kris didn't like being tied to this reception line. She kept thinking about how a sitting duck must feel in a shooting gallery. But just because handcuffs were golden didn't make them any easier to break.

She'd met the leader of the opposition, Shirley Chisel, early in the line. A short woman in a conservative suit, she'd given Kris's hand a firm shake. "I understand you and I almost met a few days ago."

Kris raised an eyebrow.

"On the mall," the woman continued. "Was that one aimed at you or me?"

"I shouldn't have been there," Kris pointed out. "Just luck. What about you?"

The woman scowled. "It was on my schedule for two days."

Kris left it at that.

"I hope we get a chance to talk again," the woman said as she passed Kris to the next senator.

There'd been a lot of handshaking since then, but nothing of interest. Kris hoped that was about to change, she was finally reaching the government.

The Americans on Eden had adopted a parliamentary government with a strong executive. Kris could never figure out why anyone would have an elected president from one party and then risk having the prime minister and his majority in parliament be from the other party.

Just another thing she didn't much care for on Eden.

The last couple of senators had been members of the government. She was now shaking hands with the defense minister, a cordial woman who actually seemed to recognize Kris. But she said little before handing Kris off to the prime minister. He was a jolly short man. With his snow-white beard Kris had to fight thoughts of Father Christmas.

His party must have an evil-looking whip somewhere among its members because the prime minister looked barely able to herd a thirsty pair of sheep to water.

Next in line was the third vice president . . . and Inspector Johnson stood at his elbow, whispering something in his ear.

So the vice president smiled at Kris and said, "I'm glad you're enjoying your vacation on Eden."

"Oh, it's not a vacation," Kris corrected. "I'm an active-duty naval officer from Wardhaven, attached to the procurement section of the embassy. I just arranged for United Sentient planets to buy a huge chunk of software from an Eden company, and build the latest of your computer designs."

"That's nice," the man said, as if Kris had agreed with him. "And I do hope you feel safe here. We do know how to take care of our people."

"No doubt you do," Kris managed to say, eyeing Johnson, and noting that he did seem to get the full double meaning. "Our people" doesn't include this visiting Rim princess.

Kris found herself being urged on to the second vice president by gentle pressure on her wrist. She and the first vice president struck Kris as more zeros. Maybe they were major players in the local political game, but if matters got deadly, they looked only too ready to be first in line for slaughter.

And would die wondering what the noise was all about.

The president didn't impress Kris, either. His smile didn't

get past his lips. His eyes were distracted, never meeting her own. And his handshake was little more than a touch.

Was Kris supposed to risk taking a bullet for the likes of these? If Martinez hadn't said these folks were worth fighting for Kris was tempted to signal retreat, get her people out of Dodge, and let the locals settle their own affairs.

Then again, she had yet to meet the competition.

Kris headed for the hors d'oeuvres.

Grant von Schrader was near the end of the hors d'oeuvres tables so he could listen in on the next important conversation of the evening.

"Where is the rest of the food, Tony?" the coordinator asked the caterer.

"It's coming, sir. It will be here. Let me check," the short round man now running "A Taste of Italy" answered, reaching for his phone.

"There's a new flu bug going around, don't you know?" Tony rambled on. "Half my crew called in sick. I had to hire all kinds of new people this afternoon. I did get you the first half of the spread here, didn't I?"

"Yes, but there's a galloping herd about two shakes away from here and this is going to vanish like a politician's honor," the coordinator noted with a sly grin.

"Well, my guys are here, sir. But they're being held up at the gate. Some sergeant insists everything on all eight of my next trucks has to be inspected."

"Oh God, give me that. The last thing we need is hungry cops pawing over my fancy food," the coordinator said, taking the phone from Tony.

"Sergeant, this is Dick Hamernack, I'm personally coordinating this affair for the president. We need that food." This was followed by a pause.

"Well, have you inspected the first truck?" The coordinator nodded as he got the answer he expected. "Good, all the trucks are like the first. Right, Tony?"

Tony nodded, actually believing the truth of what he affirmed. He would not be one of those alive in the morning.

"Well, if you've seen one, you've seen them all. Get them in here. And I mean now. Right now."

The coordinator handed the phone back. "Cops! They want to look under every bed. They'd pull up every dress if you'd let them."

Tony ruefully nodded agreement.

And Grant von Schrader allowed himself a smile.

Around Bronc, the noise of an engine going into gear drew smiles from the two sergeants with rifles. Those were quickly reflected on the faces of the kids with guns.

Bronc kept doing his own searches, just like he'd been told. Nothing new. No surprises.

Had Cara got the message out?

Were they going to kill everyone just like they said?

Bronc worked his jaw, trying to get rid of some of the tension, trying to keep his stomach from revolting at the thought of so much blood. There wasn't much he could do.

Never in his life had he wanted so to live, to grow up. To be with Cara.

His computer completed another search. Nothing had changed.

47

Kris spotted the CEO of Nuu Enterprises on Eden and homed in on him at the hors d'oeuvre bar. "An interesting guy you got as a president here."

"He meets our need," the CEO said, a man no more presupposing than his planet's government. "We can't all be Longknifes, and not every planet in space wants a legend calling the shots. If you don't mind my saying so."

"I have learned to value diversity," Kris said. "By the way, I've also learned about a fellow who's something of a player on Eden. A Grant von Schrader?"

"Him," the CEO huffed. "Not exactly what I'd call a good example of our planet, but yes, he's a player. Oh, and he's here. You want to meet him?"

And before Kris could decide how to answer that, she found herself squired down the table into that meeting.

"Grant, have you met Kris Longknife?" was followed by a pause that quickly grew pregnant.

The two eyed each other. Kris schooled her face to gentle neutrality and seemed to see the same in the face of the middle-aged man across from her. The conservative cut of his formal wear did not camouflage his ramrod military bearing—or his eyes.

Those were an icy gray that reflected back a cold calculation of the world . . . and gave away nothing about what lurked behind them. Someone could drown in the frigid water of those eyes, and the owner would take no notice.

Kris wondered what he saw looking back at him, but he reflected nothing to her.

"No, I have not had the pleasure, Henry. Thanks for bringing her over to my little corner of the world" seemed affable enough, taken word by word. The whole of the content came no where close to measuring up to its parts.

Kris offered him her hand and got a solid shake that seemed to offer to go long and tight, but held back.

Kris suppressed the temptation to tighten her own grip. If Grant was holding back, so would she.

"The sunset was quite red tonight," Kris said, turning to the weather for her innuendo.

"I noticed the river was running red in return. It can be very lovely at those times," he answered back.

And for a moment, just a split second, Kris saw the heart of a man who would delight in a river running red with the blood of the bodies it floated.

This was no man to leave the future of a planet to.

And in that moment, Kris made her decision.

There would be no retreat tonight. She and hers would fight this man. Fight him for the hopes and dreams of a world of people like Cara and Bronc, Uncle Joe and Auntie Mong and all the store owners like themselves struggling to make a living and hold the line for some minimum of civilization.

And certainly for a cop like Martinez. He who tried.

For them, Kris would risk flesh and blood to stop whatever monster lurked in the heart of the man before her.

"You have lost security," Kris said, doing her bit to dent the confidence of the man she faced. "Some of us know what is going down tonight. You will not succeed."

Grant von Schrader might have raised an eyebrow at that. Or not. Instead he turned to the woman beside him. A lovely dusky-eyed woman. "Have you met Topaz."

"No," Kris said, offering her hand again. The woman took it gently in a gloved hand.

KRIS, THAT IS ABBY'S MOTHER.

I KNOW, NELLY. CAN YOU TELL ME ANYTHING ABOUT HER?

SHE IS NOT SQUAWKING. BUT I THINK THAT'S BECAUSE SHE IS NOT CARRYING. I DETECT NO HUM OF ANY ELECTRONICS.

That would certainly be unusual for anyone.

Kris waited to see how this would develop, but it was Grant who said. "I think I see someone I should talk to. Henry, if you and this lovely lady will excuse me." And with a half bow, the man was gone and the woman with him.

The Nuu CEO watched him go. "Would you mind telling me what that was about? 'You will not succeed.' "

"It's a Longknife thing. And here's another Longknife thing. Leave. Do not look back. Do not hesitate. If you want to live a long life, be somewhere else as quickly as you can."

The CEO shook his head ruefully. "My contacts warned me that you were strange. If you will excuse me, I see some folks I need to spend time with," he said, and headed off in a direction that did not have any door close by.

"Some people are just too dumb to live," Jack said softly.

"No," Penny disagreed. "They are comfortable living in the normal and cannot believe that there is any other way."

"Wouldn't it be nice if their way was the only way?" Commander Malhoney offered.

"Well, I don't think tonight has any chance of going that way. Jack, did you get a good look at our Grant von Schrader?"

"And I didn't like what I saw. That guy's been in uniform. If he's been here for fifteen years and still has that look of sharp steel about him, I think we would be wise not to underestimate him."

"Nelly, send out the code word. Play ball."

"Sent, Kris."

And that settled the matter. Any chance that Kris might cancel tonight was now gone.

In the car park, grim Marines would be swapping out of dress uniforms for camouflage sniper kits. Others would be wandering off from the close patrol around Kris's limo and the two Marine rigs to set up their own observation points, reverting to the oldest warrior skill set, checking out the developing situation with the Mark I eyeball.

Captain DeVar got the code word, as he had expected. His reading of the history books was that Ray Longknife was hard on subordinates. As in, he lost a lot of them.

He had been none too excited about putting his Marines into the tender hands of another such legend on the make.

But this young woman surprised him.

This Longknife noticed the people around her and took them in as more than cannon fodder. And she actually seemed worried about kicking butt and taking names here on Eden.

When she'd let on that she just might call tonight off, he'd been happily surprised.

So her decision not to call it off told him that something up there settled her final reservations. And there was no doubt that here was a good cause for knocking heads and taking names.

The call came at a good time for the captain. He had his two platoons lined up below the water's edge. Two squads spread out on each side of him. One squad in reserve on his right and on his left. Technical support behind the reserve.

The Marines were ready.

"Gabby, show me something I don't know," he ordered.

The tech let a small float loose on a thin wire. It would have looked funny if he'd thought about it. Here was a big fish sending up a hook to that upper world. Only here, the hook was a camera.

Now Captain DeVar saw his target up close. The building was big, stone, and ugly. Several trucks, from a caterer if you could believe the signs on them, were backing into the service entrance to the left. Lights were still showing bright in the Gallery from every window. Several balconies showed people holding drinks and party plates.

Well, it was party time.

The Marine transferred his attention higher up. The roof of the place was festooned with antennae. Most were the usual communication clutter. He concentrated on the others.

Two, one at each corner of the building, were targeting sensors. A closer search showed him eight, no nine, auto-guns scattered along the roof line. They'd be slaved to the sensors, probably with someone in security central with his finger on the release button.

Right now, the button had to be under the thumb of a friendly. Dumb, yes, but a good guy. When it passed to the thumb of a bad guy, things would get bad for anyone caught in the open.

"Gabby, pass this picture to the front team. Advise them to check out the roof and stand by to take down their sensors. Can you identify any cameras?"

"Not at this time, sir. I don't think they've got them on. I'd say they're going for motion detection and radar. Maybe some infrared. But no sensors active other than those two suites at the corners, sir."

Which meant tonight would be a study in slowly developing hell.

Captain DeVar signaled his troops to settle in place and wait. Marines were good at waiting.

Abby had had enough of waiting. She tapped her computer; it woke up Cara's phone a second time. A green blip appeared.

"She's two blocks up, one over to the right." And then Abby held on as Sergeant Bruce took a hard right and made the turn.

Abby would have waited for the next right.

Abby would have been wrong.

A screeching left put them on the right street. A tiny figure was walking along, head down, shoulders weighted by the whole burden of a world as only a twelve-year-old can carry it.

Bruce accelerated even as he said, "We got company."

Four blocks up, a car did a slip-sliding turn into the street and gunned its motor. Abby squinted, tried to make out driver and passengers.

"Guns," she said, the same second Bruce did. And her own automatic was out. She jacked up the power to maximum and flipped the magazine to deadly.

Bruce rolled her window down as she went through the drill, so all she had to do was lean out. Good thinking on his part.

There was an arm out of the passenger window of the approaching car.

Abby fired for the passenger window.

The other people noticed that they weren't alone on the street and changed their aim from the kid to the onrushing car.

That fit Abby fine. She swept her fire right to the driver, then back to the gunner. Beneath Abby, she could feel her own car shuddering as it was hit.

Out of the corner of her eye, Abby saw Cara go down. Whether the girl was down smart or down hit would be determined later.

Beside Abby, Bruce struggled to keep control of the car, but it was fishtailing.

"They're going to run Cara down," Abby shouted as the other car began to swerve and slide out of control.

Abby found a firm hand on her slacks, yanking her back in the car even as the rig began a painfully long, slow swerve on a collision course for the other car.

A course that would intercept it a good five feet before the shooter could hit the girl.

Abby braced herself.

The crash wasn't nearly as bad as Abby expected.

Yes, there was the bouncing around the inside of the car as it fell apart, and smooth things became pointy things that cut.

And her brain must have bounced off the inside of her skull at least two, maybe three, times.

Still, all in all, it beat a jab in the eye with a sharp stick.
Barely.

And it had its nice part. Bruce dragged her out of the rig
firmly, but gently. Then he felt her all over for broken bones
and bleeding arteries.

He could have done it so much better, feeling her up, but he
was professional about it. Abby would have to schedule time
to show him how to unprofessionally take advantage of a girl.

But that would have to wait for later.

Abby was dragging herself out of Bruce's touch, and
crawling on her hands and knees to Cara.

"You okay, kitten."

"I think I got hit," the girl whispered.

To an insistent "Where?" the girl raised an arm.

Yep, she'd been creased by a stray round, flying glass,
rock, hard to tell. Abby pulled a bandage from her usual supply and stanched the bleeding while calling over her shoulder,
"Sarge, you think you can get the car going?"

That was followed by a starter turning, but no sound of
anything cooperating. "I think we're afoot."

"Advise Commander Tordon that shots have been fired,
Cara has a flesh wound, and we're afoot."

"Yes, ma'am" came back solid Marine, followed by
"Gramma Ruth says she'll try to send us wheels but not to
count on it. Kris has ordered 'play ball,' but so far there's no
report of 'batter up.' "

"Play ball" did not surprise Abby. The Kris Longknife she
knew would not leave a planet to drop into the hands of someone who tried to shoot old ladies and kids. But it was nice
working for a boss who needed convincing that people needed
killing.

"Tell Ruth that we'll manage our own wheels, or we'll ride
the tram back."

Bruce did, then grinned at Abby. "You gonna hot wire a rig
or me?"

"Which of us will take the longer?" Abby said, tightening
the bandage down around Cara's arm. "Does that hurt?"

"Not much," Cara said as Bruce gently helped her to her feet. "You wouldn't boost a car, would you, Aunt Abby?"

The look of moral confusion in those young eyes bothered Abby. But not enough to consign her and hers to the tram.

"Baby ducks, we really need to get back to the embassy, and we really need to have a doc look at that cut arm."

"Don't call me 'baby ducks.' That what Gramma Ganna calls me. I have to take it from her. And I thought you were different."

"I am, Cara, but right now I'm not sure I can afford not to boost some wheels."

"Why don't you ask Uncle Joe for his truck? He might lend it to you."

"I didn't think of that," Abby said. And between the two of them and their blackened hearts she could probably explain to the old fellow the importance of her leaving a bruise on his skull, and hot wiring the rig.

Abby let Cara lead them to the familiar street corner, followed by Bruce as soon as he checked to make sure there were no survivors from the other car.

Uncle Joe listened quickly as Cara gave him her version of what was going on, then took Abby aside.

"I hear strange things are happening around town tonight."

"I know that only too well. The shots just fired were us trying to keep some thugs from running Cara down, turning her into a drive-by."

"It is disgusting when good children get mowed down by things they have nothing to do with."

"We need to get her to medical care."

"Take my truck," the old storekeeper said, offering keys.

"I cannot do that," Abby said. "It was no accident that Cara was marked for death, and I, as well as my tall friend here, are players in the things that you are hearing about. If you are seen to be taking our side, it could cost you your life."

The old man frowned. "Then I may have to walk into a door and give myself cuts and bruises I can show off."

"We could hit you carefully."

"It would not be good for Cara to see you do that. No, you take the keys and go. I think Mong across the street can give me the wounds I need to show if things go as you say they could."

And so it was that Bruce bounced his way out of Five Corners with a lot less horsepower than he gunned his way in.

48

Kris listened to the latest report from Gramma Ruth, her gut going cold, her game face sliding into place.

"Cara has a flesh wound, but she was definitely targeted for something worse, kidnapping or death," Commander Tordon finished.

"No shots have been fired here, yet," Kris reported.

"It looks like it's only a matter of time," Jack said.

"But it's a very important matter," Kris answered back. "Let's assume we're only minutes away, team. Keep a lookout for guns. If you see one, shoot. Take a prisoner we can talk to if you can, but take no risks otherwise."

The net absorbed her orders in total silence.

Kris turned to Penny. "You're in command of this hall. Try to hold casualties to as few as possible, Marines and civilians. If you can, be close to Senator Chisel when all hell breaks loose. It would be nice if she survived the night. Good luck."

The intel woman took the orders and best wishes with a slight roll of her eyes.

Now Kris turned to the woman Marine at her elbow. She was about Kris's height and her dress was the same cut only black. "I've had it with waiting for something to happen. You ready to switch places with me."

The woman stepped sideways and Kris passed before her, half hidden by the circle of Marines around them. Suddenly the Marine's dress was red. Kris's was black. The Marine was a blonde; Kris was a brunette.

Kris took Jack's arm, and a Marine corporal stepped into place at Penny's elbow.

For a moment, the circle seemed no different, then Jack and Kris took a step back and quickly disappeared into a room off the hall. As they did, the circle of Marines slowly moseyed down toward the central dome.

Once on their own, Kris and Jack ambled among the art, talking about how good it was to get relieved for a bit and what art they really wanted to take a look at once they got a breath of fresh air. Before too long, a pair of Marines fell in a comfortable distance behind them.

As security, even in their red and blues, they passed unnoticed, as important people talked to each other, or very important people talked, trailed by their security details.

And Kris did her numbers.

The reception line had been a real herd event, say four hundred going or receiving. Say some thousand important people around to see and be seen. Add to that three, maybe four thousand security people or waiters or whomever.

Call it maybe five thousand upstairs and downstairs.

Kris eyed the security folks. And found them strangely uncomfortable tonight. How many of them were in on this? How many of their patrons were not? How many of the owners of these security details would find out later tonight that, like Gramma Ruth, they had not bought loyalty?

Everything was wrong with this picture.

Kris's history professor had once mentioned that civil wars were some of the bloodiest. This looked like it might set a new record if it wasn't over in a night.

That probably was the plan.

But then, what plan survived contact with the opposition?

Kris found herself on the west balcony, overlooking the car

park. Her limo stood out like a dinosaur among whales. She counted the number of Marines around them and came up with less than a third of those assigned. Good.

She glanced around the other cars. Most had only a driver with them. Some had a shotgun.

Kris turned and leaned against the marble balustrade. She looked up and remarked to Jack how lovely the stars were.

What she actually looked at were the auto-guns. She counted nine of them visible. There were likely another nine hidden, if she was any gauge of a defense. And she had defended a space station or two in her brief career. Well, defended one, attacked the other. She'd expect at least as many guns in plain sight as were hidden away as spares.

Whose side would the auto-guns be on? At the beginning? Middle? End of the firefight?

She would have some say in that. Or die trying.

Kris ambled in. Outside, in the shadows, Jack's uniform had undergone a change. His red coat was now black; his blue pants had taken on the same color. The distantly trailing pair of Marines now looked identical to Jack. Kris took in some art, and watched some more important people ignore their security as if they weren't there.

She leaned against the doors to the stairs. Jack said something and Kris laughed, leaning back, cracking the doors open just a bit.

Just enough for a fleet of Nelly's nanos to get in.

Before long, she ended up on the back balcony, staring at the river. The moonlight rippled off it. A perfect moment for lovers.

But Kris chose to glance up at the roof line and see the auto-guns. Those had to be stopped from mowing down her Marines.

NELLY, HOW'S IT GOING?

THE CAMERAS IN THE STAIRWELL ARE READY TO LOOP, AND THE SCOUTS HAVE HERDED THE NANOS DOWN TO THE BOTTOM FLOOR OR BASEMENT.

"Let's go, crew," Kris said with a tight smile and headed indoors. To work, perchance to live.

Once in the stairwell, Kris hardly slowed down. Nelly reported the cameras in a sixty-second loop. Physical security for the upper floors consisted of a mere gate that her Marines ducked under.

Jack handed her over it very gallantly.

They had to take Nelly's word for it that the observation nanos had been herded out of their way.

If an observant human spotted this concentration of nanos, an alarm would go off—but none did.

Neither did a guard look in on them as they climbed past the fourth floor.

On the fifth floor, there was an actually locked door keeping them from the roof level. Jack made short work of it, and they kept going.

In an area clearly intended only for working stiffs, they came to the end of their climb. Gray paint replaced the soft beige walls. Pipes were painted identifying primary colors.

At the roof level were two doors. One looked to open onto the actual roof. Kris turned the other way and led her team into a gray, shadowed corridor.

Drawing her automatic, Kris clicked it to sleepy darts.

Ahead, the first three offices were dark. Empty.

Farther down, light shown from one, its door closing even as they came in view of it.

Somewhere in the building, a single shot rang out.

It was quickly answered by weapons on full automatic.

49

Gunny Sergeant Brown heard the first shot and shouted, "Down." His Marines obeyed in record time.

Most of the civilian drivers stood up taller to get a better look at whatever was going on. Several drivers in their armored limos actually got out so they could gawk.

One saw Gunny on the ground behind the huge limo and sneered.

His sneer lasted for about fifteen seconds as the sound of automatic weapons filled the night air.

Then the auto-guns on the roof cut loose.

Gunny did not look, but from the sound of things, the guns cycled from target to target, sending a short five-round burst into every human in range.

At least, that's what the sneering guy's body absorbed. Five rounds of 20-mm general purpose.

Not much of the sneer survived him taking one round to the head.

Gunny remembered why light infantry loved the earth and hugged her well.

He checked his own Marines. They were doing their earth-hugging best to stay low. As he expected, Private Haskell managed to take a fragment. In the butt, no less.

He was screaming like he'd been filleted from nap to chap. Making more racket than any of the civilians. But then, none of the civilians were making any noise at all.

Not even breathing.

Gunny laid there, not much liking that all he could do was lie there on the receiving end. He cuddled up close to the recollection that his time to dish it out would come later.

Still, under fire for the first time in his long career, he didn't much care for this part of the battle. And knew it must be worse for the kids under his command.

"Keep it tight, Marines," he called. "The princess is counting on us to suck this up and not do something stupid that'll get us suddenly dead."

The "Ooo-hah" that came back was subdued by the earth that protected them.

Grant von Schrader smiled where he stood by the bronze in the center of the rotunda. Things were going very well.

White-coated caterers had produced machine pistols right on his signal. The most observant of the Secret Service watching from the second floor had noticed and gotten off one shot.

He and his associates had all died within seconds of that lone resistance. The agents close to the president had gone down with him, a gallant, but in the end, useless defiance.

Several of the bodyguards that would not be turned had also gone down shooting. The stream of fire that got them usually took down their patron.

That quickly persuaded most of the powers that be that they were better off holding their hands up and having their paid protection do the same.

For a brief moment, Grant considered letting that wiser protection live through the night. Maybe hire on with his people. But they had been offered a chance to join before. Could he count on them to join later?

He put that problem off for now.

Some of the more-interesting scenes took place when big-wigs found themselves herded into the rotunda at the point of a gun wielded by their own paid security. The shock on their faces was something Grant would treasure for the rest of his life.

There was nothing quite so delicious as awareness dawning too late.

As the gunfire in the hall fell silent, the auto-guns opened up from the roof. Their power rattled the windows and made the palest among those being shoved together go even paler.

Now the only fire inside was for those who refused to accept their state. "You-can't-do-this-to-me-I'm-Mr.-Big-of-Bigger-and-Biggest" got a round in the leg.

A half dozen of those, and even the dumbest of the Big, got appropriately small. Or maybe just quiet.

Grant surveyed his handiwork and liked what he saw.

While the fire on the ground floor was heavy, the actual number of deaths on the main floor were few. The president, agents, yes. But people seemed to accept that those were legitimate targets and, somehow, they were not.

The finely dressed saw themselves as different, people of value worth ransoming. They honestly believed their wealth would protect them even in the mouth of a gun.

Over in the front of the rotunda, two bodies were sprawled in blood, one in a soft burgundy dress, the other in a proud royal blue. Ruby and Topaz had served their purpose.

None of the big people really knew them, yet they all had to have seen them at this important party, that event. Now they were dead.

And you would be, too, if you don't do what the guys with guns tell you. It was an easily readable message. Yet those two were nobody that anybody personally knew. No one reached for a gun to defend either of the two women.

Still, people looked at those two familiar bodies, and looked away or tossed up their fancy hors d'oeuvres.

And obeyed the guys with guns.

This was almost too easy.

There was one more dead body Grant wanted to add to that collection. He searched for a certain red dress.

And did not find it.

So he eyed the crowd for bright red and blue Marines . . . and found them. But the women they surrounded all wore black, except for the orange thing that seemed out of place here.

Grant called up the picture of the princess arriving and, yes, there she was on the arm of the Naval officer.

He now stood alone.

The orange woman, yes, a Naval officer herself, had been escorted by a Marine officer.

Now a sergeant stood at her side.

When had that changed?

Grant eyed the brunette in a similar tight dress to the red one the princess had been wearing when he last saw her. Was someone gaming him?

For only a second he considered having the Marines hauled up to him. Then he dropped it. That they had produced no weapons, offered no proof that they were not armed. And they stood there, united, defiant in their ranks.

And other security men were gravitating to them.

That was going to be a tough nut to crack.

He'd remember that when the time came to kill them all.

Grant tapped his commlink. "I have a problem, Colonel."

"Strange enough, so do I. Who goes first?"

"Princess Kristine of Wardhaven was not caught up in our net. I suspect she is on the loose somewhere in the building with two or three of her Marines."

"That should be easily solved," the colonel said. Grant considered disabusing the man of his error but let him go on.

"The rapid reaction force is coming in," the colonel announced into the silence. "If you want a good view of their deaths, you might want to stand behind the rotunda doors."

"Take them down," Grant ordered. Just like in the old days. His smile tightened. It would be good to get back to giving orders and having powerful men snap to and obey.

Still, he did not move for a better view. It would be a shame to die gawking at an easy kill if one stray bullet got lucky.

Grant did remember the old times.

* * *

EVEN on the roof, Kris heard the roar of powerful engines. Through a window, she spotted eight-wheeled, armored personnel carriers roaring at full bore for the entrance.

The cavalry was arriving.

Maybe even in time.

NELLY, WHAT'S THE NANO SITUATION?

STRANGE NANOS ARE COMING DOWN THE HALL TOWARD US. I HAVE NEVER SEEN THIS KIND BEFORE. I AM LAUNCHING KILLER NANOS TO TAKE THEM OUT. PLEASE WAIT.

"Freeze. Go dark," Kris ordered through unmoving lips.

And Kris turned into a black hole, married to a shadow in a darkened hall. Behind her, her Marines did the same.

Along the roof beside them auto-guns opened fire. Twenty millimeter, piercing, armored shells tore into the top of the carriers. What they did to the men inside, Kris did not want to imagine.

NELLY, WE NEED TO GET MOVING.

KRIS, THESE NANOS ARE GOOD. I AM HAVING TO REINFORCE MY OWN. WE COULD LOSE THIS BATTLE.

DON'T. STRIP MY CROWN IF YOU HAVE TO. KILL THOSE NANOS. WE HAVE TO PUT THOSE AUTO-GUNS OUT OF BUSINESS BEFORE OUR MARINES TRY TO GET IN.

I AM TRYING, KRIS.

Outside, a shell hit a gas tank and the personnel carrier exploded in flames.

Four, five, six of them raced out of control, drivers dead or on fire or both. They collided with walls, trees, one another.

Kris was grateful the distance robbed the scene of human sounds.

And into that small piece of hell, new monsters trundled on tracks that would have shaken any building except this one of granite and marble.

Where did Eden get those old battle tanks? Their appearance left the question irrelevant. Troops with assault rifles trotted along in the shadows of the monsters. This was a combined arms assault by skilled soldiers.

Of course, smoke, a fire plan, and solid preparation of the battlefield would have been nice, too.

But you don't blast a battlefield loaded with the movers and shakers of your planet, now do you. Someone had ordered the heavies in without the heavy prep.

So they rumbled, but no cannon's roared. No machine guns reached out to challenge the auto-guns.

Kris would have shaken her head at the sight. But the door down the hall opened and a man with a machine pistol stuck his head out to get a personal take on the scene.

His face showed hard, alert, lit as it was by the sparkle of burning nanos. He grimaced at the battle taking place in front of his door. Then he studied the hall, marking each shadow.

His hard eyes seemed of half a mind to just spray the space with a full clip and be done with it.

Someone inside shouted something, and he scowled . . . and turned back in.

The door slammed. Tumblers of a heavy-duty lock spun.

Kris almost let a sigh out.

And the world in front of the Gallery lit up as a rocket shot from the roof to slam into the rear of the lead tank.

It hung there, burning for a second. Then it must have burned through. The rear of the tank exploded.

Another rocket led a straight line of glare to a second tank. In less than a breath, that one, too, was a flaming pyre.

NELLY, HOW MUCH LONGER?

WE ALMOST HAVE THEM, KRIS.

ALMOST IS NO HELP TO THOSE POOR DEVILS BURNING OUT THERE.

I KNOW, KRIS. I AM DOING MY BEST.

Kris knew she was. Knew that no one could do any better. It wasn't Nelly that Kris was mad at. There was a certain Grant von Schrader who was running up quite a tab.

A tab Kris intended to collect to its fullest.

"We are clear. Only our nanos are left," Nelly announced.

Kris moved quickly, silently down the hall.

50

Captain DeVar had gotten the whispered "Batter up," signal from Penny, followed by no more information than he could glean from the reflections of explosions and rocket fire as it lit up the soft afterglow of sunset around the Gallery.

He'd ordered Gunny to keep his own counsel, unsure if they'd have communications or not. The princess had warned about the possibility of jamming.

"Commander Tordon, are you on net?"

"Sounds like I'm about the only one on it."

"Are you being jammed?"

"Not that I'm aware of, Marine. I suspect if they jam us, they also jam themselves. Just now, they need to talk at least as much as us to find out what's happening."

"So what is happening?" DeVar asked.

"All hell done broke lose, son, and the devil's out to lunch" came through in an easy drawl that almost made the Marine forget how bad things were.

"There's all sorts of confusion on the main government net about what may or may not be going on at the presidential palace. Some say he's dead. Some say he escaped but wounded.

There's a whole lot of shouting on net for orders. Any orders. Any of that sound about right from your viewpoint?"

"Most of what's happening seems to be on the other side of the palace from me," DeVar said. "I see a lot of reflections of things. Is anyone being jammed?"

"Not that I can tell. But with everybody yammering and shouting, I can't tell if there's a hole in the middle of it. There's plenty of folks willing to fill any hint of silence."

"How's the rest of town?"

"There's an assault under way on that warehouse we visited yesterday. But we kind of expected that. Your Lieutenant Martinez is up to his eyeteeth on that one. Don't look for any help from him for a while."

"I wasn't expecting any. If he can hold, though, these folks out here won't be getting any extra help, either."

"So, what you gonna do? Storm the place?"

"I don't know, Commander. It don't look any too good, but I can't be sure it won't be worse in a few minutes."

"Ain't that what they call a leadership challenge?" DeVar could almost hear the grin behind that.

"Seems to me that's what it is," he said. "Let me know if anything changes on your end."

"I will. You're about the only one calling home. Ain't that sad how kids never do?"

And the familiar voice was gone.

Captain DeVar studied the Gallery, or palace, or killing field. Whatever it was.

Talk to me Kris. What's happening?

Grant von Schrader watched as the last tank backed up, a failed antitank rocket sputtering on its heavily armored snout.

"Well, it will be a long while before they try that again," he said, smiling at the sergeant at his elbow.

"No question, sir."

Grant turned back to the huddled wealth before him. Many of them had watched through the Gallery's windows as their salvation turned to failure, death, and flight. He smiled as a wave of dread swept the place. Well, most of the place.

The Marines stared back at him with hard, defiant eyes.

"What shall I do about that missing princess?" As Grant mulled that conundrum, he climbed up to stand among the greats of Eden on Landing Day. And smiled at the image of himself. It was a pleasant thought.

The Marines had formed themselves into a loose battle array halfway down the great hall's south wing with their backs to the west wall. The only good shots at them would be from the east side of the second floor walk. The officers had their backs to the wall. The Marines held the first line.

More and more of the still-armed security guards migrated to stand with them.

During the initial planning, Grant had given thought to disarming everyone immediately. And given it up as taking too much time.

Grant figured the dispirited people would be helpless and little trouble even with guns.

He had not considered that some of the guards might be Marines. Dispirited and helpless didn't seem to be in their vocabulary.

"Commander," Grant shouted, "you over there. Where's Kris Longknife?"

The Navy commander shared a few words with the woman in the ridiculous orange taffeta affair. She nodded and then stood a bit straighter.

"I speak for this detachment." The missing "sir" hung like a slap in the air.

"And you are?"

"Lieutenant Pasley-Lien, United Sentient Navy."

"Where's Kris Longknife?"

"The last place you want her, buster" shot back at him. That brought a titter of laughter to the hall.

Looking ridiculous in front of these people was the last thing Grant wanted.

"Throw down your guns, and I'll let you live."

"Our guns are all that's keeping you from slaughtering us. No way, my optimistic little friend."

Again the hall ran with that nervous twitter.

Above them came the sounds of running feet. The riflemen brought in on the last of the caterer's trucks galloped down the second-floor gallery and took up positions, assault rifles aimed down into the crowd.

With luck, they might actually hit something if they fired, Grant thought. He'd been briefed about their poor performance on the rifle range.

But no one down there knew that.

"You, security guards," Grant shouted. "You still have your weapons. Disarm those hardcases for me. You can't be afraid of a couple of Marines. Do it and you have a job with me."

The security guards looked around among themselves. Some whispered things Grant didn't catch.

One looked like he might take Grant up on his offer, but he ended up coldcocked before anything came of it. Someone picked up his pistol and joined the group around the Marines.

"You're putting a lot of people at risk, Lieutenant Pasley. You could lose everything very quickly."

"I'm a widow, buster, you Peterwald toadies already took everything I hold dear" came back in a cold voice.

A check with his computer told him what he should have researched sooner.

"You going to let a nutcase like that get you all killed?" didn't have the impact Grant expected.

"Sergeant," he shouted to one that commanded the shooters on the second-floor balcony, "throw down some plastic cuffs. If you allow yourself to be cuffed we'll move you down to the north wing. You won't get killed if we have to shoot these crazies."

The plastic stringers were thrown out, scattering as they fell. Some people did offer their wrists to their neighbors to be bound.

"Don't do it," the orange harridan shouted. "They want to kill us all. If you make it easy for them, they'll just kill you last."

The eager rush to be cuffed died.

Grant eyed the firing line on the second floor. Should he give the order to fire? Let the massacre begin? He did not plan to let anyone here out alive. The only question was when to let them in on the secret.

"Hey, Grant!" That blasted woman's voice drew his attention back to her. The tall Naval commander moved out from in front of her.

She held a service automatic. It was aimed directly between Grant's eyes.

"You die first," she said.

A second later, several of the Marines had joined her, their automatics on him. Reflexively, Grant's eyes searched their uniforms. All were sharpshooters. One a sniper.

Somewhere in the building there was an explosion.

Now Marines and armed security guards drew beads on the punks lining the upper balcony.

"You sure you want to die with a jarhead's dart between your eyes" came in the voice of a Marine sergeant.

Above, rifles wavered. One disappeared from view as someone broke into a run.

Grant waited for one of his sergeants to tell him what was happening. Better yet, for one of his sharpshooters to take that woman down.

Then the lights went out.

Grant dropped into the darkness and off of the bronzes. Behind him darts pinged off the artwork where he'd been a second ago.

Kris said a bitter word as the lights went out. That was not what she'd intended.

She'd edged up to the door slowly, examining it as she went. It was metal, with an armored-glass window, reinforced with bars. In an older, more safe world, it would have been the epitome of maximum security.

Today, it was puny.

She waved a Marine forward. He frowned at the lock,

then reached into this uniform and withdrew a coil of plastic explosives.

While he rigged the door for destruction, Kris risked a few glances through the glass.

It showed her little. Whatever was inside was far inside, well away from the door. What she did see carried the hint of observation and security.

Hopefully, this was where the auto-guns were controlled.

The Marine stepped back, signaling that he was ready to blow both the lock and the hinges.

Kris reached into the padding of her rear and pulled out two whizbangs. Jack took one. She kept the other.

The sergeant held up three fingers, then two. Finally one.

And the door exploded.

Kris launched herself from the wall in a low crouch. She hit the door low, Jack high. It went down ahead of them.

But not flat. A body was on the floor beneath it.

Ahead of Kris was a counter, a glass cage cutting off further access to the computer stations within.

There was all of ten centimeters of clearance between counter and glass to allow supplicants to pass requests inside.

Kris tossed her whizbang through the space the same moment Jack did.

Behind her, a Marine went fully automatic, hammering at a small-caliber auto-gun turning to take her under fire.

Even as Kris ducked and rolled up to the counter, the auto-gun was sighting in on her. Kris left that problem to the Marine behind her and aimed her gun at the four men sitting at the computer stations in the room.

The auto-gun put three rounds into Kris's hairdo, then coughed and spat no more.

That's going to hurt in the morning, Kris thought, as she shouted, "Anyone got a grenade?"

"Here's one," a sergeant behind her shouted. He tossed. She caught it, pulled the pin in one motion, and tossed it through the opening in the glass.

"Fire in the hole," someone shouted.

A moment later there was an explosion. Kris counted to two, then jumped up and started shooting.

Maybe she didn't aim all that precisely at any specific target. Maybe she should have.

The lights went out.

51

For fifteen seconds, only the light of muzzle flashes lit up the main hall. It was enough for people to die by.

Penny tried to trace Von Schrader's flight by the flashes of the gunners behind him, but he was in full beat-feet mode, and not looking back.

Penny did see several gunners go down behind him, so she wasn't wasting her ammo.

"Mind if we grab some grenades, ma'am" came from a Marine.

"Let's don't and say we do," Penny said. "We got a lot of civilians lying around" was her answer.

"Let's get them some protection," Commander Mulhoney shouted. He rolled behind a marble statue in front of Penny, braced his back against the wall, and pushed. What was likely a very expensive bit of art toppled over, crashing into pieces as it hit. But people could huddle behind it. Around the great hall, other statues of bronze and marble went down.

Fire from the balcony was getting light. Penny balanced that against the fire from the rotunda and ordered her shooters to concentrate there. She also sent a couple of shooters to cover the stairwells in the back. No question, she could be rushed from there.

"Let me see if I can get some of the civilians out of here," Commander Mulhoney said. He backed up, found a door that opened onto the east portico, and tried it. It stayed closed. He stood and fired at the lock. It flew open.

He stepped out on the portico. "Civilians," he shouted, "follow me. Let's get the hell out of this place." That got the attention of the people cringing on the floor.

It also got the attention of people with guns who were already outside, covering the balcony. Two rounds spun him around.

"Blast it," was his only response as he went down.

Then the emergency lights came on and Penny got a good look at just how bad hell could be.

Grant von Schrader slid to a halt behind a huge bronze vase. "Colonel, the situation is developing faster than we expected," he said into his commlink. "Tell me something I don't know."

"We no longer have contact with Security Central," he reported.

"I told you that Longknife girl was not to be underestimated."

The colonel did not defend himself or argue that there was no proof the loss of Security Central was the work of a Longknife. Instead, like a pro, he went on with their future.

"We are taking fire from the parking lot. I suspect we did not get all the Marine guards around the Wardhaven limo. I have detached a fire team to keep them busy."

"Do not ignore our back door," Grant snapped.

"I am not. I have detached two fire teams to cover the river. I'm sending a third up to see if the auto-guns can be operated locally."

"Good. Tell them to look out for that Longknife hellion. The man who gets her will get millions."

"Yes, sir. They are aware."

"And now we must say good-bye, Colonel. Activate the jammer."

"I was about to, sir. May I recommend that you fall back on my command post."

"I will see you there in a moment. The slaughter here should be over very soon."

Grant turned to the sergeant at his elbow. "Kill them all, then report to your colonel when your job here is done."

The Greenfeld men pulled grenades from their belts as Grant low-crawled for the stairwell.

Bronc stared at his computer. It was totally jammed. A rock would tell him as much as his fine computer.

One of the sergeants picked up a gun that had fallen to the balcony's floor. The young man who had held it stared blankly ahead. His forehead had a small hole in it.

Bronc had seen what the back of his head looked like. He never wanted to see that again.

"Your computer's no good. Do some shooting," he ordered.

Bronc put his computer aside and took the gun. He eyed it like some snake.

"Shoot, damn you, kid. Shoot or I'll shoot you." It didn't sound like something Bronc could argue with.

Not when the sergeant punctuated it by shooting down a kid that was running for the far end of the balcony.

Bronc edged up to the balcony. Most of the kids still shooting were lying flat on the floor, shooting through the fancy marble poles that held up the banister. Bronc slipped his gun out, and aimed the barrel in the general direction of a statue of a half-nude woman.

He pulled the trigger.

Nothing happened. The gun didn't fire and the trigger didn't move all that far back.

He squeezed harder on the trigger, but it just would not move.

"I think you have to do something with this lever," the kid

to his right said. He lay his rifle down, leaning it sideways so Bronc could see what he was pointing at.

He also made the mistake of getting higher up on his elbows than he'd been.

Something took the top off his head, spraying blood and stuff along the wall behind him.

Bronc felt like throwing up.

"Shoot, damn you." That may or may not have been aimed at Bronc, but he got his head down, pushed the lever with his thumb, and shot.

The gun fired. It fired a long burst until Bronc remembered to ease back on the trigger.

"Don't go automatic," the kid on his left warned, staying low. "The sergeants don't like that. Push the safety back a notch."

Bronc did. The next time he pulled the trigger, it only fired one shot.

"And aim," the kid said. "The sergeant hates it when you shoot but don't aim."

That kid was looking hard down the barrel of his own gun. Bronc did the same. He tried to line it up on that half-naked lady and pulled the trigger.

Some plaster above her head exploded. Was that him?

"I'm out of here," a kid shouted, down the line from Bronc, as he jumped up and headed for the stairs.

"No you ain't," the sergeant snarled, and blew his head off.

"Enough of this," the kid at the sergeant's feet shouted, rolled over, raised his gun, and put three rounds into the sergeant's belly, below the body armor that they had and the kids didn't.

The other sergeant drilled that kid, but a girl, one of the few that got jobs as shooters, put two rounds into the back of that sergeant's head.

But then she half got up and someone below put a bullet into her.

"Now what do we do?" the kid next to Bronc asked.

"I know a way out of here, I think," Bronc said.

"I'm right behind you," said several voices.

"They're gonna kill us," said one guy who was still shooting.

"You can stay here and get killed by those Marines. Me, I'm taking my chances with anyone else," said Bronc and led a dozen or more in a low crouch off the balcony to the stairwell. He'd seen his sensor sergeant go up higher when he was peeled off to back up the firing line.

Bronc led the way up, rather than down the way they'd come.

A couple of guys headed down. But a second later there was fire from that direction, and the screams of dying youth.

The rest followed Bronc up.

"Sorry, ma'am, I must have tossed you a demolition grenade." That sort of explained to Kris the mess she was looking at.

Jack's flashlight showed a grizzly scene. The counter and its glass enclosure had held, as had the windows. That left nothing for the explosives to work on but four human bodies and the electronic gear still smoldering in the room.

The walls were covered in soot and blood and bones and body parts. The armored glass wept red onto the counter.

The sergeant used his last bit of C-8 to blow the lock on the door and let them into what they had done.

"You see any switch that might turn the lights back on?" Kris asked.

"Looks like the grenade blew up on that work station," Jack said, aiming his light at one particular sparse bit of wreckage. Cables led into to it, and away from it, but there was no telling what they might have done in between.

"Do we have the auto-guns out of commission?" Kris asked.

That got only a shrug from Jack. On a well-designed ship, any station could be brought up as any station. Even if they had demolished the primary work center for the guns, was there a backup security center in the basement?

No way to tell.

"Nelly, order the Marines to attack."

"I can't, Kris. That jamming just started."

Kris said a very unprincesslike word.

"Jack, can you signal the captain?"

"Let's see how good my Morse code is."

Jack wiped the gore from a small section of the window and started flashing a message toward the river. "Let's hope this is good enough."

"Stop or I'll shot" came from the sergeant guarding their back door. He followed that up with a shot.

"Don't shoot. Please don't shoot" came in a voice that sounded familiar to Kris.

Captain DeVar knew things were changing in the Gallery when he spotted the explosion behind several windows on the roof.

"Let's get ready to ride, troops," he ordered, wondering if he was ordering them into a slaughter.

Then the lights went out.

"That sure looks like showtime to me," he said, ordering the first squad forward.

They splashed from the river and slid down on the riverbank, rifles at the ready. Nothing happened.

Then a light started flashing from the window that had been lit up a moment ago by that explosion.

It took Captain DeVar a second to realize that the light's flashes had meaning.

"FROM THE HALLS OF MON" said enough for one Marine.

"Charge," Captain DeVar ordered for the first time in his life.

"Move it, move it, move it," sergeants echoed to his right and left.

"Last one to the big house does KP next month" came from somewhere along the line.

And a hundred sharp troopers raced across the manicured lawn of the Gallery as fast as full-battle rattle would allow.

And ahead of him, on the roof, the captain spotted movement. More movement down on the west portico.

Muzzles flashed there. Dirt exploded here. A Marine went down.

"First squads, hit the deck," DeVar ordered. "Provide covering fire. Second squads, advance with me."

Nobody joined the Marines for an easy berth.

It didn't look to this Marine captain like his crew would be seeing one anytime soon.

52

Penny ordered the sergeant to reorient his axis of attack.

The balcony was silent, all the shooters up there either dead or fled. If she wasn't mistaken, Bronc had been the one that led the final flight from up there but it was hard to tell in the faint light from the emergency lamps.

She hoped he lived. They owed the kid for his warning.

Then a grenade sailed in from the rotunda, and another. And another. The general slaughter had begun.

The first grenade landed among a clump of civilians. They stared at it . . . and died as it exploded. The second landed in a group that had a Marine. He fell on it and died . . . but the others lived. Another fell among the group of Marines. One of them tossed it back to explode above the head of the raiders.

It was nice hearing screams from them.

More grenades flew. More examples of folly and denial leading to death. Or bravery and courage leading to a single death or death to the enemy.

Long forgotten virtues quickly were remembered on Eden.

The grenade toss became a full participation sport.

"Don't we have a few of those ourselves?" a Marine asked.

So Penny and a security type ended up pealing grenades of their own out of their petticoats and tossing them to Marines in the front who tossed them into the midst of the shooters and throwers around the bronze figures holding pride of place there.

A lot of art shattered. A lot burned.

But then, so did a lot of people.

A security type saying, "I was a pitcher for the Dodgers," asked for a grenade. He stood in the doorway to the west portico and tossed it toward the main entrance. There were screams. From Mulhoney came the first sign of life. Only a weak thumbs-up, but it was a sign.

But somehow, the portico force was reinforced. The sounds of a major firefight out there aimed at the car park and the one exit from the great hall told Penny safety didn't lie in that direction.

More grenades flew in. More grenades were tossed out. People died cringing in on themselves. People died fighting. But here or there, Marines shouted for more grenades or a fresh magazine. Penny found herself promoted from pack mule to supply sergeant.

How long could this keep up?

Kris watched the Marines charge from the river, hope rising in her belly. Then she turned for the door. "Don't shoot, sergeant. Is that you, Bronc?"

"Yes, ma'am, Your Highness. And I've got a dozen scared kids with me. Please don't shoot us."

And somebody fired.

Kris reached the corridor just in time to see the kids hugging the tiled floor and her Marine firing at something down the hall where Kris had lurked only a few minutes ago.

She pulled out two whizbangs and sent them flying down the passageway in company with the sergeant's darts.

The whizbangs went bang . . . and a door slammed.

"I think we got trouble on the roof. They might be trying to come around behind us," the corporal said.

"Or see if they can get the auto-guns shooting," Kris growled. "Cover me."

And Kris was out, tiptoeing through young men, who huddled as low as the floor would let them. Most had rifles, but few clutched them. Kris stooped to pick up one, pulled a bandolier off another.

She reached the door to the stairwell about the time the other stairwell creaked open again and the sergeant behind Kris took it under fire.

The next set of whizbangs brought Jack in behind Kris, along with a couple of kids who didn't take to lying on the floor while bullets whizzed by a few inches above their heads.

Even a teenager could figure that sooner or later, someone was going to lower their aim.

One of the kids was Bronc.

"The Marines from the river are taking fire," Jack whispered. "DeVar's slowed. Half providing overwatch to the half still moving."

"Can these auto-guns be fired on manual and locally?"

"Your guess about what they do on Eden is as good as mine," Jack said.

Kris flipped open the door to the roof.

And watched as it was quickly punched full of holes.

"This ain't gonna be easy," Jack said.

Kris felt around her bottom. "Whizbangs, sleepy gas, don't look all that good just now."

"I have some smoke and two frags," Jack offered.

Kris pulled out two whizbangs and two sleepy gas throwers. She distributed them among the willing kids. "Jack will toss the smoke first. Keep it close in. You kids throw the sleeping gas as far as you can. It's open air and the gas won't do so well, but even a yawn helps." That got a dry chuckle.

Kris would toss the whizbangs. Farther than the smoke, shorter than the gas.

"Ready? Jack tosses on three, the gas on two. I'll throw the bangs on one. Jack, you add a frag to the mix. Don't run out there until I tell you the smoke has thickened up. Hear me?"

"Yes, ma'am" came back just like you'd expect from a bunch of teenagers.

And so they did it. Smoke, gas, then bangs, and lastly boom. Kris waited, one hand on Bronc's heaving chest. His heart was pounding like it might punch its way out past his ribs.

Kris waited for the smoke to thicken.

"Stay low. Run now."

And Kris and Jack led the kids out, firing their automatics into the smoke, into the flashing lights.

Somewhere a man screamed. Another man cursed and hollered for a medic.

Kris ran low, then dropped to roll up behind the concrete base of some antenna. Jack picked the next one for his own.

A boy went down, sprawling from a hit. Another found a cinder-block wall to take cover behind.

There were six of them out on the roof before the smoke dissolved and a wall of automatic fire replaced it.

And somewhere down the roof, an auto-gun cut loose a long wicked burst at the ground below.

Kris didn't need to see, she could feel the Marines going down before it.

"Snipers, get those bastards on the roof," Gunny Brown called.

And got a fusillade of small-arms fire for his effort. Since this big, armored dinosaur hardly budged as it took the hits, it was no skin off Gunny's nose.

But clearly, something was happening up on that roof. From the looks of it, he'd say Marines held down the right wing up there. Probably that lieutenant and the princess.

And it looked like they could use all the help he could send their way.

Then an auto-gun opened up, thankfully, not on Gunny's side of the roof.

But it had to be shooting at something, and the old man and his platoons were the only worthwhile targets beside Gunny's fire teams.

Marines needed help and the only help Gunny could give was to the roof.

One sniper took down someone with a gun trying to work his way down behind the right wing.

Good.

Another dude up there stopped at what looked like an auto-gun and started to raise a shield or maybe it was just the top of the control box. A sniper put an end to that noise.

Now other Marines opened up, sweeping the front of the roof clean of dark figures. Those that didn't crouch low and beat a hasty retreat only stayed in place to die.

But applying pressure on the roof lighted up the pressure they'd been keeping on the front porch of that stone monster.

Clearly, a major fight was going on there.

Gunny drew up a good sight picture and dropped a guy leaning out a door to toss a grenade.

He went down. A moment later, his grenade did horrible things to the fellows around him.

Gunny grinned and swept the area, looking for another grenade thrower. He hated those things. Didn't those dudes up there know that Mr. Grenade was not your friend.

Gunny checked his fire teams. Between the half dozen around him and the two sniper crews on his flank, he could hold this car park against most any force coming at him from the front.

He spared a glance behind him. Tanks and trucks still burned fitfully. Why hadn't any of those shooters worked their way up to reinforce him? What was going on out there?

Gunny shook his head. Officers were supposed to do that kind of worrying. If he wasn't careful, someone would order him off to OCS.

Gunny sighted in on movement at a window. He blew another grenade thrower back to where he'd come from. A moment later, there was a delightful explosion.

It was nice being an enlisted swine.

* * *

Captain DeVar knew the auto-gun was aimed at him. Of course, every man up and following him felt the same way. But when the auto-gun finished its first burst, it was DeVar's legs that would no longer hold him up.

The captain skidded to a halt, the armor taking up most of the shock. His legs weren't hurting. Yet.

He put the time to good use.

"Rockets, get that gun," he ordered.

A Marine specialist behind DeVar sighted his rocket launcher on the roof. He seemed to pull the trigger the same second that the auto-gun selected him for death.

The rocket hit the roof, but missed to the right of the auto-gun, taking down two riflemen. A second rocket spec got the gun that got his pal.

For a second the fire fight seemed almost silent as only the usual rifle fire broke the evening's silence.

Then a second auto-gun opened up. Its first target was the remaining rocket man and he went down hard.

Hand grenades were hopeless at this distance. Even the 20-mm grenade launchers were hard-pressed to reach the height of the Gallery roof.

The snipers took the gunner under fire, but the auto-gun was looking for them, too.

Just about the time it started looking to DeVar that he and his men would need a miracle to cross this killing ground, the pain in his legs hit him like a runaway truck. A sheen of red covered his vision and he had to put his head down.

The battle would have to go on without him.

53

Kris knew she had to get that auto-gun.

"Jack, you still got a grenade?"

"Just one frag."

"Aim for the gun. Boys, give him cover."

She and the boys laid down cover fire. Jack lobbed the grenade.

The grenade took out the gunner, but another stepped into his place and the auto-gun kept ripping holes in the ranks of the armored Marines.

Kris felt inside her bra and pulled out the bomb hidden there.

"Cover me," Kris called.

"That can't be what I think it is," one of the boys said.

"Cover her," Jack ordered gruffly, and let off a blast of pistol fire.

Kris fired three rounds herself, dropped the pistol, rolled right to the other side of her concrete protection, and half stood to lob her bomb.

The other side of the antenna support took a pounding. But quickly the fire worked its way toward her. Kris ducked back down before any caught her.

And her booby bomb sailed past the auto-gun to explode on the next one in line.

Unfortunately, it was not in operation.

But it was fully loaded.

The bomb's explosion started a fire, which burned for a fraction of a minute before it began baking off ammo. Undirected 20-mm rounds took off for the stars, or shot off for the river.

One took the head off the guy manning the operational auto-gun. Another took the back out of the man who stood to take the dead gunner's place.

Terrified shooters fell back on the stairwell, trying to get out of reach of the mad nondirectional slaughter.

Then two rounds took off the door to the stairwell and exploded inside.

The next guy to seek safety leapt off the roof, trying to reach a tall elm.

He did manage to catch a limb. But not one that would hold him. On the way to the ground he caught another limb, but it was no stronger. He hit the balustrade of the rear porch and lay there, his back at a horribly odd angle.

There was a sudden rush for the stairs.

Kris gritted her teeth on the temptation to let them run, and joined Jack in shooting them down.

If they got off the roof in one piece, surely Grant von Schrader had sergeants waiting to rally them, beat them back into fire teams.

Behind Kris, one of her young shooters threw up.

When they had the roof to themselves, Kris holstered her automatic, but kept the long rifle at the ready. It was a commercial version of the M-6, probably made on New Jerusalem. She noticed it had been modified for fully automatic fire.

Interesting.

Jack stood, rifle in hand, and waved to the Marines below.

Many were up, trotting for the back porch of the Gallery.

Many were up, but way too many of them were still down.

The static on net saved Kris from having to ask who was

among those down. She trotted for the stairwell, blackened and blocked by bodies.

Given a choice of following that route down or finding another, she turned to Jack and they headed back the way they'd came.

On the way they put a solid burst into each of the auto-guns they passed. They would trouble Marines no more.

This was not going the way Grant von Schrader planned.

"We've lost the roof," Colonel Müller reported. His words were as dismal as the cold, bare concrete walls of his command center in the sub-basement. "Again, the militia folded like cards."

"Why couldn't your sergeants hold them?" Grant shot back.

"Because we did not have enough time to train them to have a backbone," the colonel shot right back.

Grant nodded. "We both knew we needed more time."

"Have we killed enough of the sheep?"

That was the only real question left this evening. The objective tonight had been the total decapitation of Eden's business and government. Grant had promised the wastrel side of the old families that they would inherit. They had lapped up his words.

They were cheap promises. In a month, hardheaded business men from Greenfeld would arrive, making their way into the business of this world. In a year, 90 percent of it would be owned by Greenfeld. And the workforce would hum with the efficiency that only a strong fist could produce.

That had been this morning's dream.

What was left tonight?

"Colonel, prepare to withdraw to the north as we planned. I'm going up to the rotunda to see how many more of the sheep we can slaughter. Then I will meet you at the north rally point with your sergeants."

Colonel Müller glanced at his watch. "You have ten minutes. A second more and you will find no one there."

"As I would expect of you," Grant said.

He headed for the stairs. With luck, he just might get himself a Longknife in the next ten minutes.

Kris dropped down the stairs, Jack and two Marines right behind her. Six very scared but very obedient teens tagged along behind them.

"You know, Jack, just once I'd like to end one of these dustups with a Peterwald puke to talk to. To really talk to. You know what I mean," Kris said over her shoulder.

"Sure you'd want to hear what he'd say?" Jack asked. "Sure your Grampa Ray would want that?"

Kris wasn't all that sure she cared what Grampa Ray wanted. He'd sent her into this mess with not one word of warning. Not one suggestion of what to look for. Several colorful and obscene suggestions came to her of what Grampa Ray could do.

Course, him being king, some of them might be treason.

Kris kept her own counsel.

They came to the third floor. The balcony here gave a view of the main floor below. But to actually get a shot into something down there meant showing way too much of Kris's precious skin.

She headed down another level.

The second floor had the disadvantage of being covered with the bodies left from the earlier phase of the shoot-out. The teenagers blanched, but followed Kris as she led them out, gingerly low, walking past the bodies of dead friends.

The main floor looked like a slaughterhouse. And one in special need of cleaning. Probably qualified for one of the labors of Hercules.

Bodies were piled up. Some where they fell. Others were piled in front of people who used them to absorb bullets instead of themselves.

Sculptures had been upended because their bases afforded better cover. The shattered statues had been pushed around to afford protection to the people who cowered behind them.

Here or there another hand grenade flew. A rifle barked. Automatics spat. Beneath the staccato of battle, the whimpers and cries of wounded humanity filled in the lower octaves.

And over it all was the stench of blood and death.

Kris blinked away the general picture and focused on those that mattered to her.

There was Penny. Her orange dress now covered with the red of fresh blood, the brown of dried blood. But the lieutenant was still waving orders and reaching under her dress to toss a grenade to one Marine, or a magazine to another.

Fire at the moment was desultory. Whether because ammo was running low or people on both sides had grown reluctant to risk exposure, was not clear.

Kris noticed two Marines that had acquired rifles. Probably ones that fell from the hands of inexperienced casualties on the second-floor balcony. They fired sparingly.

Kris retrieved a bandolier from one dead shooter and tossed it over the rail. For a second the fire slackened. Then one gun went to full automatic, covering the trooper retrieving the spare ammo. A moment later, the second rifle was back on line, snapping off bursts.

Kris tossed a second bandolier. It landed close to the other Marine. In a minute, he was back going rapid fire.

At the rotunda, the fire seemed to slacken off in the face of the newly energized resistance.

Kris reached the end of the balcony and risked a glance over just as the figure of Grant von Schrader dogtrotted up to the edge of the rotunda.

"What are you guys, asleep," he shouted. "You want your mamas? Did we rob a bunch of cradles? There they are. Shoot them. You got grenades left. Throw them."

Kris drew a bead on him. And she would have put a full five-round burst into him if he hadn't picked that moment to duck behind that bronze representation of Landing Day.

She would have loved to have a long talk with him, but because of his lip, the fire was growing hot again.

Kris decided today was no day for talking.

She reached into her bra and drew out the last of her booby
bombs. She considered several places to toss the thing, then
grinned.

She punched it for a four-second fuse and lofted it straight
for the center of the bronze statuary.

It sailed through the air, ignored by most below, but
watched by Kris. It plopped down right in the dead center of
the statues, bouncing off one, then landing at the foot of the
five great founding fathers of Garden City. They stood there,
backs to each other, staring out at the land they had come so
far for.

And when the explosion came, bronze feet and torsos and
arms were converted to even more ancient bronzes: daggers,
spears, and swords.

The gunners around the rotunda just kind of went to pieces.

"Good God," Jack muttered.

"Have mercy on them," Kris added, as Tommy did so
many times before. "I will not," she said for herself.

A second explosion hardly made its point with the echo of
the first one still hammering Kris's ears. But a moment later,
its source became clear.

The familiar sound of M-6s on single shot, the hallmark of
good Marines, swept the rotunda, only seconds before the
Marines themselves in full-body armor and battle rattle swept
into view.

Many still dripped riverwater or mud. But they were the
cavalry, here at the rescue. They had no bugles, no proud
streamers, but man, were they beautiful.

There were scattered cheers from Kris's side of the great
hall. Hands shot up in the rotunda.

Not everyone's. Someone got off a shot at the leading
Marine. That one died.

That was all it took to get any reluctant hands up.

Silence—lovely, empty silence—filled the hall.

Broken only by the moans and whimpers of those for
whom peace had come too late.

54

Gunnery Sergeant Brown stayed under the white dinosaur while the glass settled from the huge explosion in the rotunda. Only when the deadly glass shards finished tinkling off the cars did he risk rolling out and carefully looking around.

Darkness was back, though his eyes would hold the memory of that flash of bright light for a while to come. There was sporadic fire for a few moments. Some dude was always late getting the word. But it wasn't long before even they woke up—or died—and silence broke out in all its glory.

And the quiet stretched and grew and Gunny knew that it was good. Anything was better than the unshirted hell they'd been in for . . . he glanced at his watch.

Only the last thirty minutes!

That was impossible. He raised his watch to his ear. It was still ticking. A fine old windup watch handed down from father to son for more times than Gunny wanted to think about.

It still ticked and insisted his eternity in hell had been little more than half an hour.

He shook his head.

As the quiet stretched into something that was almost a delicious peace, Gunny glanced over his shoulder. In the distance he could just make out the revolving lights of dozens of emergency services vehicles.

Why weren't the ambulances moving?

He turned back to look for his fastest runner, someone he could send back there to get the lead out of that bunch . . .

And spotted dark figures skulking out of the north wing of the Gallery.

Not being an officer, Gunny might not know all the important stuff. But he knew the stink of rats leaving a sinking ship. Especially the stink of rats leaving a ship they had done their best to hole.

A slight change of plans here.

Gunny caught a runner's eye, but sent her off to bring back the sniper team on the south end. Then he motioned to his own fire teams in the center to start their movement north.

The northern sniper team was led by Corporal Donovan. She never needed to be told where the action was. She and her partner were already up and doing a slow, low walk from car to car, headed north.

But Gunny needn't have worried about his rats getting away.

They didn't go all that far, maybe fifty yards, before they stopped at a tree surrounded by stone flower pots.

Half a dozen faced out. Four or five talked among themselves in the center.

If that wasn't a well-organized rally point, Gunny hadn't spent twenty years in the Corps.

And they waited.

That was what professional troops were supposed to do, wait to see if anyone detached or just lost showed up at the rally.

But after that last explosion and fire, the place was pretty quiet.

Gunny sure would have been tempted to keep the bugout boogie going.

But that looked to be an officer doing the look-around from the center, so good NCOs were waiting, just like they should.

Which gave Gunny's team time to catch up, overtake, and pass them. Gunny spotted several good ambush sites and smiled.

When that bunch of rats moved north again, it would be right into his waiting arms.

As the seconds flew and Gunny's Marines set up their kill zones, he watched the one he took for the senior NCO exchange words with the guy who had to be the senior officer.

Gunny heard not a word, but he knew the drill.

"Sir, we should move on. We can't afford to lose a second."

But the officer only glanced at his watch. Who was he waiting for? Gunny would bet money the officer knew personally the one who was holding them up—likely had served under him as a junior officer.

Maybe, another time, waiting would have served a purpose. Today, Gunny was prepared to make sure it didn't.

And Gunny made up his mind.

He signaled to the crew in sight of him. Sleepy darts.

And they passed it along.

Sleepy darts were a risk, but Gunny was one of the many NCOs who were getting sick and tired of Greenfeld pukes doing this or killing that and no one living to tell the tale.

The officers might be happy not having to face the hard truth about the undeclared war they were in, but all the dancing around the truth made an honest fighting man just want to puke.

This call was Gunny's to make, and he was making it.

These rats were beaten; he could see it in the hunch of their shoulders. They were walking into an ambush put in place by good Marines.

These dudes were going to wake up with a roaring headache tomorrow morning, and they were going to sing, sing, sing.

And kings and captains could just bite themselves if they didn't like what a sweating, cursing Gunny Sergeant had done to them.

The enemy officer took a final glance at his watch. A final glance at the Gallery. Nothing moved out of it.

He signaled to his troops and a scout pair led off, quickly

followed by others as the outer guards of the rally point folded themselves into a traveling column.

It was a beautiful work of art that Gunny was fully qualified to appreciate . . . unlike much of the crap hanging in the now-smoking building.

But they were moving right into his ambush. *His* work of art.

Gunnery Sergeant Brown grinned and drew a sight picture on the officer. He and his Marines were artists in their own right.

Come and see the art we do.

55

Who said the only sight more sickening than a battle won is the sight of a battle you lost?

At the moment, Kris's addled brain refused to cough up the answer to that question. And she had better uses for Nelly.

"Are you still jammed? Can you get out a call for medical services?"

"I am sorry, Kris, but yes, I am still jammed."

Kris shook her head. The jammer had clearly lost, but either was keeping it on for pure evilness or forgetfulness.

Or maybe they hadn't given the battle up for lost.

That was not a comforting thought.

Marines in battle gear now moved purposefully into the rotunda to disarm and secure the prisoners. "Captain DeVar, what's your situation?" Kris called from the second-floor balcony.

One Marine looked up. "Ah, I'm Lieutenant Troy, ma'am. I think I'm in command, ah, Your Highness."

Told Kris a lot about the company of embassy Marines.

"Lieutenant, secure your prisoners, set up a defensive perimeter here for the hall, then send armored detachments to check out the rooms in this place. They may find civilians who managed to stay lost through the shoot. They may find shooters trying to get away."

"Ah, ma'am, I'm not sure I've got enough troops to tackle all that. And do you have any medical aid? We could sure use more out back."

That told Kris all she needed to know about her company.

She nodded, thinking through what mattered most and shortening her list of priorities. "Lieutenant, secure your prisoners and the perimeter of the great hall against a counterattack. I'll get us medical aid."

Kris turned to Jack, muttering under her breath, "Where are those ambulances?"

They headed down the stairs. "Boys, stay close to us or you may be mistaken for prisoners. You deserve our gratitude."

Admittedly, they'd turned their coats several times in the last—Kris glanced at her watch—only a half hour! Still, Bronc and his friends had done the right thing after doing the wrong thing.

"Marines coming in," Jack called as they approached the main floor. It was good he did.

They were still blacked out from head to toe, a shadow of a shadow. That camouflage had probably saved their lives tonight. But now they were approaching fellow Marines.

There had been a fight here. Kids with rifles and men in dark clothes lay where they'd fallen.

Several of Penny's hand grenades had been used here.

A statue had been rolled up to the stairwell exit. A marine and a security guard looked at Kris over pistol sights. Beside them, two or three more lay where they had died.

The Marine raised the aim of his automatic and whispered a dry mouthed "Semper Fi."

And they passed within.

The south hall had gone from being a bright, gala party to a dark, bloody, slippery mess of groaning humanity. At least it groaned where it wasn't deadly silent.

It was far too quiet for Kris's tastes. She concentrated on watching her step and getting where she needed to go.

Behind her, one of the teens added the contents of his stomach to the slime they waded through.

Penny and several surviving Marines held the middle of the hall. The Navy lieutenant and those around her were just risking sitting up.

While several of the Marines stood to greet their comrades, Penny settled for just sitting there. A long sliver of bronze had sliced through the flesh of her upper right arm.

The lieutenant eyed the spear point in her flesh and shook her head ruefully. "I survived this whole bloody mess, and then you make your usual entrance and whack me one."

"Sorry about that," Kris said, and tried to put some actual feeling into the words. Even she didn't hear any. "I'll try to get someone to look at that."

"In a thousand years after the really bad cases are cared for," Penny said, looking around. "Where *are* the ambulances?"

"I don't know." Kris hated to admit it. "And Nelly says we're still being jammed. Can't say squat."

"Kris, I think I can home in on the jamming," Nelly said. "It seems to be coming from below us."

Kris took a deep breath, and let it out slowly. So this thing wasn't over yet. Maybe she could hand Nelly over to a fresh Marine and let a couple of them go chasing into the bowels of this building.

So there is a limit to just how much a Longknife can take, a small voice said somewhere inside her.

And this isn't it, another part of her growled.

"Thank you, Nelly. Jack, you and your Marines up for another ramble through the artwork?"

Jack nodded. The "Ooo-Rah" from the Marines might have been a bit below their usual enthusiasm, but they got it out.

From outside somewhere came the familiar sound of M-6s barking on single shot. Marines had someone under fire.

The rapid staccato of machine pistols answered them, but only for a few seconds. Then the night got quiet again.

"Nelly?" Kris asked.

"I am still jammed."

Kris turned back for the stairs.

"Be careful, Kris," Penny called. "Don't be the last one killed in this shoot-out."

"I'll do my best," Kris answered over her shoulder.

"So will I," Jack shot back.

"Us, too," the Marines added.

"Me, too," came from the kids who trailed right along.

"I guess I better go along with you," one of the Marines with a rifle said. "Someone might have left a little gift behind and I suspect you'll want a demolition tech," he muttered.

And so Kris led her scratch team once more into the black mouth of hell.

56

The emergency lights in the stairwell had been a casualty of the fight here. Kris found herself searching for a foothold among the dead bodies and failing.

Jack brought up his flashlight without being asked.

The defenders above had put up quite a fight.

Kris made her way carefully, avoiding the bodies, going from one patch of damp blood to the next open bit of gore. Behind her the others followed in her tracks.

She reached the ground floor and peeked out over the sights of her rifle.

The butcher bill for tonight was going to be huge.

These people must have been mowed down early in the attack. Many of them appeared to be security types taking a break, or actual government workers who'd picked a bad night to work late. Grant hadn't considered these folks important enough to keep alive.

"Nelly, where's that jammer?" Kris bit out

"Not on this floor."

"Is there a basement or sub-basement?" Kris asked over her shoulder.

"There's a door here, in the back of the stairwell," a kid's voice called.

"Don't touch it," the demolition tech called.

Too late.

The explosion was subdued, but the boy's scream was harsh on the taut nerves left by this evening.

Kris and the Marines got back to the stairwell to find two boys bleeding. One badly.

Jack stripped off the boy's belt and made a tourniquet for the shattered arm. Another Marine cut strips from the boy's shirt and used it to bandage his chest.

The demolition expert ran his fingers around the door. It was still solidly closed.

"Why don't you wait outside?" he suggested to Kris and the rest.

Nobody argued with him.

A long moment later there was a click, and the sergeant said, "The door's open. You all stay here while I check out the stairs."

Kris felt guilty, but she stayed put.

"Do you need some light," Bronc said, eyeing the darkness yawning from the newly opened stairwell.

"Don't mind if you do," the expert said, "but you stay well behind me and don't touch anything you don't have to."

Bronc followed the sergeant, one hand holding a light, the other hand in his pocket.

The other kids and the Marines moved as far from the door as they could.

"It's clear to the next landing" came a full minute later. "Stay to the center of the stairs and don't touch the walls."

They followed, Jack first, Kris second, the remaining three kids coming up the rear.

"Is it on this level?" Kris asked Nelly.

"It is at the other end of the building, the north end, and I think it is a floor lower. Or maybe the floor angles down. I do not know, Kris."

"There's more stairs here. Give me a second to check

them," the sergeant said, and moved off, with Bronc two steps behind him.

Kris glanced up. There were emergency lights in the corners. Tiny red lights flashed, testimony that they worked, just turned off. She announced that.

"Yeah, I noticed that, too," the sergeant drawled back. "I didn't really want to see what happened if I turned them back on. Do you?"

Kris agreed to the dark.

A moment later they were descending to the next level.

Emergency lights were on here, making this concrete sub-basement seem almost cheerful after the rest of the evening.

There also were no bodies. No wreckage from the fight. Here was a simple, functional area where workers did what needed to be done to make the rest of the place work.

It seemed almost painfully normal.

"The jamming is coming from the far end of the hallway," Nelly announced.

The sergeant led off, carefully doing his job. The rest followed in his footsteps.

It seemed easy.

Right up to the discovery of the jammer.

It was in a squat black box, sitting on a table, with antenna leads connecting it to pipes and power lines.

The sergeant studied it and shook his head.

"How much do you want this thing?"

"I'd like to take it home for study. It's the only thing that's managed to jam my computer's net," Kris said.

"The only thing," Nelly added for emphasis.

"But right now we need to turn it off. Kill this jamming and get some ambulances in here," Kris added.

"This baby looks to me to be rigged to explode. Say twelve different ways to Sunday. It is not meant to be turned off," the sergeant said, shaking his head.

"You need some explosives?" Jack asked. "Penny gave me her last grenade."

"That and some wire."

"Here's some wire," a kid said.

"Don't touch it!" came from half a dozen others.

"I wasn't going to," the kid answered.

"Smart kid, you're learning," the sergeant said, pulling off his belt and beginning to unwind a long filament from it.

The others backed out of the room. The sergeant did, too, a half minute later, the end of the string in his hand.

"I don't know what's going to happen when I yank on that grenade. They could have put a small charge in that jammer, but . . . so far . . . they ain't done nothing small.

"What do you say that the rest of you mosey on down to the other stairwell. I don't think we're going to bring the whole dang building down on us." He glanced back in the room. "I don't think."

Kris and the others moved down the hall. "Nelly, could you drop off some nanos. Something to activate once the jammer goes down."

"I am doing that, Kris."

Kris and her team reached the possible safety of the distant stairwell and she waved back at the technician.

He almost closed the door to the jammer's room, stepped back across the hall, held up three, then two, then one finger.

Then yanked.

He started jogging toward them as Kris counted, "Four, three, two, one."

The grenade went off.

A second, louder explosion followed a moment later, blowing out the door to the room that had held the jammer.

"Something is going on down the hall," Nelly shouted.

The sergeant took off at a flat-out sprint.

And the north end of the corridor exploded into a roiling ball of flame, reaching out to engulf him.

The Marine reached the hall that led off to the northern stairwell. He threw himself into it.

Kris and the rest of her team fell back into their own stairwell and slammed the metal fire door shut.

A half second later, the door blew open swinging around to bash Bronc and the kid standing beside him.

Overpressure knocked Kris against the stairwell, popped her ears, and left her with an overwhelming need to yawn.

Around her, Jack and the other Marines, black as witches' hearts since Nelly turned on their camouflage, went back to wearing red and blues, their faces brown, pink, or black as they'd been born.

And Kris found herself in a gray dress.

"I am no longer jammed," Nelly announced. "But your protective coloring controls are all dead."

"I think that's okay," Kris said. "Commander Tordon, can you hear me?"

"Loud and clear. What's been keeping you, dearie?"

"This and that. And some of the other. Listen, we've had a really bloody situation here. We've got a major medical incident on our hands and require maximum medical assistance. Where is it?"

"I don't know, Kris. The rest of this burg ain't exactly been sleeping. Your friend Martinez and his Fraternal Order of Proud Caballeros managed to hold the warehouse that I have such fond memories of. The streets over there are covered with the bodies of optimistic gangers who weren't as good as they thought they were. But it wasn't easy. Martinez was talking about his stand at the Alamo."

Kris did not remark at the historical reference. It was a different planet and if the words worked, fine.

"Anyway," Gramma Ruth went on, "Martinez and some of his crew took off a couple of minutes ago to help you. Let me patch him through to you."

The sergeant rejoined Kris. He signaled that he could not hear a thing. His eyes were bloodshot, and burst blood vessels showed on his face, but he seemed about as chipper as someone in his profession could be who had faced the monster in its lair and lived to tell the story.

Carefully, Kris and company worked their way back up the stairs.

And Martinez came on the net.

"Where are you?" Kris demanded.

"I'm stopped at a roadblock."

"Well blow the dang thing."

"It's not *their* roadblock, Your Highness, it's *our* road-block. Some of my brother cops seem more interested in keeping the media reporters out of there than in letting the ambulances in."

"Oh my" was about all Kris could muster.

And as she arrived at the main floor, who should she meet coming down from the upper floors, but the third vice president. His tie was cockeyed, and his shirt's buttons were now done in the wrong order. And the gorgeous blonde following him had a very proud grin on her face.

"We spent the entire attack hiding under a table," the third vice president said, with almost enough conviction to persuade a four-year-old.

Kris knew, even as she did it, that she'd be in deep trouble for this. But it didn't keep her from reaching into her totally wrecked hairdo and pulling out her automatic.

Then she jammed it under the jaw of Eden's third vice president.

"What do you want to bet me that your Inspector Johnson is commanding the roadblock up the road from here?"

"Of course he is." It was the wrong answer for this politician.

Kris grabbed the man by his tie and hauled him out of the stairwell. She aimed his head so he got a good look at the slaughter yard that the main hall had become.

"Oh my" was the man's shocked reply.

"Tell your man to open the road. To get the ambulances in here."

"We can't do that. They'll talk to the media. This is horrible."

"Yes, Mr. Third Vice President, this place is horrible, people are dying, and you and I are talking about totally irrelevant matters.

"Tonight people have been trying to shoot me dead and blow me to bits. And I have shot people dead and hurled explosives that blew them to pieces. It would be no bother at all for me to add you to the long list of people who died here tonight."

"Oh" came low and slow to the man's lips.

"Take down the roadblock."

The politician looked down at the automatic at his throat. For a long second he eyed it, alarm growing in his eyes. Kris could almost hear his brain grinding as the pistol changed from a party prop to an instrument of death.

To the source of his impending doom.

Eden's third vice president brought his wrist up to his mouth. "Inspector Johnson."

"Yes, sir" came only a second later.

"Allow the emergency services vehicles in. Allow everyone in. Close down the roadblock. We need help here. Lots of it. Now."

"What about the media?"

"Don't worry about them. Just get help in here."

"Sir, is Kris Longknife pressuring you?"

"Inspector, do it."

"Yes, sir."

The line went dead. Kris didn't let go of the politician. She didn't lower the gun. Open covenants openly arrived at was one of her father's favorite sayings. But until this covenant started to pay off with medical care here, it hadn't been agreed to and Kris wanted this man to know that his chances of living to see the morning were not getting any better.

Gunnery Sergeant Brown kicked in the front door of the rotunda.

"I think the ambulances are moving, finally," he announced, "Yes, those blasted whirley gig lights are finally moving."

"Let me know when the first one gets here," Kris ordered, not releasing her grip on one pale, political fish. Maybe he was finally getting a good look at what lay around him.

Or maybe the closeness of his own brush with mortality was settling in.

A long minute later, the first ambulance arrived.

Kris didn't even waste a sigh when she tossed the politician aside. His knees failed to support him, and he fell on a still oozing body. The lovely blonde did not stoop to offer him solace.

She'd spotted a newsie coming in and made a beeline for him.

Lieutenant Martinez arrived in the first wave, a pair of alternate media reports at his elbow. They looked around wide eyed. One lost her lunch, but they kept their cameras rolling.

This was not something that would be lost somewhere between the happening and the eleven o'clock news.

Oh, and Inspector Johnson showed up.

He made a beeline straight for Kris.

57

Kris had a command to care for. One that had bled deeply.

Gunnery Sergeant Brown announced he was the proud owner of ten prisoners. "Would have been eleven, but dang if the officer that I personally plugged didn't managed to smash a tooth or something and kill himself."

"I sure wanted to talk to him," Gunny finished.

"So did I, Gunny, but I'm starting to think Greenfeld's powers that be don't want to be at war with us any more than our honchos want to be at war with them, official like."

Which seemed to leave Gunny Brown with something to chew on.

Kris knew that the first thing she should have done was go hunting for the ambassador. Instead, she trotted for the riverside walk to check on Captain DeVar. No surprise, the zoo collecting around her, trotted right along. Even Johnson.

The wounded captain was just being lifted onto a stretcher.

"He going to be okay?" Kris asked the nearest medic.

The woman looked worried. "He's lost a lot of blood. We got to get him to Doc fast."

"I'm too mean to let a little leakage put me down," the captain grumbled, but his words were slurring.

"Gunny," Kris said into her commlink, "we need a rig here fast for the captain." She glanced around the field. There were several casualties that looked to have been hit hard by the auto-gun. More that had been hit too hard and were beyond aid.

"I got one rig able to roll. That whale of yours needs a new tire. Once the driver changes it, I'm sending it back to the embassy with the walking wounded."

"Do that," Kris agreed. "Just get me something back here that can handle four," she said, eyeing the medic. The woman held up a hand with all fingers spread. "Five stretchers."

"Damn, was it that bad back there?"

"It looks it," Kris answered.

A Marine rig quickly arrived, shot up and limping, but going nevertheless. Tailing it were a pair of private rigs driven by loyal members of the Fraternal Order of Proud Caballeros.

And a newsie made to jam a mike under Kris's oversize nose.

Inspector Johnson got in the way. "You can't interview her."

"Why not?"

Martinez stepped forward. "Because he doesn't want you to know the only thing that stood between the liquidation of all our leaders and the survival of the few who did was these Marines from Wardhaven."

"That's not true," Johnson insisted.

"Pan your camera over this field," Martinez went on. "Who do you see down? Not Eden troops. You drove by the wreckage of our rapid reaction force. How close did it get?"

"Not very," the reporter said.

"You've taken pictures inside the hall. Did you see any of our guards still alive?"

"My producer isn't allowing us to show those pictures." The reporter shivered at a memory. "It's too bloody, but I can say that all I saw were Marines and a few private guards still alive. And some of their patrons," she hastily added.

"You can't say that," Johnson insisted.

"I just did," the reporter shot back. "And I said it to the"—she tapped her earbud—"to our ten million subscribers, including the nine million that just joined us tonight."

"I'll have your license canceled," Johnson snapped through gritted teeth.

"You and what government?" the reporter snapped back. "Shirley Chisel of the opposition has already called for new elections."

"They can't make such a call."

"They can if they're not the opposition," the reporter said with a grin. "A lot of them weren't invited to this shindig tonight. And just making an educated guess at the survival rate of those that were, I'd say the majority party doesn't have anything like a majority anymore. How many votes do you think they'll have in the morning?"

Johnson paled.

And Kris did a quick look at her options.

Eden was changing. It could never be the same after this night. Oh, people like Johnson and his boss might try, but this tide was in full flow, and only fools got in the way of a riptide.

So what did that mean for her?

King Ray would probably try meddling in these people's affairs. Kris was no longer blind to some of his less socially desirable habits. But she was here and he was not.

These people did not need a Longknife. Or rather, they'd had about all of a Longknife that they could take.

With a shrug, Kris made up her mind.

"If you will excuse me, I have wounded Marines I need to get to care before we lose them." Kris saluted the reporter and the police lieutenant, and turned away.

"And my cops and caballeros are searching the great hall for any living soul," Martinez said. "What do you say we get more pictures your producer can try to edit for public consumption?"

"Who did this?" the reporter asked as they left.

"We'll be a long time investigating that question," the cop

said carefully. "Things like this aren't accidents that just blow up one day. But at the bottom of it all, I think we'll discover that we did this to ourselves."

Kris went about her duty, hunting through every nook and cranny where a Marine might have fallen. She would leave no one behind. No one for the civilians to stumble across.

The wounded were dispatched to the embassy at first. But Doc was quickly overwhelmed. When Kris's limo took off with the walking wounded like Penny, it headed for a hospital.

The search went through the night. The embassy sent a team of Foreign Service officers to hunt for the ambassador. They found him, along with the third political officer, a lovely middle-aged woman who had taken Kris's place on his arm. They were among the dead on the ground floor. The attackers hadn't even considered him important enough to herd upstairs.

Wardhaven's officers took their leader back to the embassy.

Grant von Schrader was also found. The bronze foot of one of the landers had taken him full in the face, smashed his skull, and pinned him against the wall. They identified him by the contents of the wallet in his hip pocket. Kris ordered him left to hang there. "Let Eden pick up its own trash."

The Marines gently collected their own honored dead on the grass in front of the west portico. The last of them was gently laid out just as sunrise colored the dawn sky. The pink of the reborn sun blushed their cheeks, tried to make them look warm and alive. The lie was painful to observe.

One of Martinez's men showed up with blankets to give them decent cover.

And Kris had her final run-in with Inspector Johnson.

58

"The President wants you and your Marines out of here," Inspector Johnson started without preamble. "Off this planet. Out of the reach of these newsies and their cameras."

"Your president is dead," Princess Kristine, daughter to Wardhaven's Prime Minister, reminded the inspector. It had been a rough night. Was the obvious slipping out of focus?

"The third vice president is not dead, and he is taking charge."

Kris knew that such transfers were often automatically assumed by the uninformed. But there were procedures to be followed. "Has he taken the oath? You know, being third in line is still third in line until you raise your right hand and swear the words." Politics turned on such fine distinctions.

That seemed to give Johnson pause. He blinked several times.

Kris gave him a moment to absorb that, then went on. "Besides, if the blond bimbo I saw him with right after the shooting stopped wasn't his wife, I suspect your man is as politically dead as your president is physically." Kris, after all, did grow up on politics.

Now Johnson blanched.

"I have my orders" had to be the final fallback of any poor bureaucrat.

"Is your third vice president aware I have dead and wounded to take care of?"

Another blank stare. Of course this politician had no idea what price had been paid by fighting men while he was up with his bimbo. Of course Johnson had no idea what Kris owed the wounded or fallen. Guys like Johnson wouldn't have thought they owed them a dime.

"Nelly, get me Doc if you can."

"Doc here" came back immediately.

"You in surgery?"

"No, Your Highness, I've got the worst of them stabilized. Which doesn't mean we won't lose a few more. Your Commander Mulhoney is in bad shape. I won't know until this evening."

"Should I come for a visit?"

"Your Highness, it's not for me to tell you what to do, but everyone I've got here is asleep and needs to be. If you came, they wouldn't know you had."

"I'm being ordered off the planet, dumped into the first taxi in line," Kris said.

"Ain't that the way it goes. I keep telling folks that doing good deeds is a waste of time and effort, but who pays attention to a doctor."

"I may call you back, Doc."

"I'll probably be too busy to take it."

And Kris rung off.

"Can you get Penny?" She was on the line in a few seconds.

"What's it look like back there?" the intel officer asked.

"Quiet at the moment. What's it look like your way?"

"We got an entire wing to ourselves. They're getting around to the last of the walking wounded now."

"You still lugging that bit of statue?"

"Yep, but they gave me happy juice, so I'm feeling no pain."

"I'm being ordered off the planet," Kris said.

"Well, that didn't take long," Penny said with a snort.

"I need to know if you and yours are safe."

"About as safe as we can be. A couple of Martinez's Gay Caballeros are posted at our doors."

"I think that's *Proud* Caballeros," Kris corrected.

"Well, they look pretty happy to me. I'm told they're to keep the newsies out, but they're doing a lousy job of it. I got one newsie at my elbow. We've been getting to know each other. Good woman. She's looking forward to things changing so she can marry the father of her son."

Beside Kris, Johnson looked to be having an epileptic fit.

"You'll need to paint me a better picture than that," Kris said.

"Seems that her baby has voting rights so long as she doesn't marry or name his father. If she does, the kid's franchise goes poof. If that dead horse goes away, she'll marry, but not until."

Kris smiled at Inspector Johnson. "Sounds like a lot of people are rooting for a change."

"Sounds that way," Penny said.

Johnson just shook his head. At the inevitable?

"So I take it that you're as safe as you can be?" Kris said.

"Looks that way to me. How far they running you off."

"I don't plan to go farther than the Naval base on the space station."

"Then you go make arrangements and us walking wounded will stumble in over the next couple of days. If we need rescue, I'm sure we can count on a Longknife."

Kris glanced around as her net went silent. A new day was dawning, both literally and figuratively for Eden. There were a lot of newsies reporting it. She could spot at least six within her own field of vision.

With her wounded secure Kris asked the last question.

"How do you propose getting me out of here without a media zoo?" Kris said. She didn't expect an answer to that one.

Silly her.

"There is a shuttle in the boathouse just north of here. It was there should the president ever have an emergency need of it."

And the killers were trying to flee to the north. Now that was explained.

Kris had just one more show stopper. "How many Marines will this shuttle hold?" It was bad enough that she was leaving. She would not leave her company to slink back to the embassy.

They'd come here as a fighting unit and that was the way they would leave.

"The shuttle is a Boeing 2737. It holds a hundred."

The inspector had her there. Maybe it was exhaustion. Or maybe it was an attack of common sense. But Kris said, "Then we shall see how many form up," and called on Gunny Brown to form the company. Johnson might order her out, but there was one remaining duty Kris would not leave undone no matter how ungrateful this nation was to its saviors.

The Marines came when they were summoned. Some were still searching among the dead for any that might still live. Others had been standing guard because, after the horror of the night, people had discovered a need to guard themselves again.

The medics and lifesavers came with bloody hands and drawn faces.

They formed under Gunny's watchful eye: First platoon. Second platoon, technical support. There was no spit and polish left on them. Those who had begun the night in bright red and blues finished it as blacked and worn as those who'd charged from the river in full, dripping, muddy, battle gear.

They found their place in rank and file to stand, exhausted, used beyond reason or measure. And counted off.

The count came out painfully short, so they put their heads together to fill it up to its proper measure. Some were on the list of Marines dispatched to hospitals. Others lay under blankets or in the body bags that had been required to collect what could be found.

So when the platoon leaders turned and reported all present or accounted for, Kris could see pride in Gunnery Sergeant Brown's face as he turned to her and passed along the word.

"Ninety-eight Marines present, ma'am. Forty-seven dispatched to the hospital. Twenty-nine dead."

It was a bloody butcher bill.

Among the Marines of the Technical Support Platoon stood Bronc and eight of his young buddies. If Gunny Brown said they were Marines, who was Kris to gainsay.

"I suspect I make ninety-nine," Jack said.

"And I make one hundred. Kindly tell Inspector Johnson that we will be taking his blasted shuttle out of here. He'd better have the Naval Station on High Eden ready to receive us."

"Where will we go from there?" Jack asked.

"The Wasp came through Jump Point Delta six hours ago," Nelly reported. "It's boosting for High Eden at one point five g's. It will dock in twelve hours."

"A bit late, but not that bad," Kris said.

"You ordered them here!"

"I figured a couple of days ago that I'd need a ride out of this mess," Kris agreed.

The Marine first lieutenant trotted off to let the local cop know that one Kris Longknife would go quietly.

Well, fairly quietly.

"Sergeant, will you please have the company change front."

"Yes ma'am," Gunny said, saluting. Kris returned the honor.

"Company" was followed by "Platoon."

"About. Face." And ninety-eight survivors turned to face their dead.

Kris repositioned herself to the new front of what she could only think of as her command.

Softly she said, "Gunny, prepare to render honors."

There was nothing soft about what she said next. Her words rang out across the lawn. On the west portico news cameras from a dozen different viewpoints and persuasions recording the Marines' farewell to Eden.

"Before you lie men and women, Marines all, who fought, and bled, and died that Eden might be free. That a new day of hope and liberty might be yours. May God have mercy on your souls if you break faith with these soldiers who gave their tomorrows for your today."

Kris paused to let the words sink in. To let the realization dawn on millions of watchers.

"These Marines paid a price for all of you," Kris continued. "Rich and poor. Voters and disenfranchised. Landers families and yesterday's arrivals."

Another pause.

"Your failed policies and attempts at dodging the obvious brought you to this night. A night of guns and bombs and murder. It brought you here with no defense for your future, your liberties, your freedom, but a handful of strangers from distant stars and those among you that were willing to step up to the plate. Tonight, neither wealth nor voter card nor history mattered.

"These men and women laid out here cared. They tried. And they paid a heavy price for you. You owe them your future. For God's sake, make it worthy of their sacrifice."

Kris wanted to reach through the recording cameras. To get her hands around every man and woman who had sat comfortably, uncomplaining while their nation bore down on this crisis point. There was no way she could do that. There was really nothing more for her to do for Eden. Or for her company.

She paused for a long moment, then whispered, "Render honors."

"Hand salute," Gunny ordered.

A hundred men and women commanded their stiffened and used up bodies to pay this final respect to those they had worked with. To those who had fought and bled beside them. To those who had stopped a bullet or thrown back a grenade for them.

From somewhere came taps.

None of the Marines had brought a bugle to this battle. But one of the caballeros had. He paid the ancient honor to the fallen as beautifully as ever was done.

On the last note, one that quivered in the morning air, Gunny Brown called, "Two," and one hundred hands came down.

"Gunny, march the company for the boathouse."

"Yes, ma'am" was quickly followed by the orders to make

it so. *We march a dirge to graveside. But we always quick march from it. Wasn't that the old saying?*

And the Marines moved off. Kris never knew who started it. Was the first voice from among the battered ranks of her company? Or did the song start up there on the west portico? It really didn't matter. The song started.

"From the halls of Montezuma" was a single, clear voice.

"To the shores of Tripoli" grew in volume.

"We will fight our country's battles on the land, space, and the sea."

59

The killing wasn't over. Or at least it was a close run thing for the next couple of hours.

An admiral from Eden's fleet met Kris at the door to the shuttle when it docked at High Eden. He demanded she immediately board an outgoing liner. Kris didn't much care for the way he was rushing her out . . . or separating her from her Marines. And she had at least one major deal breaker.

"Is a certain Victoria Peterwald booked on that ship?"

The admiral was nonplus toward the question. But he did check. "Why yes, she will be."

"Then I won't. Haven't you heard? Longknifes and Peterwalds don't play well together in the sandbox. People tend to get suddenly dead around us."

The admiral failed to understand that. Gunny Brown was wise enough to have four hulking Marines, stinking from sweat and battle, edge the Navy puke out of Kris's sight before Eden lost more of its ruling elite.

Then it turned out the Navy base was unprepared to offer hospitality to a hundred tired, hungry, and war-weary Marines.

Kris got angry when an Eden chief with a huge gut told her

the mess hall would not open for anyone until 1130 hours, two hours from now. She got outraged when a voice on the phone insisted the transient barracks didn't accepted new sign-ups until after 1500 hours.

Ever-helpful Nelly told Kris that there was a fine hotel just outside the gate that had plenty of rooms and a four-star restaurant.

But the rental cops at the gate tried to put a stop to that troop movement. It seemed that neither Kris nor any of her Marines were authorized to leave the base. For a second there it looked like matters would get downright mortal.

Fortunately, the base security guards manning the gate were puny . . . and unarmed. They took one look at the hulking Marines headed their way . . . many of them still armed to the teeth . . . and decided it was time for their coffee break.

All of them. All at once.

The hotel manager was a bit taken back by the arrival of one hundred filthy, tired, and evilly disposed hulks led by one very cranky princess. But the moment he got a look at Kris's credit card, amazing things started to happen.

One entire wing of his hotel was scheduled to begin renovation that day. He shooed away the workmen and had his staff put old sheets on beds in record time.

Fifteen minutes after their arrival, half the Marines were sound asleep. The other half made a quick stop by the coffee shop for some chow before joining the others.

Kris's last word to the manager was that many of her troopers were still heavily armed. Disturbing their sleep might not go very well for the one doing the disturbing. The manager nodded and assured her that none of her troops would be disturbed.

If only Kris had told the manager that she was in the same mood and should not be bothered either.

The clock beside her bed said Kris had hardly gotten ten hours sleep when she was awoken by a gentle but persistent tapping at her door.

"Go away or you are so dead." It wasn't a very princess way to greet someone, but Kris was not feeling much like a princess.

"But you're the one who summoned me. All the way from Wardhaven." That got her attention. The voice did sound dimly familiar.

Rolling out of a bed that had seemed so lovely a short time ago, but now looked full of enough dirt to grow potatoes, Kris crossed to the door and swung it open.

There was Captain Drago of *her* good ship *Wasp*.

"What's a pirate like you doing this close to Earth?" she demanded.

"I heard a princess was in distress and decided to risk hanging in her rescue."

Kris glanced down at her dress. It was filthy, bloodied, and torn. "More likely some street urchin. I'd invite you to chow but I'm not sure they'd let me in the restaurant without sloshing me down with a fire hose and finding something else to cover my ugliness."

"I don't know of whom you speak, Your Highness, but I see a full bath through that door, and I have taken to carrying around clothes in your size just in case you need them."

"Is that a proposition," Kris said, taking the offered blue shipsuit.

The black-hearted pirate just grinned.

"I'll be with you in two shakes," Kris said.

Showered and dressed, she found that her shoes of the night before had settled into pumps. Those alone she salvaged from what must have been a very expensive ensemble. Less than a minute later, she was ordering a steak smothered and loaded, and a salad deliverable five minutes ago.

The hotel showed no further evidence that it was occupied by a Marine task force until Jack marched in from one door the moment Gramma Ruth, Abby, and little Cara came in the other.

They all headed straight for Kris's table. Which the manager immediately expanded and filled with water and menus.

"Good to see you again, Skipper," Jack said. He had managed to have his uniform dry-cleaned and his shirt washed. His shoes, however, would never again carry the shine required of them.

"Glad to be here," Captain Drago replied, "but I hope you will excuse me. I am glad I wasn't here earlier. I see that the princess has been up to her usual mischief without her beauty nap."

"Look upon that face . . . and die," Kris muttered.

"I suspect a lot of Peterwald troops did," Ruth said, under her breath.

"Where is Bronc?" Cara asked.

"Sleeping," Jack assured her. "He's got a concussion and a sprained wrist, but he's in a lot better shape than some. That young man came through for us when we needed him," he said, eyeing Kris, then Ruth. "I hope we can do something for him."

"We already have," Ruth said through a wide grin. "Seems that the requirements for a Wardhaven passport aren't all that clearly codified just yet. A good friend of mine in the visa section was only too happy to provide one for him and his mom."

Cara looked terrified. "Bronc is leaving Eden?"

"Bronc and you must get out of here," Ruth said, her face now serious. Kris knew what had to come next.

Gramma Ruth did it softly, telling as gently as anyone could a young girl that her mother and grandmother had died suddenly. Violently.

When quiet came again, the girl sat in her chair for a long moment staring at her hands. "I thought that might be why Aunt Abby wasn't letting me go home." Cara shook her head. "Gramma Ganna wanted so much to move uptown. And it killed her just as dead as the hood kills kids."

"I want to take you away from the hood," Abby said. "I want to take you away from Eden."

"Why, you were never here before?" She was blunt but honest.

"Right, I wasn't," Abby said, offering all the contrition she seemed able. "But you and I are all the family we've got. I want you here with me," Abby said, shooting Kris a glance that told one princess to keep her mouth shut. *We'll settle anything between us later.*

"Will Bronc be coming with us?"

"I don't think so," Gramma Ruth said. "My sister Mary's youngest boy has a boy about Bronc's age. Some folks may think Hurtford is a hayseed of a planet, but its got a good school system and Bronc will get a top-notch education there in a school where no one will try to kill him. I think the boy really needs that for a while."

"And me?" came from Cara in a voice already lonely.

"I think your aunt has plans for your education," Ruth said, eyeing Abby. She nodded. "And you and Bronc can send messages to keep up with each other."

"I'm not sure I like that," Cara said.

"All I ask is that you give it a chance for six months," Abby said. "If it isn't working out in half a year, we can look it over again."

"Are you going to quit your job?"

"I don't think I'll have to," Abby said, not meeting Kris's eyes.

"Then we'll be traveling around in space!"

"I'm never quite sure where I'll be from moment to moment," Abby admitted.

A waitress arrived to take orders; decisions were hastily made. And Captain Drago asked Kris what he was doing here.

"How big is your ship?" she said.

"The *Wasp* has changed a lot since you were last on her," Drago said, "but she's not a whole lot bigger than when you stole her."

"I captured her fair and square," Kris grumbled, but a schematic of the ship appeared on the table before them and it held her attention.

The ship was designed to pass for a vulnerable five-thousand-ton freighter. The command and crew space was forward. Amidship was a long spindle where shipping containers were attached to honest merchant ships. The *Wasp* could actually take quite a few.

Aft was the engine room that Kris remembered only too well.

Now, a large structure ballooned out to cover the length of the ship. And that was its secret. Smart metal could be rotated along the side of that outer skin, absorbing laser hits and radiating the heat back into space.

The *Wasp* had a warship's hide on a sheepskin cover.

"And that's not all. Nuu Research made a breakthrough. Our new reactors can strip electricity directly out of our fusion drive. No more having to use magnetic coils to coax electricity from the plasma blasting out our engines." Drago grinned. "Next time we get in a fight while in orbit, somebody's going to be very sorry they went for us."

"How many people can you handle aboard?" Kris asked.

"Still only thirty. Maybe forty if they're friendly."

"I've got a hundred, hundred and fifty marines I need to get out of here."

Drago paled at Kris's words. "I'd never count on a Marine to be friendly."

"There's a Nuu Ship repair and modification facility here on High Eden," Nelly said. "It lacks a full yard capability but it has some tools."

"For what?" Drago said.

"People are using containers to ship colonists out on merchant ships," Ruth observed innocently.

"But Eden never sends out many colonists," Drago answered. "No one here makes those kinds of containers."

"I have the designs in my innards," Nelly said. "I could direct the robot shops to make what we want."

"Thank you, Nelly," Kris said.

Drago still shook his head at the thought of loading his wonderful ship full of big, hairy Marines.

But they were ready to sail four days later.

60

Captain Drago avoided asking Kris the obvious question until they were boosting for Jump Point Delta at 1.5 g's.

"Where do I set a course for?"

Kris had been considering that quite a lot.

She turned to Abby, Jack, Penny, and Gramma Ruth. Penny, along with thirty-six bandaged, walking wounded had come aboard the day before the *Wasp* sealed locks and got under way.

There were other wounded that did not make it aboard. Captain DeVar's legs were a thousand-piece jigsaw puzzle. The docs were still debating whether to fix him up or amputate and install metal. The wounded that did come arrived in twos and threes, anything not to draw attention. Kris was none too sure that mattered.

The newsies dirtside had a lot to report . . . and they were reporting it all.

The opposition party had used a rarely applied option for them to actually put a law on the table. Now, after the slaughter, they had the votes to see that their proposal to give the voting franchise to every man or woman in American Eden was not sent off to die in committee.

Any option for the ruling party to hold the line on the vote vanished when Lieutenant Martinez pointed out that he and his Fraternal Order of Proud Caballeros had not fought that night for those of Spanish blood, but for everyone on Eden. If people could fight for everyone's freedom, shouldn't everyone be free to vote?

Kris feared the man was too logical for a life in politics, but it looked like he was headed that way.

So full voters rights were passed and moments later, an election was scheduled. Eden certainly needed to fill plenty of seats. The presidency was vacant, as well as the prime minister position. And all three of the vice presidents also ended up vacant.

As it turned out, the woman who survived with the third vice president was not his wife, and they had been in his office the whole time, not skulking under a table. He admitted to being an alcoholic and signed himself into rehab.

She admitted to being an aspiring actress and offered to portray herself in both a family version of their adventure . . . and a version for mature audiences only.

Kris did not look back as she left Eden with little or no plan to ever return.

But that did leave the question of where to go.

"Abby, have you filed your report on my misadventures yet?"

"I need to send it out today. Do you want to review it?"

"Nope, just send Nelly a copy."

Jack raised an eyebrow at how Kris was avoiding Captain Drago's question. "You should check back in with General McMorrison on Wardhaven."

"Yes, I imagine that I should," Kris said with a sigh. "But I've got this ship and a batch of Marines. Why should I let Mac or Grampa Ray decide what I do next?"

"Isn't that what Naval officers usually do: whatever kings and generals decide?" Penny said.

"And look what *that* has got us," Kris pointed out.

"There is that," Penny agreed.

"I think my little girl done grown up." Gramma Ruth beamed.

"Anywhere you'd like to go, Gramma?"

"I been a lot of places. Some I can even go back to," Ruth said with a sly smile. "Why don't you surprise me?"

"Set a course for Chance," Kris decided. Then she glanced at Abby. "I suspect if Grampa Ray or Mac don't like it, we'll hear soon enough."

Admiral Sandy Santiago at Chance had orders waiting for Kris by the time the *Wasp* docked. Neither Kris nor the admiral felt any rush to comply, so they spent a pleasant morning bringing each other up-to-date on the recent happenings in their lives. Kris found several interesting things in Sandy's report on the comings and goings of her command, Naval District 41, out here on the Rim.

The efforts to crack the newly discovered alien worlds were not going well. No surprise there.

In a similar vain, just about any ship that could hold air were being chartered and sent out to try to duplicate Kris's success at finding new worlds. Other alien worlds. Anything.

That also was no surprise. Before Grampa Ray's Treaty of Wardhaven there had been a similar explosion of discovery.

And humanity stumbled on the Iteeche and had almost been made extinct.

That was something to think about, but Kris begged off of lunch with Sandy and instead dropped down to Last Chance to see a certain Ron Torn.

He invited Kris to dinner at his favorite steakhouse and introduced her to Amelia Blang, the daughter of the new ambassador from the Helvetican Confederacy.

Their wedding was in a week. Could Kris manage to attend?

Kris was pretty sure her heart did not skip a beat. Or at least not too many. And she did remember to breathe.

After only a moment's reflection, Kris found that she must

beg off. She had immediate orders that would have her moving on before then.

The next day, the *Wasp* boosted for Jump Point Alpha at 1.5 g's.

Another good boyfriend lost. At least, on the positive side, this time Kris would not have to add another bridesmaid's dress to her collection.

61

The *Wasp* made a comfortable 1 g as it covered the distance between Jump Point Beta and High Wardhaven. The entire time, the awaited message scheduling a meeting between Kris et al and General McMorrison and whoever showed up sober never came.

So Kris started planning how she wanted the meeting to go.

"Abby, we've got to get you in uniform," Kris said at breakfast.

"Why forever should we?" Abby said.

"Oh, Auntie, I think you'd look great in uniform," Cara said. "Can I have one, too? Everyone else has one."

"The captain doesn't," Abby pointed out.

"Yes, but he's special."

Having a twelve-year-old girl at the breakfast table . . . or dinner table . . . or just on board was a whole new experience for Kris. Course, at twelve, Kris had spent most of her time drunk. Thank heavens Cara did not have any vices like that.

Still, the girl was twelve.

"Now about that uniform," Kris said, trying to wrestle the

conversation back where she wanted it . . . and feeling very much like one of those bull riders she'd seen on South Continent.

"I don't have a uniform," Abby pointed out with a sharp edge.

"I could sew you one," Nelly tossed out, ever helpful.

"You can sew?" came from several around the table.

"We have lasers aboard to cut out the cloth if someone will lay it out on a table for me. I can guide the sewing machine if someone works with me."

"Me, me," Cara squealed, raising her hand. "I've always wanted to sew and we could sew me some clothes. Something like pirates wear."

"You are evil," Abby muttered, scowling daggers Kris's way. And left to find the cloth Nelly claimed the *Wasp* had in storage.

The *Wasp* docked with still no word from Main Navy.

Kris decided two could play that game. She assembled her usual suspects. Jack and Abby in khakis, Penny and Kris in undress whites.

Gramma Ruth avoided even being asked by muttering that she'd better go hunt up that rascal Trouble.

They took the beanstalk down, hailed a cab at the station, and made their way unannounced to General McMorrison's office.

"He's expecting you," the secretary said without looking up. "Go right in."

Which begged the question of exactly who was gaming who.

Kris took three steps into Mac's office, and brought her little parade to a halt: Jack on her right, Penny and Abby on her left.

General Mac was at his desk, making a show of reading something. King Ray in civvies was sitting in the general's visitor's chair, turned around to face not Mac but the arrivals. A huge grin was spreading across his face.

On the other end of Mac's desk, Admiral Crossenshield, Chief of Wardhaven Military Intelligence was digging out his wallet and passing a bill of unidentified value to the king.

"Abby, you're in uniform," King Ray beamed.

"A bit faster than one admiral expected," Kris said, betting she knew the bet the admiral was paying off.

"Never underestimate my great-granddaughter," the king said like any proud grampa.

"The day is coming when you'll wish she wasn't so smart," Crossie said, sounding rather cross.

"Yes, like today," Kris growled.

"You handled Eden just like I figured you would," King Ray said.

"Is that why you didn't give me some help? Like maybe tell me what I was headed into. Give me a chance to think through my options. Maybe get a few less people killed?"

"Is that what's bothering you? For what it's worth, the butcher bill on the Eden op is one of the lowest ever in a major political upheaval." The king sounded like he'd done a check of his library, or more likely, of his soul, before he came to this meeting.

"Maybe it is from where you sat," Kris snapped. "But you weren't stuck searching through a darkened, blown-out room to find enough arms and legs to fill a body bag."

"Is that what's bothering you, kitten?"

"Don't kitten me. I've had it with the way you use people. I quit. Mac, you got a resignation for me to sign?"

The general shuffled through his papers. For the first time in all these counseling sessions, he came up empty. "No."

"Well, get one typed up. I will not continue to work this way."

"Hold it, hold it." Now it was Grampa Ray's turn to backpedal. "It can't be all that bad."

"You send me out on missions telling me one thing and expecting another. Maybe it was fun at first. Me, a kid, working for the legendary Ray Longknife, but the new wore off in a hurry. I'm burying too many good people for things that might have gone different if I'd known what I was walking into.

What I was walking *them* into. No, Grampa, the good old days are over between us."

The legendary Ray pursed his lips in thought, then nodded. "Okay, young woman, what do you want from me?"

Kris was surprised to see the matter coming to a head this fast. But then, Grampa Ray was not known for avoiding conflict.

As a matter of fact, neither was she.

Kris signaled her team to take seats on the couches in front of Mac's desk, and took the chair at the end that left her farthest away from the three she'd come to think of as the dirty trinity.

Everyone seated, if not comfortable, Kris lost no time. "I want to chose my next job."

"I still can't find you ship duty like you want," Mac pointed out.

"I think I've found my own ship."

Crossenshield put a hand over his mouth, but it did not hide his smile.

"Yes, Crossie, I want the *Wasp*, crew and all. I also want the Marine company presently on it."

"For what?" Ray asked softly.

"To be the law out past the Rim."

The trinity exchanged glances. Ray passed the money back to his intel officer.

"You've talked to Sandy?" Ray said.

"I know that we've got problems beyond the Rim. It's gold rush days and there ain't no law in sight."

"That's a problem that hasn't gone unnoticed," Ray admitted.

"And I want to take the *Wasp*'s guns out there. With my Marines I'd be in a perfect place to kick butts and take names. But not just Marines. I want a legally recognized judge with a broad writ. And researchers. There's a whole lot of unknown out there. Between some scientists and Marines, we should be in a position to tackle just about anything."

"There's rumors of pirates," Crossenshield tossed into the pot.

"I'll expect better intel from you than just rumors," Kris bit back.

"Sometimes that's the best we got."

"Just so long as you give me all you have. Nothing held back. Nothing in your pocket so you can see just how good the kid is at improvised dance and firefights."

"You'd write the book for the new Wardhaven Survey Agency," King Ray said.

"Something like that. Hopefully a day will come when there will be more researchers and less Marines aboard a survey ship."

"I keep forgetting how young and optimistic you are," Ray said.

"And how old and pessimistic you are," Kris shot back.

Most of the others suddenly found a need to study the ceiling. Abby discovered a loose thread around a buttonhole and pulled. The room got very quiet.

"You aren't a little girl anymore, are you?" King Ray said with a deep sigh.

"No. I am grown. I've put three, four years in the Navy and I'm starting to understand why you and Grampa Al don't get along. It must have been hell being your son."

Abby was pulling threads from her shirtsleeve. Several of the men were now studying the carpet. Penny looked desperate to be somewhere else.

The king stood. Everyone in the room stood with him. "I think we've done about as much as we can here. Crossie, you see to it that Penny and Abby have access to everything that this young Turk thinks she needs to be the law out beyond the Rim. Mac, I think a full company of Marines is a bit stiff for one ship, but I'm not about to arm wrestle my kid into giving up so much as a private. Who knows, that private might be important to her some day." Kris had never seen the scowl he sent her way.

But she refused to be quelled by it.

He looked back at Mac. "See that the *Wasp* is fully outfitted for discovery, keeping the peace, and stopping the odd and sod land grab by our Peterwald friends."

"That enough for you?" he asked Kris.

She nodded agreement.

"And get the *Wasp* out of here as quickly as you can. I'd prefer not to have a repeat of this conversation."

And the king turned to leave.

Kris felt the urge to run, to catch up with him. To hug him. To do something to bridge the chasm that had opened between them.

But she stood in her place as he left.

Hugs were not something Longknifes did.

As the door closed behind him, Kris turned to the now shrunken trinity. "We'll need to add a lot more containers to the *Wasp*. I'd like a whole new sensor suite. Have you given any thought to who the boffins are and what kind of caring and feeding of them we'll have to arrange for?"

And the room got down to serious planning.

The *Wasp* sailed within the week.

King Ray was known to have a special fondness for ships of exploration. Back while he was President of the Society of Humanity, he regularly saw survey ships off.

He was not there when the *Wasp* sealed locks.

About the Author

Mike Shepherd grew up Navy. It taught him early about change and the chain of command. He's worked as a bartender and cab driver, personnel advisor and labor negotiator. Now retired from building databases about the endangered critters of the Pacific Northwest, he's looking forward to some serious writing.

Mike lives in Vancouver, Washington, with his wife, Ellen, and her mother. He enjoys reading, writing, watching grandchildren for story ideas, and upgrading his computer—all are never ending.

Oh, and working on Kris's next book, *Kris Longknife*: *Intrepid*.

You may reach him at Mike_Shepherd@comcast.net or drop by www.mikemoscoe.com to check on how the next book is going.